# Phantoms

by Stephanie Osborn

Chromosphere Press

Huntsville, AL

***Phantoms***

© 2018 Stephanie Osborn
ISBN 978-1-947530-06-5 (print)
ISBN 978-1-947530-05-8 (ebook)
Cover art © 2018 Darrell Osborn
Fiction

First electronic edition 2018



This is a work of fiction. All concepts, characters and events portrayed in this book are used fictitiously and any resemblance to real people or events is purely coincidental.

Chromosphere Press
www.chromospherepress.com

# Table of Contents

# Chapter 1

"...So if we're going out, what shall I wear, Echo?" the svelte, platinum-haired female Agent asked her partner, the tall, dark, and handsome head of Alpha Line, the Division One's special forces department; together, the two formed the Alpha One partnership, the Division's premier field team. "Are we talking dinner-and-a-movie jeans, or do I need to dress up more?"

"I think 'dressing up' is probably in order," Echo replied to the woman he had finally asked out, after a couple of years of working side by side with her as the Alpha One team.

"A Suit?" Omega queried, a gently inquiring look in the azure eyes.

"Well, that'd be fine with me, Meg, but I think you'd probably feel better if you were dressed up a bit more..."

"A skirted Suit, then." Another curious glance.

"Mmm...think formal," Echo replied, an amused twinkle in his eyes as he steadfastly refused to yield to her subtle attempts to find out where he was taking her.

"Formal?! Ooops," a perplexed Omega replied, grabbing for her cell phone.

"What's wrong?" Echo asked, raising an eyebrow.

"I literally don't have anything to wear, Echo," Omega told him with a sheepish grin as she keyed the cell phone. "There's nothing in my closet but Suits, black jeans, and black and white shirts. I haven't needed anything else. I'm going to ask India if I can borrow something; she's about my size. Hello, India?" she asked, and Echo assumed that the distaff member of the Alpha Two team had answered. "Yeah, girlfriend, I need some help. Do you have a formal dress I can borrow tonight? Yeah, I'm going out. No, no, Mu didn't change his mind." Omega grinned at her partner. "Look, just grab a couple dresses you think will work for my figure and height, and come around the corner to my quarters, and you can find out who. He's standing here waiting for me to get ready. Yeah. Okay, thanks, India." Omega closed the cell phone, replaced it on the table, and looked up at a grinning Echo, her own expression closely mimicking his. "I give her no more than two minutes."

"With Romeo right behind her," Echo replied, glancing at his wrist chronometer.

"Uh-huh," Omega agreed, studying her own wrist chronometer. "And...India minus five...four...three...two...one..."

A knock sounded on Omega's front door.

"Leave it to the ex-astronaut," Echo murmured, stifling laughter, and Omega smiled.

"You never have asked me what I did for NASA before making astronaut," she reminded him as she headed for the front door.

"What did you do, then?"

"Scheduled the timeline of flight activities. Down to the second. Come on in, India, Romeo," Omega invited, opening the door to admit the beautiful Afro-Asian woman and the handsome black man with whom she was partnered, as Echo chuckled.

"Well?" India asked promptly, as she entered with several evening gowns draped over one arm.

"Yeah, who's the hot date with, pretty lady?" Romeo added, right behind. "Hi, Echo."

"Hi, Romeo, India." Echo acknowledged the Agents' entrance with a nod.

"So?" India pressed.

"So?" Omega grinned, moving to stand beside Echo.

"C'mon, Meg, who ya goin' out with, already?!" Romeo exclaimed.

"What did I tell you on the phone, India?" Omega asked, turning and straightening Echo's tie with affection. Echo's warm brown eyes sparkled with mischief as he looked down at his partner.

"You said he was here waiting...for you to...get dressed..." India's voice tapered off, and Echo and Omega watched with undisguised amusement as Romeo and India figured it out.

"Damn!" Romeo grinned. "Way ta go, Echo!"

"Here, India," Omega said, taking the dresses from her friend. "Come and help me get ready." She headed into her bedroom.

"I'll...be with you in a sec, Meg," India said in an odd tone, and Omega nodded, closing the bedroom door. As soon as the door closed, India rounded on Echo. "What the hell do you think you're doing, Echo?!"

Echo blinked in surprise.

"Taking Meg out."

"You're going to hurt her, Echo. As soon as she figures out you're only doing it because you feel sorry for her—"

"Feel sorry for her? Why?"

"Don't give me that! Because Mu stood her up, of course."

"India," Echo said quietly, face expressionless, "I don't feel sorry for her. I have no intention of hurting her. And it's none of your damn business."

"Let 'im alone, India," Romeo remonstrated with his partner in work and romance; a few months earlier, the pair had applied for and been granted a life partnership, the Agency's nearest equivalent of marriage. "Echo's got as much right to take Meg out as you an' I got to GO out."

"...All right," India acquiesced, glancing sharply at Echo. "I'll go help Meg." She disappeared into the bedroom.

"Listen, Echo," Romeo said in sympathetic understanding, moving to stand beside his ex-partner, "I know you an' Meg 've been kinda...lonely. Both of ya. An' if this is what you both want, I'm behind ya, a hundred an' ten percent. I think it's great. Just lemme know if I c'n help you two, any kinda way."

Echo offered the other man a slight smile and stuck his hands in his pockets, thoughtfully studying Omega's carpet with warm, dark eyes.

* * *

Omega was trying on a dress when India slipped into the bedroom. "What do you think, India?" Omega asked, modeling the full-skirted white gown.

"Mmm...try the skinny black one," India said critically, studying her friend. "The white looks really good, and the fit is great, but with your fair complexion, it's like there's too much pale, if you know what I mean. I think the black will look even better, 'cause it'll contrast with your skin and hair."

"Okay."

"Meg..." India began as Omega stripped off the white dress, "are you sure about this?"

"About what, India?" Omega replied as she hung the white dress carefully.

"About going out with Echo."

"Why not?"

"Well...go ahead and have fun. Just promise me you won't take tonight seriously, or expect any more 'dates' with him."

Omega stopped and stared at India.

"Hon', are you trying to tell me something?" she wondered. India looked away, embarrassed.

"I just don't want you to be hurt because you misunderstood your partner's attempt to be nice."

"What?! Are you saying the only reason Echo's taking me out is because—"

"I think it's because Mu stood you up." India nodded.

Omega's face went rigid, jaw squared and firm, and she didn't move for several seconds. Then she threw on her black silk dressing gown over her bra and panties, tied it closed, and headed for the living area.

* * *

Romeo and Echo were chatting about the approaching baseball playoffs when Omega emerged from the bedroom, a concerned India behind her.

"Um, listen, Echo," Omega began in a low tone, "I...I appreciate the thought, but...but I think I'll...stay here tonight..."

Echo blinked, and an emotion flickered momentarily through the dark eyes; Romeo thought it looked like intense pain.

4

* * *

"What's wrong, Meg?" Echo asked softly. "Why'd you change your mind?"

"I don't want pity, Echo," she replied, staring at his feet. "If nobody wants a...a half-alien, kludged-together kind of woman-thing as a...a romantic partner, well, that's the way it is...and I get that. But I don't want anyone taking me out just because they think I'm lonely and feel sorry for me."

"Dammit, India, I told you to stay the hell out of this," Echo said in a tight, controlled voice, throwing a hard look her way, even as Romeo gave a shocked glance at his life partner. "Come here, Meg." He caught his partner's arm and drew her through the connecting 'back door' into his own quarters. Staring at India, he pointedly closed the door, then turned to Omega. "Meg...do you honestly think I'd ask you out just because I pitied you? Do you think I'd ever ask a woman out if I didn't want to? Have you completely forgotten the hot tub conversation, up at my beach house? I'll keep reminding you of that, as often as I have to, baby, until it sticks. 'Your partner thinks you're hot stuff.' Remember?"

Omega studied Echo's face thoughtfully for long moments. Her gaze fastened on his eyes, apparently seeing something in the brown depths, and she nodded to herself, satisfied. In turn, Echo saw the doubt leave the blue eyes of his partner.

"That's more like it. Now," he tried again, "will you go out with me tonight?"

"Yes," she agreed, and smiled. "I think I'm rather looking forward to it."

"Good," he said softly, offering her a slight, pleased smile in return; her own grew wider in response. "That's a helluva lot better. Now go get dressed, baby."

"Okay."

* * *

Echo and Romeo had resumed their sports discussion, meandering on to the upcoming football season, when India emerged from the bedroom.

"Gentlemen, may I present Omega?" India said formally, stepping aside with a flourish as Omega walked through the doorway. Both men stopped in mid-sentence.

The statuesque blonde was encased in a backless column of jet black with a plunging V-neckline, exposing a hint of décolleté. The left side of the slim skirt was slit to the top of the thigh. Antique diamond drop earrings—family heirlooms—hung from her earlobes, twinkling in the light, and a matching pendant nestled, sparkling, in the hollow of her throat. One hand held a small beaded clutch. Strappy black high-heeled sandals brought the luminous blue eyes almost on a level with Echo's own. The flower he had tucked behind her ear earlier, when he had asked her out, still snuggled there, carefully woven into the now-upswept platinum tresses. Omega's skin glowed, a faint blush colored her cheeks, the azure eyes were smoky and seductive, and her moist lips were soft and full.

"Will I do?" she murmured demurely.

Romeo emitted a long, low whistle. Echo was silent for a protracted moment, eyes narrowed as he took in the vision before him.

"Echo?" Omega pressed, uncertain.

Romeo and India glanced at each other, confused at his lack of response. *He asked her out, but now he doesn't even react...?*

"Maybe I better go get that baseball bat now," Echo murmured finally, stepping forward and offering his arm. Omega smiled and tucked her hand into his elbow.

"Huh?" India muttered. "Baseball bat?"

"I don' get it," Romeo added. "Echo, you got weird ideas 'bout romantic remarks, m' man."

"Inside joke, guys," Omega noted, and smiled up at Echo as she glided gracefully through the front door on his arm. "Trust me, I appreciated it. Thanks, guys; see y'all later..."

* * *

The powerful, charismatic man in the black Suit seated his beautiful companion at their table in the famous Italian restaurant—which was rather decidedly more upscale than their usual haunt, which haunt was not shabby to begin with. The waiter smiled his approval at Echo's courtliness. "Signore, may I bring the two of you something to drink, while you peruse the menu?" he asked the couple, his accent as heavy as the pungent scent of Italian spices in the restaurant.

"Due Bellinis, per favore," Echo responded, as Omega unobtrusively surveyed their surroundings. The solicitous waiter departed immediately.

"Echo, this is lovely," Omega murmured, delicately fingering the perfect rosebud in the vase on the center of the table.

'Mm-hmm," he replied, watching her with the barest hint of a smile. *She sure is,* he thought.

"What did you order us to drink?" she asked, intensely curious, seeing the waiter approach with a tray of drinks.

"A Bellini," he told her. "I think a proper Southern belle like you will enjoy it. Try it," he said, as the waiter set the drink before her, before setting down Echo's drink as well as a couple of goblets of ice water. Omega picked up the glass and sipped it slowly.

"Mmm," she purred happily, "peaches!" and Echo chuckled.

"Told you you'd like it," he said, sipping his own drink. "This restaurant is known for their Bellinis. As well as a number of specialty dishes."

Echo ordered several courses for them both, his close association with his partner and best friend ensuring he already knew what she liked, and they tasted and sampled and chatted their way through a delicious dinner. When it was time to go, Echo dropped his *carte noir* onto the check, and the waiter responded in instant recognition.

"Yes, sir," he told Echo quietly, "it will be taken care of, signore. Have a good evening."

"Thank you," Echo replied, retrieving his *carte noir* and holding the chair for Omega. "Let's go, Meg. Our show starts in about twenty minutes. We've got just time to get there and take our seats, if we 'hurry.'"

"What show are we seeing, Echo?" Omega asked. Echo's lips curved up slightly.

"You'll see," he told her, enigmatic as ever.

* * *

Echo escorted Omega into the Majesty Theatre, and an usher promptly met them and led them to their box. Echo felt the tremor of excitement run through the woman on his arm, and he smiled to himself. Abruptly, he became the startled recipient of a delighted hug.

"Oh, Echo! You brought me to see *Phantom*! It has to be my absolute favorite! I've been dying to see it!" Omega exclaimed.

"I know. That's why we're here." Echo seated his companion, then himself. "I'd planned to do this, sooner or later. Tonight seemed to be a good time."

"Ohh...now if only..." she murmured wistfully.

"He's here."

"What?" Omega's head swiveled toward her partner.

"Michael's appearing tonight in the title role."

"He is?!"

"Yep. He came back for the current run of the show. Um... the 'revival,' I think they call it."

"Waitaminit...'Michael'? You're on a first name basis with him?!"

"Of course," Echo replied with a shrug and a smile. "Actually, I usually just call him Mike. I helped process him through when he came to Earth years ago. He said to tell you he'd wait for us in his dressing room after the show, if you want to go backstage."

"If?!"

"I take it that's a yes?"

An excited Omega smiled at her partner, fairly beaming in delight.

"Echo, you're...you're..."

"Full of surprises?"

"That, too."

* * *

Omega was totally enthralled by the performance. Echo watched, intensely pleased, as his partner became completely absorbed in the story unfolding before them, and he considerately refrained from making any comments when the performers were onstage. When he saw her lips moving slightly during the musical numbers, he leaned over her unobtrusively, then smiled—Omega was singing along, just under her breath, barely loud enough for him to detect. Then Echo glanced down, and the smile grew wider; slim, neatly-manicured fingers softly tapped the arm of the seat, in perfect rhythm with the music.

Echo put out his hand and covered Omega's, lest the faint, unconscious drumming disturb others—he wasn't worried about the singing, as an average person's breathing was louder, but he was concerned that the slight tapping sound might draw attention. Startled, Omega broke out of her reverie to glance at her hand, then up at Echo. He put a finger to his lips, then grinned and lightly squeezed her fingers. Her eyes grew round with good-humored embarrassment—which confirmed for him that she hadn't realized she was doing it—and she covered her lips with the fingers of her other hand as she mouthed a silent, "Oh!" Then she gave him a happy smile and squeezed his hand in return. Echo leaned over and breathed in Omega's ear.

"Enjoying yourself?"

"Immensely." Sapphire eyes sparkled.

"Good," he responded, squeezing her hand again. "Oh, this number coming up is a good one."

"Ohh, yes," Omega sighed. "It's one of my all-time favorites."

The song began, and both Agents were caught up in the beautiful duet as the romantic leads acknowledged their characters' love. Echo, smiling slightly, glanced down at his companion to see how she was enjoying herself, and was shocked to see the blue eyes filled with tears, the expression one of loneliness and isolation, as she watched the scene onstage. The smile on his face faded, the dark eyes narrowed, and the brows knit in concern. Wisely, however, he refrained from saying anything, pretending not to notice.

By the time the house lights came up for intermission, Omega appeared normal, except for a suspicious glimmer in her eyes.

"...Meg?" Echo began, somewhat hesitant, and she looked up with veiled expression, "...want anything to drink?" he finished, deciding to abort the more serious query for the time being. *After all,* he considered, *she's been through a lot lately, and maybe the music just triggered something that needed letting out.*

"Oh! Yes, please. That would be nice," she agreed. Still holding hands, they walked together out of the auditorium, located the lounge, and ordered drinks—Echo's favorite whisky, chilled, neat, for himself, and a white wine for his date.

"What do you think of the show so far, baby?" Echo asked with a casual air, watching her reaction closely—without appearing to do so—as they stood and sipped their drinks. Omega smiled.

"I love it, Echo, just like I knew I would," she responded with soft emphasis.

But there was a ghost of the earlier loneliness haunting the recesses of the sky-tinted eyes. He considered that ghost for a brief moment, then decided to act.

Wordlessly, Echo adjusted the flower in her hair, tucking it more securely behind her ear, the ear Omega had said traditionally represented romantic attachment—a symbolism that Echo had already known. *Because that's the message I wanted to get across,* he thought. *I want her romantically attached...to me.*

Omega blinked at his motion, and studied Echo's face as he adjusted the flower. Echo saw the ghost in her eyes recede and vanish, at least for the moment. *Good,* he thought, pleased. *That was a little reminder of 'You're not alone, baby. You have me.' And it seems to have worked. Or at least helped.*

"There," he said in a satisfied tone, dropping his hand and surveying his handiwork, "perfect."

Omega offered him another smile, and this time, it reached her eyes. Echo smiled back, pleased.

The lights flashed, signaling the imminent end of intermission, and a gallant Echo escorted his still-smiling companion back to their box.

* * *

"Ohhh..." Omega sighed, applauding enthusiastically as the curtain came down and the house lights came up. "That was simply wonderful."

"The definitive word from the hopeless romantic," Echo remarked with a grin, and Omega blushed.

"I'm sorry," she murmured, embarrassed.

"Don't be," he replied, catching her chin and nudging it up as she tried to tuck her head. "I was only teasing. I like that facet of your personality. Besides, it's kept you from getting hard and callous—which is easy to do in our line of work."

"I suppose," Omega remarked thoughtfully. "Is that what's kept you from getting callous?"

"What?!" Echo asked, startled. "Me?"

"Uh-huh."

"Are you calling me a romantic?"

"Of course not, Echo," a gently-bantering Omega said with a soft, knowing smile, as she fingered the flower he had placed in her hair. By making the gesture, she sought to remind him that he had had sentimental attachments to that particular blossom even before he and Omega had ever met, and discovering that it was his partner's favorite flower had only strengthened that attachment. To reinforce the reminder, she added, "What would possibly give me an idea like that? You, a closet romantic? Why, the thought never once crossed my mind."

Echo kept a straight face, but Omega suspected there was a hint of a gratified smile in the dark eyes. *Why yes, I do know you that well, Ace,* she thought to herself, and grinned. Echo's gratified smile made it to his mouth then, as the corners of his lips twitched upward. Rather than comment, however, a thing which she knew might give him away in public and potentially ruin his Agent Badass image, he apparently chose to change the subject.

"The crowd's thinned out some, Meg," he said. "Ready to go backstage and meet an old friend of mine?"

"Like you have to ask?" Omega responded, her grin growing wider.

* * *

"...So this is your most recent partner, Echo," the Tony-award-winning performer remarked in his soft, deliberately-cultivated British accent, as he sat at his dressing table and removed the mask that was part costume, part makeup appliance. "You're a lucky man. If she is as good an Agent as she is beautiful, the two of you must make an unbeatable team." Omega blushed at the alien actor's praise.

"Well, let's just say there's a reason we're called the Alpha One team," Echo acknowledged, and Michael smiled, impressed.

"I see," the actor said, standing. "Indeed, that says it all, right there. Now let me show you two around a bit."

* * *

The star led them about backstage, introducing the couple to actors, musicians, stagehands, and managers. Omega was fascinated, and immediately struck up an animated conversation with several friendly secondary performers. A tolerant Echo watched her in pleased, gentle amusement, until Michael discreetly pulled him aside.

"Echo," the actor began in a quiet tone, "are you and your partner here on 'business,' by any chance?"

"No..." Echo murmured, "it's an evening out on the town, just the two of us. Why? Is something up, Mike? What's wrong?"

"Oh," Michael responded, disappointed. "Well, it's just

that...I was rather hoping...perhaps Fox had heard..."

"Why? Seriously, Michael, is there something you need the Agency for?"

"Well...maybe. It may be nothing, or it may be deadly serious. I'd like to discuss it with you in private, just to see what you think, if you wouldn't mind." As Michael spoke, a clear soprano voice rose through the theater, singing the opening notes of the show's titular melody. "Would you mind doing it now, tonight? We can grab a post-show bite while we talk, and the two of you can have drinks. I'm famished, and from what you've told me, I'm sure your partner wouldn't mind an additional opportunity to talk with me about the show. Let alone spend more special time with you, judging by appearances."

"All right. Let me find Meg, and we can go," Echo said, turning to look for his date, and secretly pleased by the actor's assessment of the Alpha One relationship.

"You don't have to look, Echo. Listen," Michael said with a smile, pointing in the general direction of the stage.

"What?" Echo glanced at his old friend, confused.

"Don't you recognize it?" Michael led the way to the wings, and an astonished Echo stared out onstage, where several musicians in the orchestra pit accompanied Omega as she sang the title song.

"Meg?!" he whispered, shocked at the beauty of what he was hearing.

"Ah, my cue," Michael murmured, as he heard the appropriate bar of music, stepping onstage and letting his rich voice join Omega's in the song's duet. Omega faltered when she heard him, turning toward him and blushing furiously. Echo watched as a reassuring Michael gestured for her to continue, moving steadily across the stage toward her; Omega smiled, a bit diffident, and continued her role.

More and more of the cast and crew gathered in the wings and among the seats as Michael skillfully led Omega through the scene. Echo listened, astounded, as Omega's voice rose higher and higher toward the aria's crescendo, Michael subtly encouraging her throughout. When the musicians stopped and Omega hit the final, incredible note with perfect pitch and in full voice, the house fell silent in stunned astonishment. Then suddenly it exploded as performers and technicians alike cheered and applauded.

Omega froze for a moment, then a shrewd Echo, familiar enough with his partner to recognize the signs, realized she was adopting another character—that of an experienced, capable performer, as she bowed graciously on Michael's arm, then turned and made her calm way toward her partner...who, uncharacteristically, was rather less calm.

"Meg!" A jubilant Echo grabbed her shoulders in almost-awed elation. "Damn, honey! Why didn't you TELL me you could sing like that?!"

"You never asked," Omega said simply, "and it never seemed important. It isn't like I'll ever make a Broadway debut—or even a community theater debut—while I'm in Division One, let alone Alpha Line."

"Actually," a thoughtful Michael said behind her, "now that you mention it, that might be exactly what we need..."

* * *

"...And so I used to do a lot of community theater," Omega explained over a late-night snack in Michael's favorite post-performance restaurant. "It was my major non-work hobby. I sang with the Houston and Huntsville operas not infrequently, too. The last couple of years I was in Houston, we even started a semi-professional theatrical company, and I was their principal first soprano. They used to joke that I was the least-diva diva ever."

"Damn, baby! It seems like I'm not the only one full of surprises tonight," Echo remarked. "Meg, you sing like... like..."

"An angel," Michael supplied with a smile. "Appropriately. Omega, do you know the rest of the show's music that well?"

"Well, um, pretty much," she admitted, shy. "It's my favorite musical, and we were going to mount a production of it in Houston—Clear Lake Repertory Theatre, we called ourselves; that was the semi-pro group—when I was still there, but it fell through at the last minute because we couldn't afford to stage it properly after one of the producers had to back out of supporting it financially. I don't blame 'em; a tornado came through northwest Houston and tore up jacks, leaving a whole lotta people in a financial bind. So yeah, I'm pretty familiar with the show. But I'm awful rusty. I haven't had occasion to really sing since joining the Agency."

"So you've actually rehearsed it?!" Michael asked in excitement, and Omega nodded. "Don't worry about rusty; that, we can fix. How quickly do you learn blocking and choreography?"

"She's a damn quick study, Mike," Echo answered for her. "She loves to dance, and picks up on new steps really fast; we've been dancing together often enough now—we go dancing at least a couple times a month, when we can find time—that I can speak to all of that from personal experience. And we've staged convincing mock fights with less than five minutes' prep time."

"Well, then." Michael turned to Omega. "How would you like to be the first Division One Agent on Broadway?"

* * *

"...Wow. That's...bizarre. So there seems to be a real, live 'theater phantom' plaguing the production?" Omega verified. "Talk about life imitating art."

"Yes," Michael answered. "The way I figure it, whoever is doing it was likely inspired by the plot of the show, so he or she is deliberately paralleling events. And it falls under the jurisdiction of Division One because there is such a preponderance of offworlders in the cast and crew. Especially the crew."

"And you want Meg to step into the female lead to try to lure the phantom into the open?" Echo asked.

"Exactly."

"Why? It's an awfully dramatic tactic," Echo pressed.

"And what about the understudy?"

"It's...it's getting dangerous, Echo," Michael finally admitted. "Two nights ago, the chandelier really did fall. Do you know how heavy that thing is, with all the rigging? An experienced Division One Agent in the role is more likely to...survive...than poor Sofia. OR Kate. In fact, Kate, the understudy, is so frightened that she's taken a temporary leave from the company, under the guise of a 'family emergency.'"

There was a long, towering silence.

"So all you really want is to use Meg as bait," a grim Echo finally declared.

"Well...yes. I suppose so, in a way..."

"No."

"But, Echo—"

"No, Michael," Echo reiterated, reserved and formal. "You want to put my partner in position as a target, where she can't defend herself adequately, and I can't get close enough to do it for her. That's unacceptable."

"Echo, we've got to help," a concerned Omega said earnestly.

"And we will. But not at the risk of you becoming a permanent part of the stage," Echo answered, relenting slightly. "Come on. Let's go talk to Fox. I'll be in touch, Mike."

The two Agents stood and exited the restaurant. Michael noticed Echo's splayed hand resting lightly —familiarly, almost possessively—on the smooth, bare skin between Omega's shoulder blades, and raised an eyebrow in surprise.

* * *

"Echo, you know I've got to do it," Omega said from the passenger seat of the Corvette as it took them back to Headquarters. "If that sort of stuff keeps up, Sofia doesn't stand a chance. She's not trained to run a gauntlet, Echo. I am."

"Yes, you are. But—"

"I should be able to step into the role with only a couple of brush-up rehearsals. And Michael can coach me through the rest."

"True. But—"

"Besides, Sofia has fans, a family. An entire show depending on her. On the other hand, if something happens to me, it isn't like there's anybody to miss me."

The Corvette was silent. Then a pale Echo, staring straight ahead through the windshield, said in a low voice, "What am I?"

"What?"

"Do you really think I wouldn't even notice if something... happened to you?"

"No," she responded softly, touched. "But...let's face it, Echo. I'm your third partner. There are other Division One agents. Other partners. There's nothing special about me. Recombinant genetics notwithstanding."

"Damn," Echo said, face nearly white, a strange look in his milk chocolate eyes, "you do think I'm a heartless son of a bitch, don't you?"

"No, Echo, no!" Omega exclaimed, shocked that she had just done the one thing she had thought impossible for her to do: deeply hurt Echo. "I don't mean it like that at all! I'm just trying to be...practical. You know it's true—"

"No, I don't. Have you forgotten about the defined partnership we've got? Alpha One is us, baby. You and me. No substitutes. No replacements."

"—And you know there's a job to do," she said, pretending to ignore his statement. "You're a professional, Echo. The consummate Agent. To many in the Agency, you're the definition of what an Alpha Line Agent should be. Hell, you're the definition of an agent, period."

"Including you?"

"Including me. ESPECIALLY including me. And if anybody should know, it's me. You trained me. So...I know what I have to do, Echo."

Echo mulled over their situation.

"I seem to recall, once upon a time, you doing everything in your power to keep me from going on a mission that you knew was likely to get me killed," he pointed out.

"Or enslaved." Omega nodded. "And I recall your refusing to be dissuaded because there was a job to do."

The interior of the vehicle was silent for long moments.

"I don't like it, Meg."

"Neither did I, Echo. Neither did I."

"All right." Echo sighed. "Let's learn from that earlier experience, you and me, and make sure we communicate and work together through all this mess. Deal?"

"To the best of my ability. Deal."

"Okay. What do you want me to do?"

"Well, assuming Fox approves it—it really is way higher-profile than any agent has ever done before, and he might not—then you're gonna have to work closer with me than we've ever worked in our entire partnership," Omega told him. "Because what you told Sir Michael was right: I am gonna be basically defenseless up there. We'll need nonverbal signals..."

"We need the exact layout of the stage and sets."

"Yes, and we'll need to develop strategies intended to work around, and with, the layout," Omega added.

"And I need to watch you like a hawk," Echo finished.

* * *

"Given that you'll already be in heavy makeup, dark wig, and costume for the role, it should be fairly easy to create an undercover persona for you, Omega," Fox agreed in his office shortly thereafter. "I'll see to it that you and Echo are given whatever support you need." Omega nodded.

"Damn," Echo muttered under his breath.

"What, Echo?" Fox asked, glancing at him sharply.

"Nothing, Fox."

"I take it you're concerned about this particular new mission?" Fox quizzed the male Agent.

"Let's just say it puts Meg in a helluva bad position, Fox," Echo remarked. "Never mind that she's hardly recovered mentally and emotionally from that whole debacle with Mark Wright! Up on stage, she's a sitting duck. She'll have absolutely no way to defend herself. No way even to carry a Winchester & Tesla, as many costume changes as she'll have."

"I might be able to rig something with a warp pocket and a unitard underneath the costumes, Ace," Omega offered.

"Emphasis on 'might,'" Echo pointed out.

"That's why she has a partner, Echo," Fox reminded him. "Omega has those enhanced senses of hers, but she also has you. And you have your experience and skill. You two are more than adequate to the task, or I wouldn't even consider it."

"But, dammit, Fox, when Meg's onstage, I won't be anywhere near her. How the hell am I supposed to guard her?"

"Fox," Omega volunteered, a mischievous glint in her eye, "Echo could probably get a bit part in a walk-on role. An extra or something. That would at least get him onstage with me. A costume, a little stage makeup—"

"Hell, no," Echo rejoined. "I got more than enough of that makeup shit impersonating that actor dude on the movie set last Christmas holidays."

"Make up your mind, Echo," Fox said, irritated. "Close to Omega in a bit part, or guarding her from offstage. Those are your options."

"Point made. All right." Echo sighed. "Put me onstage."

"Echo?!" Omega blinked in shocked surprise.

"I'm not gonna let a perp pick you off, Meg, no matter what." Echo shrugged. She laid a gentle hand on his shoulder.

"I was just teasing you, hon. I don't think you have to go through all that, Echo. Madrid told me the other day that R & D has upgraded the subcutaneous transponders to two-way voice. If you wear a headset, we can communicate even if I'm onstage."

"And you can call Romeo and India in if you need more backup. It's settled, then. You start tomorrow. Now go get some sleep," Fox commanded. "I'll call Sir Michael, discuss it with him, and get it all arranged."

"Thanks, Fox," Omega said, as the two Agents left the Director's office.

* * *

Fox waited a few moments after they left his office, then stood and moved discreetly to the bay window to look out over the Core and watch the pair. A tense Echo steered his glamorous companion through a gauntlet of gawking aliens and staring agents. Echo's right hand was lightly but firmly—almost possessively—pressed against the smooth creamy skin at the small of her back. A sharp-eyed Fox observed Echo signaling his sensitive partner by subtle changes in the pressure of that hand, gently maneuvering her through the crowd, and noticed the black-clad, squared shoulders relax as soon as the elevator bank had been reached.

Fox watched until the elevator doors closed on the attractive couple, then he turned back to his desk, smiling to himself.

*About damn time*, he thought, intensely pleased. *Zebra will want to hear about this development, when I get home tonight.*

* * *

Echo walked Omega into her quarters, and both of them promptly sighed in comfort and relaxed. Echo loosened his tie, and asked, "Mind if I ditch the Suit jacket, Meg?"

"Not unless you mind my getting rid of these high heels," Omega replied, balancing on one foot and reaching down to remove first one, then the other. "Ohh...that's better," she remarked, digging her toes into the plush carpet while Echo tossed jacket and tie across the back of her recliner. "I've gotten used to the low-heeled lace-ups we wear. I can't believe I used to wear these kinds of things all the time. Want anything out of the kitchen, Echo? A late-night snack or something?" she added, padding on bare feet into that room.

"No thanks, Meg," Echo said, flopping casually onto a corner of the black leather couch. "I think I just want to unwind a bit and then crash. We've had a late night."

"True," Omega agreed, returning to the living area with a glass of lemonade and sitting down beside Echo. "But I had a wonderful time, Ace," she murmured, looking into her glass and smiling.

"Good," was all Echo said.

* * *

He settled back with a sigh, stretched out his arms across the top of the couch, leaned his head back, and closed his eyes. Omega studied him for a moment, then she blinked several times and glanced away. Suddenly she felt—and, unbeknownst to her, looked—very weary and alone.

*No good-night kiss is coming tonight, I guess,* she thought. *I suppose India was right after all, at least to an extent.*

"Pretty tired, huh?" she murmured, tentative and testing.

"Mmm...a little," he answered, eyes still closed. "Not too bad. Just relaxing."

"Was the evening so stressful, then?"

* * *

"...Parts of it." Echo raised his head and opened his eyes as he felt Omega get up from the couch; the glass of lemonade sat abandoned, largely untouched, on the coffee table. "Want to go out again tomorrow night?"

"Don't feel obligated, Echo," Omega said in a low voice, turning at her bedroom door. "I appreciate your thoughtfulness, taking me out when I got stood up. And I appreciate that it was something you sincerely wanted to do. But don't feel like you have to keep on doing it. I'll be all right. I...always am, in the end." She turned back toward the bedroom. "Turn out the lights when you go to bed, okay?"

"Meg, wait." By the time she turned, Echo was already standing beside her. "I don't feel 'obligated' to do anything." He took her shoulder in one hand and gently nudged up her chin with the other, until she met his eyes. "Now why won't you go out with me again? I thought you said you had fun."

"I did. But you didn't."

"Who says?"

"You said."

"What?!"

"You said the evening was stressful, Echo," Omega reminded him.

"I said parts of it were stressful," Echo corrected her. "The parts where you got tapped to be a fishing lure for a shark. The rest of it was a helluva lotta fun."

"Oh."

"And Meg...I know that the last time you sat over there with a date," Echo nodded over his shoulder at the couch, "things got rather...steamy. Maybe you thought this one would end that way, too. But you told me yourself, in the island safehouse on The Beach not two weeks ago, that you preferred to take your relationships slow, build 'em gradually. And...after everything you went through with Wright, I figure you're probably a little uncomfortable regarding the opposite sex right now. Being the victim of a rape attempt has to be...painful, disturbing," Echo said softly. "Am I right?"

"Yes," Omega whispered, trying to look down. Echo held her chin firmly but gently, and she was forced to continue meeting his eyes.

"One day at a time, Meg," Echo told her, keeping his voice soft. "Let it grow in its own time, what we've got, you and me. Slow and gradual. A day at a time. Don't worry about any more than that. Right now, we've come to the end of one day, so let's look to the next, you and me—how about tomorrow night?" He let his eyes urge her to say yes.

Omega studied him for what seemed an aeon, then nodded with a slight smile.

"It's a date," she said, and Echo grinned, pleased. Then she added, "Oh! But maybe we need to check my rehearsal schedule first."

* * *

"Shit, that's right," Echo said, looking blank for a moment. "I forgot about that for a second. Okay, Ms. Diva, we'll check your rehearsal schedule, then fit our dates around it. For now, you ought to get some sleep, baby. That angel's voice of yours needs to be rested for your Broadway debut."

"Okay." Omega laughed. "Good night, Ace." She turned and entered the bedroom.

Echo clicked off the lights in her living area, and scooped up his jacket and tie as he headed through the back door, but Meg thought she heard, very faintly, "Good night, Angel-voice."

* * *

Mu knocked on the doorframe of the Director's office first thing the next morning, and Fox glanced up from his incessant paperwork.

"Oh, come in, zun," he said, waving the younger man into the room. "I want to commend you on your excellent work in apprehending Mark Wright, not just once, but twice. And I do intend to put in for a FORMAL commendation for you."

"Um, thank you, sir," Mu said, subdued. "It...it needed doing, and I could do it."

"And you wanted to do it, eh?" Fox offered. "For Omega's sake."

"Uh...yes sir."

"What can I do for you, then?"

"I..." Mu bent his head. "Sir, could you arrange an immediate transfer?"

"What?! To where?" Fox said, surprised.

"To, um, field agent in the L.A. Office should do it, I think."

"What's wrong? Does Omega know? How does she feel about it?"

"No sir, she doesn't know. And I'd appreciate it if you didn't tell her. At least, not until after I'm gone. Assuming you approve my request."

"Did the two of you have a fight? Is she why you want to transfer?"

"She's why I need to transfer, Fox," Mu sighed, "but we didn't have a fight."

"Then what happened? This isn't about what Slug did to her, is it? That whole 'she's not normal' thing?" Fox raised an eyebrow in displeasure.

"No sir!" Mu said, seeming shocked that he would even think such a thing. "No, Meg is...awesome. She's just...not for me."

Fox studied the agent across the desk from him for long moments; a downhearted Mu directed his gaze back at the desktop, unable to meet the Director's eyes.

"You don't want to do this, do you?" a shrewd Fox observed then. Mu looked up at him, startled.

"No sir, I don't," he admitted. "But...I think I gotta. For her...and for me."

"Why? Did you...well, you'd only just started dating, so I guess 'break up' is hardly the right terminology...but you know what I mean."

"Sort of," Mu sighed. "Spending that much time with her, I got to watch her a lot. And...because of everything she's just been through, let's say...well, her emotions and responses are a little closer to the surface than usual, I think. So I realized that, that I wasn't the guy she really wanted."

Fox raised a thoughtful eyebrow.

"Who do you think she wants? Wait," Fox interrupted before Mu could respond. "Was it somebody in a position of relative authority, who is at the same time NOT the Director?"

"Bingo," Mu murmured, face falling. "But will probably be the Director, one day. So I see I'm not the only one to have noticed."

"Mm, perhaps. All right. But why is that any reason for you to move across the continent?"

"Because I...because I don't think I can stand to watch her on another man's arm. I heard he...took her out last night, after I broke it off."

"You were serious about Omega."

"As a heart attack. I..." he broke off, then tried again. "She's so amazing. And gorgeous. And fun. I thought I'd found...'Her.' If you understand me. And...maybe I did. Except I wasn't her 'Him.'"

"I am very sorry, zun," Fox offered, keeping his voice quiet and his tone gentle. "Yes, I can arrange for that...as soon as possible, I suppose?"

"Yes, please."

"What about Zeta, the agent we were looking at partnering you with? Is she transferring with you? Does she even know you're transferring?"

"She knows," Mu affirmed, "because I talked to her yesterday for a long time, after I broke it off with Meg. I was...hurting pretty bad." He shrugged. "She offered to be a sounding board, and I took her up on it. And then somebody texted me, all kinda joking-like, that Meg an' Echo were going out, dressed to the nines. You know what I mean—'you got competition, bro'—and it felt like somebody had put a bullet through my chest. And I knew, if they were dressed like the report said, that Echo was pulling out all the stops. Which meant that...HE probably cares about HER, too. And I realized I never had a chance...though I think Meg seriously did try to give me one. Anyway, Zeta...was there for all of it. It was her idea that maybe some physical distance, some space, might help me out. She said it was up to you and me, whether she transferred or not. She's game, though."

"What do you want her to do?"

"I...I think maybe I need a little bit of time to, to get my sea legs back, Fox. Zeta and I partner together really well though, so yeah, if you can spare her to the West Coast, I'd like for you to send her after me...but not right away."

"Understood. And yes, I believe we can do that. Do you want to move out there but not start duty right away? Perhaps take a little bit of time to get your head together, explore the area? Have you ever been to Los Angeles?"

"Once, with the President on a campaign junket," Mu said. "But I was working. I almost never got a chance to look around wherever we were going, at least for anything other than security details." He shrugged. "But I haven't accrued near enough leave time for that, yet."

"You might be surprised, zun," Fox pointed out. "When I helped set up this organization, I never liked the notion that anyone coming into it as a career move not only lost their past, they lost everything they'd accrued in whatever job they'd held previously. It didn't seem fair, somehow, and I wanted the new recruits to have SOMEthing, dammit. So I went to bat for that as a policy. I didn't succeed across the board, but for the more experienced personnel we acquired, I was able to push through a policy that we'd match whatever they had accrued at the time they left their old life. When Omega effectively recruited you, she and I discussed it, and we both felt that, as a Secret Service lead, you were a prime 'acquisition,' let us say, and worthy of applying the policy. You have fully two Division weeks of leave."

"I do?!" Mu said, startled. "That's...wow. Thanks, Fox. And, um, I guess if you can find a way to pass on that thanks to Meg, I'd...appreciate it."

"And she doesn't know you're transferring, right?"

"No. I thought...I'd wait until I was gone, and then find a way to notify her. Otherwise, I know her; she'll try to talk me out of it, or something."

"Most likely," Fox agreed. "Though you hurt her, you know."

"I did?"

"Of course. Whether or not you are the man she would prefer, I cannot say. But she likes you, Mu, and she took your suit seriously. I saw the whole thing from the window, when you broke it off." Fox gestured at the bay window overlooking the Core. "What YOU didn't see was her reaction after you left. I did see it. And I expect Echo did, too...which may explain part of why he chose the timing he did, regarding last night's evening out."

"Oh..." Mu shook his head. "Am I wrong, then? I mean, they did go out..."

"No," Fox sighed. "I don't think you're wrong. But she is fond of you and likes you, and more than likely—and knowing her—she assumes it was because of her...personal history. You know what I mean—the 'enhancements.'"

"Well, damn. I...didn't think about that." A despondent

Mu sighed. "I seem to have messed this up, twelve ways from Sunday, just by being there. Maybe you can help convince her otherwise."

"I can try," a skeptical Fox told him. "But Omega has notions of her own where this is concerned, and it is hard to disabuse her of them."

"Then I'll see what I can do, once I can...can stand to do it," Mu determined. "Meanwhile, do I get the transfer?"

"You do. But I'm going to make it conditional," Fox noted, pulling up the forms on his virtual desktop and filling them out. "That way, if you find that you want to come back for some reason, the skids will be greased. There," he said, initialing the form. "I'll notify Juliet; she heads that Office. I'll also notify your supervisor here; don't worry, zun, I'll be discreet. You have a minimum of three days' leave, and more if you want them, effective immediately. Go to your quarters and pack what you'll need, and catch a maglev west. I'll see your quarters furnishings and other personal items are sent along within a day. And Juliet will have temporary quarters for you until you get set up."

"Okay. Thanks, Fox."

"You're welcome, zun. After all," Fox said, wry, "I seem to be the general father figure in the place. I suppose it behooves me to look after my children. Especially when they're hurting."

Mu cocked his head in some puzzlement; Fox chuckled and waved a dismissive hand.

"Never mind, Mu. You're dismissed, unless you need to talk about something else."

"No sir, that about does it."

"Run on, then."

And Mu was gone.

# **Chapter 2**

"All right, Meg, here's the story," Echo told his partner as he steered the Corvette toward the rehearsal hall a little later that morning. "We've got a double layer of cover. Layer one: We're undercover detectives that Mike has hired, investigating the incidents at the theater. Layer two: Our cover as detectives is as actress and manager. You're actress Margaret Stratford—"

"Nicknamed Meg," she interjected, and Echo nodded.

"—And I'm Alec 'Echo' Williams, your rather overprotective manager, with whom you're romantically involved."

"Oh?" Omega's eyebrow shot up, intrigued.

"That way, nobody thinks twice about seeing us together all the time."

"...Okay. That works."

She glanced away, avoiding his eyes. Echo, however, scanned his partner from head to toe out of the corner of his eye.

"You're wearing your gym clothes."

"Uh-huh. I figured I'd show up ready to rehearse."

"Have you already inserted the transponder implant? Or do you need my help?"

"No, it's already in."

"I hope you didn't have any trouble with it this time. I didn't hear you yell or anything. Damn, when I saw your shoulder split open like that, up at Ipswich, I..." He shook his head. "I honestly didn't know WHAT to do. And that's...rare, for me."

"No, the extreme reaction seems to have gone away along with everything else to do with that little...interlude...with Wright. Anyway, I put the transponder right here." Omega laid her index finger behind her left ear. "I figured I could hear your transmissions easy that way, with nobody else the wiser. I'll admit it took a bit of doing, plus using a hand mirror along with the mirror in the bathroom. I almost called you to help at one point, but then I figured out how to do it; it's good. Oh, and I slipped a warp pocket into my shorts, so I'm carrying my Winchester & Tesla. You got the headset, right?"

"Yup. It's in my pocket," Echo told her. "And I've got a full complement of weapons on me. Plus a couple extra."

"Extra?"

"Yeah. I got my usual two blasters plus Winchester & Tesla. Then I added another blaster, another Winchester & Tesla, and a collapsible-stock tachyon splitter rifle. Not to mention spare battery packs for all of it." He neglected to tell her about the throwing knives, taser, and collapsible baton that were also secreted on his body; he intended to let nothing happen to this partner who was so dear to him, if he could prevent it. *And I'll beat the perp to death to prevent it, if that's what it takes,* he thought.

"Holy crap, Ace! Warp pockets?" Omega stared at him in something like shock.

"Warp pockets." He nodded.

"Okay. Well, you shouldn't need any of it today, Echo," she observed. "We're not at the theater."

"No. But you know I'm always prepared."

"I know," Omega grinned. "Are you SURE you weren't a Boy Scout?"

"Scout's honor," Echo deadpanned, pulling over and parking. "We're here."

* * *

"Ah, there you are," Michael said, coming to meet them as the two Agents entered the rehearsal hall. "Sofia, Charlie, these are the investigators I was telling you about," he said, introducing them to his leading lady and the rehearsal pianist. "This is Margaret Stratford, and this is Alec Williams, more commonly known as 'Echo' to his friends. Margaret will be filling in for you, Sofia, until we can catch this damnable saboteur." He handed Omega a schedule. "Here, my dear. This is the schedule of rehearsals and performances you'll need to attend over the next couple of weeks."

While Michael went over the schedule, Sofia scanned Omega from top to bottom, then turned to Michael, interrupting.

"Are you certain she can handle it?" she asked, cold as ice.

"She can handle it," Echo said, firm and confident.

"You heard her 'audition' last night, Sofia," Michael reminded his costar. "She'll do fine."

"Sofia," Omega said softly, "may I talk with you for a moment?" She drew the other woman aside, and they conversed animatedly in low tones as the men watched.

* * *

"Meg is a special lady," Michael remarked, offhand, as he observed the female Agent soothing Sofia's ruffled feathers.

"She is," Echo agreed.

"Echo," Michael said, throwing the male Agent a sidelong glance, "what is Meg to you?"

"I told you on the phone, Mike: I'm her agent."

"No, no, no. Forget the cover story for a minute. What is she to YOU? Personally?"

"My partner." Echo looked askance at Michael.

"Nothing more?"

"Why do you ask?"

"You seem unusually...protective. Of her. I've never seen that side of you." Michael studied the other male. "As long as we've known each other, Echo, you know you can trust me. What you say to me now goes no farther; any secrets you impart—personal, or professional—will go with me to my grave if necessary. I only want to help."

"...All right." Echo sighed. "Meg was almost raped recently, Mike."

"What?! Where??"

"In her own bedroom."

"Inside Headquarters?? How?" Michael was incredulous. Echo looked away.

"Let's just say...a perp, an old enemy of mine, intended Meg for...breeding stock...and the guy got in while she was asleep...and leave it at that, okay?" Echo's voice held a note of pain. Michael nodded.

"Is she...all right?"

* * *

"She's...fine. She woke up and defended herself as best she could, given he already had her partly pinned down, and screamed for me—I have the adjacent quarters, connected by a 'back door,' which we usually keep open these days, 'cause we get along like gangbusters, and trust each other to the max. So I came running, and...everything turned out okay in the end." *She could probably use that counseling we keep talking around,* he thought to himself. *But it's a bit late for that at the moment.* He added aloud, "Don't worry, she can handle this."

"She's important to you, isn't she?" Michael asked then.

"Like I told you, she's my...partner." Echo paused, then added, "With all that entails."

"Best friends?"

"The best I've ever had in my life."

"Ah." Michael gave Echo a knowing smile. "And...perhaps a bit more. Or," he decided, "perhaps you'd both LIKE it to be a bit more..."

"Um," Echo began, but found he had nothing else to add. Rather to his chagrin, Michael simply nodded with a slight smile.

"All right, then," Michael decided. "I understand now. Let me know if there's anything I can do to...help."

Echo could only nod.

* * *

"Sofia, I have a good idea how you're feeling right now, and I don't blame you," Omega said gently to the other woman. "Let me assure you, however, that this is not some ploy to take over the role. I already have a job I love. I'm not after yours. I can't do it justice, anyway. But I can keep you alive to keep performing for your thousands of fans. That's why I'm here. The ONLY reason I'm here."

Sofia scrutinized the female Agent.

"You're either a damn good actress, or you're completely sincere," the Broadway prima donna said then.

"I'm a decent actress, but I am sincere."

"...All right. I think I trust you. 'Why' are you taking over the role? What's our story?"

"Mmm...you injured your throat, or maybe you're warding off an illness, and I'm an old friend from chorus days?"

"That'll work," Sofia agreed. "It's fairly well known I'm protective of my voice. Let's try the illness, I think; I can have a chest cold coming on without anyone else being the wiser."

"Good. We'll go with that, then."

"Margaret..."

"Call me Meg."

"All right." Sofia gave her a smile, then sobered. "Meg, aren't you scared? You could be killed. Surely Michael told you about the chandelier..."

"Yes, he did. Been there, done that." Omega shrugged. "It just comes with the territory."

"But if something happens...doesn't your family worry about you? Your husband?"

"I don't have a family, Sofia. And I'm not married."

"Oh? Then he's not..." Sofia nodded in Echo's direction, and Omega glanced where she indicated.

"You mean Echo? Echo's my partner, Sofia."

"Oh." Sofia studied the attractive head of Alpha Line. "Is he...single?"

Omega glanced down, pretending her attention had been suddenly taken by the rehearsal/performance schedule. *Aaand there goes any hope I had of making the partnership 'something more,'* she decided, dreams sinking fast. *I can't possibly compete with her. After all, what am I, really? Just... 'damaged goods.' Deliberately damaged goods, but still.*

It did not occur to the female Agent that recent events were taking a severe toll on her mental and emotional outlook, nor that post-traumatic stress often resulted in a negative self-image. Nor did she realize that she had just endured the latest in a long string of such traumas, beginning with the revelation over a year earlier that she had been extensively modified as a child, against her will and with no anesthesia. Worse, those modifications had been designed to prevent even the galactic tech in the Cerebellar Holographic Mnemonic Re-Encoding Induction System from wiping her memories, so she was unable to forget them, having once been 'deprogrammed' and made to recall them. Worst of all, given the full extent and nature of those modifications—which included the addition of significant amounts of extraterrestrial sentient and animal DNA to her own genetic material, among other things, the former taken from kidnap/murder victims—she was no longer certain that she was worthy of anyone's love interest, let alone that of her heroic partner, a man whom she all but idolized.

So she gave the only answer that she felt was fair and honest.

"...Yes, he's...single." Omega stifled a sigh.

"Hmm..."

* * *

"Okay, that's taken care of," Omega told Echo in a low tone, as she moved to stand beside him once again. "I'm not a threat to her any longer."

"What did you do?" Echo matched his partner's tone.

"I just talked to her a bit. I made sure she understood that I wasn't angling to take over the role or anything like that. That was what she was worried about."

"Oh, okay. That's good, then. Great job. Got your rehearsal schedule figured out?"

"Yeah."

"And?"

"Well, among other things, I'll have to switch back to a twenty-four hour day," Omega said. "A forty-eight hour day doesn't give me any time to sleep, what with performances and rehearsals."

"Hm."

"Yeah."

33

"Hell. Your sleep schedule has gotten yanked all over the damn map in the last month. Are you sure you can handle it, baby?"

"Do I really have a choice?"

"No, I guess not. Well, we'll just deal with it, then. What about our date tonight?" Echo asked.

"Um...there's a problem with that," Omega answered, hesitant.

"They want you at the performance tonight," Echo anticipated.

"Yeah. I have to help Sofia backstage. I'll pick up the cues and costume changes that way."

"What about afterward?"

"I have to be back here at the rehearsal hall first thing tomorrow morning. Like, not later than eight in the morning, ish. I gather the time is a little squishy, but not THAT squishy. There's a lotta stuff they need to cover with me, to get me up to speed in time."

"Oh. So you have to go straight home tonight and get some sleep." Echo's voice was ever so slightly flat, and an expression that, in another man, might have been disappointment, lurked deep in the dark eyes.

"Yeah, Echo. I'm sorry. But it's your lucky day after all." Omega tried to be as nonchalant as possible, but she studied her schedule again, as intent on it as if it were an alien criminal.

"Why?" He glanced at her.

"You've still got a date, if you want one. Sofia thinks you're a hunk."

"What?" If it were possible, Echo's voice was even flatter than before, and Omega bit her lip, not sure whether to laugh or cry.

"She's attracted to you, Ace. She said to ask you to stop by her dressing room after the performance," Omega said, now intently watching the pianist warm up. "She wants to go out to a post-performance dinner with you."

"Didn't you tell her we already had a date?" Echo's brows

were knit, apparently in bemusement at this unanticipated sequence of events.

"No." Omega stifled the sigh that tried to escape.

"Why not?"

"One: I knew by then I couldn't keep it. And two: I'm not in her league."

"What do you mean?"

"Sofia's gorgeous, Echo. And she's a star. And incredibly talented. And really very sweet. Like I said," she shrugged, "I'm not in her league."

* * *

Echo's forehead creased as he remembered the self-image Omega had telepathically shown both Echo and Wright, her purported attempted rapist who had been modified and brainwashed just as Omega had been, only some three or four weeks earlier—a timid, plain, mousy blonde, awkward and untalented.

"Meg?"

"Hm?"

"Try looking in the mirror sometime, baby. I mean, really looking. Seriously."

Omega just stared at him, puzzled.

"Never mind," Echo sighed. "Mike's waiting to begin. Let's get a move on."

* * *

Echo spent the rest of the day sitting in the corner of the rehearsal hall, watching and listening as Michael and Sofia put Omega through her paces. By the time the intense all-day rehearsal was finished, both performers were impressed, and Echo was duly astounded at his partner's artistic ability.

Omega, however, was just plain worn out. Echo watched as she eased to the floor in a corner, wiping her sweaty face with her shirttail.

"Damn," Echo murmured to the two professional performers, "Meg looks blasted. She doesn't normally look THIS tired after a full-out training session! Is she going to be able to do this?"

"She'll be fine, Echo," Michael reassured him. "This was an intensive crash course in the entire show. If Sofia or I had put in the day she just did, we'd be exhausted, too. And probably a lot worse than she is. She's in great shape."

"Yes," Sofia agreed. "We just put her through the equivalent of three or four performances in one day. And she's still going. She'll do well." Sofia sidled up to Echo as Michael went to talk to Omega. "Did she pass along my invitation?"

"Yes."

"So I can expect to see you after the performance tonight?" the lovely brunette verified, pleased.

"No."

"Oh?!" Sofia was at once surprised and offended.

"Look, Sofia," Echo explained in a quiet, firm voice, "Meg didn't tell you, but she and I had planned to go out tonight. That date now might only be taking her home, putting some good food in her, and seeing that she gets unwound and in bed at a reasonable time, but I won't stand her up."

"I...see," Sofia remarked, staring at the tired blonde across the room, who still conversed with Michael. "Are you two... an item?"

"...Something like that," Echo replied. "A...package deal, you might say. We come together."

"So to speak." Sofia raised a suggestive eyebrow as she jumped on the unintentional double entendre. Echo remained expressionless.

"So to speak," he reiterated.

"Why did she bother to pass on my invitation to you, then? Let alone to tell me that you were unattached?"

"It's...a long story, Sofia. Meg was being Meg. Accept that that's just the way she is, and let it go at that, all right?"

"No, it isn't all right. Effectively, she lied to me about you. What else did she lie to me about?"

"Okay, look. I didn't want to say anything for the simple reason that it really isn't mine to tell, but if it helps you understand where she's coming from, she probably won't mind. Meg's past involves extensive childhood abuse—from somebody OUTSIDE her family, let me add—and several looming tragedies, including the loss of her entire family. Much more recent experiences include stalking and an attempted rape. That latter collection of events has thrown it all into a kind of...spiraling cesspit of emotional...shit. She's...having a hard time of it, from a self-esteem perspective, right now. Does that help explain?"

"Oh! Damn," Sofia murmured. "I would say so."

"Good. So that was the mindset she was coming from, when she told you I was unattached. She feels..." Echo broke off and shook his head, searching for words. "I dunno. She just doesn't feel good about herself."

"Okay. Any chance I can convince you to change your mind?" Sofia edged closer, apparently dismissing Omega—and all related considerations—from her mind.

"No."

The beautiful actress pouted in disappointment, and departed for the theater shortly thereafter.

* * *

It transpired that, while Sofia was somewhat aware of the 'mixed-origin' cast and crew thanks to a long friendship with Michael, the third lead, Sebastian, who made up the last member of the play's romantic triangle, was both human AND unaware of the presence of offworlders. This at once complicated and simplified matters, as it required that Alpha One keep him in the dark about the investigation.

"But no," Michael informed them, "I can't see how he could possibly be our malevolent theater apparition. He's a brilliant performer with a wonderful voice, but he doesn't... think...like that."

"You've known him for a while?" Omega asked.

"Oh yes," Michael noted. "And quite well. He was, at one time, my protégé."

"At one time?" Echo pressed. "He's not any longer?"

"Only because he outgrew the need for a mentor. We are still good friends, Bast and I."

"That probably takes care of that," Echo decided. "But we'll keep him under watch, all the same, Meg. Just in case."

"All over it, Ace."

"As usual."

* * *

Echo stayed backstage that night, never far from his partner or the three principals during the performance, intently observing every detail around him, and logging it in memory. The performance remained unmarred, however, and Echo used his observations to plan for contingencies. After the curtain call, he approached a clearly bone-weary Omega.

"Ready to go?" he asked quietly.

"In a little bit," she replied, handing him an armload of sweaty, dirty costumes before picking up another pile herself. "Here. Help me carry these down to the costume room so they can be cleaned before tomorrow night."

"Okay." An obliging Echo trailed along behind Omega through the guts of the theater until they came to the costume shop, where they deposited the piles of soiled clothing, then made their way back to the dressing rooms. "Now?" he asked.

"Let me check one more time with Sofia," Omega replied, knocking on the appropriate door.

"Echo?" Sofia's muffled voice said hopefully, and Omega shot a quick glance at him.

"It's both of us, Sofia," Omega replied, and the door opened to reveal the lovely actress wrapped in an aqua satin jacquard robe...and not much else. "I just wanted to see if you needed anything more before I left."

"No—not now," Sofia said, smiling at Echo. "Go home and get some rest, Meg. I feel a 'sore throat' coming on after tomorrow's performance."

"All right. See you later, Echo," Omega said, glancing at him with tired, empty eyes as she turned to go.

"Hold on, Meg," Echo said, laying a hand on her shoulder.

38

"Where are you going?"

"Home."

"But I've got the keys." He held up the keyring and jingled the Corvette's keys.

"And I've got a hand to hail a taxi," she replied quietly.

"C'mon, Meg, I'll get you home, baby," Echo said, putting an arm around his weary partner and snubbing the actress, who stood gaping after the couple. "See you tomorrow, Sofia."

* * *

"I'm sorry, Echo," a dog-tired Omega murmured. Her eyes were closed; her head leaned against the headrest in the Corvette as Echo drove them home.

"For what?" he wondered.

"Blowing your date."

"Well...it isn't as much fun as last night's, but I still enjoy the company," Echo admitted.

"Huh?" Omega raised her head and opened confused blue eyes.

"Meg," Echo told her, voice soft, face sincere, "there's absolutely no conflict tonight between where I need to be and where I want to be."

Omega puzzled that one for a bit, then sat up straighter.

"In that case, I should try to be a little better conversationalist," she decided.

* * *

After a good night's sleep, Omega woke very early. "Oh, boy, this is gonna get interesting, and not in the good way," she muttered, looking at the alarm clock. "After that whole shit with Mark, going on and off Division days? Now throw me back onto a regular twenty-four hour Earth day plus adding the physicality and scheduling of performances...this is gonna hose my sleep bad."

But when she got up, threw on her robe, and headed into her living area, the aromatic smell of chicory coffee was already wafting through the back door.

"Meg?" Echo's voice, kept intentionally low, drifted

39

through along with the coffee aroma. "I heard movement. Are you up, baby?"

"Yeah, an' I smell coffee!" she said and grinned, coming into his quarters. Echo, dressed in trousers, but no shirt or shoes—and completely unaware of how appealing such a bare-chested appearance was to his partner, even as many times as she'd seen it—met her at his kitchen door with a steaming cup. Plenty of cream was already in it, just as she liked it.

"Here. Absorb that, Angel-voice," he told her, "then you can give me a hand with breakfast."

"It's a deal. Whatcha got in mind to fix?" Omega sucked down the hot stimulant in record time.

"Will a mushroom 'n' cheese omelet work for you?"

"Yup, it works for me just great. I'll get the mushrooms." Omega pulled the fresh fungi from Echo's refrigerator, proceeding to lightly rinse, stem, and slice them. Meanwhile, Echo shredded a couple of different varieties of cheese. "Geez. Just at the moment, I really miss your mom, Echo."

"Huh?" he said, glancing up. "I'm sorry; I was going over the plans for the day in my head. What did you say, baby? Ma? Wait. Is something wrong? Do I need to go call Ma?"

"No, everything is all right. It's only that I miss Dihl, and our 'family cooking sessions,' is all. This," she gestured at the cutting board, "made me think of 'em. No big deal. Have you heard from her?"

"Yeah, I talked to her for a few minutes, the other night. It seems Angamar is putting in for a transfer to her Division; her dad died and was buried, and now, as the eldest offspring, Angamar looks like becoming the family matriarch."

"Oh. What's your mom gonna do?"

"She doesn't know yet; she's still trying to figure that out. We talked about the various options, and I did tell her that you and I both would miss her pretty bad if she put in for a permanent transfer to the Ranch. At least until such time as we decide to retire there ourselves. Unless you wanna retire to the Farm instead. Which we can do, if you'd rather."

"Aw. Well, maybe she'll split her time between here and the Ranch. And if it comes to that, Alpha One can do the same with the Farm and the Ranch. When that day arrives."

"Yeah. That'll work. And I suspect that Ma will choose the split-time option, too. She's been enjoying our 'family time' as much as you an' me; she told me so the other night. I think she's really happy to have me back, and to get you in the bargain, too."

"Good. I'm glad, and I agree. I love Zebra to death, and don't tell her I said this 'cause I wouldn't hurt her feelings for anything, but she's not quite old enough for me to think of her as a mom figure. Let alone MY mom figure."

"You've kinda adopted my mom as yours, baby?"

"Um." Omega shot him a glance, uncertain if he was offended or not. Something around his eyes, as he looked at her, told her it pleased him, however, and she offered him a shy smile. "Yeah, kinda sorta. I mean, she'll never replace my birth mom, don't take that the wrong way or nothin', but...it's kind of a relief sometimes to have an older woman I can go to for advice and junk, if you know what I mean. And know that she cares, and that she'll do the best she can by me. And the feeling is mutual, for that matter. You...don't mind, do you?"

"Of course not. I think it's great."

"Okay. Good." Omega glanced at Echo's growing mound of shredded cheese. "Ooo. What-all have you got there, Ace?" she asked, waving the tip of the chef's knife at the pile.

"Mmm...Jack, some Swiss, and your favorite."

"Cheshire?"

"Yep."

"Oh, boy! Thanks. Here's the 'shrooms." Omega handed him the small bowl full of sliced mushrooms.

"Good." Echo tossed the fungi in the hot skillet and began sautéing them. "Grab the eggs and hand 'em to me, okay?"

"Got 'em." Omega got out four eggs, and in moments, a large omelet was in work on the stove. The two Agents wove in and out as they efficiently prepared the meal together, never in each other's way, as comfortable working together in the kitchen as they were on a mission in the field.

A few minutes later, they were sharing the omelet at Echo's dining table—one plate, two forks.

"Mm. That turned out pretty damn good," Echo mumbled around a mouthful.

"Mm-hm," Omega agreed. "We should try catering sometime."

"Hey, you hush that, now. Don't give Fox any ideas," Echo warned. "That'll wind up the cover for our next assignment."

"Speaking of which," Omega veered off, "I checked the schedule, and today looks like being a duplicate of yesterday."

"Okay. I'll need to stay here for a while, then, if you're at the rehearsal hall. You'll be safe there. Get Alpha Two to give you a ride over, and I'll bring the 'Vette when I can."

"All right. Why?"

"Fox wants to see me."

"That's fine. Just tell me the next time y'all decide to fake your death, okay?" Omega smiled, but her eyes were somber, and Echo glanced down.

"Meg, you know we couldn't. Everything hinged on your believing it..."

"I know, Echo. It just...hurt."

"Well...I don't think Fox has anything like that planned," Echo informed her, trying for a touch of levity in his tone and expression; he was rewarded with the hint of a smile. "I know I don't."

"Good! Well, I'm for a hot shower, then I'm off to rehearsal. You gonna take care of the dishes?"

"Yeah, I'll throw 'em in the dishwasher."

"Thanks. Will you be by the rehearsal later?"

"Unless Fox changes my plans, which is gonna be damn hard to do, all things considered—he'll have to give me something awfully urgent to do it, let's put it like that. Take your cell phone just in case."

"Wilco. Catch you later, Ace."

"See you at rehearsal, Angel-voice."

* * *

"Morning, Fox. What's up?" Echo asked the Director, entering his office.

"Good morning, Echo," Fox said, looking up from his paperwork. "Close the door and have a seat, zun."

"Hm. This sounds serious," Echo observed, as he complied.

"It is. It's also unofficial," Fox said.

"Meaning?"

"It's a chat between old friends, Echo. I'm...concerned."

"About...?"

"It looked to me like you pulled out all the stops when you took Omega out the other night."

"We had a good time," Echo replied, deliberately evasive, and shrugged.

"Are the two of you still going out together?"

"Well...yes and no."

* * *

"What do you mean?" Fox asked, confused. "Either you're still dating, or you aren't."

"This situation with the 'theater phantom' kinda makes it hard to schedule a date, Fox. Meg's up to her eyeballs in rehearsals and performances." Echo shrugged again.

"Ah." Fox nodded in understanding. The Director watched his Agent closely, as he added, "So. Is that why you didn't want her on this assignment?"

"Shit, of course not, Fox," Echo replied immediately. "I just don't like setting Meg up as a helpless target for some crazy perp. Especially when she's still trying to get over the whole big pile of shit with Wright. Where she was an almost-helpless target of a crazy perp."

"Echo...Omega has done this sort of assignment before."

"I know, Fox, but this is a different situation."

"What makes it different?" Fox pressed.

"Well..." Echo seemed at a loss to explain; his face held a blank expression. "I...don't know how to say it, Fox..."

"There's her mental and emotional state," Fox offered.

"Yeah..."

"And the fact that you're usually right beside her, but can't be, quite, for this."

"Um, well yeah..."

"And she still needs that counseling she keeps tap-dancing around."

"Uh-huh..."

"But none of those are the biggest thing, are they?"

"What?"

"I'll tell you the biggest thing that's different, Echo," Fox offered quietly. "You."

"Me?!"

"Yes. I gather you decided to...heed my advice about not taking your partner for granted."

Echo raised an eyebrow and watched Fox coolly, without replying.

"You can't coddle her, you know. Can't keep her locked in a saferoom all the time, just because you're afraid something will happen to her, to your heart—she isn't going to LET you, for one thing. And yes, I know that's what she is to you, zun... because I've been there, myself, now. I've seen that look in your eyes...in my own." Fox shrugged. "In the mirror, at least. And I still had to let my heart come with me—on the bridge of my flagship, no less—when we went into battle against the Cortians, earlier this year."

Echo still said nothing; he sat stoically, watching his oldest friend and mentor.

"Echo...how does Omega feel? About the two of you, I mean. As...MORE than partners."

Suddenly the brown eyes faltered and looked down.

"You still don't know for certain, do you?" Fox guessed, as shrewd as ever. Echo continued staring at the floor, and Fox studied him. Had Omega been there, she would have seen compassion deep in Fox's eyes.

"Echo, I understand," a surprisingly-gentle Fox offered

then. "I remember what happened to Chase. I'm...sorry we didn't get there in time. And I'm sorry things didn't work out, to begin with. But I know why you're worried. You don't want the lightning to strike twice. And now you've decided to step out and make your partner the special part of your life that you've been wanting to...and this comes up. So that ramps up your concern, your anxiety...and your personal involvement. But—"

"Fox, where's Mu?" Echo asked suddenly, looking up. Fox raised an eyebrow at the sudden change of topic.

"He asked to be transferred to the L.A. Office."

"Really?! Why?"

"...Personal reasons."

"Hmm..." Echo mused, and Fox realized his astute successor likely understood far more than he was letting on. "Listen, Fox, thanks for the concern. I'll try not to be overly protective of Meg, I swear. But I gotta go. I got a couple of things I need to do before meeting Meg at the rehearsal hall."

"Echo—" Fox began.

Echo was gone.

"Maybe I SHOULD have made it an official chat," Fox grumbled. "That way, he couldn't walk out in the middle of it..."

* * *

Echo sat alone in his study, door closed, placing a vid-call. The viewscreen flickered to life with the image of another Division One agent.

"Mu here."

"Mu, it's Echo. Have you got a minute to chat?"

"...Um. Hi, Echo. Sure. I'm taking a few days off and exploring the area a bit before I return to duty; I don't have any place I have to be at a given time today. So, um. How's it going?"

"Fine."

"How's...how's Meg?" The now-West-Coast agent's voice was slightly wistful.

"She's fine, too, Mu."

"Did she...say any—?"

"She doesn't know I'm calling you."

"Oh."

Echo studied the other agent's image with a practiced eye.

"You've got a real thing for Meg, don't you?" he said, very quiet.

"She's...a very special lady." Mu shrugged, looking away from the monitor for a moment.

"She is, that," Echo agreed. "So why did you break it off?"

It was Mu's turn to scrutinize Echo for long moments. Finally he responded.

"I wasn't who she wanted to be with. Wasn't the one who could make her happy."

"Oh? Did she tell you so?"

"No. I figured it out after watching her some. I...cared enough to...to get out of the way."

"Is that also why you requested a transfer?"

"Yes," Mu said simply.

"Mu," Echo began, more than a little hesitant, "who...do you think Meg does want...to be with?"

"You."

"Me?!" Echo looked blank. The other man gaped in astonishment.

"Damn, Echo!" Mu exclaimed. "You're supposed to be one of, if not the, top Agent in the whole damn organization! You're one of only two surviving Originals! You've got eyes like a hawk. You don't miss a thing. How is it that you can't see what you've got, right under your nose?! I'd give one eye and both legs if Meg lit up like that when I walked into a room!"

"I...see," Echo said, astounded. "You're...you're sure?"

"Not one hundred percent, but pretty damn close," Mu sighed. "Listen, Echo. I know you took her out the other night when I broke our date; I heard about it...well, let's just say I heard it through the Agency grapevine. I don't know what your motive was, but if you were only being nice, if you're not really interested—and you're a damn fool if you're not—at least be careful and don't hurt her, all right? If you're serious about her...look, just take care of her, okay? For...for both of us. And if you...decide you don't want to be more than, than...her teammate...give me a call. I'll gladly step in for you. Maybe... if she knew that you, I mean if things didn't work out between you...well, maybe she might look twice at me then."

Echo nodded slowly, wordlessly, in the face of the other man's heartbreak.

"Listen, Echo," Mu said, glancing at his wrist chronometer to make excuse, "I've...gotta go. It's still early here, I haven't had breakfast, and I'm...starving," he lied; more, Echo knew he was lying, and Mu knew that he knew. "I hope you know what a lucky man you are. Give my...give my love to Meg."

"I will, Mu," Echo said quietly, realizing the other man was trying to escape while he could still maintain his composure.

"Goodbye, Echo."

"Goodbye, Mu."

* * *

Echo arrived some time later at the rehearsal hall. Slipping in unnoticed, he positioned himself where he could watch but remain undetected. Omega was struggling with the choreography of the costume-party scene.

"Blast it, Michael, I'm never gonna get this," she sighed, discouraged.

"Of course you can, Meg," the actor encouraged. "Why, Echo told me you're the Agency's version of Ginger Rogers."

"Suuurre he did," Omega responded in good-natured disbelief. "I know Echo better than that." Echo blinked, startled; he had, in fact, made that very statement to Michael.

"What do you mean?" Michael asked, puzzled.

"Echo's general idea of a compliment is, 'You'll do,'" Omega declared. She grinned, rueful, and Michael laughed.

"Echo is, indeed, a man of few words," Michael agreed, "but just because he doesn't compliment you to your face doesn't mean he doesn't notice, or doesn't appreciate it. You should know that by now."

"That's true, I suppose," Omega acknowledged. "Oh, well. I don't guess it matters. The last time somebody gave me a nice compliment, he dumped me and moved clear across the country, according to the email I got from Fox this morning. And the one before that tried to rape me."

*Damn,* Echo thought, disappointed and upset. *She's forgotten all about the conversation in the hot tub up in Massachusetts. It's like, suddenly, all she can think of is the bad stuff. What's going on in that beautiful head?*

"...Ouch," Michael responded, wincing.

"Uh-huh. Those kinds of compliments I can live without." Omega thought for a minute. "Echo said, huh?"

"Yes, he did," Michael verified.

Omega wiped her sweaty face, brows drawn together in deep concentration. Then she nodded.

"All right, Ace, I'm not gonna make you out a liar," Omega declared to the air. "Let's try it again, Michael."

"That's the spirit," the performer told her, as they went through the steps yet again.

Half an hour later, a perspiring Omega had the scene down cold. A watching Echo abruptly 'appeared' near the door of the room as she and Michael prepared for one last run-through.

"Hi, Ace!" Omega called, an exultant smile lighting her face. "Hey look! I been working on this all damn morning, and I finally got it! Catch this! And one, two, three—!"

An intensely gratified Echo leaned against the doorframe, a slight smile on his own face, watching his partner and her leading man dance and sing their way perfectly through the scene, seeing the way her face lit up now that he was obviously in the room. When it was over, he broke into applause, and Omega, flushed with exertion, colored still deeper in pleasure.

"Will it do?" she asked, seeming somewhat shy. "I can't really tell..."

"More than," Echo told her. "I just have one thing to say... to you." Echo turned to Michael. Omega blinked in surprise, and her face fell slightly.

"And that would be?" an impassive Michael asked, glancing at Omega's crestfallen face.

"I want my partner BACK when this is over." Echo jerked his thumb at Omega with a grin. "You're not dragging her off to star in one of your productions, I don't care how terrific a prima donna she is." Omega beamed.

"Don't worry, Echo," she said, and grinned, herself. "This is way too hard a job to do on a regular basis. I'm afraid you're stuck with me."

* * *

A mischievous, almost amorous, glimmer flashed through the smoky brown eyes, and Michael quickly interjected, "Don't go there, Echo. Not 'til you get her home, at any rate!" The two men, one human, one alien, grinned at each other. Omega rolled her eyes toward the ceiling, and an idea struck. She threw a sly glance at the pianist, who returned it knowingly.

"Hit it, Charlie! Just like I told you!" she told the pianist, grabbing her partner as the musician broke into a rapid Latin rhythm. Michael watched in amusement as the two Agents expertly cha-cha'ed twice around the room, Echo grinning, Omega giggling like a schoolgirl.

"Very good," he commended, applauding as they slowed to a stop. "No one told me Ginger's partner was named Fred."

"We do all right on the dance floor together," Echo understated with a grin.

"See what I mean, Michael?" Omega shrugged with a smile, and Echo sobered thoughtfully, suddenly understanding what she had been trying to say earlier. "Eh bien. What's next on the schedule?"

"That's it," Michael said. "You've got the show down. Your call tonight is at 6:30 local. Go home and get some rest until then. You debut two nights from now."

* * *

"So what did Fox want?" Omega wondered as they navigated Manhattan in the Corvette.

"Nothing much," Echo hedged. "He sorta wanted an update on, uh, what was going on with this whole theater thing, and if we'd found out anything yet. And," he shrugged, "if we enjoyed our evening out, the other night."

"Aw. So you told him it was a mixed bag?"

"I told him we still weren't sure of anything regarding the theater, and that we both had fun on our date, but that the rehearsal schedule was hosing our attempts to go out again," the male Agent admitted.

"Okay. So just a little update for him, huh?"

"Yup."

"It surprises me that he'd ask about our date, I guess," Omega decided.

"Nah. Remember, I told you, all the agents are Fox's 'kids,'" Echo reminded her. "And since you've kinda created our little family, with Fox as the father figure, he's got even more interest in you an' me, and Romeo an' India, as his special kids."

"That's...really sweet," Omega observed. "Whatever you do, do NOT tell Fox I said that, though. I can just imagine his face, upon his actions being called 'sweet.'"

"Ha! Don't worry, I won't. 'Cause you're right! Have you had lunch yet?" Echo asked his partner.

"No. And I'm starved," Omega replied. "I burned off bazillions of calories in rehearsal this morning. Have you eaten?"

"Nope. I'd say it's time for lunch, then. Whatcha up for?"

"Right now, if it's remotely human food, I'm game. I'd even go for some of the off-world stuff, as long as it doesn't eat a hole through my stomach."

Echo chuckled. "Pizza?" he suggested.

"Trifle's?"

"Yep."

"Let's do it!"

* * *

Minutes later, they were seated at their favorite table in

the Antarean felinoid's restaurant, being served their usual kitchen-sink pizza. Omega dug in with significant enthusiasm, replenishing her depleted reserves given her artificially-amped metabolism, and Echo watched for a moment with hidden amusement—no less affectionate, for all that—before starting in himself. After giving his partner time to blunt hunger's edge, he tossed off a casual inquiry.

"It looked to me like you were glad to see me, back there. Was Mike being too rough on you?"

"Oh, no," Omega replied, glancing up from her pizza with a smile. "Michael's a nice guy. Funny as hell, too. He's got a great sense of humor."

"So you two are getting along well?"

"Uh-huh."

"Why were you so glad I showed up, then?"

* * *

"I'm always glad to see you, Ace." Omega looked up at him, nonplussed. "You're only the best friend I've got. We're together so much that when you're not around, sometimes it feels like I left half my brain at home." She smiled, and Echo returned the smile, a warm glimmer deep in the dark eyes.

"Well, it's nice to be wanted, I suppose," he remarked, half-teasing.

"I...really wouldn't know," Omega said, withdrawing slightly as she returned her attention to the pizza. Consequently, she failed to see the pained look that flashed across Echo's face.

* * *

"Come on, Meg, you know better than that," Echo said softly.

"The data points are running pretty consistently one-sided, Echo," she replied in a low voice.

"I thought you and your best friend were starting to see each other fairly regularly," he deadpanned. Omega gave him a tired smile as she deposited the last pizza crust on her plate.

"Nice try, Ace. But you and I both know you're just being kind, hon. If you'd really been interested, you'd have asked me

51

out a long time ago."

"Now that's not true," he declared. "It's taken me all this time to decide if you'd even go, never mind be offended and wanna break up the partnership, or something equally bad."

"Aw." Omega glanced at him, uncertain. "You really mean that?"

"Hell, yeah. As for being needed...have you forgotten Ma and the Ranch?" he wondered.

"Huh?"

"Back in June, when I thought Ma was dying," Echo reminded her. "I needed you then, and I've told you so. I leaned on you hard, baby."

"Meh," she murmured. "Yeah, I guess, but it wasn't like you needed it to be ME that you leaned on. You just needed a friend there. Joe coulda done as well."

"No, he couldn't, baby," Echo protested. "I needed my BEST friend there. I needed the woman who knows me so well that I don't even have to say when I'm hurting, because she already knows. I needed YOU there."

"Nah. To be honest, I never even knew that you WERE leaning on me, Echo. It seemed like, whenever I'd try to reach out to you, to get you to open up or let me help, you only brushed me away. Like..." she glanced at her hands, "like crumbs on your fingers." She wiped her hands on her napkin, dabbed at her mouth, and stood, as Echo stared at her, speechless. "C'mon, Ace. I need to get home, get cleaned up, and rest a bit before tonight's performance."

* * *

Later that day, Echo wandered over to the back door to ask an offhand question of his partner, to find she had fallen asleep on her couch.

He came into her living area and stood beside the couch, gazing down at Omega, for a long time. His expression was wistful, almost yearning.

A feather-light touch of her arm ascertained that she was cold, and he grabbed the threadbare old throw off the back of the couch, spreading it over her and tucking it in gently. She hummed softly, apparently glad of the cover—though she never awakened—and turned over, curling up and facing away from him.

He bit his lip, disappointed.

Then he sighed and went back into his own quarters.

* * *

The next morning's rehearsal was brief.

"No, we only want to reinforce the blocking and choreography with Omega," Michael told Echo, as Sofia took Omega through several details of one of the scenes. "And she's already proving she took to it like bread and orgnath."

"Orgnath? I haven't heard that one."

"Oh." Michael flushed slightly. "Even as long as I've been on Earth, I occasionally forget myself. That's Yelfflan for 'jam.' She took to it like bread and jam."

"Oh, okay." Echo filed the information away in the part of his brain reserved for linguistics.

"We'll be done well before lunch, at this rate. And there is no performance tonight; it's our regular evening off, to allow the performers to rest. And," Michael added, turning a firm gaze upon Echo, "that's what we want HER to do tonight, too. Oh, have some fun if you two wish—go see a film or whatnot—but don't keep her out late, and don't make her spend the day in the office, doing paperwork. Just because she's not here doesn't mean she's not working on our show; I've set her a bit of homework, though it shouldn't take long. We want her fresh for her debut tomorrow night!"

"No, finding your perp is our assignment, so if Meg needs time off to recuperate and prepare for the show, that's acceptable," Echo agreed.

Thirty minutes later, the quick brush-up rehearsal was over, and Echo carried Omega back to Headquarters, where she showered and changed into casual clothes for her day off.

# Chapter 3

"Hey, Meg?" Echo slipped through the back door a bit later, to find his partner pacing, a book in hand.

"Yeah, Ace?" Omega answered, not even looking up.

"Whatcha doing?"

"Oh," she said, finally glancing up at him. "This is the script; I had a copy from years ago, and Michael verified it's pretty much exactly what they're using for this run of the show. I'm just going over it to make sure I have all my lines down. I told Michael I had it, so he gave me an assignment to read through it by tomorrow night."

"Aha; that makes good sense, baby. Hey, listen, it's still late morning, so we have plenty of time to plan, but I was thinking. Since there isn't a performance tonight for you to go to, I was wondering...would you, maybe, like to go out?" Echo offered her a tentative smile. "It doesn't have to be anything fancy, and I swear I won't keep you out late. Besides, I promised Mike I'd have you home early! Anyway, I know you need to rest up before you do this show. Maybe just a nice dinner someplace, and then...oh, I dunno. You can pick what we do, if you wanna. Or we can come back here and just sit and talk. I only wanna spend some special time with you."

"Um, I appreciate the gesture, Echo, but I really think I need to just stay here and work on this," Omega murmured, looking up at him and waving the script. "Don't feel like you have to, you know, keep me occupied or something." She returned to reading, her lips moving from time to time as she mentally ran her lines.

Echo stopped where he was, staring at her, as a burning sensation of rejection washed through him like a flood of lava.

*Damn,* floated through his mind. *Talk about being blown off. I laid it all out, even admitted I wanted special time with her! I offered to let her choose the activities for the evening! And she's got the rest of the day today and all day tomorrow to read that damn script. Mu musta been dead wrong about her wanting to be with me. Because, sure as hell, I've been friend-zoned. Dear God. What the hell do I do now?* He drew a deep breath, trying to tamp down the pain that was overwhelming him. *Might as well get it out in the open, I guess. Make her say so, one way or the other. At least I'll know.*

* * *

"Look, if you really dislike the idea of me as a lover that much, just tell me up front," Echo demanded, finally showing the pain he felt. "Quit this ignoring every attempt I make to get close to you and flat TELL me."

Omega gaped at him, the script apparently forgotten; it fell from her limp fingers to the floor, unheeded.

"What?" he wanted to know, irritated.

"Are...are you trying to say...that you're...seriously... interested...in me...?" she whispered, pale and seeming shocked. "Romantically, I mean?"

"Isn't that what I just said?" he wanted to know, still irked and hurting.

"I...I..." was all she managed to get out. Her face paled.

Echo stared at her, eyes narrowed, studying her features, and suddenly realized he was seeing an expression that he had rarely, if ever, seen on his partner's face: Omega was completely clueless and confused.

*She doesn't know what to do or say,* he decided. *She honestly doesn't know how she's supposed to react. I guess I caught her off guard by being so direct, this time.* He relented sufficient for an explanation, but found he could not face her, even so.

"Baby, I've been trying to flirt with you for...damn, I dunno, Meg. A long time now," Echo said, finally turning away in an effort to hide how very deep the pain ran. "I'm crazy about you. I've done everything I could think of to ease into it, or at least broach the subject, and you either ignore me, change the subject, or find some way to blow it off. I thought, I mean,

55

I hoped...when we were at The Beach, and you...but I guess it was all just...just biochemical." His shoulders slumped. "Well, you don't have to worry about it any more. I'm pretty persistent, and I don't take no for an answer very easily, but I guess you finally got your point across."

"Echo, I...I had no idea..."

"Aw, Meg, don't give me that!" he spun to face her, anger now layered on top of the hurt. "Don't lie to me about it! Just tell me that's not what you want—that I'M not what you want—and have done!"

The last of the color drained from her face, and she swayed. Echo blinked in surprise, then leaped forward to catch her as she started to crumple. He swept her up into his arms, taking two steps to her couch and laying her on it, grabbing the throw pillows and shoving them under her feet. He knelt beside the couch and watched, puzzled; of all the reactions he'd considered she might make, passing out wasn't any of them.

Eventually she stirred, let out a soft groan, and tried to sit up. He caught her shoulders and held her prone.

"No, stay there," he told her. "You passed out. I wanna make sure your head is gonna stay put before I let you sit up."

"Oh, okay," she breathed, then lay there looking up at him in silence for long moments, her expression unreadable even to him. Then she put up a tentative hand and brushed his cheek with her fingertips.

Despite himself, his eyelids fluttered closed at the gentle touch, and he let out a breath. Warmth filled him at the slight but intimate contact, and when he opened his eyes, she was watching his reaction.

"What are you thinking?" he wondered, voice soft, gazing down into cerulean blue orbs.

"That I am an idiot," came her response.

"Why?"

"For not seeing what you put in front of me." She turned her head...just as he caught a wet gleam in the corner of her eye.

"Whoa, whoa, wait," he said, catching her far cheek in his palm and turning her head back to face him again. *There ARE tears in her eyes,* he observed, surprised. *What's going on here?* He shook his head. "I'm...not gettin' it," he admitted.

"Can I sit up?" she asked.

"Are you gonna explain yourself once you do? This isn't a diversion, is it?"

"No, I promise."

"Okay."

He helped her sit up, and she patted the sofa beside her. He turned and sat where she indicated; she drew a deep breath.

"I honestly...didn't see it," Omega murmured. "Obviously, you're sure I did, but I swear to you, Echo, I had no idea. I'm evidently pretty clueless about some stuff."

He gaped at her.

"You're joking."

"No. I wish I was. Um, look," she said, keeping her voice low in both volume and pitch; the effect came across as more than a little ashamed, and a whole lot embarrassed. "I've always been too driven to, to have much in the way of romantic relationships. We talked about that some, when I first came aboard here."

"Yeah, I remember that. So...are you saying that you...just never learned to recognize when a guy was flirting with you?"

"I...I..." Omega stared at him, a kind of blank expression on her face, as she considered his question. "I...dunno. I guess maybe it depends how 'in your face' the guy is with it. You... you're subtle, and gentle, and you don't press. I, I'm starting to think about stuff now, things you've done over the nearly two years we've been together that I didn't quite understand at the time, and..." She put her face in her hands. "I am so stupid!"

"As close as we are in other ways, Meg, did the idea not even occur to you that we COULD have a relationship?"

"NO!" she exclaimed. "Well, yes, initially, but...I, I mean, after—look, after Slug, and all his machinations and tinkering and all—nobody wants me! You've seen it yourself, in action!

Oh, guys might be interested for a little bit, maybe even intrigued, but when they find out what I REALLY am, what really happened to me—!"

"I'm not 'guys,' Meg," Echo pointed out. "I'm me. I'm your partner, and your best friend. The guy who thinks you're hot stuff. I'm in it for the long haul. Why have you been shoving me away?"

"Because it never actually crossed my mind that YOU, of all people, would be seriously interested in the creature engineered to KILL YOU!" Omega exclaimed, as upset as he had ever seen her. "Echo, don't you understand?! I didn't see your interest, because it didn't occur to me to look!"

Echo sat back at that. *It makes a certain sense; a body does have to be looking for something in order to find it, generally speaking,* he considered. *I guess it's kinda like when you see somebody you know, but it's somewhere you don't expect to see 'em, so you don't recognize 'em,* he decided...

...Right as Omega remarked, "It's like when you don't recognize somebody you've known a long time, because they're not where you expect them to be." She ran a distracted hand over her platinum hair. "I didn't expect you to be...'here'...so I didn't recognize what you were doing, I guess. Honest, Echo, I haven't been trying to hold you at a distance or anything. I've told you lotsa times, you're a looker, and a good catch. I mean," she began, and dropped her gaze as her face flushed, "that's pretty much why I...approached...you like I did, at The Beach. I thought...since we were best friends, and you'd said you thought I was pretty...maybe we could have...made it work, somehow. And I wondered if maybe...you might...I mean... well. But even then, I didn't really SERIOUSLY consider that you were already interested, Echo! I swear!"

"So you're saying you'd have accepted, if you'd recognized...?"

"I...up until Mark Wright showed up and the whole backup to the backup plan of Slug's started going down, probably, yeah." She dropped her gaze to her hands, which were fidgeting in her lap. "But...but now, maybe I oughta push you away, after all..."

"Hold on a damn minute. What the hell is that supposed to mean?"

"It means, Echo...what if this is exactly what Slug wanted to have happen?" Omega explained, patently miserable. He watched as her fingers gripped each other tightly enough to whiten her knuckles. "What if he engineered me to be attractive to you? What if he programmed a response? What if...your being attracted to me now...was the backup to the backup to the backup plan?"

"Meg, get real for a minute," Echo said, finally grasping what she was saying, and trying not to snort in amusement. "Last I checked, neither of us sleeps with our blasters in bed. Within reach, sure, but damn, baby! I doubt you're gonna blow my head off right in the middle of us making love or something. And frankly, even as good as you are, you're still not gonna be able to kill ME with your bare hands...any more than I could do that to you, these days."

* * *

"No, that's not what I meant," she said, feeling her cheeks heat at his remarks. When the mental image he had just conjured for her—the two of them, naked, bodies entwined—popped into her thoughts, her face got even hotter. Then another thought occurred. "Wait...are you saying you..."

"Am I saying what?"

"You said you were crazy about me. Is...I mean, do you..." Omega was afraid to come out and say it, in case she was misunderstanding what he really wanted. *I mean, it could just be he wants, like, partners with benefits or something,* she considered. *In which case, I am way off in left field on THAT.*

"Yeah, I think maybe so," Echo said, very, very quiet. "I've thought so for a while now."

"How...how long?"

"I dunno." He shrugged. "A while. Maybe even since you went off to find yourself, and came back to me. I just didn't realize it until a few months later."

Fear gripped her.

*It's Slug, it's Slug, he did it, it's happening, oh God help; what do I do...?*

* * *

Echo saw the terror that filled her sapphire eyes, and something inside him threatened to break, something that had never broken in him before, something that would be irreparable; and he knew he would never be the same if it did. *But,* he thought, morose, *I dunno if there's any way to stop it. The lady isn't willing.*

"Okay," he finally capitulated, turning away and starting to rise. "I see that look in your eyes. I get the message. I'll...go to Fox and ask for a transfer. Is a different field office far enough, or had you rather I went off-planet?"

"What?!" Omega exclaimed, grabbing his near shoulder in both hands. "What are you talking about? I never said anything about you transferring!"

"When you look that scared when I tell you how I feel about you, I just kinda figure..." Echo said, trying to pull away gently. The something inside him got closer to breaking.

But Omega hung onto his arm with a tenacious kind of gentle strength he didn't know she possessed, because he couldn't free himself, yet it wasn't causing him physical pain.

"Stop," she declared. "Echo, please stop. If...if you're really...serious, then I know this has to be hurting you something awful, and I'm sorry. I wouldn't hurt you for anything. But just stop and listen to me, please. Hear me out. I'm struggling just to get words together to explain, but you're reacting before I can manage to finish."

"All right," he sighed, settling back down. "I'm listening."

* * *

"It isn't you, or how you feel about me, that I'm scared of, at all," Omega said then, deciding to simply blurt it all out, before he could misinterpret something else and react negatively. "It's what it might lead to."

"What do you mean?"

"You were talking, a second ago, about...about lovemaking," Omega reminded him, trying not to stammer in her embarrassment. "But we already know that Slug engineered me to...to m-mate...with Wright. And whatever offspring that produced...were intended to be assassins sent after you. By their very nature. Genetically programmed predators, keyed on your template as prey."

"Yeah, the damn bastard," Echo cursed. "I mean Slug, by the way. Wright only got caught up in Slug's schemes, the same way you did; by the time I saw what was really happening, I felt kinda sorry for the poor guy, to be honest. But we managed to outwit that whole mess. It's over and done."

"Did we? Are you so sure?" Omega wanted to know, feeling her insides starting to tremble.

* * *

Echo blinked in surprise and stared at her, as a fuzzy idea began to form itself in his mind. *No,* he thought, astounded, *surely not. Is THAT the problem?*

"Keep going, Meg," he murmured. "Explain."

Omega shrugged, released his shoulder, and returned her attention to her fingers fidgeting in her lap.

"It's really simple, Echo. What if...if it didn't MATTER who the father was...? What if," she swallowed hard, threw him a brief, pained glance, then dropped her gaze, "ANY children I had...ended up as 'Echo assassins' regardless? I mean, okay, so any kids Mark and I had woulda been some kinda super-predator things, but...what if that's the ONLY difference it made?" Her voice cracked, and she started to stammer despite herself. "If we...a-and you...and I got...our ch-children...Echo, I don't want my children, OUR children, to commit patricide! I...it would...I...don't think I could stand it..."

"Lemme get this straight," Echo said, running a hand through his thick, dark hair until it stood on end. "You're afraid if we become lovers, and you got pregnant as a result, that our kids would grow up to kill me, because of Slug's genetic programming of..."

"Of my eggs," Omega finished for him. "Yes. Maybe... what you feel for me...isn't of your own volition, Echo. Maybe, some way, I've been programmed to...seduce you."

* * *

"I sincerely doubt THAT," Echo said with a slight chuckle, finally starting to understand a few things in his partner's head. "If he'd done that, I'd have expected you to catch on to me a lot sooner than all this. Hell, I'd have expected you to come on to ME, if that was the case."

"C'mon, Echo! Listen to what I'm saying. He did a lot more to me than mere mental programming, you know. And you've already seen what the pheromonal components can do, first-hand. After all, isn't that kinda what I did, at The Beach? Come on to you? Big time, at that! Take it seriously, please!"

"All right, I'll try. And I guess you got a point, especially about the pheromones. Look, Meg, you have the memories now; it should be easy to find out—did Slug program you to seduce me, or not?"

Omega stared at him for a moment, blinking, and he realized in some surprise that she hadn't thought to check the recovered memories. *Probably the poor baby doesn't even like to think about it if she can help it,* Echo considered, remembering what she had shown him of them. *God knows, I sure wouldn't, in her shoes.*

Then he saw her eyes defocus as she turned her attention inward. She closed her eyes and swallowed hard, and Echo instantly regretted telling her to revisit those horrific memories of torture. When her brows furrowed and she paled, he realized she was concentrating hard, determined to search those dreadful memories in excruciating detail to see if she was putting Echo in any kind of danger merely by being around him.

*She cares,* he realized, and warmth filled him. *Enough to revisit those damn memories and screen through 'em bit by bit, merely in an effort to keep me safe. I dunno how much she cares, or if it's anything like how I care about her...but she*

*DOES care.*

After several minutes of this, during which he remained as silent as he knew how to be, she finally opened her eyes and gazed at him, though her pale face still looked a little drawn... which Echo considered completely normal, given the nature of those memories she'd just analyzed...and which he had been honored to share, a few weeks previous.

"Well?" he wondered.

"I don't see anything like that in there," she admitted. "But then, there wasn't anything in there about the 'mate' Slug engineered for me, either. He just figured the hormones would be enough to force THAT to happen, I suppose."

"True," Echo admitted, hiding his distaste; of all the things Slug had done to his partner over the years, that one ranked right up there with the torture of the enhancements— both were equally dehumanizing. *But I'm not gonna risk her misinterpreting my reaction. It'd be just like Meg to think I was disgusted by HER, instead of what Slug did.* So he tamped down his response very carefully.

He fully understood, however, that he had no true idea of just how bad those enhancement procedures—done without any sort of anesthetic or sedation—might have been, and even when she had finally shared those memories telepathically with him, Omega had refused to allow the full measure of the agony and pain to reach him, choosing rather to block them, so he would not have to endure it...as she had. *As she still does, at least in memory,* he added.

"It occurs to me," she said then, aborting his train of thought, "that maybe we need to see how much the Agency has learned about gastropoids, specifically Snails, in the time since we took out Slug." She headed for her study, and he followed.

"Why?" he asked, as she woke the laptop there.

"Because I need to try to understand how he thought, figure out what he would have considered and what he would have rejected, if I am ever gonna feel comfortable about, about being with someone—anyone. But especially you."

"But why didn't you do all this when you dated Mu?" he asked, then shook his head. "Never mind—you didn't know about the mating thing when that first started."

"Right. That all went down right after he first asked me out, and...well, to be honest, I didn't think about these kinda ramifications until just now. Besides, I..." she shrugged, "kinda figured it wouldn't last, a relationship with him. And it didn't."

"Why did you think that?"

"Eh, I dunno. I just had a feeling. In hindsight, I think it's possible he was only interested in a, an 'exotic' experience... and maybe a little dangerous, into the bargain; you know, like I was a sexy thrill ride or something. Then, when the whole thing with Wright went down, he musta come face up against what he was really getting into. Oh, he tried to go on with it, once I got back, and he was nice enough. For a bit there, I thought it might actually work. He cleared out soon enough afterward, though, so I guess he'd had plenty enough 'danger' to satisfy him."

With that, she initiated a search in the PGLEIA archives and sat back, as Echo dragged up the extra chair to wait with her...wondering if he ought to tell her the truth: that Mu was in love with her, but decided he couldn't be what—or who—she wanted. But there was another matter that needed getting out in the open, because Echo wasn't sure how much his secret actions might have factored into the situation, either.

"Damn good thing for him, too," Echo muttered, making his decision.

"Huh?"

"Don't think I didn't see how much it hurt you, when he dumped you. Or that I'd be above putting a black eye—or worse—on the guy who did it."

"Oh..." She blinked. "But...if you felt like this...didn't it hurt?"

"Well, hell, Meg, of course it did," Echo confessed. "But if he made you happy, I'd have found a way to deal with it... somehow. But he didn't. He pressured you, and then he dumped you and hurt you. I...didn't..." he hesitated, then continued the confession. "I, uh, I didn't tell you at the time, but after he... kinda pressured you to sleep with him—"

"Well, sorta, but not," Omega interrupted. "I mean, he assumed I would, yeah, because he assumed that was just what everybody did, I guess. But when I explained that I wasn't 'everybody,' and I was a little more reserved than that, he backed right off, Echo."

"Well, he still shoulda checked, first," Echo fussed. "Anyhow, I pulled him aside that next day and told him he damn well better treat you right, or he'd be answering to ME as well as you. Then, right after Mu transferred, Fox made a little 'offhand' comment to me, in an email. It wasn't direct, not from Fox, but what it told me was that Mu MIGHT have been clearing the hell out to stay outta Alpha One's way. I'm sorry about that; I know you took it personally. But I'll confess to you, the whole thing might have been my fault—I might have been what scared him off; I might be the reason he dumped you, or at least A reason—" he broke off, thinking, *Maybe not the primary one, if Mu was telling me the truth, and I've got no reason to doubt him...but I'm sure it didn't help.* He sighed. "...And I'm...sorry, baby. I guess I shoulda told you, but I didn't really get a good chance until just now."

"Um, oh. Okay. Well," she considered, "that actually does... make me feel better about it. On a lotta levels."

"Good, then. I'm glad I 'fessed up, if it helped," Echo said, gruff, deciding to let sleeping dogs lie for the rest, at least for the time being. *I'll have to tell her the rest sooner or later, I suppose,* he decided, *including the fact that I talked to him the other day, and that he's probably in love with her, but things are getting complex enough right now without throwing a third party's feelings into the mix. Especially as upset as she already is. I'll let things settle for another day or so, get us two on an even keel, then look at telling her more of all THAT.*

They fell silent, watching the tablet display as it searched for recent data on gastropoids. Omega had set the search to specify anything discovered in the last two years, since anything that had been uncovered before likely would have come up in their original investigations. So they waited patiently, blonde head and dark bent close together over the screen, to see what would pop up.

Five minutes later, the search came back with...nothing.

"Well, shit," she fretted. "Echo, I swear I'm not trying to put you off. I just...before I can even think about answering you, I HAVE to know this. I mean, I know it's something that would be...we wouldn't be jumping into, into bed right off, I know; I only...I don't wanna have what should be a good thing turn into a nightmare...or worse."

"Given what we now know about your personal history, Meg, I understand that, and I agree with it," Echo gave her his honest answer. "I wouldn't be happy with an outcome like that either. So what do we need to do now, to make you comfortable with the idea? Enough that we can at least start our relationship heading in that direction?"

"Would you object," she began, scrunching her face, "if we discussed it with Fox? If anybody's gonna know about new Snail data, it'd be him. We don't have to tell him the full reason WHY, necessarily, just that..." Omega sighed. "Well, look—after that whole mess with Wright, I'd already started wondering if Slug had expected me to have an affair with you, if that was another layer of his planning that simply never happened, for whatever reason...but almost happened, down at The Beach. And then today you come up with this, and..."

"Aw, shit, baby," Echo grumbled in sudden understanding, covering her near hand with his own. "I stomped right over one of your secret fears. NOW I get it! Damn! If I'd known that, I'd have approached the matter completely different."

"I know," she offered him a rueful half-smile. "I probably keep too much stuff to myself. But damn, Echo, can't you imagine me trying to approach THAT topic with you? 'Say, partner, have you ever had the hots for me? I was just wondering if Slug tinkered with me that kinda way, see...'"

Echo laughed.

"Yeah, but let's face it, you'd sure have been damn surprised at my answer," he told her.

"Yup, but it would only have confirmed my worst fears."

"Probably, going down like that. C'mon, let's go talk to Fox. He knows how I feel anyway. Has for some time now."

"You told him? But not me?"

"I didn't have to tell him. We've known each other since the time I came aboard as a kid. I think I still hold the PGLEIA record for youngest human Agent. Maybe youngest Agent, period, I dunno. Anyway, he reads me about as well as you do, and he's seen it happening. He asked me quite some time ago if there was anything I needed him to do, to, uh, help things along. I told him no, either it would happen or it wouldn't. In retrospect, I'm wondering now if he hadn't already realized that you weren't picking up on my attempts to get your attention, and thought maybe a gentle nudge in the right direction might line you up to recognize what I was doing. Hell, for all I know, he figured out how I felt before *I* did."

Omega offered him a slight smile. His hand still covered hers, and now she turned that hand palm upward, wrapping her fingers around his hand...just like she had done on the beach outside Ipswich. Warmth filled him.

"Let's go, then," she told him. "It sounds like we have an ally, there. One that I sorely need, right now."

"Well, given the time, how about we slap together some sandwiches first?" Echo suggested, glancing at his wrist chronometer. "I think he just entered his monthly meeting with the other Division chiefs about ten minutes ago, anyhow. I got the feeling this isn't gonna be a quick search for info, and that'll give him a chance to finish his meeting before we descend on him."

"Okay. Yeah, that works. I got fresh hoagie rolls..."

"I got some sliced, smoked turkey and honey-cured ham."

"Let's do it."

* * *

"Well, for that, we need to ping Zarnix," Fox told the pair as they sat in his office right after lunch. "He's been digging out information on Snails ever since Slug's second attack on you, Omega...if we also style your abduction as an attack, as I'm sure both of you do, as well as myself."

"Damn straight," Echo muttered, and Omega nodded, tight-lipped.

"All right then, let me get him up here."

* * *

"You want to know how Snails reproduce?" Zarnix asked, puzzled.

"That'll do, for starters, if you know," Omega confirmed.

"I do, now," Zarnix averred. "I have done quite a bit of research since your little adventure, and have learned a great deal about that particular gastropoid species, not merely medical and biological. Once, all we knew was that the Snails and the Shells had a symbiotic relationship. Initially we weren't even completely certain they were the same species! And I can now tell you that they are, in fact, not only the same species, but mates. Almost without exception, the Snail is male and the Shell is female. They are attached via a constant coital coupling."

"WHAT?!" Omega exclaimed, shocked. "Surely I didn't hear that right."

"I heard it, too," Fox said, grimacing, "and I rather wish I hadn't. Oy gevalt."

"So they're doin' it...ALL the time??" Echo wondered, not sure if he was more curious or disgusted. *After all,* he considered, *I'm betting it's crossed just about every human male's mind at SOME point. Probably a buncha female minds, too, I guess.*

"Essentially...yes, they are," Zarnix confirmed.

*Oh hell,* Echo thought, feeling his face heat.

* * *

"I am so glad Romeo is NOT here right now," Omega murmured, flushing despite herself.

"No shit," Echo muttered agreement. Omega glanced at him and discovered his face was as red as she suspected hers was...especially when she saw Fox lean back in his desk chair and hide a smirk in his hand.

"Keep going, Zarnix," Fox said. "Or, well, maybe Omega has specific questions."

"Omega?" Zarnix offered.

"Yeah. Do they have live births, lay eggs...?" Omega wondered.

"Something of a combination," Zarnix noted. "The Shell produces eggs approximately once every one to one and a half orbital periods of the homeworld, give or take, which from a practical standpoint amounts to every three to five Earth years. These are almost immediately fertilized by the Snail, and gestation takes about a year and a half, Earth time. Whether the eggs are laid or not seems to depend upon the couple's decision. Some prefer to lay the eggs and nest, others prefer an internal gestation. As for Slug specifically—or Azeln, as he was known then —and his Shell, whose name was Nelé, according to, erm, we shall term them 'marriage records' on the homeworld? I can tell you for certain that she was in fact gestating at least three eggs when Agent Echo killed her. I went back and studied both the in-situ photographs and the forensics reports, and there were indeed developing eggs, well over halfway through gestation, found inside the dismembered body of the Shell. The medical examiner of record did not entirely recognize them for what they were, being as unfamiliar with gastropoids as the rest of us were at the time, but the descriptions of the 'internal organs,' as he put it, confirms my diagnosis: Slug and its Shell—or rather, Azeln and Nelé—were expectant parents when the fight occurred. Mother and babies were all lost as a result."

"Wow," Omega whispered, appalled. "Damn."

"What she said," Echo agreed, an odd, disturbed tone to his voice. "That...sure explains a lot."

"It surely does," Fox said, surprised.

"Yeah, including why Slug never replaced the Shell," Omega added. "He was grieving his wife and babies."

* * *

"Damn," Echo murmured, shoulders slumping as his face fell in dismay. "I didn't mean to kill innocent children. No wonder he kept calling me a monster."

"You had no way of knowing, Echo," Fox declared. "Don't do that to yourself. Slug wouldn't have thought twice about killing you. He was trying to, as it was. Which was the direct reason why his own family died—Slug was, very literally, playing mind games with you."

"Yeah, Boss, but still. I'm a baby-killer...and I had no idea. I, uh...maybe I need to, I dunno, turn myself in?"

* * *

"Absolutely not," Fox declared, sterner than they had ever seen him...save when Omega had tried something similar, upon discovering the source of the sentient genetic material which had been spliced into her own, without her consent, had all been murder victims. "If Slug didn't have enough sense to leave his pregnant wife at home on a dangerous mission, then the fault is his. Besides, you were targeting Slug, as I recall, not the Shell! It was Slug's own fault the shot went wild and hit his mate."

"Well, true. But damn, Boss—!"

"Listen to me closely, old friend," Fox said, relenting his sternness, but remaining firm. "It was. Not. Your. Fault. I will, however, be sure to formally report the ENTIRE thing to the Galactic Council, along with the fact that you willingly offered yourself for disciplinary action. Which I, in turn, declined to take, as unneedful, given that it was the perpetrator's interference which caused the deaths, not your intent, nor any sort of poor technique on your part."

Echo ran a distracted hand through his hair, unsatisfied, but unsure what else to do. *Of all the things I expected to learn from this quest of Meg's, that was NOT one,* he thought, disturbed on a very fundamental level. *I mean, damn! Babies! Because of me, three babies died! If I'd known at the time...I'd have done something different. I dunno WHAT, but something.*

"Hey, Echo," Omega said softly, laying a gentle hand on his arm, her grip warm and soothing. Her thumb, hidden from the others by his arm, lightly rubbed his inner forearm, near his wrist, in reassurance, gradually nudging inside his sleeve in order to caress his skin and increase the calming effect. "Shush, hon. I get why you're upset, in spades, 'cause of my whole 'the genetics came from people Slug murdered' thing, but it's all right. And Fox is correct. Besides, WE know what happened." She gestured with her other hand, to indicate the four beings in the room. "And Fox and I both are more than willing to tell the whole damn galaxy the truth, if we need to. It's okay. You didn't know—NOBODY knew, until..." she threw a querying glance at Zarnix.

"About six months ago, when I discovered their mating practices, I began to suspect," Zarnix admitted. "I thought it made sense, given Slug's behavior after that. You see, we knew that there had been neural feedback from Nelé's death which caused brain trauma in Azeln; now we know that there was ALSO neural feedback from the developing minds of their three children. And that was IN ADDITION TO the grief from the loss of his entire family...and possibly some survivor's guilt. Not to mention real guilt...because, on some level, Azeln had to know that HE was himself responsible, even if he did try to blame you, Echo."

"Damn," Echo breathed.

"...It took me about another month, or perhaps a month and a half, to dig up enough of the incident reports and autopsy records to start to confirm my suspicions. So, let us say four months, give or take; I have known the truth of what happened for about four months. I have been meaning to write up a paper to submit to Fox, but when the Harrnakian influenza epidemic hit the planetside alien population earlier than usual this year, I had my hands too full of sick people to do it. But we have that under control now." He nodded an apology to Fox. "I will get on it as soon as may be."

"Good. I'll append it to the report to the Ennead," Fox decreed. "Echo?"

"I'm still not satisfied, Fox," Echo admitted, still distressed. "But I guess it'll have to do. I...honestly didn't know. And you're right; I wasn't aiming for the Shell. For years, I didn't know WHY I hit the Shell...until Slug attacked Meg, and pulled the same shitty trick of reaching into my nervous system and causing my bicep muscle to twitch. My whole damn arm went cockeyed for a second. It even affected my trigger finger—my finger contracted and hit the trigger before I even intended to."

"Ahhh," Zarnix hummed in understanding. "And that explains some readings India took when she treated you in the aftermath, which Zebra and I have long puzzled over."

"Meaning you have medical evidence confirming Echo's story?" Fox wondered.

"We do. Which effect would ensure that Echo had NO control over where the shot went. And that, in turn, means that the shot striking the mother was sheerest coincidence. And you could not possibly have been aiming at her, because had you been doing so, you COULD NOT have struck her."

"And there is our answer," Fox noted. "Zarnix, can you write that up as a separate white paper, please? It doesn't have to be long; just a couple of pages explaining the physiology, based on Echo's first-hand eyewitness accounts, and your confirming evidence."

"I'll be happy to, Fox," Zarnix agreed.

"Echo? Better?" Fox asked.

"I suppose so, Fox," Echo said with a shrug. "I'm still bothered that my actions—at least in inadvertent conjunction with a murderous perpetrator—resulted in innocent babies dying, along with their mother, but despite our best efforts, accidents happen, I guess."

"They do, zun," Fox murmured. "Don't worry. I will see to it that you are exonerated of any possible accusation or repercussion. As for your own mind's recriminations, try your best to let them go; you could not have known—NO one knew, until the last couple of months, DECADES after the incident— and you couldn't do anything about it. Then, or now. All right?"

Echo paused for a long moment, then finally nodded without looking up.

"Good. Now, back to our original inquiries. Omega, tekhter?"

"Ace, are you okay?" Omega murmured, tucking her head to try to look up into his face. She invisibly stroked the skin of his wrist with her thumb again.

"Yeah, Meg, I'll be all right," he said, slightly hoarse, but meeting her eyes. "Go ahead; it's fine."

"So, um, okay, now I need to know some linguistics, and maybe syntax," Omega decided. "This relationship between Snail and Shell...what did they call it among themselves? What connotations did their term have?"

"That, I cannot tell you," Zarnix confessed. "We Chesharilzi are not telepathic, whereas gastropoids are ENTIRELY telepathic, and I have not been able to understand the gastropoid language as a result, despite considerable effort on my part. You will have to ask a native telepath. I recommend Zz'r'p, as he and I have already discussed my findings together, and he aided me with respect to those 'marriage records' I mentioned." He shook his head in bemusement. "Which, I might add, are very different things from what we would consider records, when unsighted, telepathic beings are responsible for them."

"In that case...any more questions for Zarnix, you two?" Fox addressed Echo and Omega. "No? Okay, Zarnix, you're dismissed to head back to the medlab and handle your patients. Thank you for your time and effort. I look forward to reading those reports, and with your permission, will send copies to Alpha One as soon as I receive them."

"By all means," Zarnix agreed. "I had planned to copy them on the message, in any event."

"Very good."

* * *

It transpired that Zz'r'p was awaiting a personal communique, so he requested that the two Agents come to his private office in the Arcturan embassy, upstairs in the Headquarters building. Fox also had coordination for an upcoming diplomatic envoy to plan, so he sent Alpha One to Zz'r'p's office alone...then surreptitiously contacted the Arcturan ambassador on the HQ-internal vidphone to let him know what was in the wind before they could arrive. Had the Deltiri had eyebrows, they would have shot up in surprise.

"Ah, so! And Echo has finally chosen to act upon what he has felt for all this time?" Zz'r'p said with a delighted laugh.

"That's what I suspect is going down, yes, though they didn't QUITE come out and admit as much to me. I don't think it's so much that he finally chose, as it is that he finally figured out that Omega wasn't catching on to his attempts to be subtle," Fox pointed out. "From what I've been able to read between the lines plus what I've seen firsthand, she just wasn't seeing it, and he's been interpreting that as a brush-off."

"Oh, yes." Zz'r'p sighed. "I am not surprised. She believes she is unlovable, that no worthwhile man will ever be interested in a 'thing' like her. While you and I know it is not true, I cannot say I blame her for feeling so, given that damned gastropoid's machinations. Fox, you cannot imagine what he did to her. I am not merely an innate telepath by nature of my species; I am a highly-trained adept. And it still took all my skills to shield the core of my being against the onslaught of remembered pain and terror which came flooding out of her, once the memories were released." The Deltiri from the Arcturus system shook his head in grief and distress, and Fox winced. "And realizing as she did, as you and Zebra and I have finally done, that he meant it to degenerate her into a bestial-but-intelligent creature he could control, only makes it that much worse. The fact that she can continue working for the Agency, and still be as effective as she is, is testament to the strength of her will, the indomitability of her spirit...and the determined love she bears for her partner."

"I wondered about that," Fox murmured. "Suspected, even. So she loves him, too."

"She does," Zz'r'p averred. "I am certain you can see it as well as I. It takes little of my telepathic skill to know that, especially after all this time working with her—I have gotten to know her, and so I can read it in her actions, in her protectiveness of her partner, without the need to invade her thoughts to ascertain it. Though I am positive she would deny the nature of that love at this point. And her actions now are a desperate effort to push Echo to what she believes to be a safe distance, without hurting him any more than she can help."

"What?! But I thought this was about proving that it's safe for them to..."

"It is, for Echo. But remember, Echo is her hero, as well as the love of her life. And as such, deep within, she believes herself unworthy of him. She is trying to protect him from herself, and any possible repercussions accruing from what was done to her."

"So she's looking for an excuse to refuse him, without driving him away totally?"

"I believe that to be the case, yes. I will know more when I see them."

"But...could she be right?"

"It is unlikely," Zz'r'p said thoughtfully, pondering. "It took biochemical manipulation to force her back into Slug's schemes this last time—and she still fought it, 'tooth and nail,' as you humans say—ultimately successfully, too. She drew strength from her determination to be her own person...but she also drew strength from her love of her partner, and her resolve to see him unharmed." He met Fox's eyes through the vidcall. "That does not automatically mean that there could be no hurdles to be overcome in such a relationship, however. The matter of children, should they desire them, is apt to be most problematic, for instance. In any of several different ways."

"Ooo. Yes, I get that," Fox said, wincing again. "Maybe I'd better start Zebra and Zarnix and Dihl to work on how to get around that whole tinkered-to-hell 'programmed genetics' thing. If they start now, then maybe by the time it's needed, they'll have a workaround."

"Precisely. Alpha One should be here any moment, friend Fox, and it would not be good for them to find us in this particular conversation..."

"Right. Keep me posted, as much as you can without betraying their confidences, Zz'r'p."

"I shall be glad to, my friend. For I can tell, you have only their best interests at heart. You want them to be happy, even more than you want them as effective Agents."

"Well..." Fox felt his face heat. "They're my top Agents, and it's really good having them running Alpha Line. That said, though, those two have been through more than most, if you understand me. I think they've earned a 'happily ever after,' several times over. IF we can convince 'em both to accept it. And, knowing them, it isn't like it's apt to stop 'em working. I asked Echo once, what would happen if he actually won Omega as his mate, and they had children."

"I would hazard a guess that he indicated Alpha One would leave field work and run Alpha Line from the office?"

"Bingo. On the money. Those two...they're in this for the long haul."

"Indeed they are, because it has become their life— together. What we must do, you and I, is convince them both that there can be more to that life together. And I think that is doable, though there will be rough spots along the way. I will call you later with the outcome. Zz'r'p out."

"Fox out."

* * *

"Oh, you're kidding!" Zebra said, a huge grin on her face, as she talked to Fox on a personal vidcall. "They ARE?!"

"It looks that way, bubeleh," Fox averred.

"So wait, lemme get this straight. Not only did Echo ask Omega out the other night...and Omega went...AND they pulled out all the stops..."

"Yes. Now they are beginning to talk about a life together," Fox confirmed. "Including the possibility of sex and children." He ran a hand through his salt-and-pepper hair. "Though I think Omega is still rather afraid, especially of that last item."

"Well, after that whole ball of drek with Wright, who can blame her, sweetheart?" Zebra wanted to know. "If I were in her shoes, what I'd be trying to find out right now would be whether or not it made a difference, Wright versus Echo as the father of said children."

"On the money, meyn teyere," Fox observed. "That is exactly what she is trying to ascertain, insofar as I can tell. Is there any chance that you might know? Zarnix did not seem to, though perhaps he simply did not quite pick up the nature of their inquiries..."

"No," Zebra huffed. "I have no clue. And I should have thought about that when it was all going down." She rubbed her hand across her cheek. "And it probably also behooves us to start looking at that sitch, with an eye to undoing whatever Slug did to her ova."

"I was going to suggest, yes."

"All right. I'll get with Zarnix, ping Dihl, and 'the Omega team' will start looking at the problem. I assume there's no rush...?"

"No, I don't think so," Fox considered. "I expect this will be a slow courtship, partly because Omega is so worried. Zz'r'p thinks she will resist it, though she does not want to, in order to keep Echo at what she feels is a safe distance, in order to protect him from herself. Except, knowing Echo as I do..."

"That won't fly," Zebra finished for him.

"I seriously doubt it," Fox agreed. "Zz'r'p is convinced that she loves him as much as he loves her—and that, without the need to telepathically read her feelings!—which means she's already predisposed to want the relationship. And Echo can be exceeding persuasive, when he wants to be. As soon as he is convinced of her love, nothing will stop him going after making her his mate, wife, whatever you choose to term it."

"Which also means we'll need to go find a 'wedding' present," Zebra said, practically wiggling in delight. "Why is it I wanna sing that old kid's song?"

"Ha!" Fox laughed. "I know the one! 'Echo and Omega, sittin' in a tree...'"

"'K-I-S-S-I-N-G!'" they finished together, then burst into happy laughter. Finally they sobered...only slightly.

"I am SO happy this looks like finally coming together," Zebra said then. "Those two deserve to be happy. I'm delighted for them."

"I know, bubeleh. As happy for them as they were for us," Fox agreed. "Shall we break out one of the bottles of Emdali wine tonight, by way of celebration?"

"I think that sounds like an excellent idea, hon," Zebra said, dimpling with a smile. "And just because THEY aren't ready...doesn't mean WE aren't."

"Exactly, meyn teyere gelibte. Exactly."

* * *

"...So what you really want to know is, how did Slug view his mating, and would he have considered a partnership such as you have had with Echo in the same fashion?" Zz'r'p asked Omega.

"Um, pretty much, yeah," she agreed, blushing deeply and looking down at her toes. Echo bit his lip to keep from grinning.

*She's so damn cute when she's embarrassed!* he noted, then turned his attention to Zz'r'p's response. The blue, fishlike alien shot a half-grin at Echo, and the Agent knew he'd picked up the thought and agreed.

"Well, it would seem that he and his...mate, the Shell named Nelé, did consider each other as partners in a work sense, and I think, under the circumstances, most gastropoids would," Zz'r'p considered. "It would almost be necessary, as once mated, they are only separated in death, according to my understanding, based on the recent discussions I have had with Zarnix. Whether or not Snails understand that human work partnerships do not necessarily function the same way might be questionable; however, let me present some food for thought on the matter."

"Okay," Omega said, glancing up at the Arcturan with a hint of uncertainty in her demeanor.

"Go ahead, Zz'r'p," Echo said, easing an arm around his partner's shoulders by way of encouragement and comfort. "We're listening."

* * *

"First of all," Zz'r'p began, "there is virtually no such thing as homosexual relations among gastropoids. It simply does not work that way within their species. The symbiotic relationship cannot occur between, say, Shell and Shell, or between Snail and Snail; they all communicate telepathically, but the bond can ONLY occur between Snail and Shell, because of the way the respective brains are...'wired,' let us term it, never mind the physiological, ehrm, parts—the sexual coupling. Now, the few gastropoids I have encountered DO understand the concept of gender in other races, not just their own. And they understand that other species may be more or less complex with regard to intimacy and reproduction."

"So they understand that humans can be more complicated, or that the Xemlon have more than two sexes, an' stuff," Echo offered.

"Precisely. That said, occasionally there are genetic gender inversions within the species; according to my understanding, the Snail is generally male, and the Shell female, but this is not always true. Very rarely, a Snail may be born female, or a Shell male. These inversions comprise the few instances where what other species might term homosexual mating can occur. They are rare enough, however, that unlike most other planets, the majority of gastropoids do NOT understand non-heterosexual mating; it is foreign to them. It is not that they object to it, any more than to the Xemlon, with their four genders, all required for mating and reproduction; they just do not comprehend it. Therefore, Slug would have recognized that, for instance, X-ray and Echo—who were partnered during Slug's original attack—were of the same gender, so it likely would not have occurred to him that it could possibly be a sexual relationship."

"Not that it was," Echo said. "X-ray kinda halfway took my dad's place in my life. Not quite, 'cause I only lost Dad a few years before I...got 'recruited,' but he was a father figure, for sure. Between him an' Fox, I...did okay."

"Understood," Zz'r'p said, nodding. "And I remember X-ray training you, when you were little more than a boy, yourself. He did indeed treat you as if you were his son. As did—and does—Fox." The alien turned to Omega. "Do you understand what I am saying, Omega? Slug would not have considered an Agent partnership as a spousal or mated relationship. He would have recognized it as a working relationship, with, perhaps, friendship overlaid, at least in most instances."

"Yes, I get that," she murmured, obviously thinking hard, "but so why didn't he pick a boy to work with, instead of me...?"

"Oh, I can answer that one, Meg," Echo said, turning her to face him and meeting her eyes. "And I haven't even seen anything but the original reports on the stuff. He picked you because you were far and away the best candidate for getting a top-level agent embedded in Division One."

"That is correct, as nearly as I have sensed," Zz'r'p agreed. "It had nothing to do with your being female. With your innate abilities, intellect, and skills, you were simply the best agent candidate, period. And that was to be my second point. No matter what he did to you after, my dear girl, it is important to remember that—out of all the young people Slug viewed as candidates, YOU were the smartest, strongest, fastest, with the quickest wit, the greatest ability to adapt, to think on your feet." *And now is the time to provide that encouragement I discussed with Fox and Zebra,* the Deltiri decided. *Though undoubtedly it will need reinforcement from time to time. At least this is a start.*

"Lucky me," Omega noted then, wry.

"I want you to remember something, young one," Zz'r'p

added, earnest. "Will you do that?"

"I'll try. What is it?"

"That, no matter what Slug intended for you, he FAILED," Zz'r'p pointed out. "Because he failed to take something vital into account."

"He didn't take into account the essential Meg," Echo noted, assured.

"Exactly, Echo, exactly!" Zz'r'p exclaimed.

"Huh?" Omega said, looking at both males with a blank, confused expression.

"It is simple, my dear. He did not factor your personality—your heart, your spirit, your CARING, your concern and love for others—into his equation." Zz'r'p met Omega's gaze. "And so he failed. Echo is alive; you are alive...but Slug is dead. And all of his plans, even 'the backup to the backup,' as you put it, failed with him. Because YOU chose to fight back."

"Because you refused to be his tool, his hand, baby," Echo added. "Don't think for one minute, when your programming kicked in to force you to shoot me, that I couldn't TELL you were fighting back, either. Your movements were slow, jerky, almost...almost spastic, kinda."

"And that very fact," Zz'r'p tag-teamed Echo, "enabled Alpha Two to get there in time and put a halt to matters."

"Barely," Omega grumbled.

"But still," Echo insisted. "Your caring and your sense of, of inherent RIGHT, that's what Slug didn't take into consideration. That's where he messed up."

"No matter what he may or may not have done to your body, Omega," Zz'r'p agreed, "no matter what programming he forcibly inserted into your mind, your SPIRIT overcame all of that. And it continues to do so, to this very day...or you would not be here, now, in my office, asking the questions you are asking."

"Okay, okay. I see what you're saying, guys. I'll...I gotta think about that, some. But what about...I mean, the whole thing with Mark Wright...? How does that affect us now?"

"That was more of his long-range planning in work, Meg," Echo explained. "If you'd been a guy, Slug woulda just picked a comparable woman in the place of Wright."

"Precisely," Zz'r'p averred. "So the plan did not depend upon the gender of the...'lab rat,' I believe you are wont to term it."

* * *

"Okay." Omega accepted the comments at face value. "So far, so good."

"Now, that being said, it is just possible that he thought something MIGHT happen between you and Echo...but," Zz'r'p noted, even as Omega grew agitated, "I believe that the entire affair with Wright—" he broke off when Omega flinched, apparently having surface-read her negative reaction to his phrasing. "Oh, I am sorry, Omega; it was a poor choice of words. Forgive me. Let me try again. I believe that the entire sequence of events with Wright would have had a secondary purpose, if the two of you—that is to say, you and Echo—had developed a romantic and sexual relationship in the interim: namely, that Echo should have had to watch you in the arms of another man. And more, to bear that other man's children, instead of his."

"Urg," was the disgusted sound that Omega made then, and Echo had to agree with her.

"But you think that was something Slug didn't specifically intend?" Echo pressed.

"Actually, I think it probable that he did not even like the very idea," Zz'r'p pointed out. "He viewed Omega as his weapon, his personal tool; his own hand—well, pseudopod— in action, if you will—as you remarked, moments ago. To have his personal tool willingly in his enemy's bed for no other reason than to take pleasure in it would have been abhorrently offensive to him. Now, had it occurred in the weeks leading up to his end game, it might have been marginally acceptable, since it meant she would have been all the more important to you, and rendered it the more painful when he killed her slowly in front of you. But it did not happen thus, and by all accounts, he did not appear to be perturbed by the fact."

"But...but..." Omega began. "Zz'r'p, I can't say this in front of Echo..."

Pain shot through the male Agent.

"You don't want me knowing something?" he wondered, voice very quiet. "I can leave..." He started to rise from his seat, already half-turned toward the door.

"No, please stay," Omega pleaded, grabbing his forearm in the same strong but gentle grip she had used earlier. "I...I don't think I mind your knowing, I just...can't bring myself to say it."

Echo sat back down, puzzled. He watched as Zz'r'p locked eyes with Omega, and suddenly the Agent realized there was a conversation going on to which he was not privy. Abruptly their gazes broke, and Meg glanced down with a soft dry sob, as the Arcturan shook his head in dismay. The tall blue alien turned to Echo.

"What she just showed me, what she wants you to know, Echo, but cannot bring herself to say aloud—to ANYONE, let me note—is that, while she was abducted and the various procedures performed, the pre-pubescent Omega was forced into a sexual climax, apparently by the stimulation of the cerebral enhancements. No, no," he broke off, raising his hands as he read Echo's unvoiced agitation, "he did not actually rape her, at least not in the sexual sense, although the entire experience can be viewed as a form of rape, in that it was a gross violation of her being, both mental and physical. No, she has just shown me the memory, and I have reviewed it with her, and explained to her what happened. The entire procedure, which was intended to enhance all mental faculties and sensory responses via enlarging the neural network, created what are sometimes called 'phantom sensations' throughout her body— itching, tickling, burning, and the like. A telepath would be able to take note of these various sensations and know if the specific step of the procedure was working...which is apparently one reason why she was forced to endure the entire thing with no anesthesia or sedation. There are certainly other, more benign, ways to do it; he simply did not bother."

"But why?" Echo wondered. "Why create...those kinds of feelings...in Meg, if...?"

"That was my question, too," she murmured, still staring at the floor in shame. "I didn't even really understand what was happening, at the time; I was too young. And it was immediately followed by awful pain in the same places..."

"Aw, baby," Echo whispered, suddenly understanding one reason she was afraid.

* * *

*Yes, Echo,* Zz'r'p's voice sounded in his head. *You are correct. She has a deep-seated fear of sexual intimacy, resulting from this experience. The sad part is that the specific sensations in question were entirely extraneous to Slug's purpose; they were the merest side effect of his procedures. They HAD no purpose. Unfortunately, the subconscious recollection and reaction is almost certainly one reason why she has avoided romantic relationships most of her life. You have your hands full, attempting to create a complete life with her. It will be difficult, at least in the beginning.*

*Well, damn,* Echo thought, embarrassed himself. *I didn't really think I'd get it by a telepath of your abilities, but I didn't mean...*

* * *

*No, no. It is quite all right, youngling. To be honest, Fox is not the only one to have known for some time. Not that I had to use any real skill; I normally surface-read most humans with whom I interact, merely in order to ensure I have correctly interpreted body language and intonations of a species with which I was not raised. And your affections, for someone with that ability, have been quite near the surface for a goodly time, and thus easy to read...for me, at least, though not to non-telepaths. But—to paraphrase a particularly astute human I once met, some few years ago—a wise Deltiri does not always admit to everything he knows.*

*Does...does SHE love ME? I mean, like...that. Or can you tell me? I don't wanna violate her privacy or anything. The good Lord knows, she's had enough of that already.*

*I think to tell you outright would be a violation of her privacy and my principles,* came the answer. *However, I can point out to you that you already know the answer. Stop and think about your history together: how much she trusts you, how happy she is in your company, the fact that she prefers to be with you even in her off hours, her willingness to give everything—up to and including her own life—to ensure your safety. What does that tell you?*

*That...she loves me.* A brilliant flash of joyous light appeared to Zz'r'p to erupt within the male Agent at that moment. *But... so why has she held me off, all this time?*

*Can you not understand? What does she call herself, in reference to what has been done to her? 'Lab rat.' 'Frankenstein's Monster.' 'The Thing.' On and on.*

* * *

*Yeah, but...wait. Are you saying she really thinks of herself like that?* Echo was astounded and not a little horrified. *I mostly thought she was trying to joke about it. You know—dark humor.*

*It is no joke, though she does attempt to gloss over it in that fashion,* Zz'r'p replied. *She does, indeed, think of herself thus. She does not consider herself worthy of you—worthy of anyone, but especially of you, the man who is her personal hero. And now, especially since we know that Slug's last resort was to mate her with another altered human to produce a brood of super-assassins, she is even more revolted by herself. She is also, as she has told you, afraid that mating at ALL will create those same assassins—perhaps not as powerful, but conceivably as effective, if you will excuse the rather bleak pun. And since you have now declared your interest, her mind has analyzed potential future repercussions, and also as she told you earlier, she is now utterly terrified that your own children by her—assuming there would, or COULD, be any, depending*

85

*upon precisely how her eggs' genetics were modified—will kill you.*

*Which would break her.* A different kind of pain washed through Echo.

*It would. Which is another reason why I said that, if you choose to pursue this relationship, it will be hard work. You will have to discuss this with her, and decide together what you want to do about children in advance—advance as in, BEFORE YOU BEGIN the relationship; as in, start the discussions NOW—it is, after all, what this visit is about, when all the social and Agency trappings are peeled away. AND... you will have to ensure that she is unable to become pregnant in the meanwhile.*

*I'm not worried about 'in the meanwhile.'*

*It does not matter if it worries YOU. What matters is that SHE is worried. If you hope to convince her to let you love her, you will have to face HER fears, and overcome them.*

*Oh...*

* * *

It was Omega's turn to sit and watch the silent conversation to which she was not party, seeing the fleeting, barely-there expressions on Echo's face and attempting to read them: horror, embarrassment, confusion, happiness, shock, grief, more confusion. Finally she read comprehension dawning in those brown eyes that she knew and loved, and she sighed and averted her face.

*He gets it now,* she thought, as sorrow and loneliness filled her. *Why I can't do what he wants. Why I have to push him away. He's...he's probably the most incredible guy I've ever met. He's a thoroughbred stallion, and I'm an intergalactic... mutt. And if we had kids...dear God. I couldn't face it, couldn't live with myself, if our own children...killed him. And that's assuming they were even normal-looking human children. With my luck, they'd be green with blue and orange polka-dots, half a dozen eyes on antenna stalks, three legs, and tentacles with pincers for hands.*

*Stop that,* Echo's voice told her.

Omega glanced up, to see Echo and Zz'r'p both watching her.

"Huh? Did you say something, Ace?"

Zz'r'p looked at her partner, and Omega heard the Arcturan's thoughts again.

*Explain to her.*

*Okay,* Echo said. But his lips didn't move.

*Zz'r'p? What. Have. You. DONE?* an incensed Omega demanded.

*Let him alone,* Echo told her. *There's a lot I need to tell you, Meg. But I told him I didn't have words to tell you very well, and he suggested he facilitate a mental conversation between us. We didn't mean to come in, in the middle of your musings, but I think I'm glad we did.*

*But...how much did you hear?* a horrified Omega wanted to know.

*Not everything, Omega,* Zz'r'p averred. *I heard your entire thought as I 'tuned in,' but he only heard you berating yourself and any offspring of yours. But would it have been so bad if he had heard all? It was only complimentary.*

*I'd have been twelve kinds of embarrassed.*

*Well, that's neither here nor there, Meg.* Echo cut to the chase. *Look. I need you to give this a chance, give ME a chance. If you're scared, we don't need to have kids. The birth control injection India gave you is still in effect, right?*

*Um, yeah.* Omega felt herself blush. *And Zebra confirmed that I'd already had two—one when I processed in, and another, just to make sure, when I came out of the regen pod last winter. So...I guess the matter's handled unless I decide otherwise. Or unless Slug managed to figure a workaround for that, too.*

*Unlikely,* Zz'r'p determined. *There is only so much the damned creature could do. I suspect you would have reacted to the injection, much as you did to the implant, if he had.*

*That,* Echo agreed. *Okay, baby, then leave it. If it gets to that point—and to be honest, I hope it does—then either we won't let you get pregnant, or we'll set the medical research team loose on the problem and see if we can find a way to ensure healthy, normal human offspring. I'm not too keen on the idea of my kids taking me out either, especially after we saw that seventh Interstellar Wars flick together just recently.*

He gave her a lopsided, mischievous grin, and that got a laugh out of her, despite herself.

*That's better, baby. Now, would that help ease some fears?*

*Yeah, I guess so, Ace. A little.*

*Zz'r'p, is she consciously aware of the other fear?*

*Not entirely, Agent Echo, no. Agent Omega, do you realize you have a fear of sexual intimacy, arising out of your abduction experiences?*

*I...hadn't been, but I'd begun halfway suspecting something like that in the last couple months or so.*

*Zz'r'p,* Echo asked, *can you, um, give us some privacy to talk, but still maintain this link for us? Or is that too hard?*

*I am trained and duly certified as a counselor, Echo; I can do as you ask. Stand by a moment. You will both feel my presence diminish and disappear from the conversation, and at that point you will be able to converse in private.*

Alpha One waited until the sensations the Arcturan had described were in effect. Then Omega tried a tentative, *Zz'r'p? You there?*

No answer.

*I guess we can talk,* she decided.

*Okay, Meg, it's time for me to lay a few things on the line for you, just so you know some stuff up front. The first is that, like I've alluded to a few times, I've had a couple lovers.*

*Yeah, I gathered.* She tried hard to clamp down on a certain amount of jealousy and envy, but the slight grin she saw on his face told her it was a lot harder to hide in a telepathic conversation than an audible one. *All right, behave,* she told him.

*I was gonna say the same to you, but okay. So. The first one, I was little more than a kid. I'd only just turned 21, and...*

*well, Nreefluvan was a Kochavi, and I was a curious kid. Need I say more?*

*A Kochavi? The 'sexpots of the universe'?* Omega asked with some amusement. *No, that says it all, right there. How long did you see each other?*

*Oh, a few weeks. Maybe as long as a couple of months. Not long. I think she didn't have a good feel for just how young and soggy behind the ears I was, as a human. It wasn't real serious, but it still hurt when Ree finally broke it off. So...yeah, I've been dumped, too.*

*Aw. I'm sorry, hon. Did you at least learn anything fun?*

*A few things.* He grinned, a dark, rascally, impish grin. *I was hoping to show you, one of these days.* She felt herself flush.

*Um, okay, maybe. Keep going.*

*Hold that thought, though, because we're coming back to it. A few years later, there was an ambassador that came through on...well, there had been a new administration installed on Tu'Ven and that was the first time they sent an envoy to Earth, officially recognizing us as part of the Coalition. It was a big deal. And I was flattered when Kar'nun took an interest in me.*

*So she was number two. Is she still planetside?*

*No, she was recalled when the administration changed again, a couple years later—it was actually a promotion for her. And no, we weren't lovers that whole time. We decided it wasn't working for us, and broke up after about six months or so. It was an amicable breakup, so there were no diplomatic repercussions...which was a really good thing. Every now and then Fox gets a communiqué from her homeworld, and passes on a message that she sends greetings. And I tell him to respond in kind.*

*Any more?*

*Just one. Chase Martin. Dr. Chase Martin, later Dr. Chase Martin-Collins. Yeah, that Chase. You already know all about that from our conversations last Christmas.*

*Yeah, I figured that's who it was. I felt really bad for you, hon.*

*It's okay. It was still kinda new then, the...the way it ended, and all.*

*All right. So tell me about her.*

*Well, I met her on a mission...*

*Which one?*

*Um...the Zaglaxan sabotage thing?*

*Oh, okay. I remember that report.*

*I'll bet.* He grinned. *Sometimes I don't think you forget anything much.*

*Not about you, anyway.* Her grin was more a devilish smirk, and she watched as he flushed. But, she decided, he also looked pleased, though he tried to hide it. A quick check of the link revealed the truth, and she grinned wider.

*Um,* he said, flushing deeper, seeming to realize she'd read him. *So that was about a year and a half, not quite two years, before you and I met. Not that long after X-ray died, actually. I'd gotten Romeo up to speed, but...* He shrugged. *I dunno. There was something missing in my life, and I knew it. Anyway, she turned out to be a big help in undoing the sabotage and setting the gadget back to what it was supposed to be doing. She was a professor of mechanical engineering at MIT, see. And we hit it off, but I had to brain-bleach her when it was all over. She didn't really know what I was actually doing to begin with, but I thought she'd make a great agent, with that kind of knowledge base and skill set. So I did what I had to do to slap an end-bracket on the incident, then came back and talked to Fox to work out the details, and took about six months off. The idea was to try to see if I could build something with her, build a relationship. And if I could, I was gonna try to recruit her. If she was open to the idea, all well and good, and she'd have come back with me, got the brain-bleached memories back, and gone to work in one of the support departments, while Romeo and I went back out in the field. And then I'd have had somebody to come home to in the evenings. That was what I hoped would happen. But if she wasn't open to recruitment, I was willing to...I was gonna retire—get brain-bleached and everything— and stay with her. Fox and I already had a background worked out for me, 'cause it was my cover for going back to her.*

*Wow. Then you and I would never have met. I'd be a regular astronaut, dinking around in low Earth orbit and trying hard just to get to Mars. Your mom would be dead. And Slug woulda been pissed, tryin' to find you to get his revenge.*

*I guess so. Once he found me, though, I'd have been dead meat. Totally defenseless, and without a clue what was happening. 'Cause no memories of it.*

Omega winced.

*So what happened? With you and Chase, I mean.*

*Nothing, really. It turned out, in the time it took for me to work things out with Fox for the whole plan, she met somebody else. They weren't a done deal by the time I got back to her, though, and I did spend the night with her a couple times—at her place, let me add; so there's no memories associated with anywhere I lived, for you to deal with—but anyway, she did have some feelings for me. But I also got to know her better. I found out more about her...and she wasn't into big guns and fast cars and action movies, and shit like that. All the stuff you and I like. In fact, she was kind of a guns activist. And you know me. It just...didn't work.* He shrugged. *So 'Alex Robertson' died in a car crash, and I came back here. Shortly thereafter, Fox designated me his successor, and we started talking about instituting a concept that eventually became Alpha Line. She did grieve me for a while, which...well, this is gonna sound bad, and I don't mean it like that, but...I was sorta glad, you know? I appreciated the fact that she grieved me. It helped ease a little of the pain of the breakup, and told me I'd meant SOMETHING to her, at least. Last I'd heard, she'd finally married the other guy, AND become vice-chair of the department, with the likelihood of very shortly moving into the department chair role, since the chairman was almost retirement age. She was happy; it was what she wanted. And I was happy for 'em. Lonely, but happy for 'em.* He paused.

*And then Slug took 'em both out, damn him. Right as they were starting to... 'come into their own,' I guess you could say.* He shrugged again, and Omega instinctively reached out and covered his hand with her own.

*I'm sorry, Ace.*

*Hey, it's okay,* he said, taking her hand in his own. *She wasn't you.*

It was Omega's turn to flush. She dropped her gaze as she felt her cheeks heat. She tried to think of a response, but came up empty. Sensing that fact, Echo continued.

*Anyway, baby, it was long over with by the time I met you. Translated, there's nobody you have to be jealous about.*

*Um, okay.* Omega tucked her head. *I just...* She broke off, uncertain how to finish.

*I can pick up on that one. You just don't understand why I'm interested.*

*Yeah.*

*Well, lemme show you something, then.*

*What?*

*This is why I needed Zz'r'p's help. You know me; I'm a man of few words, and didn't know how to describe it, let alone whether I could manage to force it out past my lips. But they say a picture's worth a thousand words, and I CAN show you THAT. At least I can, THIS way. You've seen this first one before, but you were kinda distracted, because Wright was in here with us. I want you to have a chance to actually LOOK at it, this time.*

And an image flooded Omega's mind.

It was a woman in a black Suit. She was tall, with long, platinum-blonde hair, so pale it was nearly silver, hanging down her back in a sleek French braid. She was possessed of wide cheekbones and bright blue eyes, and a nigh-perfect hourglass figure, strong but voluptuous. She stood with feet spread, arms akimbo, fists on her hips, in the classic superhero pose. A wide smile graced her face, those blue eyes sparkling like sapphires. She reached into a pocket, extracted a pair of wraparound 'sunglasses,' and donned them.

*That,* Echo told her, *is the first time you ever wore the Suit of an Agent.*

*That's...me? It's really me?*

*Yeah, it's you. You don't recognize yourself?*

*I didn't know I was that pretty.*

*Aw hell, baby, you're beautiful.*

Suddenly an entire montage flowed past her mind's eye: Megan McAllister running the obstacle course for the first time; Omega leaning over Echo's head to help him rack the barbell in the gym, her strong arms and shoulders grabbing the heavy weight, taut abdominal muscles flexing beneath her sports top, shapely legs and posterior clad in skintight spandex.

The same lovely female Agent crouched in front of a frightened alien toddler, comforting it. Carrying several human children through a toy store. Running full-tilt at her partner's side down an ice tunnel. Leaping through the air to take him out of harm's way; protecting him from almost certain death beneath a launching spacecraft; displaying the severed rattle of the snake that bit her. Floating in space, wide-eyed, at the end of her tether; in a spacesuit, in a compression suit, in a cowboy hat. Laughing, crying, moaning in pain, glaring in fierce determination. Screaming in equally fierce anger. Sharing a pizza with him; drinking beers together as they watched their favorite movies on television. Sitting beside him at a baseball game; at a football game; in a movie theater. Watching the stars while lying beside him on the roof, in the desert, on a remote island, on a grassy hilltop, in the middle of a pasture, on an Andean mountaintop.

It went on for what seemed like a long time, memory upon treasured memory that Echo shared with her, and she was astounded: she had never realized how much it all meant to him until that moment. *How much* I *mean to him,* she thought.

*Now you're startin' to catch on, Meg,* he told her.

*Echo? No. Alex.*

*Echo's fine. It was my nickname even before the Agency,*

*like I've told ya. But Alex sounds good too, when you say it.*

*Echo-Alex,* she addressed him, and they both grinned, *when...when did you...I mean, the first time I wore the Suit?!*

*Oh. When did I realize you were...so important to me? Is that what you wanna know?*

*Yeah.*

*I dunno for sure. I guess maybe guys don't pay such close attention to stuff like that. At least, this guy doesn't, I suppose. You sorta grew on me, to be honest. I admired you from the first, though. You were one cool, gorgeous chick. Nothing seemed to really faze you, not even getting dumped into the middle of the Agency. Oh, I knew it hurt like hell to leave NASA, to leave your dream behind, but I saw the moment when you realized you might make it even farther here than you could have there, and it excited you. I knew you were a keeper after the Antarctic mission, but when you left after your deprogramming, I didn't know what to do with myself. I convinced Fox to hold off on finding me a new partner—I didn't WANT a new partner. I wanted you to come back. Fox pointed out that looked unlikely, and I told him that I'd run Alpha Line from a desk if necessary, but I wasn't replacing you, dammit. And that's when—and why—he created the special designation of defined partnership, expressly for us. By Christmas of that year, I realized I was really attracted to you, but I wasn't sure what to do.*

*Why not?*

*Several reasons. One was pretty simple. I wasn't sure yet if we could maintain the professional level needed to keep us from getting killed, if we became lovers—I mean, we hadn't even been partners a solid year yet. The second was that I was still getting over the whole thing with Chase, the grieving part—it hadn't been that long since she'd been discovered dead with her husband, see, and that...hit me hard. Partly because I felt responsible. MOSTLY because I felt responsible, if I'm honest with myself. The last reason was that whenever I'd try to show any interest, you either ignored it or seemed to reject it. In retrospect, I probably sent you all kinds of mixed signals, baby, so it's no wonder.*

*To be honest, Echo, I...I'm afraid I missed any little flirtation attempts, or the like. It's like I told you, back in our quarters. In all truthfulness, I had been considering it during the whole Houdini mission thing last Halloween...until I discovered the truth about who, and what, had been put into me.*

*Huh. I remember you wanted to talk to me, after we got home at the end of that mission, and then suddenly you didn't want to talk after all. You said the subject had been overcome by events. Is that why? You found out the details of what was done to you?*

*Yeah.* She dropped her head. *That was what I wanted to talk about—about whether or not we might...might take our relationship to the next level. Only then I had the talk with Zebra about my modified genetics. And I found out the truth. About all of it.*

*And you were ashamed to even consider it, after that.*

*Yeah. There's still stuff I...can't bring myself to tell you.*

*Like you mentioned to me at my beach house?*

*Yeah. Anyway, after I found out all that, it just never occurred to me that, that anybody who knew about me, about what I was after Slug was done with me, could ever...* Omega broke off, dropping her gaze to the floor. *Especially you.*

* * *

Echo leaned over and put a gentle hand under her chin, lifting until he could look into her eyes again.

*Why especially me?*

*Well, never mind the fact that you were my designated target. Just...well. 'Cause you're...you. Top Agent. One of the last, and the youngest, of The Originals. Head of Alpha Line, and second in command of the whole damn organization, at least for Division One. The guy who's eventually going to BE in command of it. You've always been my benchmark, my measuring stick, to see how I was doing at this whole thing. Dying has never been my greatest fear in this job. Oh, I don't WANNA, don't get me wrong. But I was way more afraid of disappointing you, of not being able to keep up with you, than of dying. Especially given...what I was trying to live with. There were times I honestly think dying would have been a relief.*

*Damn, Meg. You never let on, any of that. Did I—DO I—intimidate you that bad?*

*No, I don't intimidate easy, to begin with. But you...you let me in enough that I never felt INTIMIDATED, but it was... important to me, to know that, that...*

*That your hero approved of you.*

*Hero? Where on earth did you get that term?*

*Several people have used that of me, where you're concerned, from time to time. Is it true?*

*...Yeah. If I'm straight about it, with myself and you, I guess it is.* She tried to look down again, but the hand under her chin was still there, gentle but firm, allowing no deviations as the brown eyes gazed deep into the blue ones.

*So. Can you learn to love your hero?*

*I...I don't know. In a lotta ways, I already do, I just...it may not be the way YOU want, at least not at this point, 'cause I'm not really sure...about anything, really. I...you're gonna have to go slow, I think. At least to start. 'Cause...I'm scared. In a buncha ways. And, and Zz'r'p was right. That whole intimacy thing...it HURT, Echo. I want...*

*Hush, baby. I understand, and it's okay. Remember I told you to hold that thought, about what I learned from Ree, the Kochavi woman?*

*Um, yeah?*

*One of the things I learned was that slow and gentle can be just as sexy, just as passionate, as hot and heavy. And I learned how to BE slow and gentle. For a kid as young as I was, that's not easy, either—but I did. And I know—pain is not supposed to be part of it, Meg. Um, I guess maybe the first time for a woman, it is, just for a few seconds, but after that, I think...I think we could blow each other's minds, babe. But I completely comprehend that you need to go slow in getting there. And it's your prerogative to decide you don't want to go any farther, at any time. I just want you to let me in, let me try to guide you to that place in your life, in your mind and heart, where you want to get there...with me.*

To Echo's shock, a huge tear suddenly welled up and spilled down Omega's face. He reached out with his other hand and drew the back of his fingers across her cheek, wiping it away.

*What's wrong, baby? Did I say something wrong? Do you not want to?*

*No, Echo, you said everything right. And saying it this way, with Zz'r'p providing the conduit, it seems like it comes straight from the deepest part of you. I think...I do wanna try, hon. You just gotta understand that I'm kinda scared...okay, really scared...um, freakin' scared half out of my wits...about several things, and I may knee-jerk on ya a little bit. Or a lot. Especially after...after recent events. Try to be patient with me, as much as you can.*

*I'm gonna tell you a secret, Meg. Back when I was working with X-ray, and then later with Romeo, I was NOT known as a very patient man. If you don't believe me, just ASK Romeo! I was impatient as hell, to tell the truth. But with you? I know who you are. I know what you can do. If you need time to adapt, I have always been willing to give you that time, because I've come to realize that, once you get the hang of things, it's gonna be something wonderful to behold. And it is, every time. So if it's true in matters of work, of missions and training and stuff, how much more is it gonna be true with you and me personally? In a caring relationship together?*

*Aw.* She blushed furiously, and he felt her skin heat against his hand. He cupped her face in that hand briefly, then tapped her nose and her lips with his index finger in a gesture of familiar affection. But as he did, he felt an electric shock run through his being as she pursed her lips to deposit a quick kiss on the sensitive pad of his fingertip. He gasped despite himself.

*You...you might just catch on...to that slow and gentle stuff quicker than I thought,* he told her, and she laughed.

*You liked it?*

*Hell yeah.*

*Okay. I'll remember it.*

*You do that.*

They both laughed again.

*So, as Romeo would say, 'Are we a thang now?'* he wondered.

*I believe we are a thang, hon,* she decided. *A slow and gentle thang, but a thang, just the same. Only I think we better let Zz'r'p have his head back before we give him a headache, though.*

*Damn. I was kinda liking this. But you're right.*

*I am available for future in-depth discussions, should I be needed,* Zz'r'p's mental voice re-entered the conversation. *Do not fear; I only returned when I heard Omega mentally call my name just now, and have overheard nothing. Have you resolved your concerns?*

*Well, not entirely,* Omega admitted. *We still have some things that have to be worked on for the future. But for now, yeah, I think so.*

*I can tell from the state of Agent Echo's thoughts that he is pleased with the current state of...affairs,* the Arcturan deliberately offered the double entendre this time, his smile as evident in his thoughts as it was on his face.

*Abso-damn-lutely,* Echo agreed, with a slightly abashed chuckle. *Thank you, Zz'r'p, for all your help. From damn near the beginning.*

*It has ever been my pleasure, Echo,* the alien said sincerely. *I would be deeply honored if the two of you would consider me a friend.*

*You've already got it, Zz'r'p,* Omega answered, her deep gratitude obvious. *I owe you more than I can ever repay.*

*Given the happiness I sense in both members of Alpha One at this moment, you might be surprised how easy that repayment is, child. I am happy for your current resolution, and wholeheartedly hope your relationship progresses smoothly and well.*

"Okay, Meg," Echo said, resorting to his voice once more, and finding it unexpectedly hoarse, "shall we head home? It's getting late anyway, and I'm sure Zz'r'p would like a break."

"All right, Echo," she agreed, standing and moving to his side. "Let's go. Thanks, Zz'r'p! Maybe we can take you out for dinner sometime. Or have you over for a meal, or something. We're both good cooks."

"I may take you up on it, young one," the Deltiri replied, smiling.

* * *

To a casual observer, there was nothing different about the Alpha One team as they meandered back to their quarters, side by side. They were their usual reticent selves, saying nothing to each other or anyone else. They did not touch, or even look at each other. But a closer observer would have noticed a certain relaxed calmness, a content gleam in blue eye and brown, that might have bespoken a successful mission completed. Perhaps.

When they reached Omega's door, Echo followed her in. But even this was not unusual, since they had adjoining, connected quarters.

* * *

The door closed behind them, shutting out the rest of the world, and Echo followed Omega into her den.

"Whaddaya wanna do about dinner, Ace?" she asked him. "If we start something cooking now, it'll be time to eat when it's ready."

"Let it wait," he told her. "We can slap together some more sandwiches, throw a frozen casserole in the oven, or maybe go out to eat, later. Or go on that date I suggested, that started the whole thing this morning. Right now, Meg, I need your permission for something."

"What?"

"Now that we have...something of an understanding, at least," he said with some hesitation, and an uncharacteristic uncertainty, "can I...finally...kiss you? Properly, I mean?"

"You want to?"

"Oh HELL yes."

"Um, okay," she murmured, sidling close, adorably shy. She leaned up and brushed her lips against his, then started to withdraw.

"Nuh-uh," he said, catching her and easing gentle arms around her. "That's how you kiss when somebody's watchin'. I wanna kiss you the way I've wanted to for months now. The way it happens in my dreams." One hand came up to cup the back of her head and hold it steady, as he bent his head to hers.

"Um, oh...I..."

"Just relax, baby," he whispered against her lips. "A kiss is all I want, and you know it isn't gonna hurt."

So she let her lips part, and his tongue entered her mouth, exploring tenderly, as Echo practically drowned in the taste of her, the scent of her. When her arms slid around his neck and she began to return his kisses, Echo let out a sound that was somewhere between a growl of desire and a howl of pleasure, his arms tightening around her.

After several moments, he eased back, reluctant to do so, but unwilling to press her too hard; he didn't want to go too fast and make her uncomfortable. To his surprise, she didn't pull away, but met his eyes. Her fingers twined in his hair kept his head bent to hers, and she rested her forehead against his.

"You taste good," she murmured.

"Mm. So do you. I could have you for dinner, all to myself."

"You'd regret the lack of calories in the gym tomorrow."

"Probably. It'd be fun while it lasted, though."

"Are you wanting to..." Omega nodded at her bedroom.

"No. Well, yeah, but that'd be way too fast. I want you to be ready and comfortable with it when we get there, however long that takes. And I know about your beliefs and stuff. We'll have to discuss that in detail, 'cause it's a little bit of a wrinkle— the Agency charter doesn't include marriage, remember—but you already know that, from talking to India and Romeo. Fox can explain the history behind it best, I guess; I never did understand why they did it that way. But for tonight, I thought we could just, I dunno, sit on the couch and make out for a little while, maybe."

"Okay. I think I'd like that."

"Even in my lap?"

"Especially in your lap."

With a delighted grin, he swept her up in his arms and carried her to the couch. Sitting down, he deposited her in his lap, then bent his head back to hers.

# **Chapter 4**

They ended up spending the majority of the evening on the sofa, except for the time it took them to throw together more sandwiches for dinner, once Omega's belly protested enough to get their attention.

The night was spent, as Echo had promised, in separate bedrooms. But neither felt alone; memories of the evening's kisses accompanied them, along with a tentative feeling of belonging, and both slept well.

Echo was waiting for her when she emerged from her bedroom the next morning, with a mug of coffee and a kiss. The coffee was set temporarily on a handy bookshelf nearby, priority being given to the kiss, which took a while to deliver, at least in the thorough manner Echo felt was necessary.

Then, with a smile, he led her into his quarters, where breakfast was already waiting.

* * *

The morning was quiet.

Omega finished the 'assignment' that Michael had set for her, and Echo used his tablet to review emails and paperwork.

The fact that they both worked on Omega's comfortable sofa—Omega slouched at one end; Echo sprawled his considerable length along it, propping one sock-clad foot on the far arm, while resting his head in his partner's lap—didn't affect their concentration in the slightest.

The fact that, from time to time, they paused to kiss, might have.

* * *

A knock sounded on the door of Omega's dressing room as she put the finishing touches to her makeup on her opening night.

"Who is it?" she immediately asked, without turning.

102

"It's me, Meg," Echo's voice answered.

"Oh! Come on in, hon," she called somewhat distractedly, as she concentrated on the delicate task of applying the last coats of mascara. The door opened, and she heard familiar footsteps behind her. "Hang on juuust a second, Ace."

"Take your time."

Omega finished her makeup, then tightened her favorite black silk robe around her and turned to her partner. "There. I—oh!" she exclaimed, as Echo gently laid a large bouquet in her arms.

"For my favorite leading lady," he said quietly, and dropped a light kiss on her forehead, as she looked in stunned amazement from the bouquet of two dozen stargazer lilies to her partner's smiling face. "Knock 'em dead, Angel-voice." He glanced around the flower-bedecked room. "I see I'm not the only one to send flowers."

"Oh," Omega said again, looking for a vase for Echo's flowers, "no—these here are from Sofia, with a thank-you note attached; those over by the table are from Michael. That big one over there by the door is from Fox and most of Division One, I think. But you're the only one to bring them to me personally." She smiled up at him. "Which makes them even more special."

* * *

"That reminds me," Echo said, as Omega sat his bouquet front and center, "there was enough interest, both at Headquarters and the field Offices, that—with the producers' approval, and a certain, um, small financial agreement, mostly because of the rights—Fox decided to pipe the performance over one of the Agency vid channels. It's going worldwide. You're a real star tonight, Meg."

"What?!" Omega blanched. "Oh no. 'Scuse me, Echo—!" Omega darted into the adjoining restroom, slamming and locking the door. Seconds later, Echo heard the sounds of Omega becoming violently ill. He pounded on the locked door.

"Meg?! Meg, are you okay? Baby, say something!"

"Give...give me a minute, Echo," Omega gasped from

the other side of the door. He heard the toilet flush, then the faucet ran for a few moments. Moments later, he could hear her spitting. After a little bit, the door opened, and she wobbled out. "S-sorry."

"Meg, what's wrong?" Echo asked, concerned.

"Nothing major, Echo," she replied sheepishly. "It's only stage fright."

"Stage..." he stared at her. "You're kidding." He pulled the dressing-table's chair out for her, and she sat, throwing him a grateful look.

"No, it's stage fright," she answered, confident. "I swear it is. Opening-night jitters. MAJOR opening-night jitters."

"But you've faced down alien murderers and psychopaths, cool as—"

"It doesn't matter." She shrugged. "Whole different ballgame, here. Remember the first time you took me ice skating? Last Christmas? Been there, done that...only this is a couple orders of magnitude worse. And I do this every time."

"Damn, hon," Echo said in sympathy, laying a gentle hand on her shoulder. "Mm. Even your shoulders are tight. Here." He began lightly massaging them, attempting to relax her.

"Don't, Echo," Omega said softly, and he stopped, looking quizzically at her in the mirror. "I know you're trying to help, Ace, but this is actually a good thing."

"Good?! Shit, Meg, you gotta be kidding me. It's almost as bad as it was before the Cortians arrived. You're not QUITE as stiff as a fence post through your shoulders and back, but you aren't far off. You'll hurt yourself, if you stay like this."

"Yeah, Echo, I know, but it's still a good thing. And I won't stay like this. See, as soon as the curtain goes up, all this undirected nervous energy, tension, and adrenaline will get channeled into my performance, and everything will go fine. If I relax too much now, I'll fall flat on my face when I get onstage. Trust me on this—it's happened."

"Oh. So...that's why you didn't want me to take you to dinner until after the performance," Echo realized, jerking a thumb at the bathroom. "And why you ate a big breakfast, but a light lunch."

"Yeah. It wouldn't have done any good for me to eat dinner; I'd have flat lost it. And since you always take me to nummy places, it woulda been a dreadful waste of delicious food."

"But you need to eat. You've gotta keep that supercharged metabolism fueled. Especially with all the dancing an' other activity. I mean, you're going nonstop for several hours, here."

"It's okay; I have been. I got some mild nibble-y stuff down here," she waved at a tote bag tucked under the makeup table, "that I've been snacking from. Sliced Swiss cheese 'cause it's mild, an' crackers, an' some grapes. Bite-sized stuff. If I eat just a little bit at a time, it absorbs faster and has less chance of getting barfed into the toilet."

"Oh. Well, if you're sure..."

"I'm sure. Broadway it wasn't, but I've got some experience with opening nights, all the same, Ace." Another knock sounded on the door. "Who is it?"

"It's Cecile, Miss Meg."

"Come on in, Cecile. Cecile, let me introduce you to my manager and my, um, my boyfriend. Echo, this is Cecile; Cecile, this is Alec Williams."

"His name is Alec, but you call him Echo?" young Cecile wondered, puzzled.

"Yes; his...what's the word; oh! His nickname is Echo."

"But...why?" the girl asked, confused.

"Because I'm a good mimic," the male Agent explained. "So call me Echo, please," he offered with a slight, friendly smile.

"Oh, I see! Pleased to meet you, Mr. Echo," Cecile said with a wide smile. "Miss Meg has already told me all about you—except for your nickname."

"All good, I hope," Echo said with a grin.

"Yes, very good!" Cecile turned to Omega. "He is every bit as handsome as you said, Miss Meg."

Omega blushed scarlet, but Echo grinned.

"Well, thank you both, then," he noted. "I'm glad to know that my looks hold up to the standards of the famous stars in this show."

"Oh yes, Mr. Echo," Cecile averred. "You could be IN the show, with your looks."

As the pretty young woman bustled on into the room, arms filled with various garments, Omega explained, "Cecile's my dresser, Echo, so it's time for you to scoot on out of here so I can get dressed in my first costume."

"I can't watch?"

"Echo!" Omega protested.

"You're wearing a unitard, Meg," Echo pointed out. "I can see it under your robe."

"No, Mr. Echo, even so," Cecile told him. "You see, by the time we are done with all the petticoats and voluminous skirts, there won't be enough room in here for all three of us! Let alone all the lovely flowers. And this is one of the biggest of the private dressing rooms."

"Aw," Echo murmured, disappointed.

"It's okay, Echo," Omega told him, soothing. "Everything is fine for now. And I'll see you back here after the performance. Where are we going?"

"It's a surprise. You'll find out then," Echo told her.

"But how will I know what dress to wear?"

"Wear something like you wore the other night when we came here to watch," Echo said. "That'll fit in just great." Then, instead of turning toward the door, he stepped closer, slipping his arms around his partner and pulling her against him, as Cecile smiled knowingly. "It'll be fine, Meg," he murmured in her ear before dropping a light, chaste kiss there, realizing she would be embarrassed to kiss him full-on with a spectator in the room—and so would he, as yet. "You'll do terrific. And I'll be nearby if you need anything. So go out there and knock 'em dead, baby."

"The proper term is 'break a leg,' hon," Omega told him with a smile.

"Huh?"

"Theater is laden with all kinds of superstitions," Omega explained. "Like, you never mention a certain Shakespearean play by name inside a theater; it's always referred to as, 'That Scottish Play.'"

"You mean MacB—"

"SHUSH!" Cecile and Omega both exclaimed at the same time. "It's very bad luck, Mr. Echo," Cecile added.

"And likewise, you never actually wish someone good luck before the curtain," Omega continued, "because otherwise, the opposite might happen. So instead, you tell them to go out and break a leg, and that's considered wishing the opposite."

Echo cocked his head to one side and stared at the two women.

"That is the craziest thing I've ever heard," he declared, "and I've heard some doozies."

"It's tradition, Mr. Echo," Cecile murmured. "We theater people take it VERY seriously."

"All right, then. Heaven forbid something bad happened because I couldn't follow tradition." Echo pulled his partner back into an embrace, and this time, he did kiss her on the mouth. "In that case, 'break a leg,' Angel-voice."

Omega's eyes shone as her partner left the dressing room.

* * *

Echo, his transponder headset on, stood in a backstage corner as Omega moved past him and took her place in the wings, awaiting her cue. He saw the slight trembling in her frame, and worry filled his thoughts despite his best efforts.

*Damn it; it's bad enough that she's terrified of the performance,* he thought, *but she's putting her life on the line on top of it. I really don't know how alert she can possibly be, keyed up like that. Hm.* After a moment, and by way of simultaneous test and encouragement, he murmured into the tiny microphone, "Stay cool, Angel-voice."

Omega clasped her hands lightly behind her back, giving him a subtle thumbs-up, and he grinned to himself.

107

"You knew I was here all along?" he whispered.

Another thumbs-up.

"Did you recognize my pheromones?"

A third thumbs-up.

"Are you still nervous, baby?"

She gave him two simultaneous thumbs-up, that time.

"Aw. Are you gonna be okay?"

Two thumbs-up. Then Echo heard her soft voice in the headset, "Cue coming up."

"Go get 'em, Meg. You got this. Er, break a leg, rather."

Echo watched in something approaching awe then, as his partner seemed to metamorphose right before his eyes: Suddenly, instead of the nervous Agent, there stood a dreamy, sensitive, aspiring young opera singer. Omega ran lightly out onstage, all trace of fear gone, to begin her Broadway debut.

Echo smiled to himself, then started on yet another systematic check of the theater environ.

* * *

The performance progressed without any glitches that were obvious to the audience, although a few minor incidents and mishaps occurred.

*Maybe they're just little screw-ups,* Echo thought, checking the rigging on the fly-rail after a brake slipped slightly, *and maybe not. Shit, Meg, be careful, sweetheart.* He glanced down at the stage from his location on a rigging catwalk to check on her, just as the title song began, and stopped dead, fascinated. "Damn," he breathed, admiring.

So powerful an image did Michael and Omega present, so beautifully intertwined their voices, that the entire theater focused on them and them alone. Echo was spellbound as the song progressed to Omega's aria. When, once again, she emitted that final, breathtaking note, there was a momentary hush in the theater, then thunderous applause.

Blown away by the performance, Echo joined in the applause, murmuring softly into the headset mike, "Brava! Bravissima!" and he smiled when Omega threw a quick, surreptitious glance toward the ceiling.

* * *

Omega's first Broadway performance had ended with no untoward incidents, and Echo waited for her backstage as she took her curtain call with Michael. When the curtain finally closed, an exultant Omega came running offstage, straight to Echo, laughing exuberantly. He stepped forward to meet her, smiling as he caught her up and spun her once, full circle through the air, then he set her down.

"I did it, Echo! I did it!" she exclaimed, exhilarated.

"You did it," he agreed with a slight smile, his hands still on her waist. "You definitely did it, baby." *And I've got all I can do to keep from kissing you breathless, right here and now,* he thought, gazing down into twin sapphires and trying not to lose himself in them.

"Did you like it?" Omega asked, suddenly uncertain. "Was it all right?"

"It was marvelous, my dear," Michael's voice interjected from behind, even as Echo opened his mouth to speak, and the two Agents turned. "You were brilliant. Do you have post-performance plans?"

"Well..." A hesitant Omega glanced up at Echo.

"I'm taking her to dinner, Mike," Echo answered for her. "Meg, why don't you run on and get changed? I'll be along in a minute," Echo said, removing the uncomfortable headset.

"Okay. See you in a few, hon!" A happy Omega fairly danced through the backstage door, as both men watched.

As soon as she was gone, Echo leaned over and whispered something to Michael with a grin. Michael gave him an *Oh, really?* look, and Echo nodded, whereupon Michael laughed and agreed.

* * *

Echo knocked on Omega's dressing room door. "Meg? It's Echo."

The door opened with explosive swiftness, disclosing a pale Omega.

"Echo?! Where have you been?? Why don't you have your headset on??"

"I wanted to have a private word with Mike," Echo said. "Why? What's wrong?" Then, taking in her shaken appearance, he grabbed her shoulders. "What happened? Did the theater phantom attack??"

"No—but I saw him, Echo! I talked to him!"

"What?! Where??"

"In the mirror, Echo!" Omega drew him into the room, closing the door, and pointed at the reflective surface. "Just like in the show!"

"Shit! I'm sorry, Meg. I should have been here..." Echo began investigating the mirror, running his fingers along its edge and trying to pull it from the wall, then tapping it lightly.

"It's all right, Echo. But...I really wish you'd been here."

"Meg," Echo looked up from his intensive sleuthing, "there's no way anyone could get back here. The mirror's attached to the wall, and the wall is solid concrete and cinder block."

"I know, Echo. I already checked. But it doesn't matter."

"Why?"

"Because...I saw who the phantom was."

"What?!" Echo exclaimed. "Who? Who the hell was it?"

"You're not gonna like this."

"Tell me."

"Slug." She met his worried gaze. "It was Slug, Echo. And now he's after both of us."

* * *

Echo stared at his partner, stunned and worried, as Omega continued.

"He was...taunting me, Echo," she whispered, pained. "He said...he said he'd planned for every contingency. That's why he...why he engineered me to kill you, and, if that failed...my... my children..." Echo watched silently as Omega's shoulders sagged. "He gloated, Echo. He laughed at...at what happened in Fox's office the night Wright triggered the...the biochemical...

the...he said that I deserved the humiliation, for siding with you against him." Slowly she doubled up, ashamed. "He's been watching us, Echo! The whole time! All these last couple years! I didn't believe it—I thought it was a hoax. But he told me exactly what he did to me, exactly how my body reacted to Wright. He crowed over the look of pain on your face that night. He struck at you through me—again."

Unsure what to say, not even sure what to believe, Echo took her shoulders without a word, and Omega leaned heavily against him.

"He said it wasn't over, Echo," Omega continued, barely audible. "My voice...isn't really mine, he said...this is another one of Slug's plans...aimed at us both."

Abruptly, Omega's knees buckled, and Echo suddenly found himself carrying his badly-shaken partner.

* * *

A disturbed Omega was lying on the tiny couch—really more of a love seat—in the corner of the dressing room. Echo, lines of worry creasing his forehead, sat on the edge of the couch beside her, holding her hand and absently stroking the back with a fingertip. She looked up at him, letting him see the sadness in her eyes.

"You don't believe me. You think I've gone over the edge," her low voice accused.

"Honey," Echo said very gently, "in the last couple of weeks you've been stalked, almost raped, had your biochem yanked all over the damn map, fooled into thinking I was dead, stood up by a would-be lover, and thrown head-first into a Broadway musical. Never mind finding out that I'm...interested, and getting blindsided by that. All that shit is a lot for anyone to handle, baby." He smoothed her hair back, attempting to soothe her, to get her to settle into a calmer state so he could assess her mental condition.

"I'm not losing it, Echo," Omega told him, deadly earnest. "Look, if it had been any other entity, I'd agree with you. I know Slug is dead—I was there, remember? I aimed the tachyon-

111

splitter rifle, and you pulled the trigger. But Slug was one of the most powerful telepaths we've ever encountered. Not to mention a complete psycho. And totally fixated on getting his revenge on you."

"And posthumously responsible for your stalking and near-rape. Baby, you've probably got some serious post-traumatic stress—"

"Echo, listen to me!!" Omega cried in frustration. "He's a telepath! What if we only killed his body?!"

Echo stopped, startled, mulling over the concept.

"Well, I suppose it's possible," he admitted at last.

"We're the Division One's Alpha Line, Echo," Omega said. "We're the special forces unit, and you and I are the TOP team in that department. We get ALL the weird shit! It's more than 'possible.' But look. Let's just go home, and I'll get India to check me out. That should prove I'm not hallucinating."

"Well, we can at least go out to dinner first," Echo amended. "You're probably starved."

"Yeah, I am, at that. Um, can I ask a favor—?"

"Sure. Whatcha need, baby?"

"Uh...I need to shower and dress to go out..."

"You want me to step out?" Echo turned to go.

"NO!" Omega exclaimed, grabbing his arm. "Echo, whatever you think, I know Slug was here. I'm not too keen on re-enacting the shower scene from 'Psycho.'"

"You DON'T want me to go."

"Eee-zackly."

"All right," Echo acquiesced. "Do you want me in here, or in the bathroom with you?"

Omega blushed at that, but looked at her partner frankly.

"I don't know. What do you think? If you think you need to be in there with me to ensure I'm safe, then that's what we'll do. Just...expect me to turn thirty-seven shades of red."

Echo sighed and bent his head in thought. *She's not comfortable with the idea of being nude with me yet,* he realized. *And I get that, 'cause I'd probably be uncomfortable too, quite yet. We simply haven't gotten to that point in our relationship, though I hope it's coming. But she's also willing to do whatever it takes to maintain security and safety...including being nude in the shower, with me watching, because I'd be watching out for her. There's gotta be some way I can protect her sense of privacy and dignity for now—which, the good Lord knows, needs a defender, lately—while still protecting HER.* Without raising his head, he surveyed her intently. *Umm...wait a minute. Maybe there is.* He pulled out the headset.

"Go get in the shower," he told her, "but don't lock the door. And take your Winchester & Tesla. Yell if ANYTHING happens. I'll stay here and monitor."

"Deal."

* * *

Omega had finally relaxed under the hot water, and was rinsing off soapsuds when she heard Echo's shocked expletive through the transponder behind her ear.

Within seconds, she had leaped from the shower, reaching for a towel with one hand and her weapon with the other; moments after that, a towel-swathed Omega, platinum hair streaming water, lunged out of the bathroom, Winchester & Tesla in hand and at the ready.

"What?!" she demanded.

Echo stood rooted to the floor in the center of the dressing room, both blasters aimed at the makeup mirror, staring in stunned dismay. Slowly he replaced the weapons in his shoulder holsters and turned to his partner, motioning for her to stand down.

"I...owe you a major apology, Meg."

"For what?" The female Agent lowered her weapon and hitched up the towel a bit. Echo waved a hand at the mirror.

"Because I just saw Slug, too."

* * *

"How's this, Echo?" Omega asked, emerging from the bathroom only a short time later dressed in evening garb. The black dress was long-sleeved, with a turtleneck collar; but the fit was almost skin-tight, showing off Omega's rather voluptuous figure to perfection. The floor-length, straight skirt had a rear kick-slit to mid-thigh, allowing glimpses of strong, shapely, golden-tan legs. Black, high-heeled pumps encased her feet, adding curve to her legs and height to her already-tall frame. The smooth silver-blonde tresses hung long and loose down her back, but the front of her hair was upswept in an intricate, face-framing braid, rhinestones glittering in it. Her face was flawless, the sapphire eyes smoky, soft pink lips moist and full.

"Fine, Meg," Echo said absently, without looking. "Everyone else is gone. Hurry up and let's go. I want to clear out of the theater until we figure out what's going on here—it's not safe to stay, just us. Not after tonight's events, not until we know more. If it really is Slug, we need to understand how, and we need a plan before confronting him again."

"Okay," a wistful Omega agreed, glancing down at the painstakingly-chosen—yet unnoticed—dress, then preceding Echo out, as he locked the doors behind them.

* * *

"Wait a minute, Echo," Omega said, confused, as they exited the Corvette in front of the conference center in Brooklyn, "this isn't a restaurant."

"No. Oh, that reminds me." Echo reached into the back seat, and firmly tucked the scarlet hibiscus he retrieved into her hair, just behind her left ear. "There we go. Now we're ready." He offered his arm, which she accepted, and escorted his puzzled companion into the apparently deserted building. They walked down a dark, dimly-lit corridor and around a corner. Light and sound emanated incongruously from a door at the far end of the poorly-lit hallway.

Omega shot a suspicious look at Echo; his face was completely expressionless as they approached the doorway. Echo ushered Omega through the door and stopped.

Omega blinked, speechless in complete surprise as the assembled alien ambassadors and Division One agents broke into wild applause. Glancing at Echo, she saw the slight grin on his face, and murmured, "Echoooo...what did you do...?" His grin only got wider.

Fox came up to the Alpha One team just then.

"Congratulations on your Broadway debut, Omega," he said with a benevolent smile. "Not only are you one of the 'cream of the crop,' but it's become highly evident you're an excellent and very talented artist, as well. We—Echo and I— thought you should have a proper opening-night party. And everyone agreed." He waved both hands around the room.

"Thank you," Omega said, flashing them both a brilliant, happy smile. "Echo said you piped the performance over the vid channels..."

"Yes, and put it on one of the big wall-panel screens in the Core," Fox confirmed. "Zebra is on duty, but she caught what she could of it, and plans to watch a video of it later; she sends her love, tekhter. Likewise Dihl watched at the Ranch, and sent delighted congratulations to you both; Joe and the ranch hands were thrilled and surprised, she said. Oh, and Bravo and Lima were fascinated. They want to discuss the play with you when you have time. It seems neither of them have read the classic book on which it is based—a matter which I'm rectifying; I loaned them the copy from my personal library."

"Okay," Omega laughed, as Echo went to get plates of food from the buffet, and India and Romeo headed over. "Are the guys here, then?"

"No, they're still on duty," Fox answered. "But they sent their congratulations and said they hoped they'd see you tomorrow."

"Woo, pretty lady, lookit chu," Romeo said with a grin as he walked up, India on his arm. "Way to go, baby!"

"Meg, you were wonderful!" India smiled with enthusiasm.

"An' lookin' mighty fine now," Romeo added. "Right, India?"

"Beautiful," India agreed. "The single red flower in your hair sets off the whole look." Omega blushed. "Don't you think so, Echo?"

Echo handed a full plate of heavy hors d'oeuvres to his hungry partner, answering, "Think what, India?"

"That Meg looks lovely tonight."

Echo glanced at Omega, then responded, "Meg always looks good," and popped a stuffed mushroom into his mouth. India nearly gaped in surprise at Echo's rather generic response.

Omega met India's eyes, glanced surreptitiously down at her dress, and shrugged unobtrusively, a rueful smile on her face. India's eyes widened, unbelieving. Omega nodded slightly in affirmation. The three men, used to intense observation, gradually took notice of the women's subtle, wordless exchange.

"What the hell are you two going on about?" Fox finally bit.

"They're talking about Meg's new dress," Echo interpreted for the other two men. "India helped Meg settle on it for her opening night, and even went and picked it up for her, and they think I didn't notice, because I haven't said anything— yet." The other four Division One Agents in the little group stood blinking at Echo in a kind of shocked amazement. Then Omega nodded in understanding.

"Since when has Echo ever said everything he was thinking?" she asked the others rhetorically, then turned to Echo. "Well?"

"Later," he told her, blunt. "There's a little matter of champagne, then we need a battle plan."

"Champagne?" Omega echoed.

"Battle plan?" India asked.

* * *

"...And you both saw him?" Fox verified, after many bottles of bubbly were opened and poured, with multiple accompanying toasts to Alpha One in general and Omega in specific. "You're sure?"

"Yes." Echo was definite. "If I hadn't taken off the headset for a couple minutes, I'd probably have seen him twice."

"At least I know now why you took it off," Omega

remarked, raising her champagne flute to Michael, who waved at her across the room, grinning hugely—and devilishly—as he raised his own glass. "But for a few seconds there, I thought I was about to be toast, and that you already were."

"What do you and Omega need, Echo?" Fox asked.

"Well...psych profiles, for starters," Echo said. "Let's make certain Meg and I aren't suffering from delusions. After all, Meg is a low-level telepath these days—"

Omega, slightly behind Echo, dropped her eyes to the floor, pain surging through her.

"—And if I'm going through some sort of mental breakdown from all the worry in recent weeks—or from getting telepathically slammed across the room—she may be experiencing the effects of it."

Omega's head popped up, startled; she had expected the inverse explanation, given recent events. Then she impulsively stepped forward to Echo's side.

"Or I may be projecting my hallucinations into you," she declared, offering what she considered a more probable interpretation. "I'm the one that a shit-ton of...junk...has happened to, lately. You're right, Echo. Let's both get checked, then take it from there," she volunteered.

"I don't think it's gonna find anything in either of us," Echo decided, "but we need to be thorough, all the same."

"Right."

Fox nodded and pulled his cell phone, and Echo looked down at the woman beside him, meeting the discerning sapphire gaze. Neither spoke, but suddenly both smiled just as Fox said, "All right. Quick psych test for both of you at 02:00 D1 tomorrow."

"Uh, Fox..." Omega began, worried. "Look at the time."

"So?" Fox glanced at his wrist chronometer.

"I'm on an Earth-day schedule of performances, Fox. I have to sleep some time." Omega paused in thought. "Or maybe I don't. We ARE talking Slug, here. Blast it, Echo, I wish I could shield your mind, too." Fox extracted his cell phone again.

* * *

"But then I'd have to stay awake with you," Echo replied, concerned. "At least one of us needs to stay rested."

"Not really," Omega corrected. "Only the person maintaining the telepathic block has to stay awake to keep it erect. That would be me. You could sleep any time you felt like it."

"It's a moot point," Fox informed them, replacing his phone. "And I've rescheduled your tests for 10:00 D1. I don't want you sleep-deprived until we know there's a need."

"Fair enough," Echo said.

"Thanks, Fox," Omega told the Director. "Echo, it's 46:30 D1 now. Much as I hate to, maybe we should think about leaving soon..."

"Nope," Romeo interrupted.

"No?" Omega echoed.

"No," India and Fox agreed firmly.

"Why not, Fox?" Echo asked.

"We want a couple of things, first," India declared, then smiled, tapping a fork to her champagne flute, and the room hushed.

"And those are?" Echo pressed.

"One: We want a dance from Fred an' Ginger!" Romeo grinned. "That's Alpha One, in case you didn't know."

"And having 'one' implies 'two'..." Omega observed.

"And two: An encore performance," India filled them in. "We want to hear Meg sing her solo from Act Two, and Sir Michael and Meg do the love song, in person."

Omega paled. Echo steadied her as she swayed.

"What's wrong?" India asked, noting Omega's pallor and sudden unsteadiness with concern. "Are you sick, honey?"

"Meg's—" Echo began, but Omega interrupted.

"A little tired," she finished for him, meeting his eyes pleadingly, and he could have sworn he heard her voice in his head: *Don't tell them I have stage fright—please. Just help me get through this.*

"You have had a busy few days," Echo smoothly picked up, giving her an out. "Are you sure you're up to it, Meg?"

"Please please please please!" Suddenly several Hypothenemoids were clustered around Omega's feet, tugging gently but insistently on the hem of her evening gown with their prehensile antennae and babbling. "Pretty lady sings good! Echo an' Meg dance good! Wanna see! Wanna see!"

"Echo...?" Omega sighed. Echo waved Michael over.

"I'll tell you what, guys," Echo struck a deal. "Meg and I will dance one number—one—then Meg and Mike will do the love song—only if Mike agrees. He's not the one she normally sings it with."

"I always like encores, Echo," Michael said and smiled, and Echo mentally muttered expletives.

"All right. A nice, slow waltz, Meg?"

"Emphasis on slow, Echo," Omega nodded, and Fox signaled the musicians. The center of the room cleared as Echo took Omega in his arms and swept his weary, stressed partner into the opening, as the band struck up the Moonlight Waltz.

"Sorry, Meg," he murmured in her ear as they danced. "I tried."

"I know, and I appreciate it," she responded. "I'm just praying I don't humiliate myself in front of everybody."

"Anything I can do to help you?" he wondered, as their synchronized bodies followed the music.

"You're helping now. I'm getting used to the audience, and I'm keeping my energy level up, but directed."

"Good."

"One more thing," she requested, seeming hesitant, "stand where I can see you when I sing?"

"Why?" Echo looked into anxious azure eyes.

"It's...the psychological factor," she said, and shrugged, slightly sheepish. "That way, I'll have a friendly face to look at, to focus on. Somebody that I know...cares. After...well, after everything that's happened in the last couple of weeks, you know me as well as I know myself—horrible secrets and all—but you've never hesitated to stand by me. And invariably, you've stayed as close by my side as you could get. And believe me, I appreciate that, more than you can possibly know. More than any words I know could express. So I also know something like a missed note isn't gonna bother you."

Through the entire conversation, they glided gracefully, automatically, around the room, their bodies moving in complete rhythm to the music and each other, without the need to think about it.

"Meg," Echo murmured gently, "I told you once, when you were learning to ice skate—way back last year, during your first Christmas with us—that you could fall flat on your face and knock me down with you, in front of 'bazillions' of people, and it wouldn't change what I think of you. Do you remember that?"

"Yes. I remember." Her face glowed in soft, warm reminiscence.

"Well, that hasn't changed, baby. It never will change."

Omega smiled up at her partner, rubbing her hand lightly on his shoulder with grateful affection.

* * *

The love song went off smoothly, without a hitch. Echo stood silently in the front of the crowd of aliens and agents, directly before Omega, with Fox on one side, and Romeo and India on the other, a swarm of excited Hypothenemoids chattering at his feet. Irokin, Omega's personal friend among the squat beetle-like creatures, tugged at Echo's pant leg with a prehensile antenna, and Echo obligingly picked up the diminutive coffee-loving alien and sat him on the nearest table to watch; the fact that Irokin filled most of the tabletop didn't seem to bother anyone.

Omega smiled as the musicians began the number; then, with Echo as her calm anchor, proceeded to sing her heart out. Echo sighed once, inaudibly, almost wistfully, as he listened to the beautiful love song. *I...really wish she was singing that to me,* drifted through his mind.

Abruptly he squared his shoulders as a realization struck. *Waitaminit. 'Stand where I can see you when I sing'? Maybe she IS singing to me!* Echo's gaze zeroed in on his partner's, meeting her eyes for a moment...before she scanned the room, smiling at this or that person in it. *Oh. I guess she WAS only using me to settle. Dammit.* He tried not to sigh in disappointment, and glanced down...thereby missing the moment when Omega's gaze shifted back to him, just as she fairly beamed in happy pride. *Give her time, Echo,* he told himself. *She's still getting used to us being 'a thang.' And so am I.* He looked back up, inadvertently meeting her eyes once more, and his breath caught at the look she gave him. *Then again...* he considered, as his insides seemed to turn cartwheels. *Wow.*

The room was silent but for the music. At its end, there was a hush, then a collective—almost dreamy—sigh, then incredibly respectful applause. The Hypothenemoids scampered over to Omega, as Irokin performed a controlled tumble off the table to the floor, to join them.

"Pretty lady, do it again!" Irokin pleaded, and his companions joined in, "Yes yes yes!"

"Sorry, y'all," a worn-out Omega protested with a smile. "That takes a lot out of me, and I have to do it all again tomorrow night. I've got to take a break."

"You've got to go home and get some sleep," Echo insisted. "Time for us to leave. Good night, y'all." He took Omega's arm gently but firmly, and led her out, as the rest of those assembled celebrated on Omega's behalf.

* * *

Omega was drained and Echo was preoccupied with planning for various contingencies at the theater when they arrived back in their quarters.

"Go on back to your bedroom and get some sleep, Meg, baby," Echo told her. "I'll see you in the morning. Good night," and he disappeared through the back door.

Omega stared after him. Then she sighed, and headed back to her bedroom.

121

* * *

About forty-five minutes later, Echo was sitting at the networked laptop computer in his study, reviewing the database on gastropoids and Slug in particular, trying to find a clue, when a recollection hit and he sat up straight.

"Oh, shit!" he muttered in dismay. "I completely forgot, what with everything else going on. Then that dance, and the song, all unexpected...damn." He stood and strode swiftly across his living area and through the back door into Omega's darkened apartment. He moved directly to the partly-closed bedroom door and knocked. "Meg?" he called softly, pushing the door open carefully. "I meant to tell you, tonight you looked—"

By the soft glow of the nightlight in the windowless room, Echo saw Omega's exhausted form curled up in the bed, sound asleep. He also saw a small, dark puddle of something on the floor in the far corner, almost hidden in the shadows. He tiptoed silently across the carpet and picked it up.

It was the black turtleneck evening dress, lying forlornly where it had been flung.

* * *

A stiff and sore Omega crawled out of bed slowly when the alarm clock went off the next morning. She stumbled across the bedroom toward the bathroom, muttering to herself.

"Mmh. Feels like I need to sleep for...about another week... at least..."

She climbed into the shower and let the steaming water run for a while, trying to wake up as much as to loosen stiff muscles; the amount of dancing required for the show was more than she was used to doing, and rather different from Alpha One's usual workouts. *Specificity of activity, I guess,* she decided. *And after a couple of days of it,* she added, *it's not surprising that it finally caught up with me. Never mind opening night tension.*

Eventually, Omega exited the bathroom and headed, towel-wrapped, for the closet to get dressed. Halfway there, she spotted the black dress on a clothes hanger, suspended from the top of the closet door frame. She stopped, puzzled, and glanced at the corner of the room, then back to the dress.

*What the hell...?* she wondered, studying the dress. *How did it get up there...?* She jumped when she heard Echo's considering voice from the doorway.

"It just doesn't do as much for the clothes hanger, somehow. Maybe it's the lack of drop-dead hourglass curves inside it."

Omega spun to see Echo leaning against the doorframe, already dressed in black trousers and black polo shirt, and holding two coffee mugs, from one of which he now sipped. She walked over to him, and he handed her the other mug—chicory coffee, heavy on the cream, just as she liked it.

"Here, baby. I figured you'd need this to get going today." He leaned forward and dropped a light kiss on her lips, but did not try for more, evidently noticing that she was still tired and stiff.

"You're a mind-reader," Omega told him, wrapping her fingers around the mug and sipping the hot, fragrant, creamy liquid. "Not to mention a life-saver. I swear the sandman hit me with his entire bag last night. Hard. Then hit me three more times."

"Damn, really? I can't imagine why. You only debuted as a star on Broadway. Never mind all the other stuff, good and bad, that cropped up around it. Stage fright, an' debut parties, an' old enemies an' shit. Not to mention looking gorgeously sexy and elegant for said debut party...which I shoulda said last night, except I wanted to tell you in private, but I let myself get distracted by dances and songs and planning and junk."

"Oh, hush, you. Mm. That's better," Omega said with a somewhat bashful—but pleased—smile, polishing off the coffee quickly. "Now I can get dressed."

"Actually, I've got breakfast ready," Echo told her.

"All right. Give me a moment to throw something on."

"Why? You look fine in what you've got on. So to speak," Echo deadpanned, eying the towel wrapped around her with considerable appreciation. Omega felt herself flush fiercely. "Whoa," he added, watching. "Did you know you blush all over?"

"Oh, shut up!" she ordered, then shoved her empty mug into his hand and pushed a grinning Echo out of the bedroom door. "Go get me another cup of coffee," she said, smiling self-consciously as she closed the door behind him. "I'll be out in a minute."

"Three...two...one...mark," Echo's voice came from the other side of the door, and Omega knew he was timing her.

"Echo...you wouldn't."

"Omega minus fifty seconds and counting. Or maybe that's Echo minus..."

"He would." Omega flung the towel in the general direction of the bathroom door and ran naked around the room, collecting items of clothing—leggings, undergarments, and sport top—and throwing them on as fast as she could go.

"Omega minus thirty..."

"GO GET THE COFFEE!!" Omega cried, as she drew on thong underwear and a pair of leggings, then wormed her way into a compression-style sports bra. "Damn, I wish I had a different kind of athletic bra," she grumbled under her breath; that particular style had no hardware or fastenings, and required pulling it on over her head and shoulders, like an extremely tight-fitting shirt. "Ack!" she exclaimed, as her left arm got caught and refused to budge. She wrestled the bra back off her arms and shoulders, straightened it, then tried again.

"...Twenty..."

"THIS IS NOT A LAUNCH!" she yelled at the door. She finally got the bra positioned properly on her body, then bent and scooped her breasts into position inside it.

"Says you," came the reply from without.

"Hell yeah, says me. And I oughta know," she shot back, then turned and looked at herself in the dresser mirror. "Nope. Way too skimpy. That's a whole lotta skin, girl. Need a t-shirt, t-shirt..."

"I could go for skimpy," came the external commentary. "Of course, the towel was the best..."

"COFFEE!" she yelled back.

She yanked out a dresser drawer and pawed through it, eventually extracting an oversized workout shirt.

She wrestled the t-shirt over her head, pulling it down over her torso, then trying to straighten it, only to get the sports bra underneath it twisted again. She pulled the shirt back off, straightened the bra top, then dragged the shirt back on. "Aw damn it," she grumbled, "now it's backwards." She hauled it off again, turned it around, and donned it a third time. "Shoes, shoes..." she muttered, dropping to her hands and knees and looking under the bed. "Where the blazes are my SHOES?! Oh, the hell with 'em! I'll find 'em later."

"...Ten...nine...eight...seven..."

A quick comb through damp hair.

"...Four...three...two..."

Omega opened the door.

Echo stood there, holding her fresh mug of coffee, with a grin. He held it out in offering.

"I was out of eggs, so I didn't think you'd mind if I made breakfast in your kitchen today," he told her.

* * *

For the psychiatric testing later that morning, Omega and Echo were taken into separate rooms and asked a barrage of questions by trained psychologists, who jotted their responses onto electronic tablets, along with observations about the Agents' behavior and reactions during testing. It was not an especially fast process.

Shortly before lunch, Echo and Omega met up in the waiting room of the psychiatric offices of the medlab, and just stared at each other.

"You look wiped," they told each other at the same time, then both chuckled ruefully.

"Do you feel as mentally wrung out as I do?" Echo wondered.

"Oh, HELL yes, Ace," Omega murmured. "And trying to figure out how to honestly answer some of those questions, after the...shit...that Alpha One has been through in the last month? 'Oy vey,' as Fox would say."

"Mm," Echo hummed, frowning. "Did you manage to talk about any of it?"

"Not...really," Omega admitted. "I told her to, to talk to Zebra about it, instead. I...hon, it's just not...not something I can talk about. Not yet."

"But you need to get it out in the open, and you need to get the counseling, baby."

"Please, don't you start, too, Ace," Omega pleaded. "India bugs me about it, Zebra bugs me about it, Zarnix bugs me about it. Even Fox has been hitting me up with it every couple of days."

"Okay, okay," Echo said, holding up his hands in a *hold on* gesture. "I didn't mean to dogpile you, baby. I just want you to get help in dealing with it, and that's kinda beyond my ability to help with."

"I know, and I don't mean to complain," Omega told him, softening her voice. "I know you're trying to help me. I just... well, look. Turn the tables around. Let's say it was YOU in that kinda situation."

"Given the respective, uh, 'equipment,' not to mention the hormones an' junk, I actually couldn't, I don't think," Echo pointed out. "Which is one reason why I can't help you with it, so much. I just dunno where to even start."

"Oh, I bet I could come up with a scenario, Echo," Omega decided. "Like...let's say the Cortians had actually gotten you. From what India has told me of the short an' ugly communiqués the Agency had with the Cortians while you and I were crashed on that protoplanet last spring, one of the things they wanted you for was your genetics. They intended to 'harvest' 'em."

"They what?" Echo said, voice flat in disbelief.

"Yeah, you got it," Omega averred. "They were gonna breed you. Probably whether you wanted to or not. Which means they had ways of getting around the 'respective equipment' issues."

"Shit," Echo whispered, eyes widening. His face paled slightly.

"So let's use that as our scenario. Assume you got taken by 'em, and it took us a while to rescue you. They'd likely have stripped you down to skin, shackled you, and..." Omega considered, "based on my experience with Slug, shot you up with a buncha junk to ensure things proceeded the way they wanted, whether YOU wanted it or not." She met the brown gaze, her own steady. "You can decide whether or not we rescued you before anything more happened or not—before it progressed further, I mean. And you can decide whether it makes that much difference to your sense of personal autonomy, whether they'd actually succeeded in raping you or not."

A horrified Echo merely stared at her.

"So, all that goes down; we rescue you and bring you home, get your body back to normal...and then tell you that you need to have counseling, to deal with the rest of it." Omega cocked an eyebrow. "Tell me, Ace—would YOU be able to open up and talk about it to a perfect stranger? Knowing that stranger was going to want every detail of what they did to you laid out and described, so he or she could assess your mental and emotional state? Somebody who doesn't even know your personal history, who doesn't know YOU, who doesn't know—but would probably insist on knowing—all your inmost secrets?"

Alpha One was silent for long moments. Echo simply continued to stare at her, aghast.

"That's...that..." he tried, after several seconds. Finally he raked a hand through his hair. "Okay, Meg," he muttered, conceding. "Point made. No, I couldn't. So I shouldn't expect you to, either."

"Thank you," she murmured, relieved. "That's all I wanted of you, Ace, simply to understand, to grasp where I am, mentally and emotionally. And...I'm sorry I had to upset you like that, to get you to understand."

"It's...it's okay. You put it on a, a level I could grasp. But..."

"I know, I know," she continued, anticipating him by the worried expression in his eyes. "I know I need the counseling. I'm not on an even keel about it, and I know that. But I'm in an untenable situation, hon, and I haven't figured out a solution yet."

"Well, I'll keep it in the back of my mind," Echo offered. "Maybe, between us, we can figure out SOME kind of a workaround."

"Okay. Maybe, if we can ever find the time when I got the gray matter to spare, we could even sit down together and try to brainstorm it or something."

"All right. And, um, by the way, baby..."

"Yeah?"

Echo shrugged, then held out a hand.

"...Thanks...for making sure the Cortians didn't...get me."

Omega smiled, and laid her hand in his.

"No problem, Ace. I've got your back, just like you've always had mine."

"All right," he said, wrapping his hand around hers and swinging it gently. "What say we go find us some lunch? It'll be another hour or two before we get the results, anyway."

"It's a plan," Omega decided. "You wanna walk down to the deli, or go farther afield...?"

* * *

After lunch at the deli, Alpha One met India and Fox in Fox's office to check the results of the psych profiles. India looked over the charts on Fox's personal electronic tablet.

"You two are clear," India told them. "Oh, Meg's still a little skittish after the near-rape, true. Okay, make that a LOT skittish. There's strong indications of insecurity and isolation in her test results. Possibly a tendency toward depression, too. All perfectly understandable, though, after being stalked by a sexual predator, no matter how unwilling the predator. There's a certain amount of PTSD that comes with that particular territory."

Omega stared at the floor; Echo watched his partner out of the corner of his eye in sudden understanding of certain recent behaviors. *Not that I'm really THAT surprised,* he decided. *I just didn't think about a couple of things, that's all. And now everything fits together, all the puzzle pieces. No wonder my baby is so unsure of herself.* India continued.

"And Echo..." India studied the chart, a twinkle becoming ever more prominent in her eyes, "Echo is...doing just fine." India met the male Agent's gaze. "Keep it up, Echo. You're doing everything right. Just keep going the way you're going, and I think things will work out."

*Well damn,* he thought, disconcerted. *It looks like the psych testing picked up a couple things I didn't think about. And now even MORE people know how I feel about Meg. And it looks like that includes India. Shit. Well, at least Meg herself knows, now. And I guess it was gonna get out sooner or later, especially now we're dating semi-sorta regularly, kinda.* Echo stared inscrutably at the former emergency room physician, who turned to Fox.

"Absolutely no indications of delusions, hallucinations, or other abnormalities," she reported. "In either one of 'em. Whatever it was that they saw, I can tell you definitively, it was NOT a figment of their imaginations."

* * *

Alpha One went back to their joint quarters after that, to allow Echo to change into his Suit, then they headed for the theater. The plan was to get there in time for Echo to do a thorough scoping-out of every room and space in the entire venue, looking for any way of physically doing what appeared to be happening there. That way, they hoped to be able to determine if the theater phantom was an actual telepath, or someone masquerading as one. If necessary, Omega could join him in the analysis, if he found anything, prior to needing to prepare for the performance herself.

So when they arrived, he dropped her off at her dressing room—after ensuring she was well-armed and the dressing room clear—and headed down the hall for the main women's dressing room at the far end, deciding to start there and work his way through all the dressing rooms first, then move into the rest of the venue.

# **Chapter 5**

But when he arrived at the door, Echo realized that he and Omega hadn't arrived early enough; several voices floated through the doorway, indicating quite a few of the women in the chorus had already arrived and were preparing for the evening's performance.

*And they're not happy,* he concluded, pausing to decide what to do. Among other things, he was trying to ascertain if everyone inside was decently attired or not—he needed to make a sweep through it to check for anything that might be related to their situation, but did not want to do so while any of the girls were *en deshabille*; that way lay all kinds of misunderstandings. But he also needed to determine the nature and target of their pique. So, after checking the hallway to ensure no one was watching, he decided to eavesdrop for a few moments.

"...What I want to know is, who the hell does she think she is?" Echo heard one of the chorus girls grumbling. "That should be one of us up there! Instead, this complete neo comes waltzing in, and takes over the lead role!"

A small chorus of "Yeah! Damn straight!" answered.

*No more than two or three overall, though, I don't think,* Echo considered, listening carefully.

"I think somebody needs to complain to the producers!" another voice demanded.

"What do you think they'd do?" someone else asked. "They approved her, after all."

"We need to demand that one of the regular cast gets elevated to the role, not this privileged little bitch Sofia and Michael brought in!"

* * *

Echo stood just outside the door, still listening to the

chorus girls gossip. His eyebrow went up as he listened, and considered the discussion to which he was inadvertently privy.

*This could be bad,* he decided. *If there's that much resentment of Meg, they could wind up sabotaging our whole operation, just for spite. And then somebody is gonna die. I only hope it isn't my baby.*

*Then again,* he realized, *there's not really that many voices complaining, though it sounds like easily a dozen women in there; it may just be two or three chorus girls who are a little too full of themselves...I wonder...*

* * *

"Oh, shut up, Marcie," another member of the female chorus noted. "You're just jealous because you don't have a speaking role in this gig."

"You're damn right! I had the title role in my last show! What the hell did they think they were doing, sticking me in the chorus?"

"You took the job, didn't you?" a third voice remarked, sarcastic. "If you didn't like it, you shoulda held out for a better role."

Harsh laughter filled the room.

"Aw, shuddup yourself, Jeanie. You're just interested in the bitch for yourself."

"She's pretty, all right, but that's NOT the reason I want her around," Jeanie, the third voice said; and Echo realized that not all of his competition might be the same gender—not that he'd noted Omega leaning that direction. "And if you can't figure THAT out, you need to get a clue."

"I still say it shoulda been one of us," Marcie averred. "Who the hell does this Margaret Stratford think she is, waltzing in here and taking the lead?"

"She's a DETECTIVE, you utter moron!" Jeanie declared, voice dripping scorn. "SHE'S here to keep Sofia and the REST of us ALIVE! Didn't you notice how fast Kate developed a 'family emergency'? Do you really want the chandelier dropped on YOU?!"

"What?" Marcie said, flat. "You're shitting me."

"Nope. She and her manager boyfriend are both really private investigators that Sir Michael brought in, to try to get rid of the joker playing the show for reals."

"Wow. I wonder why she decided to go into a career like that, with a voice like she's got," another girl wondered.

"Maybe she was good at it," someone else speculated. "Maybe she liked something else better. Or maybe it was as simple as a steady income."

"Oh, good point," someone said.

"Wait just a damn minute, now," Marcie remarked, defiant. "You mean the blonde bimbo is really Sherlock Holmes? And Mr. Hunk is a private eye like Philip Marlowe or something? No way in hell."

* * *

Echo now debated on whether or not he should confirm the rumor. *But if one of them is the perp,* he thought, *then they'll KNOW to center on me and Meg. And that puts Meg in more danger. On the other hand, the others may just try to sabotage her performances to make her look bad, and that sets her up for the 'theater phantom' to strike...and succeed. Damn. Decisions, decisions.*

Finally he came to a conclusion.

*To hell with states of dress,* he decided. *None of 'em is gonna be half as gorgeous as Meg. And I've undressed her and put her to bed, so I KNOW what she looks like. And it doesn't sound like any of this bunch is gonna be especially embarrassed, if I was to see 'em stark naked. False accusations down the road are a definite consideration, but with all of 'em in there, and a mixed-bag of support, probably some of 'em would vouch for me. If I keep my distance, it should be okay.*

"Knock, knock!" he called, and stepped around the corner and through the doorway.

"Ooo, speaking of," one of the women—a wiry brunette of average height, with a long, narrow, somewhat unpleasant face, and oversized teeth in a wide, gummy mouth—said, and he recognized the voice as Marcie's.

"Excuse me, ladies," he said, laying on his suavest, politest manner, hoping it would pour oil on troubled waters if he were as courteous as possible. "I don't mean to interrupt, or to catch any of you in, uh, a state of undress. But Mike asked me to have a quick look around the place, and he's waiting for me to get back with him on my impressions."

"See?" another woman muttered, but he couldn't identify her voice. "Investigating."

Marcie, wearing only a bra and thong, sidled up to him, brushing his upper arm with her breasts, before trying to maneuver her thigh to catch his hand. Echo quickly balled his fingers into a loose fist and turned slightly to prevent the inappropriate contact.

"You can look around my places any time, big boy," she murmured. "Go ahead and have a peek." She tilted her shoulders and folded her arms in an effort to make the most of her somewhat meager cleavage and offer his tall form a viewing advantage. Echo turned away.

"I thought I got here early enough to do this before anyone else arrived, so I wouldn't bother anybody, but apparently not! You're obviously all very dedicated actresses. This won't take long, and I promise I won't disturb any of you, so y'all go on about whatever you were doing," he noted, ignoring the blatant come-on and moving systematically around the large and well-lit room. From time to time he ran a questing hand along a wall or mirror frame, then he turned for the mass bath area. "I don't hear water running," he noted, then turned to the chorus and jerked a thumb over his shoulder at the showers and toilet stalls. "Y'all know if anybody is in there?"

"No, Mr. Echo," one of the girls affirmed. "Nobody's in there right now. Go ahead and take a look. My name's Jeanie; feel free to check with me if there's anything you need to know." She glanced around at the others with a raised eyebrow. "I'll give you the straight dope without any head games, unlike some of these bitches."

"Right, Jeanie; thanks," Echo said, and ducked into the bathroom area.

* * *

Behind him, the chorus girls clustered around Jeanie.

"Whoa, Jeanie, it looks like you were right," one said in a low voice.

"Hell no!" Marcie protested. "He just came in here, hoping to get an eyeful of naked women, that's all. He's probably a pervert."

"Well, he sure didn't want what YOU were selling, Marcie," another remarked, eyebrow raised, voice dripping with snark. "Didn't you guys see? He balled up his hands into fists rather than risk touching her!"

Laughter erupted.

"He ain't no private eye, though," an offended Marcie continued to deny. "He only came in here to get a look. Just because he ain't touchy-feely don't mean nothin'. He probably can't get it up."

"That's not what I've heard," one commented. "They say he's crazy for that woman who took over from Sofia—Meg, her friends call her. *I* heard they've got a hot affair going."

"Still no detective," Marcie averred.

"Oh, you numbskull," Jeanie hissed. "Do you actually think he's gonna TELL us?? Why the hell would he be doing a check of the dressing rooms, if he's not looking for clues an' shit? Why would SIR MICHAEL ASK him to?!"

"Ooo," came the general chorus, as a disgusted and secretly disappointed Marcie—who had no rebuttal to that—turned away, sitting in front of her makeup station with a huff and starting to apply foundation.

* * *

Just then, Echo—who had heard the whole exchange from the adjacent room; his partner wasn't the only member of Alpha One with good ears—emerged from the bath area.

"Okay," he observed aloud with a manufactured smile, "everything looks fine, as far as I can tell. I'll get out of your hair now. Sorry for the interruption, ladies."

One of the girls, apparently emboldened by his friendly expression, stepped forward, most of the other girls not far behind.

"Mr. Echo, sir?"

"Yes, ma'am?"

"Is it true that you and Miss Meg are investigators, here to protect us from the theater phantom?"

"Oh, no ma'am, we're nothing like that! Meg is a lyric soprano, and I'm her manager—though Mike did mention something about that situation."

"You call Sir Michael 'Mike'?"

Echo grinned.

"Oh yeah; we're old friends, Mike and me. I've known him since way before he was 'SIR Michael.'"

"You're not from New York," one of the other chorus girls observed. "Your accent isn't from any of the boroughs."

"No, but I've been here long enough that most of my native Texan has worn off," Echo admitted, then deliberately let a good bit more of his native dialect slip through, as he launched into the detailed cover story. "This is what Ah usedta sound like. Daddeh made 'is money in th' oil fields, see, only Ah wasn't so much interested in th' business. Ah wanted t' come t' the Big Apple an' do theater stuff. The oil company is still doin' fine, 'cause mah big brother is runnin' it now, but Daddeh left me a nice inheritance when 'e died 'bout fifteen year ago, an' Ah invested wisely—got a degree in business management— then started a theatrical management agency, like Ah always dreamed 'o doin'. I've...worked...with Mike before, an' Meg was my first, an' best, client. She an' Sofia have known each other since their chorus days."

"Then why did he ask you to look around the theater?" the first girl demanded to know.

"Oh, well, he did tell Meg an' me about this supposed 'phantom,' because like he said, it was only fair," Echo continued the cover story. "Then he got this thoughtful look, an' asked me t' have a look around, while he an' Sofia got Meg ready fer the role. Way he figgered it, see, he thought if Ah came in fresh, Ah might see somethin' nobody else had." Echo shrugged. "Ah told him Ah'd try, but Ah don't really expect to find anything. 'Cause I'm NOT a private eye, see." *Which is true,* he thought...but did not say. *Investigator of sorts, yeah. PRIVATE investigator—not.*

"If you wanted to do theater," another asked, "why don't you perform? Why did you start an agency?"

"Aw," Echo said, offering a sheepish grin, "Ah've been known to, once in a while. But it didn't take long before Ah realized Ah just wasn't quite talented enough. Besides," he remembered a certain film shoot the previous Christmas, "it turns out mah face doesn't take too well to all the makeup. Ah'm allergic or somethin', I guess. Th' skin just gets downright raw, an' Ah cain't hardly even shave."

"Ooo, ouch," came the murmur from several voices, and they all winced. "Didn't you see a dermatologist?" one of them asked.

"Aw, well, yeah, Ah saw a doctor for it," he noted, not telling them it was his partner, nor that her doctorates were not in dermatology—or any branch of medicine. He also began reining in his Texan dialect a bit, returning to his normal daily speech patterns. "She seemed to think things weren't gonna change, though she did recommend a good, um, moisturizer before applying makeup. I tried it, but I didn't think it helped that much. My face just gets that raw, see. Doesn't seem to matter what I use, either."

Another joint groan went up.

"What's the name of your agency?" Jeanie asked. "I might like to look into new...representation."

"Oh, that'd be the New Worlds Talent Agency," Echo said smoothly, giving them the name of the Division One Agency's undercover organization for offworld talent—not that any of this particular group qualified—that he knew about, at least. "But our East Coast auditioner left, and we haven't got him replaced yet, so you'll have to ping Juliet, in our West Coast office. Don't worry, though; she can set up an audition for you." He pulled out business cards, which Fox had procured for him for this express purpose, and handed them around.

"Oh, that's okay," Jeanie said, suddenly a bit shy. "I've, um, heard of them, Mr. Echo. I think they'd be perfect for me. If you could, uh, give me a good word?"

Echo met the woman's gaze, recognizing her familiarity with the front company. *And if that's the case, she may not be from 'around here,'* he considered. *Lessee; what did Juliet tell me to ask...?*

"Where are you from, ma'am?" he asked then.

"Smalltown, Kansas."

"Never heard of it, I'm afraid," Echo lied; it was the coded answer he'd been told to expect of an offworld talent. "But you've been really helpful, and I'll be happy to put in a good word for you."

"Thank you, sir," Jeanie said with a smile. "Anything I can do to help, just let me know."

"Will do."

"Hey," Marcie said, turning from the mirror, "is it true that this Meg, that took over from Sofia, is your girlfriend?"

"Yup," Echo agreed with a proud smile. "She's my baby, all right. I'm crazy about her." *And that's no lie, either,* he thought.

"And you don't think that's a conflict of interest?" Marcie pressed.

"Not at all. People in theater have been doin' that for..." Echo shrugged. "For as long as there's been theater, I guess. In fact, I think it's a good thing. By having a specially-vested interest, I do an even better job representing her."

"What about your other clients?" someone asked.

"When Meg and I decided to get involved, I took a junior partner," Echo explained, continuing the cover story. "I manage Meg pretty exclusively, and Romeo can handle everybody else."

"Do you ever see somebody on the side?" Marcie wondered,

rising and slinking up to him again.

"Nope," Echo said, as blunt as he could manage to be. "I'm a straight shooter, an' I don't cheat on my girl." Then he turned to Jeanie. "Thanks for the offer of help, ma'am," he told her. "If anything comes up, I'll remember that. Y'all go ahead and get back to it, now. I'm gonna slip on out, finish having the look-see I promised Mike, then go help Meg get ready."

And he left.

* * *

Most of the secondaries had yet to arrive at the theater, so it was not hard for Echo to scope out those private dressing rooms; he found nothing of significance in any of them. But when he arrived at the male chorus dressing room at the far end of the hall, there was another gaggle under way.

"...No, I don't mind her," one male voice noted. "Not that Sofia was bad or anything. But she always seems aware of the, uh, 'protocols,' let's just say. And Meg, you can tell she knows about 'em, but she's rather more...what's that word... oh—egalitarian. She doesn't talk down to us simply because we're in the chorus."

"Yeah, she's like the girl next door with a terrific voice," another remarked. "A beautiful woman, but friendly and down to earth. Like, maybe she isn't even aware she's pretty; she's just herself, you know?"

"Ooo, and honey, her manager is a dreamboat!" declared a third.

Echo flushed; he wasn't used to being the recipient of such compliments, and while there were some Agents who had similar preferences—their numbers within the Agency were comparable to the percentage in the general public—they tended to be more subtle in their approaches. *But that remark sure wasn't subtle. This could get complicated quick,* he decided. *Maybe I better see where the wind is blowing before I march in here.*

"Oh baby, isn't he, though!" yet a fourth voice observed. "I could get into him. In more ways than one." The room erupted in laughter.

*Nope. Not subtle,* Echo thought, and chuckled to himself. *Way the hell past the come-on that Queen made, that time. I'm glad I was able to let him down easy; he's been a good friend, all these years. Never mind ribbing him about the appropriateness of his code name. This situation might end up being a lot different. I hope not, though. Maybe I should play up the relationship with Meg a bit more, especially when the rest of the cast is around.*

"Back off, boys," someone said just then. "Credible rumor has it, he's taken."

"By?"

"Miss Meg. I heard Sir Michael telling one of the producers, they're a hot item. I gathered they're crazy about each other."

There was a general chorus of groans of disappointment. Echo grinned. *And maybe that took care of it for me. Though it isn't gonna hurt to reinforce it, a little bit.*

"Mmm, I dunno," another voice observed. "Looked to me like Sofia might have a say in that."

*Uh-oh,* he thought, eyebrows going up. *Well, shit.*

"Good luck to her. He looked gobsmacked over Meg, to me."

"Either way, looks like he doesn't swing OUR way."

"Nope." More groans of disappointment. Echo's grin grew wider...

...And he slipped around the doorframe, into the dressing room.

* * *

"Hi, guys," he offered, noting without comment the various stages of undress of the men in the room. A general refrain of friendly hellos answered him. "Mind if I check out the place? Mike asked me to have a look around. Something about a real-life 'phantom,' and he wanted me to see if I saw anything out of the ordinary."

"Sure, handsome, go ahead," one of the younger men remarked, offering a wide grin. "Let us know if you see anything you like."

Echo let out a snort despite himself.

"Sorry to disappoint you, but I'm already spoken for," he observed. "Your new leading lady is MY leading lady, too. Not to mention first, last, and only."

*And given that nobody before her ever came close to her, that's not too much of a fudge,* he decided. *It'll do to ward off interest here, anyhow. Nobody but Meg needs to know my personal history.*

"Aww," half the group groaned in disappointment; the other half merely grinned, muttering variants on, "Toldja."

"Hey, Mr. Alec," the forward young man greeted, holding out a hand. "Welcome aboard, and no hard feelings for a bit of flirtation, I hope?"

"Nah," Echo said, shaking his hand. "I got the same thing in the women's dressing room just now, so I guess I've had my share of ego-boost for the day."

The whole room burst into laughter.

"My name's Jake," the young man said. "You investigating the whole 'phantom' thing, then? Is that why you're really here? The grapevine has been flyin', see, and some of the girls were saying, well..."

"Meh," Echo said, waving a dismissive hand. "There's rumors, yeah, and then there's the truth. The truth is, Mike is an old friend of mine—like I told the ladies when THEY asked a bit ago, I knew him before he was 'Sir'—and Meg and Sofia knew each other from their chorus days. So when Meg agreed to fill in for Sofia when she started having throat trouble, Mike felt like he had to tell me about this...'phantom.' We got to talking over dinner the other night, and he thought, with me coming in fresh, I might see something nobody else had, that would help solve the little mystery." He shrugged. "It seemed reasonable, and it was simple enough. Plus, I get to look around and familiarize myself with the house...so I agreed."

"It makes sense," one of the other actors decided.

"Exactly," Echo said. "So...mind if I take a quick look

around? Y'all go ahead and do your preps; don't mind me. I don't expect to find a thing, but I promised Mike I'd look."

"Sure, go for it," Jake agreed with a shrug. "Ain't like you've never seen a guy's junk before."

"Nuh-uh. I been in a gym locker room once or twice, never mind dressing rooms." Echo moved about the dressing room while the men went through their various pre-show rituals: changing into costumes, stretching, applying makeup, vocal warmups, and the like. He kept his inspection as casual as he could, well aware that most of the other men were watching him surreptitiously. When he was done with the main room, he slipped into the bath area and had a look around, then came back out.

"Anything?" Jake wondered.

"Not a damn thing," Echo noted, completely sincere. "I'm not sure what's going on here, but my first guess would be that somebody's pulling a prank."

"Damn dangerous prank, then," one of the other guys said, shaking his head. "The chandelier nearly landed on Sofia the other night."

"Yeah, Ethan," Jake agreed. "That was a close one. And it sure didn't seem like any practical joker to me. That looked like a murder attempt, if the TV shows are anything at all to go by."

"Which they aren't," Ethan observed, "but I know what you mean. If that was a prank, somebody has a really sick sense of humor."

Echo had no answer to that.

* * *

That evening's performance was a near-duplicate of the previous night's, good and bad. Omega's stage fright kicked in once again, and once again she refused Echo's help when she grew ill...though, this time, she did not forget herself and automatically lock him out of the bathroom while she threw up. Instead, he slipped in behind her and slid an arm around her middle, cupping her forehead in the other hand and thereby

142

helping to support her wobbly body under the force of her retching.

Again the nervousness transformed as soon as the curtain rose, and the performance proceeded relatively unmarred. Echo patrolled the theater continuously, in constant contact with his partner over his headset, but nothing definitive surfaced.

* * *

Echo met Omega backstage after the curtain call, and accompanied her to her dressing room. When he opened the door, they both froze, staring, then they slowly entered the room and closed the door.

On the makeup mirror was a message scrawled in black eyeliner pencil:

*You're history. A. is mine.*
*-S.*

"Echo..." Omega whispered, agitated.

"Stay cool, Meg," Echo murmured, soothing. "Nothing is ever what it appears to be. You know that by now." They moved to the mirror and studied it carefully, without touching anything.

"Echo—look," Omega observed. "Whoever it was used what was handy." She pointed at the eyeliner pencil she had left on the makeup table before the performance; the tip had crumbled from the pressure of writing on the smooth, hard surface. "Spur of the moment? Carpe diem?"

"Probably," Echo agreed, analyzing the handwriting. "It was written by one of the actresses."

"And you think that because?"

"Feminine hand, bold, and stylized. Very 'artsy.' Besides, Snails don't have hands, so it wasn't Slug."

"Unless the way he managed to keep on 'living' was to take over another body. Then he'd have hands."

"Mm. Good point. Then we need to dig deeper, and find out who left this. Is anything missing in here?" Echo asked, glancing around the room. Omega turned to survey the dressing room in detail, taking her time and looking for any discrepancies.

"Yeah—the big tube of makeup remover..." Omega said after a moment.

"Makeup remover?" Echo reiterated in amusement.

"Don't laugh, Ace," Omega told him. "That's an important clue. One, it verifies your conclusion that it was a woman, 'cause it has a floral scent...not something one of the guys would use. Besides, that brand has a separate line of cleansers made expressly for guys. Two, if we can determine who uses it in the cast, we'll know who left the threat."

"Damn, Meg, everybody in the cast uses makeup remover. How do you figure that?"

"Because I'm a woman, in case you haven't noticed—"

"Oh, believe me, baby, I've noticed."

Omega stuck out a mischievous, mildly defiant, tongue at him. A now-grinning Echo responded in kind, grabbing for her tongue with one hand, and she quickly retracted it.

"If this were a less-serious situation," he murmured, brown eyes darkening, "I'd challenge you to a tongue duel."

"A wha? How the heck...?"

"How do you think?" he told her, puckering his lips briefly and making a popping sound, as if about to blow a kiss. Omega felt herself flush, and he grinned again. "Anyway, you were saying...?"

"Um...right, so, uh," she said, as she tried to get her train of thought back on track, "...I'm a woman, I know how women think. See, I forgot my own the other night, so Cecile brought me a tube of stuff. I don't know where she got it, but maybe the name Chanel rings a bell with you."

"Shit," Echo remarked, eyebrows flying upward. "That's sure as hell not the drugstore stuff."

"Exactly," Omega agreed. "Nor something that, for instance, members of the chorus would likely use, just based on cost factor alone. And you also have to realize, Echo, that we women are very particular about what we put on our faces. I use my own stuff almost exclusively. And it's not Chanel. I'll use something else in a pinch, like last night, but I won't keep using it. Tonight, I brought my own."

"So you wouldn't splurge using the free tube of Chanel cleanin' stuff, just because it isn't what you usually use? Sorry, Meg, but that just seems damn stupid to me. Besides, I thought most women liked to be pampered occasionally."

"We do." Omega grinned. "I don't know that I want to be lumped into the category of 'most women,' though. And Chanel makes lovely stuff, don't get me wrong. I used to use some of their products, when I was younger. But if it was only a matter of labels, or prestige, you'd be right, Echo; it would be stupid. But it isn't," she explained. "Let me ask you this—does the fragrance that I wear smell the same on India?"

* * *

"I dunno," Echo replied with a shrug. "I've never smelled it on India."

"Yes, you have, at the opening night party. I'd told her the other night, when she was helping me get dressed for our date, that she could try it sometime if she liked it, and she agreed. She ran out of her own, so she told me she borrowed some of mine last night for the party, and was gonna run out today and get some more of her usual perfume."

"Shit! You're joking. I noticed she was wearing something different, yeah, but it didn't smell anything like you. It smells way better on you. I mean, it didn't smell bad on her or anything, it just...I think it smells better on you."

"Thanks, but that's my point—although I gathered Romeo approved, rather decidedly. Anyway. It's body chemistry. It so happens my skin just doesn't like Chanel cleanser. I love the feel of it, and the way my skin feels after I've used it, but if I use it for more than a few days, my face tends to break out. Given my, um, particular brand of genetic conundrums, I guess it isn't surprising that I have to have something custom-made for my skin. But India, for instance, loves it, and she swears by

145

it. In fact, she uses the whole line."

"So you're saying somebody came by to grab their favorite face goop, and seized an opportunity," Echo anticipated.

"You got it, Ace." Omega grinned at his terminology. "If we can figure out who uses Chanel 'face goop' in the theater, we might find out who left that message."

"And likewise, who Slug is taking for a ride," Echo added. "All right; I see what you mean. Let's do a few things here." He pulled an image scanner from a warp pocket and used it to record the scene in detail, paying special attention to the mirror and the liner pencil. "I brought this thing along, just in case, and now I'm glad I did. There. We can look for any fingerprints in the images later. Okay, I got it; let's clean this up."

"Why?"

"One: there will be fewer questions from the humans in the cast and crew, if they don't see it," Echo explained. "Two: if we go on like nothing happened, maybe we can unnerve the perp."

"Gotcha," Omega replied. "Okay, then. Hand me one of those baby wipes."

"Baby wipes?!" Startled, Echo handed her the plastic canister of wipes.

"Yeah. This is a little trick of mine, something I discovered during my community theater days," Omega said with a smile, as she used the wipes to clean the mirror. "I like to use grease stick theatrical makeup—it works on my skin better than water-based pancake, which tends to make me break out really bad, not to mention leave my fingers chapped—but it's heavy and thick. So I use these things to wipe away the worst of it, before I use my regular 'goop' to clean my face—which also saves money, since I don't have to use as much 'goop' that way. Look—like this," she said, swiping her face with a fresh wipe and studying her disappearing makeup in the now-clean mirror. Echo watched with interest.

"You've pretty much got this down to a science, don't you?" he asked.

"Not really," Omega demurred. "But at my age, I've had plenty of time to figure out what works for me."

"Well, it does."

"Does what?"

"Works for you. Not that 'at your age' is especially old, but hey."

"What exactly did that mean?" Omega narrowed her eyes teasingly and considered Echo. "It sounded suspiciously like bordering on a compliment."

"Did it?" Echo said, slapping on an innocent expression. "It was simple observation and deduction. A woman who looks a good ten years younger than her true age, has flawless skin, and turns the head of every man she walks by, probably has her beauty routine figured out pretty well."

Omega blinked.

"Echo—are you feeling well?!" Her eyes twinkled.

"Never better."

"Then where in the hell did all that come from?" she wanted to know.

"Like I said—observation." A sense of satisfaction washed through the male Agent. *There,* he thought, pleased. *I think I'm starting to get the hang of NOT understating my compliments to Meg...finally. And if I play games with her, and make out like it wasn't, she gets that it was, without getting embarrassed by the compliment...or worse, dismissing it as 'you're just trying to make me feel better.' Because she gets to banter with me about it.*

"Well, all right. We've talked about the age thing before, and my skin is in pretty decent shape," she decided. "But... turning men's heads?! Where on earth did you get that idea?"

"Shit, Meg, you gotta be kidding, baby," Echo said in surprise, seating himself and putting on the headset as Omega headed for the shower. "You can't mean to tell me that you haven't noticed. It happens every damn day. And the last few evenings we've gone out, with you dressed to kill, I've seen 'em all but drool. To be honest, it's been kinda fun to watch 'em turn sixty-seven shades of green when you walk away on my arm. Never mind being proud of having you ON that arm."

"Riiight," Omega's disbelieving voice came through the headset, along with the sounds of flowing water.

"Have you forgotten the hot tub conversation?"

"Um. Well, now that you mention it..."

"Uh-huh. Thought so. That's one you really need to remember, baby. It's important. And it was, and is, every word the truth." He paused, then reminded, "Your partner thinks you're hot stuff. And you kiss good, too."

"...All right. I'll remember that."

"Good. So what are you wearing tonight?" Echo asked, interested.

"Are we going out? I wasn't sure. You didn't say anything..."

Echo blinked, dismayed. "I...didn't, did I?" *Damn damn damn damn,* the refrain banged in his head. *I screwed THAT up.*

"No." Omega's voice was quiet.

"Shit."

"'Shit' what?"

"I guess you figure I took you for granted."

"Not necessarily." Omega opened the bathroom door, robe-swathed, hair in a towel. "Between the short day, the psych testing, and the performance, you've been as busy as I have. Never mind last night's performance, and the party. And it wasn't like we did a whole lotta talking, the night before." She offered him a mischievous grin before moving to the dressing table, where she toweled off her hair and proceeded to comb it out. "Look over there in the wardrobe." She waved the comb in the direction of the tall cabinet as Echo removed the annoying headset, tucking it back in a pocket.

Echo opened the door of the wardrobe and stopped dead. Inside was a simple evening gown, in a vaguely Grecian style, made of some soft, flowing material. The hue of the dress was the exact shade of Omega's glowing sapphire eyes.

"It's blue," Echo remarked absently, studying the lines of

the dress and trying to picture it on its owner.

"Mm-hm. I decided to seize the opportunity to wear something besides black and white." Omega began applying her regular makeup. "Why? Did I break a rule?"

"No."

"Then you don't like it."

"No, I think it's...very pretty. I just...wasn't expecting...a color," Echo finished. "I don't think I've hardly ever seen you in anything but black and white. And never in blue. Even up in Ipswich, you wound up in one of my black pairs of shorts, with a white tee. You had a khaki pair picked out, but never got a chance to wear 'em."

"You know, that's right," Omega mused. "I was even wearing flat black the night you first ran across me, because I was observing with my telescope." She finished her minimal—but exquisite—makeup with a soft pink lip color. "I guess you'll get to see me in a different light tonight, Echo—literally." A knock sounded on the dressing room door.

* * *

"I'll get it," Echo said, opening the door with caution. Suddenly long, graceful arms wrapped around him.

"There you are, darling," Sofia exclaimed with affection. "I should have known you'd be looking out for your partner! Are you ready to go?"

"Ready to go where?" a suspicious Echo responded. Behind him, a certain pair of blue eyes grew wide in shock, then looked away and closed, in terrible pain.

"Out on the town, silly man," Sofia purred. "Like we arranged in our little note."

"Sofia, I don't know what—" Echo began, removing the clinging arms.

"Don't worry about it, Echo. I'll take care of things here," Omega said, standing and moving to the door to pointedly usher them out. As she passed the wardrobe, she pushed it closed. "I understand. Go on and have fun. I'll see you tomorrow."

"Meg," Echo began again. Then he saw her closed face

149

and realized she was no longer listening. Silently he exited the dressing room with Sofia. He heard the click as Omega closed and locked the door behind them.

* * *

Sofia grabbed his arm and pulled him toward the backstage entrance, chatting obsequiously. Finally Echo had had enough.

"Take. Your hand. OFF. My arm," he ground out through gritted teeth.

"What?" Sofia looked up at him brightly.

"Let. Go." He raised an eyebrow, delivering his patented Yellowstone glare. "NOW."

Sofia looked into the dark eyes for a moment, blanched, and abruptly released Echo's arm.

"I don't know what the hell kind of damn little game you're playing, Sofia," Echo said quietly, controlled fury just beneath the surface like roiling magma, "but I don't put up with being manipulated."

"But...but...didn't you get my note?" Sofia asked, confused. "I told you, if I didn't hear otherwise, I'd be here waiting..."

"I didn't get any note."

"Dammit!" Sofia was almost in tears. "I told Jimmy to make sure you got it!"

"The secondary stage manager?" Echo verified. "Stage right?"

"Yes!"

Echo spun on his heel and headed into the depths of the theater.

"Alec! Alec, wait!" Sofia called after him.

Echo just kept walking.

* * *

Echo retrieved the note from Jimmy, who apologized profusely for letting it slip through the cracks, then went straight to Omega's dressing room.

"Meg?" he called, knocking on the door. When there was no answer, he tried the knob; it was unlocked. "Meg?" he put his head through the door, "Sofia's playing some sorta damn game—"

The room was empty. Echo moved to the wardrobe and opened it. The blue dress was gone.

Echo pulled Sofia's note from his pocket, cursing under his breath. Then he stopped, scrutinizing the note intently. He strode into the corridor, where he spotted Omega's dresser carrying an armload of costumes.

"Cecile? Cecile, did you see Me-um, Ms. Stratford leave?"

"Yes, Mr. Williams, Miss Meg left with Mr. Michael right after you and Miss Sofia." Cecile cast him a sympathetic glance. "Mr. Michael was being very solicitous, and Miss Meg did not look happy. Is everything all right? You and Miss Meg have had a lovers' quarrel?"

"More like a...misunderstanding," Echo remarked with a sigh. "A major misunderstanding."

"Don't worry, Mr. Echo," Cecile said confidently. "The two of you are right together, somehow. Just love her. It'll be okay." The little dresser moved off.

"Cecile? One more thing," Echo said, on a hunch, and Cecile paused, turning around. "Meg asked me to pick up some makeup remover for her, but I forgot to ask what she uses. Was that her Chanel remover I saw on the dressing table the other day?"

"Oh, no, Mr. Echo," Cecile replied. "Miss Meg has hers made especially for her; I don't know where."

"Whose was the Chanel, then?"

"Oh, that was a tube that Miss Sofia left here."

"Mm-hm," Echo responded noncommittally, satisfied. "Thanks, Cecile."

"You're welcome, Mr. Echo."

* * *

Back in his quarters, Echo sat in his study and analyzed the evidence late into the night. At last he nodded to himself. "Yep, it sure looks like it to me," he muttered, and scowled.

Then he heard the front door of Omega's apartment open and close. He walked to the back door, where he stood rooted to the spot, speechless with admiration, as an unaware Omega floated gracefully through her den in a blue cloud that alternately draped and clung to her body almost like a living thing. Finally he managed to relocate his speech center.

"I guess the term 'angel' doesn't only apply to the voice," he murmured.

"Oh!" Omega jumped, startled. "What?"

"...Nothing."

"You're home early. Did you and Sofia have a good time?" Omega made a business of bending down to remove her high-heeled shoes.

"I wouldn't know," Echo remarked. "I spent the evening here, going over evidence. I have no idea what Sofia did."

"Echo, that wasn't very polite! Take it from me—it hurts when somebody breaks a date. No matter the reason."

"Meg," Echo told her patiently, "I didn't break a date with Sofia, for the simple reason that I never had a date with Sofia."

"But the note..."

"Was from her. I never even saw it until afterward. She's playing head games. Come take a look."

* * *

Omega followed Echo into his study, where he handed her the assignation note. "Anything look familiar?" he asked.

"Um...yeah, but...what...?" Omega pondered.

"Check this out." Echo brought up a graphics file on his laptop. "This is data from the image scans of the threat on the mirror."

Omega looked from the note in her hands to the image onscreen, and back again. "Oh. OH. It's...the handwriting, is..."

"A perfect match," a grim Echo observed. "Sofia wrote that threat. Her fingerprints are also on your eyeliner. And guess who uses Chanel face goop?"

"Wait, wait, wait. Sofia is Slug?!" Omega sat down in Echo's desk chair, dumbfounded.

"No, I don't think so," a thoughtful Echo said. "It doesn't make sense, for one thing. Sofia is the one being put in danger by this theater phantom, which apparently is Slug, trying to bait us in. But why would Slug try to kill his host?"

"To bait us in," Omega responded instantly. "Just like you said. For the same reason he was prepared to kill me, even though I was his little programmed failsafe." Omega's tone was bitter despite her best efforts.

"So who dropped the chandelier?"

"What?"

"Sofia was onstage when the chandelier dropped. If Sofia is also Slug, then there had to be an accomplice to drop the chandelier. And there's been no sign of such an accomplice. Never mind the risk to Slug's mind, if he's in Sofia and she gets killed. Slug was a lotta things, but he never struck me as a personal risk-taker. He only confronted directly when he calculated he had the upper hand, by a significant margin."

"Hm. True. On all points."

"Besides," Echo said, "look at this, Meg." He tapped the computer screen. "The reference to me is the initial A, NOT the letter E."

"Oh, I get it," Omega said, grasping his point. "Your cover name is Alec, and whoever it was, was addressing you as Alec. But Slug would have known your codename is Echo, and used an E..."

"Exactly. And probably without a period after it, since E is formally just the shorthand for my codename within the Agency."

"So what was—oh."

"Now you're getting it," Echo said in satisfaction.

"Sofia just wants you for herself," Omega observed, "and she thinks I'm in the way."

"'Thinks'?" Echo reiterated. "More like IS, baby. You're 'in the way' like an impassable mountain range. Yeah, I think that's it. Inadvertent red herring, but not the Theater Phantom."

"T.P.," Omega grinned. Then she went off into a fit of giggles as the pun struck her. "He's rolling the whole damn theater!"

* * *

"Yeah," Echo agreed, amused. He chuckled along with his partner for several moments, releasing tension together, before they both sobered.

"Well, that's a relief," Omega decided, standing and heading for the door. "At least we got that one figured out. See you tomorrow, Ace."

"Wait a minute." Echo caught her hand as she walked by. "How about dinner and dancing tomorrow night after the show?"

"I'm history, remember?" A rueful Omega smiled; it was a sad expression.

"Meg," Echo declared, "Sofia is too damn devious and scheming for my taste. I lean toward women I can trust with my life." He let his brown eyes smile. "So how 'bout it?"

"What...shall I wear?" She looked down, seeming uncertain.

"Wear the blue dress again; I didn't get to see it on you until a couple minutes ago! Besides, I have yet to see you in anything I didn't like." Echo grinned with mischief. "Although most restaurants' dress codes prohibit bath towels. I could get into it, though." He remembered something one of the chorus boys had said, and added, "In more ways than one."

She smacked him on the shoulder.

Then laughed.

Echo joined in.

* * *

The next day, after a joint combat-room session in the Headquarters gym to work out some strategy, Echo and Omega cleaned up and headed for the theater. Omega had her usual bout with stage fright, then sat down at the mirror and focused on applying makeup. She had just begun moisturizing her face when there was a knock at the door.

"Who is it?"

"Me," Echo's voice answered. Omega got up right away to let him in.

"What are you doing here? I thought you'd be scoping out

the theater."

"I already did," Echo replied. "Everything's SitNom."

"Situation Normal?"

"Yup."

"So...what's up?"

"Nothing major. You got my curiosity up last night about your makeup. Mind if I watch?"

"Sure. Pull up that chair. I'm just getting started."

"What are you doing?" he asked, dragging the chair over and sitting beside her.

"Well, I've cleaned my face, and now I'm moisturizing," Omega explained as she worked. "That helps keep my skin from soaking up the makeup. You know, getting all down in the pores an' stuff." She dotted on grease stick foundation next, and commenced blending it with a sponge.

"That's awful damn dark against your skin, Meg," Echo remarked, pursing his mouth critically.

"It'll look fine under the stage lights, trust me. As bright as they are, I'd look like a ghost myself if I matched my pale skin—even with a tan; my good tan is a lotta people's normal skin tone! And I kinda feather the edges, so it isn't noticeable. Now I'm going to contour." Omega applied darker grease stick under her cheekbones and on the sides of her nose and temples. "I'm 'shaping' my face, Echo. It's like a painting—you start with the background, then add highlights and shadows, to create a three-dimensional image."

"But your face is already 3-D."

"True. But it won't look like it in the stage lights unless I do this. See, they're so bright, and so uniform—since they're designed to evenly light the entire stage when the whole set is active—that they wash out all shadow. Everything, including faces, goes flat. So you have to add the shadows back in— shadows recede—and then you have to add highlights, which appear to come forward."

With that, she added a paler shade to the very tops of her cheekbones, the ridge above each temple, a relatively broad stripe at the top of her forehead, and a thin stripe down her nose, blending it all very carefully.

"Oh! I get it," he decided, watching closely. "It's all an illusion."

"Exactly. Move back a bit; I don't want to get this all over your Suit, 'cause now I have to set it." As soon as Echo shifted position, Omega powdered her face liberally with a big fluffy puff, then whisked away the excess with an equally-fluffy brush. "I'm doing this now, but if I was using cream-based colors for blush, eyeshadow, an' junk, I'd wait and set everything last. But I like to use powder colors, and the grease paint would grab way too much color—and wouldn't let me blend it—if I didn't set it now."

* * *

Echo watched with interest.

"Okay, your face is 'shaped,' but it looks..." he said, trying to decide on a proper descriptor.

"Bland?" Omega supplied. "Like a mask."

"Yeah. Exactly."

"That's where the color comes in," she said with a smile. "Watch." With a deft flick of her wrist, another brush, not quite as fluffy as the powder brush, applied blush, sweeping it from the apples of her cheeks up the cheekbones toward the temples.

"Damn, Meg," Echo muttered in mild distaste, "you got a little bit of cheek color on, there, baby."

"Uh-huh. Why do you think?"

"Bright lights?"

"You nailed it. Anything less and you couldn't tell I was wearing any—it just washes it all out. But I understand where you're coming from. When I was learning, I had trouble getting the intensity right, so my theater mentor told me, 'Think hooker, and you've got it.' So I did, and I did."

"Hell, Angel!"

"What?"

"I don't associate you and hookers in the same sentence."

Omega smiled again, adding eyeliner and shadow with a

steady hand.

"Thanks, Ace," she said softly. "After..." Abruptly she stopped applying makeup as her hand shook. "After...everything that's..." Her head bowed. Echo took the liner pencil from her limp fingers and laid it down. Then he slipped a gentle arm around her shoulders, pulling her into his chest.

"Hush, now. It's all right, Meg," he murmured softly, stroking her hair. "Slug did a helluva lot to your body when you were young. I know that—I know what he did; you showed me the memories, and I'm incredibly honored you trusted me with them. And yes, it brought on...an urge to mate...when Wright showed on the scene." Echo phrased it as delicately as he could. "But it was artificial, Meg. And you fought it. Successfully. It wasn't you; it was Slug. It's okay. Everything is okay, baby. Just relax." He felt her shoulders shake. "Shh. No, no. Don't cry, Meg. It'll mess up your pretty face. Not to mention that angel-voice. Relax, that's it. Shh."

Omega took a deep breath, and suddenly all sign of emotion was gone, replaced by a cool calmness. Echo blinked, taken aback by the abruptness of the change, and released her as she gently pushed away from him. *Shit,* he thought, shocked, *she sucked that all back inside like a Bardothian sponge-rat. That can't be good.*

"You're right, Echo," Omega said, suddenly all business, as she reached for the eyeliner once more. "We've got a job to do, here. I don't have time for emotional hogwash." A rock-steady hand drew a perfect line around each eye, 'winging' the outer corners ever so slightly, then she applied mascara. "Almost there," she remarked, outlining her lips with a deep reddish-brown lip pencil.

"Let me try," Echo suggested as Omega picked up her lip brush.

"What?"

"All I have to do now is fill in the line, right?" Echo took the lip brush from her and dipped it carefully into one of the pots of color.

"Right..." Omega blinked several times in dumbfoundment; Echo decided she hadn't expected him to actually try his hand at it.

*But hey,* he thought. *It might come in useful, being able to do this kinda thing, one of these days. Never mind the fact that it gives me a chance to hold her face, AND play with her mouth. Score.*

* * *

Echo grasped Omega's chin lightly in his left hand, careful not to smudge her makeup; with his right hand, he painstakingly applied the lip color. An astonished Omega studied her partner's face as he concentrated on her lips.

"Open your mouth."

Omega complied. Echo dabbed lip color on her lips with the brush.

"Now pucker up."

Again Omega complied. Echo considered a moment, then dipped the brush in a slightly different shade and applied it to the center of her lips, blending carefully.

"There." Echo laid down the brush. Omega turned to look in the mirror. Her lips were perfectly tinted, full, and moist, with the slightest hint of a pout, as if she were waiting to be kissed.

"That's...perfect, Echo," she murmured, surprised.

"I thought so."

"I'll make a thespian of you yet."

"Not if I can help it," he shot back. "I just figured it might be a useful skill for both of us to have."

"Okay, I'll let you play with my face tomorrow night." She smiled. "Deal?"

"Deal." Echo grinned.

# **Chapter 6**

Once she was dressed and in makeup, Echo had ducked out of Omega's dressing room, while she did her vocal warmups. "'Cause it kinda embarrasses me," she had admitted. "It's all these weird noises an' sounds, and running scales, and flexing my mouth, an' junk like that, an' I think it looks and sounds kinda ridiculous, though it does the job I need it to do." So he had agreed to allow her privacy until she was more comfortable with him watching, and slipped out to make one more quick sweep backstage before the opening curtain.

But as he nosed about in the dark recesses of the backstage area, he discovered a tiny nook in the far corner, carefully hidden by an angled curtain leg and some stacked set flats.

*What the hell...?* he thought, ducking behind the curtain leg and turning his cell phone's flashlight app on the secret chamber. *There's a mattress in there, and...what the blazes is that...?* Echo bent to focus the light on something lying on the mattress. *It's...a sex toy...?*

"Well, well," a soft male voice said behind him, as a hand on his buttock shoved him forward, caressing lightly as it did so. "I've got a visitor, come looking for me. Hey, handsome. I'll be glad to take care of your needs, good-lookin'. Just give me a minute."

Echo spun, trying not to trip on the mattress, to see Jake standing there, smirking as he pulled the curtain leg closed behind him. More, there was a suspiciously swelling bulge developing in the crotch of the other man's costume. *Oh, great,* Echo thought in exasperation. *Just what I don't have time for. How many times do I have to tell him, I'm taken already?*

"I think you've gotten the wrong idea, here," the male Agent tried. "Mike told me to keep my eyes open, and when I realized there was a space back here, I thought the Theater

Phantom might be hiding in it..."

"Uh-huh," a disbelieving Jake murmured, moving closer and adjusting his costume to accommodate his swelling groin. "It's okay, honey. You don't have to explain. And no reason anybody has to know."

"As long as you're not the phantom, I don't really care," Echo noted, stepping to the side and making to move past Jake. "I have places to be, and I'm sure you do, too."

"Nuh-uh, big boy," Jake said with a leer, blocking Echo's exit and boxing him into the corner. "There's no rush. I've got plenty of time before my first entrance to take care of you."

"I don't think you understand," Echo said, cool. "I'm not interested."

"Then you wouldn't be here."

"I'm here because THIS is here," Echo said, waving his hand around at the cranny.

"Exactly. And I'm here because you're here."

*Aaand THIS isn't gonna end well,* Echo thought, growing irritated. *He doesn't take NO for an answer. Other than his dance ability, he's not in top shape; I could take him down pretty easy, with one hand behind my back. But I'd rather not have to manhandle him to get outta this; we want to have good vibes among the cast and crew, not to antagonize somebody. Never mind that we don't need an injured actor right before opening curtain.*

"Echo?" Michael's voice called softly, just then. "Meg said you were backstage, scoping things out. Are you here, Echo? I have someone I need to introduce to you..."

"Over here in the corner, Mike," Echo announced, rather loudly. "Behind the curtain leg in the corner."

"Oh, damnation," Michael grumbled. "Don't tell me."

"It sure sounds like it, all right," another male voice remarked.

Jake spun in surprise as the curtain was jerked aside, revealing a very annoyed Michael with a man that Echo recognized as Sebastian, the actor portraying the show's third member of the love triangle.

"Echo, are you all right?" Michael asked, eyeing Jake's distended crotch with distaste.

"I'm fine, Mike," Echo noted, completely calm. "I think we had a little misunderstanding. I was on the lookout for your 'Theater Phantom' like you asked, and found this little hiding place, only Jake seems to think I was looking for him, personally. I tried to explain that I'm taken, but he didn't seem to believe me."

"Does he ever?" Sebastian murmured.

"Jacob, I've warned you about this," Michael declared, scowling. When he caught sight of the sex toy lying on the mattress in the beam of Echo's flashlight app, he grew even angrier. "Mr. Alec is a personal friend of mine, and believe me when I say that he isn't interested in the likes of you."

"Says you," Jake said, insolent. "*I* heard he came looking for me."

"Given that nobody else even knew I was backstage except Meg, and even she didn't know I was in this specific spot, I seriously doubt that," Echo noted, cool, then turned to his old friend. "Had you not interrupted, Mike, I was pondering which sprained joint would cause the company the least trouble during the performance."

"Huh?" Jake said in confusion.

"He means, dimwit, he was trying to figure out which one of your limbs he could afford to injure, right before the opening curtain," Michael almost snarled.

"Yeah, like pretty boy here could do that," Jake scoffed.

"I dunno, he looks pretty beefy to me," Sebastian decided.

"I guess it never occurred to you that I might study martial arts as part of my fitness regimen?" Echo suggested, raising an eyebrow. *Among a lot of other things,* he added mentally, and watched as Jake paled. "I have the equivalent of several black belts, in a couple of different forms. Do you know how little force it takes, applied at the correct angle, to blow out a knee... permanently?"

Jake went white.

"It doesn't do to underestimate Mr. Williams," a grim Michael noted to Jake. "I've known him long enough to be well aware of that. Now get out of here, and don't let me see you anywhere near this corner until after closing curtain. And once tonight's performance is over, I expect you to clear this," he waved a hand at the mattress and its adornment, "out of the theater entirely. If I catch you pulling a stunt like this one more time, I swear unto you as God is my witness that I will go straight to Signore Ormund, and have you thrown out of the company. I don't care what you do on your own time, in the privacy of your own home. You will NOT harass the other men and women of the company at the theater."

Still pale, Jake said nothing, but he glared at all three men and left.

"Well, that was an unpleasant little situation," Michael decided, scrutinizing Echo carefully. "Did he get his hands on you?"

"Not to speak of," Echo said with a shrug. "Oh, I got a small pat on the ass, as he was shoving me farther into his little love nest, but I was bent over trying to see what was in here, so it was the logical thing to push. I restrained the instinct to mule-kick him in the groin."

"Ha! You should have," Michael laughed. "It would have taught him a lesson."

"You're lucky, then," Sebastian said, cocking his head to the side. "That guy is a pain in the...well, he's a pain in the ass. He doesn't seem to know how to take 'NO' for an answer. Half the men in the company have been harassed by him, regardless of which way they 'go'—including me, though I discreetly pulled rank on him and ended that little matter. And some of the women, too; he swings both ways."

"I gathered," Echo agreed. "At least about not taking 'no' for an answer. I'm just glad I didn't have to hurt him in order to get past him."

"He's the only sour note in the lot, that I'm aware of,"

Sebastian added. "The rest of the guys get along great, regardless of orientation. But Jake? He sets everyone's teeth on edge. He's a good dancer, and a fair singer, but his personal predilections...well." The other man shook his head.

"He hasn't made a move on Meg, has he?" Michael asked, concerned.

"Not that I've seen, or she's mentioned," Echo noted. "I sorta gathered that maybe she didn't take his fancy, but I did."

"That fits," Sebastian averred. "He has a thing for brunets of either sex...almost a fetish, really. And your lady friend is a pale blonde, at least under the wig, so he probably isn't attracted to her, so much."

"Okay, that's a good thing, then," Echo decided. "Meg's had some...well, she had problems with a stalker recently. He even broke into her...apartment."

"Ooo," Sebastian remarked, wincing.

"Oh, damnation; I'd forgotten you told me about that. And that has just decided me to go to Ormond anyway," Michael determined. "He's the executive producer, Echo; you met him the other night. And I wanted you to meet Sebastian, here. You already recognize each other, I'm sure, but you haven't been formally introduced. Bast, this is the gentleman I was telling you about."

"Yes, the, um, private investigator?" Sebastian murmured, keeping his voice low. "The one no one is supposed to know about?"

"The same."

"And now the comment about hurting a joint makes even better sense," Sebastian said, taking Echo's proffered hand and shaking. "We're glad you're here, sir. And that means that your lady friend, our new prima donna, is your colleague?"

"It does," Echo confirmed. "But nobody outside of the principals, the primary producers, and I guess the director, are supposed to know."

"Right. I won't tell a soul."

"Eventually we need to introduce you to the director, I

suppose," Michael told Echo. "Not that the director is really that involved, at this point, and he doesn't even bother showing up at all the performances any more; the revival has been running for months, and the stage managers handle most of it now. And they, uh, 'know' you already, from...some of your other work."

"Got it," Echo noted, realizing that was Michael's coded message for *They're not from around here.* "Anyway, pleased to meet you, Sebastian; Meg and I really enjoyed your performance the other night, when we came to see the show before joining its ranks."

"Thank you," Sebastian said, appreciative of the compliment. "Given her talent and skill, your colleague's approval means a great deal. As does yours; you obviously know your way around. And you're both very much appreciated for your work in keeping us safe."

"You're quite welcome, and Meg would say the same, but it's our job," Echo said with a smile. "Now, I'm sure the two of you have preparations to make, and I need to finish my backstage sweep..."

"Right," Michael agreed. "Sebastian, would you like to support me in a quick chat with Signore Ormund, before the call for places?"

"I'd be delighted, Michael," Sebastian said, as the two men headed across the stage. "It's about time someone took some action on the lecherous bastard. Why, just last week..."

Echo turned and resumed his work.

* * *

On the far side of the stage, another conversation was taking place, just inside the backstage door.

"What do you make of the new female lead and her manager?" Tatiana, one of the chorus girls, wondered. "Aren't they both just the 'beautiful people' sort? And so talented!"

"They're both awful nice," Pat decided. "I talked to her for a few minutes the other evening, and she was just so friendly—not stuck-up at all. And Mr. Williams always smiles in such a friendly fashion whenever I see him, and always says hello! I hope they're with the show for a while. I like them."

"Well, I heard Sofia was retiring, and Meg was taking over the role permanently," Isaac noted archly. "And I think that's the best news I've had all week."

"Why?" Melissa wondered.

"Because that means her hunky agent will be around, too," Isaac smirked. "Honey, that guy is the best view since oceanfront property."

"He IS easy on the eyes, isn't he?" Juanita laughed. "I could look at him all week!"

"Mm-hm, baybee," Isaac hummed. "Ain't it the truth."

"Doesn't anybody here think Miss Meg is a looker?" LeBron asked, somewhat plaintive. "I think she's really pretty and very sweet."

"Oh, she's very nice," Isaac said, dismissive, "but honey, give me that Alec any day. Still, if Meg is staying around, that means Alec will be, too. So yay for Meg getting the role!"

A low laugh went around the group.

* * *

On the other side of the curtain leg from the gossiping troop, and hidden from them thereby, a particular chorus girl listened in silence, then scowled.

"Oh, no, no, no," Marcie murmured, peering into the corridor just off the stage left wings and watching through the open door of the star's dressing room as Omega, through with the more unusual of her vocal exercises, continued to warm up her voice before the curtain. "I think it's about time your theater career ended, bitch. Preferably tonight. And I know just the person to do it, too."

Marcie slipped from behind the curtain, moved to the corner prop table, and studied the items on it.

* * *

All began well in the first act of the performance, although the catwalk set descended rather jerkily during the title number, and Omega and Michael had to walk gingerly along it as they

165

sang. Echo checked it out, but it appeared to be the same old problem with the fly-rail brake, a known condition of the much-used equipment, and he dismissed it with a mental note to suggest that the stagehands do some routine maintenance.

*Still and all,* he thought, *things are going well. And Jake is staying out of everybody's way. Including mine, I note.*

* * *

But things did not remain well.

As Omega, in full costume with voluminous period skirts, ran from her dressing room, through the hallway, and into the dark backstage area in preparation to go onstage for the first act finale sequence, she tripped over something, hidden in the dark. With her hands full of skirts and nothing close at hand to grab to steady herself, she went down hard, tumbling across the wooden boards with a clattering series of thuds. She grunted twice, then lay still.

"Oh shit!" Echo exclaimed in a low voice, and ran to kneel beside her, just as several stagehands also ran up. Michael arrived scant seconds later, having seen the incident from the far side of the stage.

"Hold the curtain!" the lead actor hissed to the stage manager, who nodded and spoke into his headset before yanking it off and coming to help.

"Baby, are you okay?" Echo murmured in deep concern as his partner sat up slowly.

"That's gonna leave a mark or twelve," she grumbled, panting and rubbing various body parts. "I dunno, Echo. Gimme a minute."

"Our poor girl fairly tumbled ass over teakettle," Michael noted in astonishment. "What in heaven's name caused you to fall?"

"I tripped over something in the dark," Omega said, and immediately the stagehands began searching the area where she fell, pulling out red flashlights to scan the stage. "Something HARD...that didn't move. I've been through there I dunno how many times by now, and there was never anything there before."

"Here's what did it," the principal stage manager—Adam by name—said, picking up a small, Victorian-style cashbox in one hand, and a black scarf in the other. "Damn, it must be made outta lead."

"It's the prop cashbox for the theatre in the show," Omega noted, seeing it.

"Yeah, the one that Arthur uses in the next scene," one of the stagehands—Jon by name—declared, his face grim. Adam opened it.

"Well, no wonder it's so heavy," the stage manager grumbled, hauling out an H-shaped block of pig iron. "There's a damn fly-rail counterweight in it! And it was covered up by the black scarf, so nobody would see it," Adam added.

"Then it was no accident," Echo said with a scowl.

"It wasn't there when I came through just a few seconds before, though," Jeanie, one of the chorus girls—the only alien among the chorus girls, and the one who had been admiring of Omega—said. "And I came through in the exact same place."

"So it was targeted at Meg," Echo said, body seeming to swell as anger filled him. "Somebody was TRYING to hurt her. And that...pisses...me...off."

"Do you think you can finish the show, my dear?" Michael asked, crouching beside Omega, opposite Echo.

"Yeah, I think so," Omega decided. "Y'all help me up."

So Echo grabbed one of her hands, and Michael grabbed the other, and they pulled her upright.

But as soon as Omega tried to step forward, she stumbled with a cry of pain and almost fell again.

"Uh-oh. What's wrong, baby?" Echo wondered, grabbing her near arm and letting her lean on him.

"Foot an' ankle I tripped on," Omega said, awkwardly hobbling over to the chair a solicitous stagehand produced, as Echo allowed her to put most of her weight on him. "Uhn. That hurts awful bad, Ace. I'm pretty sure the ankle is sprained, and the foot may be broken."

"Oh damn," Echo said in dismay. "Hang on, baby. Michael, stay put right here, and watch over Meg. The rest of you, don't move."

The others nodded, and Echo headed for the rear stage entrance at speed.

* * *

He was back moments later with the special field medikit out of the Corvette. Immediately upon seeing it, the stagehands—with Jeanie's help—spread out and formed a perimeter around the pair of Agents; Echo had already ascertained that the majority of the show's alien contingent was in the tech crew. Now that crew ensured that no one else could get a good look at the advanced equipment Echo would use on his partner.

"Okay, baby, let's have a look," Echo said, opening the kit and getting out several pieces of equipment. First he examined it with the medscanner, and hummed to himself.

"What?" Omega wondered. "How bad is it?"

"I dunno," he decided. "It looks like the ankle is sprained, yeah, but I'm not sure about the foot. What do you think?" He handed her the scanner and let her study the readouts.

"Oh. I see what you mean," Omega said, scrunching her face. "There could be green breaks in there, or there could be bruising, or...just an unhappy foot." She considered for a moment. "Hm. I sure wish we had India here."

"Right. But we don't. And we don't have time for her to get here. So let's treat this like it could be broken, and see about getting you through a little bit longer, until I can get you to Zebra. She'll know what's what, and be able to fix you up, good as new. If this weren't a mission, I'd take you straight to her, right this instant. But I guess we need to try to get you through the rest of the show, if we can. If we can't, I'll still take you straight to her."

"Okay."

"Lessee here, now." He selected a micropore syringe from the kit. "Gimme your arm, hon. This'll help it not hurt so much, while I stabilize the foot and ankle enough so that you can get through the show, and afterward I'll see about taking you back to the medlab to get patched up."

"All right. As long as I'm not too loopy to remember my lines."

"No, I thought about that already. This'll work."

Omega offered her arm to Echo; he injected the pain medication, then eased off the dance shoe on her injured foot, beginning to examine it more directly.

"Mm. It's starting to swell," he observed. "If I get this strapped up fast, I can minimize swelling, and you can finish this out. I can't guarantee you can wear that shoe, though."

"I'll run to the costume shop and get a couple sizes bigger, and she can try 'em when you're done, Mr. Echo," Jeanie offered. She picked up Omega's discarded shoe and checked the size, then scampered off, coming back within moments with a selection of dance shoes for her to try when Echo was done. "Here we go, honey," she said, crouching down and placing the shoes beside Omega. "Something in this ought to fit, even over the bandage. It won't match, but they're close enough to the same color that nobody will notice from the house."

"Excellent," Michael decided, while Echo worked on Omega's foot and ankle, applying a topical medication, then reaching for the specialized bandages. "I know that Sofia has been relieved to be safely out of the way while we figure out this little mystery. I'm glad that the two of you should be able to continue that task, though I am very sorry that Meg got hurt."

"Meanwhile, I guess we need to find out what Arthur has been up to," Omega decided, watching Echo wrap a stabilization bandage on her wounded foot with infinite care, occasionally glancing at her face to ensure he wasn't hurting her. "We may have found our Theater Phantom."

"Oh, I can tell you what Arthur has been doing, Miss Meg," Adam informed her. "He's been frantic, running around looking for this damn cashbox."

"It could be a ruse," Echo considered. He finished strapping up the foot and ankle. Jeanie crouched beside Alpha One and together, the three tried on shoes until they got one that fit comfortably over Omega's swollen foot AND the bandage. Echo pulled the strap across Omega's instep and fastened it, ensuring it was snug but not tight; having the shoe slip, or at least as bad, come off, in the middle of a dance number would only make matters worse.

"No, I don't think so, Echo," Michael disagreed. "Because that box is supposed to get transferred from the stage right wings after he exited his previous scene with it, to the stage left wings here, for his next scene. And since it wasn't here, he was over there, with me, looking for it—because he reasonably assumed that it didn't get carried from one prop table to the other; such things happen, from time to time. I saw Jeanie go on stage safely, and then a few moments later, I saw Meg here take her header in the same area...all while Arthur was pawing frantically through the props on the table, looking for it, right next to me."

"No, no," Pete, one of the stagehands, declared. "I grabbed that thing from the stage right props table and brought it straight over here, as soon as Arthur sat it down." He stepped to the stage left props table and pointed. "I put it right there."

"And I saw it there, not five minutes ago," Jon averred. "As well as Pete, headed back across the stage, after setting it there." He pointed behind the backdrop.

"Which means somebody took it after it got moved over here, but before Arthur usually picks it up to go on," Adam observed. "Did you see who, either of you?"

"No, I was having some issues with my costume—the quick-change didn't go smoothly tonight—and I had paused to re-fasten my cape," Michael admitted. "I'm sorry."

"And I had to go handle the set transition," Jon said with a wry shrug by way of apology.

"Hm," Echo hummed again, thoughtful. "Then that adds even more significance to the black scarf used to hide the cashbox prop."

"Whose was it?" Omega wondered. "Was it a prop too, or

part of a costume, or...?"

"I know whose it was," Jeanie averred. "It was part of a costume. I recognize the jacquard pattern in it."

"Whose?" Echo demanded, rounding on her.

"Marcie's."

"Sonuvabitch," Echo cursed.

* * *

"Don't worry, Echo," a furious Michael noted. "I'll handle this one with the director and producers. It may take a day or two, but rest assured, she's done with this show. And very likely in the theatrical community," he added in deep disgust, "once this hits the grapevine."

"You really heard her saying all that shit, Ace?" Omega wondered. "And she KNEW you heard her?"

"I don't think she actually stopped to wonder if I'd heard or not, baby," Echo explained. "It was kind of, 'out of sight, out of mind,' I think. She couldn't see me, so I must not have been anywhere around, you know? She didn't strike me as exactly on your level, intellect-wise. But come on to me, she definitely did. Of course, so did some of the guys, in no uncertain terms, so hey."

"Oh my," Omega murmured, trying not to laugh; she knew from many detailed conversations with her partner, let alone watching him react to various women, in real life and on the small and large screens, that he was firmly in the hetero camp. *Never mind the other night's smooching, and the way he responded to it,* she thought. *So I can imagine just how much headway the guys made.*

"Well, hey; to each his own, I guess," Echo said with a slight grin. "Just because it doesn't float my boat..."

"Nah, I was just wishin' I'd been there to see, Ace," she told him with a smirk. "I'd have loved to see you turn that red with embarrassment. Oh well. I got more immediate considerations, like whether or not I'm gonna be able to finish this performance."

"I think you can, if we use the modified blocking and

171

dance steps Sofia and I showed you," Michael decided. "We developed them for just such a circumstance, because accidents do happen...though this was NOT an accident. I'll help as much as I can, and Adam, you grab Sebastian and tell him to use the injured-player blocking and steps. Let him know—privately—that Meg, here, has taken a bad tumble. We don't want it getting around what happened until I have a chance to act on things."

"Will do, Sir Michael," Adam agreed, shoving his headset back on and murmuring into it as he sought to locate the other principal actor. "Okay, stage right acknowledges, and is sending him over here with Arthur, who has to fetch his prop, anyway."

"Good." Michael turned to Omega and held out a hand. "My dear, can you stand now?"

Omega took his hand and stood gingerly, then tried out the foot and ankle. She scrunched up her face, but then nodded.

"It still hurts, but not as bad," she decided. "Let me walk around a minute or so, and then we'll give this a shot."

"Oh dear," Arthur said, coming up, as Omega paced slowly. "I heard there had been an accident. What happened?"

"Someone used your cashbox as part of an obstacle course for our dear Meg," Michael noted, voice clipped in his annoyance. "That series of thuds you heard a few moments ago? That was Meg, tumbling across the backstage area."

"Oh damn!" Arthur exclaimed. "No wonder I couldn't find the stupid thing!"

"With this in it," Adam said, hefting the fly-rail weight.

"The hell you say!" Arthur expostulated, patently horrified, as Sebastian walked up. "Meg, why are you even walking, girl?!"

"Wow," Sebastian murmured, eyes wide. "What Arthur said."

"Alec, here, strapped it up for me," Omega pointed out, "and I'm going to try to get through the rest of the performance using the modified blocking and dance steps, then he's gonna take me to the ER to see about it. I'm hoping nothing is broken."

"So Sebastian, you and I need to ensure we support her as much as possible, without the audience noticing," Michael added.

"Aha. I see," Sebastian agreed at once. "Certainly. We had to do that for the actress in the role before our Sofia, as well, Meg—do you remember, Michael? When Jeannette managed to trip on the setpiece stairs and break her ankle, although no one knew it at the time?"

"Oh, damnation! I'd forgotten all about that silly goose," Michael said with a fond smile, watching as Omega tried several little dance steps with reasonable success, while a protective Echo hovered nearby to catch, should she stumble. "She was a dear girl, but how in heaven's name she ever managed to make it in dance, as accident-prone as she was, I don't know!"

"Well, it ended her dancing," Sebastian said, solemn. "I saw her a few weeks back, and it turns out the broken bones damaged the tendons...irreparably, she said. She still sings, and takes roles that don't require any fancy footwork, but the days of her doing a show like this one are over. I can't imagine," he added, shaking his head. "I've no notion what I would do, in her shoes."

The others cringed.

"Okay, I think I've got this," Omega decided. "Echo, I might, um, need a little help over intermission, though..." She sent him a very subtle coded message that said, *I might need more of the pain medication by then, so don't put away the medikit.*

"Got it," Echo agreed, casually gathering up and stowing the medikit items, closing the case, and shoving it into a warp pocket. "We'll get you through this, baby. Then I'll get you to the doctor, straight off."

"Ready for the curtain?" Adam wondered.

"Hold on while I get across stage," Michael said, suiting action to word.

"All right, everyone," Adam murmured into the backstage sound system, watching as Michael scampered across the stage behind the curtain. "Places for Act I, Scene 10, everyone. And...raise curtain."

* * *

Echo watched for several minutes as Omega launched into the last scene of the act, wanting to make sure she was able to do it without undue pain.

*But she looks like she's doing fine,* he decided. *Other than the subtleties of the changes to the dance steps and the...what was it they called it...oh yeah, the 'blocking,' which I guess means where they're supposed to go onstage...I don't really see a difference. I hope the strapping holds through all that activity; I did the best I could with it. I'll check it again during intermission. I might need to redo it.*

And he resumed his cautious surveillance of the entire theater.

* * *

At intermission, the two Agents checked in with one another in Omega's dressing room.

"Anything, Echo?" Omega asked.

"No, nothing that I can see, Meg," Echo responded, kneeling beside her to check the way he had strapped up her foot and ankle. "Okay, this looks good. Have those enhanced senses of yours picked up on anything?"

"Not really," Omega replied. "I heard a lot of activity, off and on, up among the overhead pipes and battens and stuff over the course of the act, but with the catwalk glitch, that's to be expected. And I suppose Marcie had to go find a suitable weight she could use."

"Yeah," Echo agreed, dragging the visitor chair around to face her. "Here. Put that foot up, as much as you can, when you're not on stage, baby. Now where's that cold pack I had? There it is." He applied the pack to her injured extremity. "No, some of that activity was me, checking it out—and you're probably right about the little bitch—but there were stagehands up there looking at it, too. I already popped word to the chief stage manager—Adam, wasn't that his name?—that the fly-

174

rail brake thing needs some serious maintenance, preferably immediately, and he agreed. He's gonna have the fly-rail tech guys go over it in detail after final curtain tonight."

"Yeah. Maybe the presence of Division One Agents scared off our little phantom," Omega guessed. "Especially given we're Alpha Line, which I've gathered is developing a bit of a reputation."

"Maybe." Echo's tone was doubtful. "I mean, yeah, it's developing some notoriety as a department full of serious badasses, which is what we wanted, for a lotta reasons. But I don't think it would be that easy to scare off the phantom. Especially if it's Slug."

"Hey, I can wish, can't I?" Omega joked.

"You can, as long as you don't stop preparing in case your wish doesn't come true."

"No, I get that."

"Do you need any more pain medication?"

"Not right now. I think I'm good. Keep it handy when you meet up with me each time I come offstage, though, just in case."

"Wilco."

Just then, Adam's voice came over the speaker, murmuring, "Places for the next act."

"Well, here goes Act Two." Omega squared her shoulders, lowered her leg, and stood, headed for the door to backstage.

"Go get 'em, Angel," Echo said, following her through the door. "Er, uh, I mean break a leg. Just not another foot."

"Thanks, Ace," floated back to him as she disappeared in the dark of the backstage blackout.

* * *

When Marcie saw the female Agent step onstage for the big costume party scene that opened Act II, her shock was noticeable, even through the ornate mask that was part of her costume; she fairly gaped at Omega.

"And that tells the tale," a still-angry Michael murmured in Omega's ear, during a momentary lull in which the audience's attention was on a different actor. She nodded subtly, then subvocalized to Echo.

*"Look at Marcie in the red and gold costume. Her mouth is hanging open."*

*"I see her,"* came the clipped, sharp reply in her transponder chip, and Omega realized that Sir Michael wasn't the only one who was angry. *"And she's the ONLY one with her mouth hanging open. She didn't expect you to be able to continue at this point."*

"Let me guess," Michael said, as Omega blinked at her partner's vehement, infuriated tone. "Echo is at least as angry as I am."

"No shit," Omega murmured, as their cue approached. "Okay, here we go..."

* * *

Echo gave his partner one additional shot of the low-level painkiller halfway through the act, and that took care of her pain until the final curtain. Omega made it through the rest of the show without further incident, with Sebastian and Michael determinedly assisting. She was grateful for their insistence that she lean on them whenever possible, to take the weight off her injured foot; while Echo had done an excellent job of sophisticated field first aid, the wounded foot and ankle were simply not going to be able to bear her entire weight through a dance routine without far more skilled, professional medical attention.

Michael and Echo met her backstage, ensuring that she got safely to her dressing room; while Jeanie diverted Marcie's attention, Echo swept his partner up in his arms, skirts and all, and carried her across the backstage corridor and into her dressing room. Michael escorted the pair, ensuring everyone and everything stayed out of the way. Even little Cecile slipped into the dressing room as well, beginning the process of stripping the last costume from her mistress; since, as Echo had observed, Omega was wearing a nude-toned opaque body stocking underneath, the proprieties were maintained for the reserved female Agent. Michael closed the door, as a curious Echo watched the disrobing process with interest.

"Damn," he murmured after a moment, as the yards of cloth piled up around their feet, "I see what you meant the other day, Cecile, about not having any room, with all those skirts an' slips an' shit."

"Exactly, Mr. Echo," Cecile said with a grin. "These will be going to be cleaned after this, so Miss Meg and I don't need to worry so much about getting them on the floor and such now. But before the show, when we're trying to keep everything looking good for the performance, it gets complicated!" She turned to her mistress. "Miss Meg, are you all right? I heard about your fall from Adam, the stage manager; he wanted me to make sure you had everything you needed, just in case."

"I'm...okay, dear," Omega averred, trying not to wince as she stepped out of her dance shoes. "I've been better, and Echo is gonna take me to see a doctor as soon as we're done here. Oh, keep that extra shoe there," she pointed, as Cecile picked them up. "I know it doesn't go with my regular pair, but it fits over the swelling and bandaging. I might need it tomorrow night. Whatever happened to my original shoe? Does anybody know?"

"Oh no! It isn't broken, is it? Your foot?" an agitated Cecile wondered. "I heard you hurt your foot?"

"Foot and ankle," Echo noted. "But I doubt it's broken, or she wouldn't be up and walking on it. It's probably just bruised, with maybe a bit of an ankle strain. I have a doctor that sees to Meg when she's injured, who can practically work miracles. I'll be very surprised if she's not doing fine by tomorrow night."

"And don't worry about your shoe, Miss Meg," Cecile said. "Jeanie brought it to me after intermission. It's over here in the wardrobe already. And she told me that, if we need her help, all we have to do is ask."

"Tell her thank you, would you?" Echo murmured.

"Indeed," Michael agreed. "Grabbing those shoes for us to find one that worked probably helped save tonight's performance."

"Of course, Mr. Echo, Mr. Michael."

"Oh good," Omega murmured, finally sitting down with a sigh, as Cecile's efforts eventually uncovered the dressing-table chair, which had been buried in yards of cloth. The injured Agent seemed to collapse in on herself for a moment, in relief. "Ohh, that feels better."

"Cecile, we would appreciate it if you said nothing that you hear in here tonight," Michael addressed the girl. "You see, Miss Meg's tumble was no accident. Someone did it deliberately...and we know who."

"Oh?" the girl wondered, scowling in anger. "It wasn't Marcie, was it?"

"It was," Omega averred. "She was foolish enough to use a piece of her own costume as part of the deadfall, and to react ON STAGE when she saw me come out anyway."

"Why did you think it was her?" Echo wondered, kneeling to check the binding on Omega's ankle as Cecile cleared away the last of the costuming. Then the petite dresser brought Omega her workout clothes in lieu of the evening gown she would have worn, had she and Echo gone out as planned. Both Agents sighed in regret when Cecile put away said gown— it was the blue one Omega had worn the night before, but which Echo had not had a chance to enjoy thanks to Sofia's machinations; so that morning he had reiterated his request for her to wear it again, for him, and she had agreed.

"Because she has had nothing good to say of Miss Meg from the beginning," Cecile observed, tart and annoyed. "And not much good to say of you either, Mr. Echo." The girl shook her head. "She has been trying to turn the rest of the cast against you both. But you're both so nice that she's starting to just get everybody mad at her."

"What's her major malfunction with us?" Omega wondered. "Why does she care?"

"Oh, I have heard all the talking, so I can tell you that—she had the lead in an off-Broadway production over the summer,

Miss Meg," Cecile informed them. "I think it went to her head. She thought, when Miss Sofia grew ill, that she should have been named to the role."

"But she isn't even Sofia's understudy," Michael pointed out. "She's simply not good enough for the role. Sofia's understudy is Kate, who is one of the offwor-ah, off-West-End actors," he corrected himself swiftly, and both members of Alpha One nodded understanding of the subterfuge, "and I checked with Kate before bringing the two of you in! She was relieved to have experienced, uh, investigators, on the case and in the role. She was...badly frightened by the whole thing. I think the, ah, the 'family emergency' she had was something of a reprieve for her."

"I know that, and you know that, sir. But it doesn't seem to matter, Mr. Michael," Cecile said with a shrug. "Marcie thinks so, therefore it must be that way, apparently."

"I'm thinking that it may be time to teach Marcie a little lesson," Michael said with a grim smile. "Would you lot be interested in going along with me, in doing so?"

Echo and Omega exchanged glances, then looked at Cecile, who offered them all a wicked grin.

"I think the three of us are in, Mike," Echo declared. "What did you have in mind...?"

* * *

"All hands meeting out front," Adam announced on the backstage intercom, moments after Michael left Omega's dressing room. "All hands. Cast, crew, production staff. Out front as soon as your duties are finished, and the show has been reset."

Moments later, a puzzled show staff, crew and cast had gathered in the front seats of the theater auditorium, murmuring to themselves. Abruptly the curtain opened partway, disclosing four figures on stage.

Adam the stage manager, Sir Michael, Echo, and Omega.

All four were scowling.

They stepped to the edge of the boards, as the lone

stagehand who had opened the curtain hurried to his seat at the end of a row.

"I called this meeting because I wanted everyone—but especially the director and producers—to know about tonight's scurrilous events," Michael announced, his rich baritone voice carrying to the farthest corners, even as it did during a performance. "Tonight, a deliberate effort was made to sabotage the show, by injuring our leading lady: Margaret Stratford." Michael held out his arm to his leading lady, as the house gasped in shock. Marcie, sitting in the far back of the group, near the end of one row of seats, squirmed anxiously. "The only reason it didn't succeed is because our dear Meg was in a spare pair of dance shoes that were too large, and she had to pad the toes," the actor lied glibly. "As it was, it was one of the worst tumbles I've seen in several years, and she is apt to be quite battered and bruised on the morrow."

A general hubbub rose, with two questions rising to the top—"Who did it?" and "What happened?" Adam stepped forward and held up an object.

"The prop cashbox was swiped off the props table," he told them, "and then a fly-rail weight put in it. It was placed in Miss Meg's path after everyone else had gone through, and covered with this scarf, to ensure it would be invisible in the backstage blackout." He held up the black scarf in his other hand.

"As for who did it," Echo added, "that was easy, because of the scarf. We know it wasn't Arthur—"

"Because he was on the opposite side of the stage with me, hunting frantically for the cashbox," Michael amended.

"—So the owner of the scarf, who never thought to report it missing, has to be the culprit," Echo concluded. "And according to some of the other chorus girls, and Meg's dresser, the scarf was part of...Marcie's costume."

A gasp went up. Marcie paled and shrank back in her seat.

"And as the attack was against the leading lady, and I submit to you that the so-called Theater Phantom was also attacking the leading lady," Michael averred, "I believe we may have found our rogue phantom.”

The entire theater troupe fell quiet. It was not a relaxed, pleasant silence. The tension in the air was nearly palpable. Most of the troupe directed angry glares at Marcie.

Finally the executive producer, one Robert Ormond, spoke.

“Well, I seriously doubt she’s really a ‘Theater Phantom,’” the older man declared, rising to his feet in the audience. “But considering this stunt, it wouldn’t surprise me in the least if she had bumbled her way into making people THINK we had a Phantom.” He shook his head and turned toward Marcie. “You’re evidently also too stupid to trust not to pull a stunt like this again. Never mind the legal implications. Pack your things and get out.”

“What?!” Marcie exclaimed, leaping to her feet. “You’re going to fire me on the word of a stage manager and a man who isn’t even part of the cast OR crew?!”

“And our principal actor,” Ormond pointed out. “The accusers comprise our male LEAD, our lead stage manager, AND—that man who ‘isn’t part of the cast or crew’ happens to be our current leading lady’s agent and manager. I’m sure he speaks with her full authority.”

“He does,” Omega noted, crisp and succinct. She took Echo’s arm, and Echo put his opposite hand over hers, curling his arm for her to grasp the elbow. It also subtly gave her the opportunity to put her weight against him, easing the stress on her injured foot.

“You agree with the accusation, Miss Stratford?” Ormond verified.

“I do,” Omega said, tilting her head in a haughty fashion. “The fact that myself, Sir Michael, and Mr. Alec all noticed her dumbfounded shock in the costumed-ball scene when I took the stage after the incident was only confirmation of our suspicions. She did not expect me to be on stage. And she was the ONLY actor—out of the entire cast, all of whom were on stage at that point—to react in that fashion.”

“You’re done,” Ormond reiterated, turning to Marcie. “Get

out."

"My contract says a week's notice," Marcie declared, responding to Omega's presumed haughtiness with arrogance of her own...except it wasn't feigned.

"Your behavior nullifies the contract, because it invalidates the willful malice clause. You have twenty-four hours, without pay, to clear the theater," Ormond snapped. "And you won't be performing again. Tonight was your last performance with this company. Or any other, if I have my way. You'll gather your things tonight under observation, and when you leave, you are not to come back. Try to harm any of our people again, and I'll see you arrested for assault and battery."

He signaled the theater security, who had been standing at the doors per Adam's advance word, and they escorted the disgruntled actress out of the house, back to the female chorus dressing room to fetch her things. Then he turned back to the cast.

"Jacob?"

"Yes, sir?" Jake said, standing.

"You're done, too. I've had too many reports of your sexual escapades, and tonight's report from Sir Michael, corroborated by Sebastian, was over the top. Get your things and go."

Jake gaped for a long moment, turning very pale. Then he hung his head, turned, and left the theater.

* * *

"And that," Michael averred to the house, after the two were gone, "is the end of the Theater Phantom. Meg, my dear, would you be so kind as to see us through Sofia's recovery from her throat ailment, and Kate's unexpected family emergency?"

"I would be delighted, Sir Michael," Omega accepted.

The cast and crew applauded.

* * *

While Michael, Adam, Jeanie, and Cecile ensured Marcie stayed away from the stars' dressing rooms as she packed her few belongings, Echo escorted Omega through the dressing-room area and out the backstage door, to the little parking lot reserved for the cast and crew. He tucked her into the passenger seat of the Corvette, ensuring she was as comfortable and secure as he could make her, then got in himself.

Moments later, they were en route to Headquarters and the medlab.

# Chapter 7

"Well, that takes care of one scheming bitch, hopefully," Echo grumbled as he drove.

"Yeah, it gets her out of both of our hair," Omega agreed. "Never mind the guy who was annoying you. And maybe it even gave whoever is hosting Slug the notion that we think the problem is taken care of."

"Right. In which case, 'they'—meaning, I guess, the Slug/other-person symbiont—might get careless."

"We can only hope," Omega noted. "With a telepath in the mix, it's kinda hard to know for sure."

"Well, that's true," Echo decided. "Anyhow, right now I wanna get you to Zebra, baby, and let her tend this foot of yours. The way you were starting to hobble a little, there at the end, I'm getting worried it's busted. Maybe bad."

"I won't deny it hurts," Omega said with a sigh. "Even with the pain meds you gave me. But I think if any of the bones ARE broken, they'll be hairline cracks. Nothing feels...off. You know, out of place or anything like that. Everything feels like it's where it's supposed to be, it just hurts."

"Wow. You must have the tendons from hell."

"Why?"

"If I'd done what you did, I mean trip like that at near-full speed, I'd expect to at least have some minor dislocations in my foot," Echo pointed out. "X-ray did something like that once, and he had I dunno how many bones out of whack in there. And don't forget how that Security guard kicked the end of her bathroom door in the night, a couple weeks back, and busted things all up. Remember, the one who was supposed to be teaming with Yankee, while Tare was on sabbatical?"

"Oh shit, that's right," Omega recalled. "Yeah, you've got a point; I coulda messed this up but good. Ugh. I guess we'll have to wait and see what Zebra says, then."

"Coming into Headquarters now, baby," Echo told her as he turned into the parking garage that hid the entrance to the vehicle hangar, down the street and across from Headquarters proper. "And there's the medics, waiting for you. I contacted Fox during the second act and told him what happened; he said he'd have Zebra on alert, and emergency medics waiting for us when we got here, complete with a medical antigrav chair. That way, you don't have to walk on it any more than we could already help. After all, doing the rest of the show was only mandated by the mission...and I wasn't real happy about THAT."

"Good, an' yeah," Omega said, as Echo parked the 'Vette and the medics came to her side of the car. "This might end up being an interesting night, sleep-wise."

* * *

"Yep, there are some hairline fractures in there, all right," Zebra averred, half an hour after Alpha One arrived in the medlab. "And some of the tendons in the ankle are mildly sprained. Nothing too bad, and by the time I'm done with her, Omega ought to be good to go."

"What about the performance tomorrow night?" Omega wondered. "We're still chasing whoever has been causing 'accidents' in the theater, you know. I need to be there..."

"...Or we need to call off the performance," Echo amended her statement. "And Zebra needs to be the one making that call, Meg."

Omega sighed.

"Well, what if we just see how she is in the morning, first?" Zebra suggested. "I'll do a few things tonight, including hooking her up to an IV of regen fluid and putting the whole thing in a removable cast from the knee down..."

"Oh lovely," Omega fussed. "No sleep for me tonight."

"That's what you think, honey," Zebra said with a grin. "The cast things we got these days are the most comfortable they've been yet. They'll let your foot and ankle move in the directions they're supposed to go, without letting 'em go in the directions the injuries want 'em to go. Besides, did you really think I'd forget about pain meds? Echo, I'll give those to you, and I want you to see that she gets a full dose every six hours... whether she's awake and coherent or not. And be forewarned, with the stuff I'm gonna give her, she may LOOK at you—she may even talk to you, all logical-sounding and everything—but believe me, she's not gonna remember it."

"Oh," Omega said, concerned, and glanced at Echo, who was grinning. Abruptly he sobered.

"Wait," he said, worried. "Does that idea bother you, Meg? I mean, I haven't really come into the bedroom in your quarters since...everything. I mean, you know...Wright and all. And you'll be doped to the gills, it sounds like..."

"Oh," it was Zebra's turn to say. "That's a good thought, Echo. Meg, dear, if that WILL bother you, I can always set you up in a room here, in the medlab, and ensure a female medtech is the one administering the meds..."

"No, I don't think I mind if ECHO does it," Omega decided. "I was only wondering if I'd do something stupid that he'll carry me high over for the next three weeks."

"Other than missing your mouth with the pills, or maybe spilling your water, I doubt it," Zebra said with a faint chuckle, then she paused to consider, rubbing a hand across her face. "Although bathroom trips might be a bit problematic, come to think about it. There's a muscle relaxant built in, and your knees will go every which way."

"I got an idea," Echo suggested. "Meg, how would you feel if I dragged one of the recliners into the corner of your bedroom, over by the closet, and crashed there for the night? I'll bring in a pillow and a sheet an' maybe a blanket, and I can set an alert on my phone to wake me when it's time for your meds. And that way, I'll know if you get up in the night, and can help you navigate. Or," he added, watching her ponder the idea, "I can bring in that air mattress again, like we used in Ipswich..."

"I think I'd rather the recliner, if that's okay," Omega decided. "But...well, if the air mattress is more comfortable, use it. I want you to be comfortable, Ace. I just...it reminds me..."

"I get it," he murmured, laying a hand on her shoulder. "And I'll be fine in the recliner. Lord knows, I've slept in mine AND yours enough. It'll take me a bit of maneuvering to get it through the door, is the only thing. I might need to call Romeo to come over and help me carry it..."

"Nope," Zebra said, going to her tablet on the counter in the exam room and swiping a fingertip across it. "I'll put in an 'Urgent' level medical requisition to Facilities, and they'll use the warp to adjust the layout and positioning of the chair—AND let's add an extra side table an' a lamp, so you've got room for stuff like the med bottle, a book, your phone, and whatever else you'll need for yourself—before you two even get out of here. Then, when I put in an all-clear in a day or two, they'll move it back the way it was, while you're out and about on duty."

"Terrific," Echo said with a pleased grin. "That helps a whole lot, Zebra. Thanks."

"Now let's get your girlfriend hooked up to 'the purple shit,' I think you called it last time you were in, Echo," Zebra laughed, "and we'll get this healing on the way."

Neither of them saw Omega's blush at the personal terminology.

* * *

An hour later, a dilute form of the regeneration fluid, targeted to broken bone and strained or torn connective tissue, was circulating in Omega's bloodstream, and Zebra was putting on the removable cast.

"Tell me if this is too tight, or doesn't feel comfortable," she said, as she adjusted the fit.

"No, that actually feels pretty good," Omega concluded. "It helps support it, like the way Echo wrapped it up in the special bandage stuff. It eases the pain some, that way, 'cause I don't

187

have to try to support it myself."

"Exactly. Great," Zebra said, and reached for an adjustable metal cane. "Now, for tonight, I want you to use this, whenever you have to be on your feet. Even with the cast, you're gonna feel a little unstable, and this will help prevent any more falls." She fitted it to the female Agent, then handed it to her. "And the two of you, head straight home. Have you had dinner?"

"Not yet," Echo noted.

"Okay, FEED her first, THEN get her in bed, BEFORE you give her these. If you do it any other way 'round, she's only gonna go face-down in her food." Zebra put a prescription bottle in Echo's hand. "And make sure she's ready and in bed before she takes it, or she's gonna be a puddle on the floor before she can GET in bed. This stuff takes effect fast. Dosage is on the label. Follow it. There's only enough for tonight, with an extra dose for in the morning, ONLY if she needs it; when she wakes up in the morning...which might take a little longer than usual...get her dressed and fed, and bring her back here. You'll probably be stiff and sore in the morning despite the 'purple shit,' honey," Zebra addressed Omega. "By the look of things, you took an awfully bad tumble."

"Mike described it best, I think, when he said she went 'ass over teakettle,'" Echo pointed out. Zebra winced, and Omega gave them both a rueful, slightly sheepish grin.

"Ow. That says it all, right there," Zebra averred. "Okay, you two run on home, and if you have any problems, CALL me. I'll be going off duty in about half an hour, but I'm on call JUST for you two. And Fox already knows and approves that."

"So he won't mind if I wake y'all at oh-dark-thirty to tell him that Meg's got a problem and for you to come quick?" Echo said, grinning as he ribbed the physician. Zebra grinned back, turning a bit pink, then shrugged.

"Knowing him, he's liable to throw on clothes and come with me," she said. "He thinks a whole lot of you both, guys. He'd want to make sure everything is okay, and not wait for me to remember to call him and tell him so. Especially since I'm the absent-minded doctor type, and might not even think about it until I was coming back through our front door."

"Aw," Omega murmured, easing off the exam table and gingerly putting weight on the injured foot. It was her turn to wince. "Ow."

"The foot, or the cast?" Zebra asked immediately.

"The damn foot," Omega fussed. "That went from my toes clear up to somewhere above my knee. Like a lightning bolt. And then exploded."

"I'm not surprised," Zebra noted. "You did a number on it, girlfriend, as India would say. That's why I want you to get home, fed, and in bed as soon as we can get you there, so you can take the pain meds. What you had in you has worn off now, and you need this new stuff in you A.S.A.P. The more you relax, the quicker it'll heal."

"Should I just carry her?" Echo wondered. "I really don't want her on that foot any more than she's already had to, tonight..."

"Not again," Omega breathed. Zebra and Echo both heard.

"What's wrong, baby?" he asked, perturbed. "I'm just trying to help."

Omega opened her mouth to speak, but only a sigh came out.

"I expect she feels like you've had to carry her a lot lately," Zebra observed, shrewd. "And maybe not just physically."

"That," Omega said, nodding. "It seems like every time I turn around these days, you're carrying me—literally, or metaphorically, through a mission."

"I don't mind. You know that, right? Hell, the good Lord knows you carried me emotionally through that whole mess with Ma's cancer. And you physically carried me to the car after I got shot last Christmas...though how you managed it, I'm still not sure."

"Adrenaline," Omega responded, wry. "An' lots of it."

"...Never mind looking after me when I got that compound fracture infected after we crashed our saucer, last spring," he continued. "By rights, I shouldn't even be here now. A couple times over." Echo reached out and gently nudged Omega's chin upward until he could look at her face. "It's called a partnership, baby. That's why we're a team. It isn't about keeping score, it's about supporting each other, getting each other's backs. Whichever one of us goes down, the other picks up, and we keep going."

"And you're a damn fine team," Zebra declared. "But no, Echo, I don't want you carrying her; it wouldn't feel good, that cast dangling from your arm, for either one of you. It's designed to flex, but not THAT much! Grab an antigrav chair for her on the way out; you can leave it outside her front door and bring her back in it tomorrow morning. I'll log that you've got it, so nobody goes looking for a missing chair."

"On it," Echo said, and they headed out.

* * *

"Once again, we're grabbing sandwiches in the den instead of the nice dinner at the restaurant where I had reservations," Echo sighed, as he and Omega sat on her couch and ate; he ensured her foot was propped comfortably on some pillows on the coffee table while they did so. "At least I thought to call and cancel, right after I called Fox from the theater. I'm sorry, Meg. This mission is hosing our dates bad."

"It's okay, Ace," Omega murmured, chowing down on her sandwich, which Echo had made for her, and which was loaded with ham, smoked turkey, and roast beef, Swiss and provolone cheeses, significant quantities of lettuce and tomato—but no onion; they were both out—on hoagie rolls plastered with mayo and mustard. As hungry as she was, Omega thought it tasted delicious, and said as much. "It's food, it tastes awful good, and I'm starved."

"Yeah, I know, baby. But eventually I'm gonna get to see that blue dress on you for more than five minutes as you head to bed."

"I take it you like blue."

"On you? Hell yeah."

190

"We'll manage it eventually," she decided. "I gotta admit, though...tonight, I'm really tired. Like, I almost gotta think to breathe, tired."

"That stands to reason, baby. And Zebra warned me to expect it, but I'd already figured it would happen. See, you had an adrenaline rush going for the performance, so you didn't feel the pain so much. You had it, you just couldn't consciously feel it. Now, you're coming down off the performance high, the adrenaline is fading, an' you're gonna be hurting pretty bad, pretty soon. And pain will wear anybody out."

"Ooo," she realized. "So I really DO need to hurry up an' get this in me, get in bed, and take the pain meds."

"Bingo. I mean, don't bolt it or anything, but don't dawdle, either."

"Okay."

* * *

They concentrated on eating, then Echo grabbed the disposable plates and napkins he'd chosen to use, chucking them in the trash, while Omega rose stiffly, grabbed her cane, and hobbled into the bedroom.

"Are you gonna need any help changing?" Echo called through the barely-open door.

"I don't THINK so," came the answer. "It's a good thing I changed into workout shorts today before we headed for the theater, 'cause it was so hot outside; I can get 'em off over this cast thing. But I left the door partway open, just in case. I figure if I fall over, I'll yell and you'll come running."

"Exactly." Echo moved near enough to the door to burst through if he were needed. He had his own bedtime prep to make, but wanted his partner safely in her own bed with medication in her, before he started on that.

"I'm glad I took my makeup off while sitting at the dressing table at the theater, though," floated through the doorway. "I'd hate to think I had to stand at the vanity and do it at this point."

"Hurting pretty bad now?"

"Gettin' there awful damn quick, yeah."

Echo heard some rustling, then the sound of uneven footsteps padding across the carpet, accompanied by a few grunts.

"Okay, you can open the door now," she called. "I'm gonna try to brush my teeth, here, then pile into bed."

Echo pushed open the door, to find Omega clad in her usual pajama top...and boxer shorts, brushing her teeth right inside the bathroom door. He cocked his head and raised an eyebrow. She took his meaning, but since she had a mouthful of foamy toothpaste, she held up a finger in a *hold it a second* gesture.

"Well, we're sharing a bedroom again," she pointed out moments later, after spitting and rinsing her mouth. "And I might haveta get up and do something in the night, in which case I'll be loopy an' you'll be guiding me. So I figured I might as well be nice an' not flash ya."

"Not that I'd mind," he said, giving her a wicked smirk. She flushed, then offered him a sheepish grin. "Still getting used to that idea, huh?"

"Um, a little, yeah." She shrugged. "I mean, I know by now you've seen...well, probably most of me, at least...and maybe one of these days, I'll...I'll show you more, but...I'm still shy."

"I know. I understand, honey," he offered, moving to the recliner—which was now in the corner by the closet—and adjusting its position so he would have a better view of the bed in case she tried to get up. "And I'm reserved about that sorta thing too, remember. I'm just teasin' ya. I kinda wanted to get your mind off your foot for a few seconds, if I could; your forehead's all puckered up from the pain."

"Yeah. Okay." She grabbed her cane, propped on the vanity. "Here we go."

Echo came to her side and helped her ease across the bedroom and into bed. He noticed when she cast a glance at a certain pink resin block, in which was imprisoned a red rose, but said nothing. Next to the resin block was a small bud vase on the bedside table; he was pleased to see it held a stargazer lily and a scarlet hibiscus—both surprisingly fresh, given they were several days old, and he suspected she had put some sort of preservative in the water. But she did nothing more than look.

*Still,* he decided, *there's a couple marks of her sentimentality where I'm concerned, sitting right there, I think. She's got the flowers I put in her hair—for our first date, and for her debut party—in the vase, and she's taken enough care of 'em that not even the hibiscus has wilted yet. And that cube is the rose I brought to her in the medlab back at Valentine's Day, all preserved. With...* He broke off, and surreptitiously studied the resin cube while, exerting considerable effort, Omega clambered between the covers as he held them open. *Damnation. Is that a LIP print on the top?! She's KISSED it?! YES!*

Somehow Echo managed to damp down the jubilation to undetectable-by-an-observer levels. Omega settled into bed, only partly reclined, and a secretly-delighted Echo tucked the covers around her, very gently.

"There. How's that?" he asked, affectionate.

"Fine." She offered him a tired smile, and he could see the fond gratitude in it.

"Now the meds. Lemme fetch a carafe and a glass. I'll be right back."

Echo headed across Omega's quarters to the kitchen, where he'd already prepared a carafe of water with its matching glass, having done so as he was preparing dinner. He grabbed it and carried it back into the bedroom, setting it on the nightstand, then fished the prescription bottle out of his pocket.

He sat down on the edge of the bed and read the dosage instructions, while Omega poured herself a glass of water. Then he extracted two pills.

"Open up."

Omega opened her mouth and stuck her tongue out slightly. Echo carefully placed both pills on her tongue; she retracted it and raised the glass to her mouth, washing down the medication.

"Bleh," she muttered, smacking her lips and tongue. "Yuck."

"Yeah, it's meds; stands to reason it'd taste like meds. All right, we got it down the hatch," he observed, as she scooted all the way down into a prone position. "You stay right there while I go get my shit outta my bedroom and bring it all over here. I'll put on shorts and a tee in your bathroom, then brush my teeth, and pile up in the recliner for the night."

"Okay."

Ten minutes later, Echo was ready for bed, and put his cell phone on the small table that had been placed next to the recliner by Facilities, along with an extra bedside table lamp; none of it was part of Omega's usual décor, so he assumed Zebra had ordered the lot like she'd suggested, thereby ensuring that Echo had something to work with while he cared for his injured partner.

After they had finished dosing medication earlier, he had moved the carafe with glass to Omega's dresser, where they were within reach but she was unlikely to knock them off with a groggy hand, and now he set the pill bottle on this new side table, next to his cell phone.

There was also a packet of his favorite snack crackers and a water bottle that he usually kept by his own bedside, in case he woke in the night with the munchies. Not long after being shot the previous Christmas, he had gotten up in the night, headed for the kitchen for a midnight snack, but had missed the bedroom door; the loud thud as he ran into the wall had awakened his partner all the way in her own bedroom. Omega had come running, and found a confused Echo, doped on his own pain medication, trying to find the door by the faint nightlight, his eyes barely open.

Fortunately for the modesty of both members of Alpha One, he had been wearing a pair of lounge pants, as he had stayed up too long after taking the pain medication, and Omega had had to get him TO the bedroom, to begin with.

She had gotten him back into bed, then scurried into his

kitchen and fetched him a bottle of water and a packet of the very same snack crackers, and made him stay in bed while he ate. Belly satisfied, he had all but collapsed onto the pillow, out like the proverbial light thanks to the powerful medication. Omega had apparently tucked him in, then returned to her own bed, leaving what was left of the water and crackers on his nightstand. She had teased him over the incident the next morning, especially upon finding that he was neither bruised, nor recalled any of it. But the event had resulted in the habit of keeping water and the crackers on the bedside table, ever since.

*It made a certain amount of sense, after all,* he realized, looking at the packet of crackers. *I never have been exactly awake when I get up in the night; even X-ray used to give me grief about it. And now turn about's fair play,* he decided, glancing at her bed.

Echo sat down in the recliner, arranged his covers, shoved his pillow behind his head, and addressed his partner.

"How ya doing over there?"

"Reeeaaal good," Omega drawled, her voice badly slurred, very Southern, and incredibly cheerful. "'M not feelin' no pain no mo.'"

*No no no,* Echo thought as he desperately stifled a laugh. *Not now. Not when she's finally outta pain. Don't do it, Echo. Keep your mouth shut. Do NOT laugh.*

"Great," he told her, switching off the lamp; the orange nightlight kicked in, suffusing the room in a soft, warm glow. "There we go. Time to kick back and get some good sleep, you an' me. You sound nice and relaxed."

"Ohhhhh yeaaaaaah."

This time a snort got past him. He clapped a hand over his mouth and nose, trying to stifle any further noises.

"Awright, go 'head an' laugh," she told him. "Ah kin hear mah own self an' Ah soun' worse 'n drunk. 'S damn funny." She giggled at herself.

"Um, yeah." Echo bit his lip; no matter how adorable it was, he flatly refused to laugh at the woman he loved, merely because she was legitimately high on much-needed pain medication. *The relief from pain must be huge, if she's this relaxed now,* he decided.

"But it feels sooo good af'er hurtin', Ace," she said then, confirming his suspicion.

"I bet, baby. I'm real glad you feel better, sweetheart. Lay down there and go on to sleep now, okay? I'm right here, and other than maybe goin' to the bathroom myself, I'm not goin' anywhere."

"Hokay..."

And she was asleep.

* * *

Echo pushed back in the recliner and raised the footrest, settling in. He could hear his partner's soft respiration across the room, and he smiled.

*That was as cute as could be,* he thought to himself. *Zebra advised us right, to get her in bed before taking that medication! Wow, I don't think I've ever heard Meg that looped before. But she was hurting a good bit by the time she got in bed, so I'm really glad it stopped the pain.*

*I wonder if she's gonna be up to a performance tomorrow night,* he wondered. *If not, I'd better be prepared to call Mike and tell him to cancel the performance first thing tomorrow after visiting the medlab, though I'm sure the producers won't like refunding all the money for the tickets. But they'd like it even less if something bad happened to her—or to one of the other cast members—all because Alpha One couldn't be there, and they had a performance anyway...though I dunno who would play the female lead, without Meg. Well, we'll see how she's doing in the morning, I guess.*

He cast one last glance at the shadowed, sleeping form of the woman he loved, then relaxed, letting himself drift off to sleep.

* * *

*Echo was standing in the wings, watching Omega sing, and utterly enthralled by her voice, when Michael's disembodied*

196

*voice—as the Phantom—echoed in the theater.*

*"Ah, my dear, I have you now," he declared, and laughed. "Die! Die! DIE! And I shall have your partner soon!"*

*A clanking and clattering came from the flyspace above the stage, and abruptly, the giant prop chandelier fell...*

*...With Omega directly under it.*

*"NO!" Echo screamed, lunging forward.*

*But an army of Marcies and Jakes grabbed his arms, his legs, holding him back.*

*He could only watch in horror and grief as Omega was crushed beneath the chandelier.*

* * *

Echo woke with a start, panting, in a cold sweat. Darkness surrounded him, only faintly illumined by the orange nightlight, but he knew he was not in his own bed. *Where am I...?* he wondered briefly, before memory returned. *Oh. Meg's bedroom. Her foot. Right.*

He eased the footrest down as quietly as he could and sat up, casting the covers aside, as he tried to school his rapid respiration into a more normal rhythm. With an effort, he got his sleepy eyes to focus on the bed. The body in it seemed okay, but the dream had been vivid, detailed...and intensely disturbing. *Way more so than my usual dreams,* he considered. *That was almost like a flashback...except it hasn't happened. Please God, may it NOT happen.*

But he decided to revert to his practice when he did have a flashback dream, so he rose and moved to the side of Omega's bed, studying her face, her body, by the faint glow in the room. He bent and brushed her hair from her face, so he could verify that she was in no pain...just as the vibrate-mode on his cell phone caused it to buzz on the table and alerted him to the fact that it was time for more pain medication.

"Mmph," she mumbled, and turned over. "Ace? Tha' you?"

"Yeah, baby, it's me. It's time for your meds."

"Hokay."

In the aftermath of the Cortian debacle last winter, when

Echo had been suffering from PTSD after being forced to watch Omega burn under the Cortians' ion drive, they had had to use several different techniques to overcome his traumatized responses; these had included long talks with his partner, among other things. One of these techniques had been the replacement of her bedroom lamp.

At the counselor's suggestion, Omega had swapped out her usual lamp with one that had a dimmer control, so that, if Echo had what he took to terming, "A bad dream, but not a full-up nightmare," he could come in and check on her without having to wake her up, thereby quickly proving to his subconscious that she was all right. This had had the immediate effect of settling his nerves, and eventually the dreams had quit occurring. But she had never gone back to the old lamp.

So he made use of it now, raising the light levels just enough to see the room clearly. She pushed up in a wobbly fashion as he turned up the light on the bedside lamp to its lowest level, poured a glass of water, and got out her meds. Once again she opened her mouth, and he placed the pills on her tongue, offering the glass to her and helping to steady it this time, as she drank. Moments later the pills were on their way to her stomach, and he took the glass from her and set it aside.

"Wha's wrong?" Omega asked then, rubbing a fist in one eye.

"Huh?"

"You look...upset."

"Um...yeah, a li'l bit." He sat down on the edge of the bed. "I, uh, I had a bad dream."

"Dat face you got looks more like it was a nigh'mare, hon."

"I guess."

"Wasn' da Cortian mess, was it?"

"No."

"Wanna talk?" she offered, still groggy, but apparently observant. "Or you jus' gonna sit dere an' monosy-monosyllable on me?"

Echo sighed.

"It's only this mission," he admitted. "I dreamed the chandelier fell on you."

"Oh." Omega shrugged. "It's hokay, Ace. I'll be fine."

She held out her arms and urged him into a gentle hug; it was a gesture that was open enough to be mildly out of character, which told him the medications had lowered her reserve. *But that means it's coming from the heart,* he decided, so he accepted...and abruptly found himself holding her tightly.

"I'm just...it was really vivid, baby. More like...like one of my flashbacks, than a regular dream. Except it was something that hasn't actually happened."

He shook his head, and forced himself to ease back and release her. Then he wondered if he only imagined the disappointment on her face.

"Huh." Omega cocked her head to one side, as if thinking.

"What?"

"Iss just," Omega began, slurring her words even more as the medication kicked in again, "'member how I had th' bad dreams b'fore Slug attacked? Th' ones 'at turned out t' BE Slug?"

"Yeah?"

"They 'uz like that, sorta. Made me think of it."

And she pole-axed backward, into the pillow, sound asleep.

*Uh-oh,* Echo thought, even more concerned. *Why don't I think that's a good thing?*

* * *

Having obtained her permission for such things months previous, in order to help him get over the PTSD after 'the Cortian mess,' as she tended to term it, a still-badly-perturbed Echo now chose to use another of the coping techniques: he gathered his sleeping partner back up in his arms, pulling her into his lap, and held her for long moments, until he settled in mind and heart. His counselor had brought Omega into one of the sessions and recommended it, as replicating Echo's physical reaction to the sight of her charred body, when he had initially thought her dead—he had pulled her into his lap and cradled her gently, grieving and in shock. Eta wanted to try to replace the emotions of that memory with an awareness of her living, healthy body, overwriting the horror and grief. Omega had been touched by the realization, and promptly agreed, but it had worried Echo...though not for the reason that Eta or Omega thought at the time.

This was only the second, or perhaps the third, time he had ever done it, outside of that session with Eta; it had been entirely too revealing of his feelings for her, for him to risk it, except in the most extreme cases. And she had been soundly asleep each time; he preferred not to disturb her if he could help it. *After all,* he had thought at the time, *it's better if ONE of us is sleeping, at least. And she's already told me that she doesn't mind.*

But now, he considered, she knew how he felt, and he felt freer in acting on it. He tucked his face into her hair, breathing her scent, listening to her respiration, and feeling her body's warmth against his own, letting the sensations soothe him until he was calm once more.

Then he tucked her back into bed, dimmed the lamp to black, and returned to the recliner, kicking back and putting the dream firmly away from his thoughts.

Both members of Alpha One slept soundly the rest of the night.

* * *

The next morning, Echo let Omega wake on her own; he woke at his usual time, checked on her, then slipped out of the bedroom to use her kitchen to make breakfast, leaving the bedroom door wide open to listen for movement. Unsure when she would wake, however, he decided simply to put in one of their premade-and-frozen breakfast casseroles to heat—he could keep it warm in the oven until she was ready to eat it, however long it took.

Then he moved to the dining area and laid out plates and silverware, popped back into the kitchen and started a pot of coffee—he expected she would need it, the way that medication was kicking her ass—and generally made sure all would be ready whenever Omega was.

About the time the casserole was properly heated through, he heard Omega start to stir in the bedroom. He cranked the oven down to <warm>, then headed into the bedroom.

* * *

Omega was just sitting up when he entered.

"Oh man," she muttered, rubbing her hand across her face and up into her hair, "what hit me?"

"Well, depending on your point of view, a prop, a fly-rail weight, the stage, and Zebra's meds, in that order," Echo told her with a slight smile, as he moved to the bedside. "Although, arguably, it could be said that you hit the prop, the weight, and the stage, I guess."

Omega just glared at him.

Echo laughed, then bent and dropped a light kiss on her lips.

"C'mon," he said. "I got breakfast ready for you, with a whole pot of coffee; I figured you might need it. And then I want to get you dressed and back to the medlab for Zebra to check out. You can shower and junk when we get back after that."

"Okay," she agreed. "Lemme see how I do here, on this foot, first."

"Fair enough."

Omega swung her legs off the bedside and grabbed her cane, as Echo moved into position to assist. Seconds later, she was upright, her cane in one hand and Echo on the other side, steadying her.

"That looks promising," he decided. "You don't look like you're hurting. Are the pain meds still working?"

"I dunno," Omega considered. "I don't feel groggy, particularly. But lemme tell ya, I don't remember much at all last night, after you gave me the first dose."

"What about telling me you were feeling better, as it kicked in?"

"I...think I maybe remember that, yeah. I sounded awful loopy."

"Just a little, maybe. Do you remember me waking you for your next dose? And chatting with me?"

"Nope. Not a thing. Sorry, Ace." Omega offered him a wry expression. "It wasn't intentional, I assure you."

"No offense taken, baby," he noted, thinking, *I only wish you remembered the discussion about the dream, and your remarks.* "Given the way you pretty much toppled back into the pillow afterward, I can't say I'm surprised."

"Oh..."

* * *

After a substantial breakfast, Echo laid out some basic clothing for Omega, ducking out long enough for her to dress. After that, he got her settled on her couch in front of the TV, while he disappeared into his quarters long enough to shower, brush his teeth, and throw on some jeans and a t-shirt. Then he came back to get her and take her to see Zebra.

The medical antigrav chair was still in the hallway, nestled against the wall between their front doors, so Echo put Omega in it and pushed her to the medlab.

"After all, we gotta get it back anyway," he pointed out, as he pushed. "And it ensures you don't put weight on that foot for very long until Zebra can have a look."

"I'm not complaining," Omega observed. "As busy as I've been with the show, I don't mind the rest."

"Good."

* * *

"Oh, this looks much better," Zebra noted, as she examined Omega's foot and ankle. "All those hairline fractures are closed up, so we just have to get the soft tissue inflammation down, and I think this'll be good, guys."

"Lotsa protein and...calcium?" Echo wondered. "In her meals, I mean."

"Yeah, but broaden that to minerals in general," Zebra said. "We want to keep them in proper balance for good, solid remineralization in the bones. In fact, I'm gonna give Omega a special supplement to help with that. Don't worry," she told Omega, "I've heard about the stage fright; I'll make sure it's easy on the tum. No sense in making you MORE prone to barfing your poor guts out."

"How did...?" Omega began, wide-eyed.

"Um, me," Echo confessed, shamefaced. "I figured she needed to know, before I brought you in last night. I was afraid you were losing nutrients that would make healing harder. I'm sorry, baby; I breached your confidence. But I felt like I HAD to."

"No, it's okay, Ace." Omega offered him a smile. "I was gonna ask about that very thing anyway, I just didn't know how she found out before I could say anything. You haven't, um, mentioned it to Fox, have you?"

"No," Zebra averred, drawing a hand across her heart. "And I won't, unless you expressly tell me to."

Echo crouched beside Omega, as she sat in the exam chair.

"Baby, will you do something for me?" he asked.

"What?"

"Have Zebra tell him. He won't tell anybody else, but I really want him to know what you're going through. As far as I can tell, you're going above and beyond the call, an' all that shit, and I want him to know."

"You want him to give her a commendation, don't you?" Zebra analyzed, that shrewd look on her face again.

"It had occurred," Echo admitted. "If he doesn't put her in for one, I probably will."

"I don't want or need one, you know that, right?" Omega murmured, dropping her gaze. "I'm not sure I deserve one. Not for barfing up my toes every night, 'cause I'm afraid to go on stage to begin with."

"Omega, look at me," Echo ordered, but gently. She glanced up, meeting the dark gaze. "Courage is not about doing something that doesn't scare you, that doesn't bother you. Courage is being terrified, scared half to death...and doing it anyway."

"Listen to the man," Zebra declared. "He is absolutely right. Besides, Fox needs to know stuff like that, so he'll know how much you can deal with. He's told me he never wants to load too much on his agents. He says it's one thing to be stretched to your max in the course of a mission. It's another to be broken because you couldn't withstand the load you've been given. He never wants to accidentally break one of his agents because he didn't know they'd reached their limits. And," she added, "he already knows you've been through hell recently, and haven't figured out how to get counseling for it. And no, I'm not fussing," Zebra told her, keeping her voice low and compassionate. "I started in on Echo last night, when he called me to give me a heads-up that he was bringing you in, and he cut me off and gave me a few things to think about, evidently based on some talks you two have had. So I think I understand where you're coming from, now. I've been trying to figure out a way for us to make it work, but I haven't puzzled anything out yet, either."

"Let her tell Fox, baby," Echo reiterated. "Please. For my sake, if not your own."

An uncertain Omega glanced back and forth, from one sincere face to the other. Finally she nodded.

"All right," she agreed in a quiet voice. "Tell him. But I don't want it getting around that I get stage fright or something."

"No, and I agree with that," Echo averred. "If I'd stopped and thought the other night, I wouldn't have come remotely close to mentioning it. But you're right; it could undermine your authority as the Alpha Line assistant chief if people think you're a coward just because you get stage fright. Besides, what it really is, based on what you've told me, is a kind of free-floating energy, as you gear up for the performance; it seems to go away as soon as you set foot on stage. Or rather, you can then channel it INTO the performance."

"Ooo," Zebra murmured. "That makes sense."

"It does," Omega confirmed, "and it really is. But YOU

TWO understand that, and Fox will probably get it; not everybody would."

"Right," Zebra confirmed. "I'll tell Fox, but nobody else, and make sure he keeps his mouth shut. Which I doubt would be a problem anyway, because he's gonna see that potential for abuse, too."

"Okay. What about the performance tonight?" Omega wondered. "Do we need to cancel it, or can I go on, or...?"

"Echo said you had special steps and stuff, for injured performers?"

"Yeah."

"Okay. Then I want you to do those for two more days. Echo, I want you to see to it that she does some therapy exercises I'm going to give her, for that same two days; they're not strenuous or exhausting, they're more about flexibility and maintaining everything in proper alignment. After that, unless you're still having pain, Omega, you'll be good to go back to a regular performance. If you're still having pain, come back to see me."

Zebra moved to the pharmaceutical cabinet and began dispensing some pills into a small prescription vial.

"Leave the cast on until you get ready to head for the theater this afternoon, then take it off; you can probably leave it off at that point, but if you come home and you're hurting or it feels kinda 'out of whack'—you know what I mean; if it feels off some way—it wouldn't be bad to sleep in it one or two more nights. You shouldn't have much in the way of pain in the meantime, but if you do, take one of these. Not more often than one every four hours, though. No," she anticipated by the look on her patient's face, "these won't make you loopy at all; I know you need to have your wits about you for this mess. It's a stronger, oral version of what Echo gave you last night to get you through that performance." She handed the capped vial to Omega, who tucked it in a pocket. "Now let's see about showing you those therapy exercises..."

* * *

Zeta had arrived the day before at the Los Angeles Office, and Mu was helping her get settled into her quarters, which were adjacent to his and connected via a back door, not unlike Alpha One's joint quarters.

"How are you doing?" Zeta asked, her voice soft. Mu slit the packing tape on another box and opened it, extracting items and handing them to his newly-assigned permanent partner.

"I'm okay," he noted, somewhat flat.

"You miss her."

"...Yeah." He shrugged. "Not that it really matters. I doubt she's missing me much."

"Aw. Have you been exploring L.A. at all?"

"A little. Fox sent me out here with some leave time before I had to report for duty."

"That was nice of him."

"Yeah."

"Maybe you can show me around. I've never been to the West Coast before."

"You'd probably be better off getting one of the locals to do it," Mu told her. "I barely remember where I went."

"Did you go to Disneyland? One of the studios?"

"I...dunno. I think I did one of the studio tours." He shook himself. "Listen, don't mind me. I'm...still trying to figure shit out. That's...why I don't remember. I spent the whole time thinking, and the 'playing tourist' was just for show, in case Fox asked Juliet how I was doing, or something."

Having emptied that box, Mu turned and reached for another. Consequently, he missed seeing the forlorn expression that crossed Zeta's face.

* * *

"Well, how's about, when we get done here, I fix us a nice, homemade dinner?" she wondered, pasting a cheerful smile on her face as he turned back around with another of her personal items. "Then, afterward, we can go down to one of the beaches or something and look around? Or take a drive up the coastal highway? Just us two? Maybe go to Disneyland on our next day off..."

"If you want to," Mu murmured, pulling out a stack of books and handing the lot to Zeta.

*Ow,* Zeta thought, trying not to wince. *This is gonna take patience, and time. And even then, I dunno if he'll ever sit up and take notice. The 'Omega bar' might be too high for me to reach. She's somebody special, and I'm...just an ordinary human.*

She sighed, accepted the books, and moved to the bookcase to shelve them.

* * *

The rest of the day, according to the plan in Echo's head, would be spent resting and working out the kinks in Omega's musculature from her tumble. As soon as they got back to their quarters, Echo contacted Michael and ensured everyone knew that Alpha One would be at the performance, but that 'due to stiffness and a few muscle strains,' the modified footwork and blocking would still be in effect for a couple more days.

Then he helped Omega get set up for a shower; Zebra anticipated their needs, and had Facilities leave an adjustable-height shower stool for Omega. Echo positioned it in the shower, then started the water, tweaking the tap until the water flowed at a comfortable temperature, while Omega gathered her robe and other items, placing them on the vanity within easy reach. Then Echo took her back into the bedroom and sat her on the bed, unfastening and easing off the tall boot cast, which had been intended to stabilize her entire lower leg; he tossed it onto a corner of the bed, to be donned again later. Omega grabbed her cane and hobbled into the bathroom with his help.

Echo slipped back into the bedroom and closed the bathroom door, leaving his partner to strip and shower in privacy. Meanwhile he foraged through her closet and dresser, and fished out suitable clothing for the day, all the way down to bra and panties, laying it all neatly on the end of the bed. Then he moved over to the closed bathroom door, hearing the water now running somewhat irregularly inside, indications of a body under the flow. He rapped lightly on the door with his knuckles.

"Hey, baby, you makin' it okay in there?" he wondered.

"Yeah, Ace, I'm doing all right," came her answer. "I'm glad for this stool, though. I was afraid I'd slip and really mess things up."

"Ooo, that woulda been bad, all right," he agreed. "Is everything in reach? Do I need to help with anything?"

"No, I'm good. Don't go far, though. I'm a little afraid of slipping when I get out."

"Roger that. I'll park my ass in the recliner and wait for you to yell if you need me."

"That works."

* * *

It took Omega longer than usual to shower, but that was to be expected, in the circumstances. When she was done, and the soapsuds sluiced away, she turned off the water and opened the shower door, to find that Echo had closed the toilet lid and spread a fresh towel over it before leaving; it was waiting for her as a makeshift seat. He had also spread a clean towel on most of the floor that the bath rug didn't already cover, ensuring wet feet would not slip on the tile.

She reached for one of the towels on the shower door rack, wrapping her hair in it, then gingerly eased herself from the stool in the shower stall over to the terry-draped toilet. The transfer proceeded without incident, and Omega reached for the second towel on the rack, beginning to dry her body with it. Once she was mostly dry, she picked up the tub of body cream that sat on the end of the vanity, and worked the cream into her skin, noting a couple of bruises that had showed up from the fall. But they were already starting to fade under the influence of Zebra's treatments.

"You still doing okay in there, baby?" Echo's muffled voice came through the door. "You're not having trouble slipping and sliding, are you?"

"No, everything is fine," Omega agreed. "You got everything laid out real good. It's only, well, I'm movin' kinda slow, as we used to say about the astronauts who got space-sick. I'm fixing to put my robe on and try to come out. My hair's still in a towel, though. I might need a little help combing it out and doing something with it."

"Are you that stiff?"

"Well, a bit, I guess. My shoulders are less than happy; I found that out trying to wash my hair."

"Are they injured? Does Zebra need to have a look?"

"Nah, they're only a little stiff. I tried to catch myself at first, instead of rolling with it, when I tripped. Got some bruising in a few places, too, but it's fading already."

"Okay. Well, I can't do that fancy braid-thing you do, but I can comb it out for you, and maybe help you get it in a basic ponytail."

"That'll work. I'm not picky. I'm just glad I'm still able to get around. Hang on a sec." Omega pushed herself slowly into a tentative upright stance, then slipped the black silk robe over her naked form, belting it firmly, and reached for her cane.

* * *

Echo was well aware that Omega was wearing nothing but the silk robe, and in different circumstances he might have spent a few seconds to appreciate the fact, but he set the thought aside in favor of being useful, given her decreased mobility. So he helped his partner over to the bed, then stepped out of the bedroom while she dressed, remaining close in case of difficulties. Once she called, he came back in and eased the cast back onto her foot and lower leg. Then he pulled the stool out of the shower, drying it off and placing it in front of the vanity, raising the height so Omega could sit on it and look into the mirror.

"Here," he said, as she appeared at the bathroom door, and pointed at the stool. "Park it."

Omega sat down in some relief, and Echo hooked the cane's handle over the doorknob to prevent its inadvertent escape, while she towel-dried her hair as vigorously as she dared, given her shoulder discomfort.

"No, baby," Echo said, seeing what she was doing. "Here, let me do that."

He took the towel from her and wrapped it around her hair, scrunching and squeezing to absorb as much water as he could. Then he gently tousled her hair with it, ensuring her hair was only damp by the time he was through.

"There," he decided, running testing fingers through the platinum strands. "That's a lot better. Let's get this combed out and into a ponytail for you."

So she fished a wide-toothed comb from a drawer. "Here," she murmured, and handed it to him.

"You want it parted someplace?" he asked, accepting the comb.

"Nah," she decided, pulling out a wad of hair elastics from the same drawer and extracting one, laying it on the vanity, then replacing the others. "Just comb out any tangles, pull it all back from my face, smooth it down a little, and tie it off."

"Okay."

Echo wielded the comb with his usual dexterity, gently combing out Omega's hair and secretly enjoying working with it; the silky feel of it in his hands was decidedly sensual, and he had no problem concentrating on the task. All too soon, he had her hair pulled back in a sleek ponytail, high on the back of her head.

"Thanks, Ace," she told him.

"You're more than welcome, honey. Now, is it gonna air-dry properly, like that?" he wondered, handing the comb back to her.

"Yeah, it'll be fine. In the summertime, I usually let it air-dry, so I don't have to fool with it," she told him, returning the comb to its drawer, "even if I braid it. It's generally pretty wavy when I take it down, but sometimes that's kinda fun to play with."

"Okay. Maybe I can play in it sometime." Echo glanced

at his wrist chronometer. "It's almost lunchtime. How about I plunk you back on the couch and go fix us some lunch? We got several different frozen casseroles I can pull out and heat..."

"Cottage pie!" she decreed cheerfully.

"How did I know you were gonna say that?" he declared with a smirk. "Okay, cottage pie it is. Maybe with a small salad on the side. And afterward I'll throw the dishes in the dishwasher, then it'll be getting close to time for me to put on my Suit."

"All of that works for me. But," Omega added, as she eased off the stool and reached for her cane, "are you sure you don't want me to, I dunno, drag a stool in the kitchen and help?"

"Nah. I'm just gonna pull it out of the freezer and throw it in the oven," Echo pointed out, shadowing her into her den and getting her seated on the sofa. Omega promptly turned slightly, lifting the injured foot and stretching her leg along the seat of the sofa; Echo pulled her throw off the back of the sofa and spread it over the injured leg, wanting to keep it warm and flexible. "There. I may—or may not —throw together a salad to go with the pie; I haven't decided yet. While the casserole is heating, though, I thought I might use my massage training to see if I can't help you work out some of that stiffness. Would that be good?"

"Yeah, THAT would be really nice," Omega decided. "I got stiffness in places I woulda never thought."

"I would," Echo noted, shaking his head. "I saw you fall. Damn, baby, you rolled, like, three times. And then didn't move for a few seconds, there. I wasn't sure what you'd done to yourself. Or what I was gonna find once I got to you."

"Ugh."

"Yeah. Okay, lemme go get lunch started, then I'll come back and see about limbering you up."

"Then after lunch, you need to get dressed and probably run down to the Alpha Line Room and see if anything needs doing," Omega suggested.

"Oh, good point," Echo realized. "We've been outta the

office, you an' me, for several days now. Will you be okay here alone, while I do that?"

"Sure. Put the remote in reach and I'll watch TV, or maybe read."

"Looks like I have a full afternoon."

"And I'm gonna rest," Omega declared.

"Which is exactly what you need to do," Echo agreed.

* * *

Alpha Line proved to be in good shape; Alpha Two had been filling in with Fox's help, while Alpha One was on assignment.

Echo returned to Alpha One's joint quarters in time to watch one of his favorite movies, sitting on the couch cuddled with a relaxed, slightly-sleepy Omega—she had been napping while he was dealing with department matters—before it was time to help her get ready for the performance.

# Chapter 8

When they arrived at the theater that evening—sans leg cast—Echo escorted Omega straight to her dressing room, where Cecile was waiting to help her; the petite young dresser was worried about her 'Miss Meg,' and insisted upon being there to help with more than simply attire. With an affectionate smile, Echo left the two women to their work, and he headed out on his routine loop of the theater environ.

First he swept the dressing-room areas, and ascertained that all was as it should be there. Then he swung through the costume shop and the prop room, where the appropriate tech crews were already hard at work. Backstage—now lacking Jake's little 'love nest'—appeared secure, as did the fly-rail area; the fussy brake showed fresh signs of work, and a shiny, brand-new part had been installed. Echo got one of the fly-rail techs to show him the repair work, and the brake now appeared to be much better than it had been.

*So far, so good,* he decided.

He headed for the front of the house.

* * *

"Oh!" Omega said, as she reached for her makeup kit. "I almost forgot."

"Forgot what, Miss Meg?" Cecile wondered.

"Well, Echo expressed some interest in my makeup last night, and I was gonna offer him the chance to help me put it on tonight, by way of learning more."

"Do you want me to find him?"

"Um, no," Omega decided, worried that the smart young dresser would figure out too much, if she came upon Echo sweeping the facility. "I know where he should be; I'll run find him real quick. It won't take long. You go ahead and get the costumes sorted out."

"All right, Miss Meg. Be careful, and don't hurt that foot again."

"I think I'll be all right, but I'll be careful."

* * *

Omega grabbed her cane and headed out into the theater, systematically checking each location for Echo. After a few minutes, she heard his voice, conversing with a woman out in the audience area.

"Who's he talking to?" she wondered to herself. "Nobody should be allowed in the house yet; it's nowhere near time for it to open."

She slipped up to the edge of one of the curtain 'legs' screening the stage left wing, and peeped out.

* * *

Echo was systematically checking the house, one row of seats at a time, looking for anything out of the ordinary, when he looked up and found a certain ex-chorus girl waiting for him at the end of the row.

*Damn,* he thought in intense annoyance. *What the hell does she want? I thought she was supposed to be outta here.*

"Hi there, handsome," Marcie said with a seductive smile. "I do hope Miss Margaret isn't hurt too badly. It was only a practical joke, you know."

"The hell you say."

"No, really! I never meant to hurt anybody," the uncommonly-poor actress lied; Echo could see her eyes darting this way and that as she extemporized. "It was just a little hazing joke. We do it to all the new cast members, and I drew the short straw this time."

"Uh-huh," Echo said, disbelieving. "Then why didn't any of the other cast members mention that?" He made to push past her to continue his sweep, but she caught his arm and clung to it.

"Seriously! Look, I know 'Sir Ego' made a point of getting me in bad with the producers, but I'm sure you could help me out; you're an agent, right? You're Ms. Stratford's agent! I was thinking, if you represented me, it would be worth your while, you know—I only took this gig until a better one came along; I was the leading lady in the production earlier in the summer! Besides...” She smiled, a sly, provocative expression, sliding her hand up the inside of his arm toward his chest as she arched her back to lift her 'assets' and make her somewhat minuscule chest more prominent. “...I'm sure I could find a way to make it...more interesting...for both of us. By way of a little thank-you. You know what I mean.” Her hand slithered from his arm to his chest, trying to slip inside his Suit jacket.

Echo's other hand moved like a striking cobra. He snatched her wrist in a firm, tight grip and yanked it away from his body, holding it out and rotating his forearm from the elbow until his palm faced upward; this had the desired result of forcing her to move away from him in an awkward effort to avoid having either her elbow or shoulder—or both—dislocated as her arm was twisted. She squirmed, as her body arched clumsily.

“STAY. AWAY. FROM ME,” he declared, in no uncertain terms. “I'm not interested in the likes of you! Meg is my girlfriend, I'm happy with things that way, and a little hussy like you can't hold a candle to her! You're lying, and it's obvious. Quite aside from the fact that that means you're a terrible actress, after what you did to Meg, I wouldn't represent you for all the gold on the planet!” he snarled.

Echo raised the fingers of his other hand to his mouth, and delivered a piercing whistle, which he repeated twice. Within seconds, a pair of armed, uniformed security guards burst in from the lobby, weapons at the ready.

“Lady and gentleman,” he addressed them, “this woman is not supposed to be here. Not only was she escorted off the premises last night with orders not to return, she was just harassing me. Perhaps you'd like to take her to see Signore Ormond, if you please? He may have some ideas about what to do with her.”

“Yes, Mr. Williams,” the man said, as he grabbed Marcie's upper arm from Echo; the other guard grabbed her free wrist.

"Come this way, miss."

"But we were discussing business!" Marcie protested.

"No, we weren't," Echo declared, "because I have no business to discuss with you."

And the guards marched her out.

*　*　*

Echo stood and watched her go in some satisfaction.

"That little stunt ought to piss off Ormond enough to get her a nice interview with the cops," he decided. But before he could turn and resume scoping out the house, he heard applause from the stage. He spun.

Omega stood near the edge of the stage, applauding, a huge grin on her face. Her cane was hooked over one arm, and her stance was even and comfortable, he saw to his relief.

"Nice job, Ace," she told him, as he moved down the aisle toward the stage. "Really, really nice. She looked like she'd been hit upside the head with a two-by-four, and all you did was pull her hand off YOU. I expect Ormond will call the cops, now." She shook her head. "And it couldn't have happened to a nicer person."

"Ain't that the damn truth," Echo grumbled. "I'd have reacted sooner, but I honestly couldn't believe she was pulling that shit on me. Do I look that stupid?"

"Nope," Omega vouched. "She did."

"Oh. Right. Well, that's kind of a relief, I guess."

"Yeah. I, uh, I especially liked the line about the little hussy not holding a candle to your girlfriend..." Omega offered him a slight smile. Echo grinned back.

"Well, she can't."

"To Meg Stratford, anyway, I guess."

"To any version of you, baby. For instance: her entire nervous system doesn't have the same mental capacity as half of one side of one lobe of your brain." He shook his head. "Her voice sounds like she's been gargling gravel, and you sound like an angel. Never mind looks. She's...coarse and, and common. You're...gorgeous."

Omega blushed, but smiled.

"Why, thank yuh, kind suh," she murmured, kneeling on the edge of the stage as he leaned up to plant a tender kiss on her lips.

"You're always welcome to that," Echo told her. "What are you doing out here, though? Shouldn't you be back in your dressing room, getting ready?"

"Yeah, but I came looking for you," Omega noted. "Last night, you expressed an interest in my makeup, and we'd discussed continuing the lesson tonight. I wanted to know if you still wanted to."

"Well, shit," Echo grumbled, checking his wrist chronometer. "I would be interested, yeah. But that little incident with Marcie ran me late; I'm still not done sweeping the place. And now I wanna go back and double-check the fly-rail, to make sure she hasn't had access since grabbing that weight last night..."

"No worries. Go finish your sweep. We can do it tomorrow night."

And they parted, Omega to return to her dressing room, Echo to finish scoping out the house and the lobby, as well as double-checking the fly-rail.

* * *

Echo ascertained that Marcie had not had access to the fly-rail since the previous evening, given that the technicians didn't leave the evening before until after she was known to have been escorted out, and they had been working on it all day, since early that morning. So he was satisfied with that; he had taken the opportunity that afternoon to check out all of the techs with Juliet, the chief of the L.A. Office, and verified they were all legitimate and trustworthy.

Then Sofia showed up.

* * *

"Oh, THERE you are, Alec!" Sofia said, taking Echo's arm just as he reached Omega's dressing room. The door was open, as Omega had been expecting him, in full anticipation that he would want to at least watch her apply her makeup; he managed a surreptitious eye roll at his partner, who bit her lip. "I am SO interested in what you're doing! I want to follow you ALL around tonight, and learn from an expert!"

"I'm...not sure that's a wise idea, Sofia," Echo tried. "It could be dangerous."

"Oh, I'm sure YOU'LL keep me safe," she purred, caressing his arm. Echo closed his eyes and drew a deep breath.

"I also have to keep Meg safe, and try to find this 'phantom,'" he pointed out.

"Oh, don't you think Meg can take care of herself?" Sofia wondered, apparently trying for ingenuous...and failing, at least as far as Echo was concerned. "After all, isn't she your partner? Surely she can handle it."

"Please keep your voice down, Sofia," Echo warned. "We're supposed to be undercover, after all."

"Oh, riiight," Sofia murmured, dropping her voice. "All very hush-hush; I get it. But I'm sure Meg can take care of herself, while you show me the ropes."

"Actually, it's a bit much to expect her to handle her role AND keep an eye out in all directions," Echo noted, turning and leading the diva away from Omega's dressing room, aiming for Michael's. "That's one reason I'm here, to begin with. As her partner, I'm responsible for watching her back."

"Surely, just for one night..."

Echo knocked on Michael's closed door. "Mike? You in there?"

The door opened abruptly.

"Right here, Echo," Michael said. "Is everything all right? Oh—Sofia! What are you doing here?"

"Well, hello, Michael, darling," Sofia simpered. "I'm here to let Echo show me around and teach me about what he does."

"I've just been trying to explain that it could be dangerous, Mike," Echo interjected smoothly. "I have to watch Meg's back, and after last night..."

"Oh, yes, I'm sure," an understanding Michael said, easing

into the breach. "Sofia, dear, this is probably not a good time for it; you may not have heard, but there was a little...incident... last night..."

Despite her reluctance, Michael resolutely drew his sometime leading lady into his dressing room, nodding at Echo just before closing the door.

Echo drew a deep, relieved breath, murmuring, "Thank You, God...and Mike," before turning and heading back to Omega's dressing room.

* * *

"...You farmed her off on Michael?" Omega wondered, as Echo watched her apply the last of her makeup.

"More or less," Echo agreed. "In a polite sort of way. She seems to have gotten the idea that I'm available."

"Well, let's face it," Omega said, concentrating on applying mascara, "you really are."

"Then you haven't been paying attention."

"Oh, you know what I mean," Omega pointed out. "It isn't like we're permanently attached or anything. We're not life partners."

"Yet."

"...And she's pretty, and talented, and successful, and all that stuff," Omega said, outlining her mouth with lip pencil, then picking up a pot of lip color and a brush. "And she's got normal human genetics, and doesn't have a lot of telepathic mental baggage dragging behind her."

"And you're beautiful, and talented, and successful, and you've been all over the galaxy," Echo noted. "And you've got way cool skills, and you're interesting, and you don't play head games with people, and I don't CARE about the genetics, and we'll eventually figure out how to get you some counseling to deal with the shit you've been put through."

"Whatever, hon." Omega diligently focused on applying lip color.

"Look, Meg, there's something you're not thinking about," Echo said, trying to break through her insecurity. "What does

219

Sofia do for a living?”

“Duh. She acts and sings on Broadway.”

“And how much notoriety does she get?”

“Um...a lot.”

“And what is Fox going through to ensure you do NOT get a lot of notoriety and attention, to protect your status as an Agent, and keep anybody from your old life from recognizing you? Never mind the wig and makeup an’ junk. Do you have any idea how hard he’s worked to ensure that you aren’t being mobbed by the press and paparazzi? Did you know there’s a contingent of field agents set to sweep the theater district every night you perform, to head off any reporters from *Variety*, or that TV entertainment channel? Or hell, the entertainment section of one of the local newspapers, for that matter?”

“...Oh.”

“And what would it mean for any Agent who became involved with Sofia? Because there’s not really a lot she could do WITHIN the Agency, so we can’t ‘draft’ her like we did you.”

“Oh,” Omega repeated, then paused and looked at him, blue eyes wide.

“So I’d have to do a full-up retirement, complete with brain bleach, and learn to like it, if I was gonna be her ‘significant other,’” Echo pointed out. “And I’m not remotely interested in retiring. I enjoy working beside you, and running Alpha Line, way too much to consider that. Never mind our plans for the Ranch and the Farm, one day. Presumably AFTER I head the Division, and you head the department, for a few years...or decades. Never mind the possibility of me semi-retiring and YOU becoming Director for a while, first.”

“Really?” Omega offered him a shy smile. “I mean, about enjoying working with...with me, an’ junk.”

“Really,” he told her, as openly sincere as he knew how to be. He returned her smile, then wiped his lips with the back of his hand before dropping a light peck on her cheek. “There. I didn’t smudge your makeup or anything.”

She laughed.

"That's better," he noted, right as the stage manager gave the five-minute call. "And that's MY cue. Break a leg, Angel-voice. I'll see you backstage."

* * *

Act I went off with its usual aplomb; the fly-rail brake still slipped a little, to the annoyance and chagrin of the techs who had worked on it, but otherwise, there were no untoward incidents.

Echo met his partner in her dressing room during intermission, checking her ankle and foot before ensuring she had no need of pain medications.

"No, Ace, I'm doing pretty good," Omega decided. "Whether it's Zebra's doctoring, or the adrenaline for the show, or both, I dunno. But I'm not hurting."

"Good. Still, let's put that foot up for now," he said, pulling the extra chair around and easing her leg across it. "It could still swell, and that wouldn't be good for it. Do I need to go get you another bottle of water?"

"No. Cecile has been keeping me hydrated. There's a supply in the...I think it's in the back of the prop room," Omega informed him. "A fridge or something, where bottles of water are kept for the cast. If your throat dries out, it's bad for singing in general, and can damage your vocal cords."

"So that's where all those empty plastic bottles have been coming from, after all the performances," Echo realized, waving at the small waste can in the corner. "I knew the thing was always full after the show, but I never noticed you drinking..."

"That's because they're the little bitty four-ounce things, and I can down 'em in about two seconds," Omega said with a grin. "But that's all I need at a go. She usually brings me one with each of my costume changes, and I chug it while she's unfastening or fastening, and be done."

"Okay. Good. You're staying hydrated, at least."

"Yup."

"Places for Act II," Adam murmured on the intercom.

"Okeydokey, here we go again," Omega said, lowering her foot to the floor, standing, and fluffing out the skirts of her elaborate costume. "Catch you backstage, hon."

"You got it," Echo said, cheerfully accepting her light kiss, and not worried in the least about any lipstick she might have left behind.

* * *

The costume party scene was, as always, a spectacle. Omega danced and sang her way through it surprisingly well, given her foot and ankle; Echo smiled as he watched from the offstage-left wing, the barest hint of what might have been pride in his demeanor as he remembered how hard she had struggled to learn it—never mind coping with the modified blocking and steps. He eased around the cross-over to meet Omega as she exited the stage in the offstage-right wing, verified that she was still in no pain and doing well, and remained there for the subsequent scene.

The 'correspondence' scene following the costume party elicited laughs initially, as usual, but when Michael's disembodied voice, as the Phantom, echoed through the theater with its menace, Echo felt an uncharacteristic chill run down his spine. *That...sounds all too much like last night's dream,* he thought in foreboding. He dismissed it as the stage darkened for the scene change.

When the stagehands cleared the stage, the lights came back up. Habitually, Echo glanced around, checking his surroundings. Out of the corner of his eye, Echo noticed the huge setpiece catwalk begin to sway overhead, hidden from the audience among the battens and curtains in the flyspace, but visible from his position backstage. His attention focused on it. Then he saw the cables suspending it. He glanced back down at the stage, to see Omega alone—directly beneath the catwalk.

"Oh, shit," he whispered. "There's no way she can make it in time!" He began to run.

But before he could reach the stage proper, he heard the sharp *SNAP!* as the cables parted on one side. An earsplitting metallic screech—that ended abruptly—denoted the failure of the fly-rail brake on the other side.

"NO!" Echo shouted. Omega turned at his shout...

* * *

Omega was preparing for her solo in the second act when she heard Echo's murmur through the subcutaneous transponder, but since it seemed to have no bearing on her, she ignored it, assuming it was an aside comment to a stagehand. Then she heard the loud, gunshot-like report above her, followed by the shrill scream of failing metal. Before she could react, she heard Echo shout, "NO!" and Omega spun on instinct, to see him sprinting toward her, faster than she had ever seen Echo run before. He glanced upward, and she followed his gaze into the flyspace overhead, then frowned, confused; her mind temporarily refused to grasp why the catwalk appeared to be growing larger.

Omega watched, stupefied, as Echo made a desperate, flying leap. He caught her in midair, carrying her downstage with him, as the huge catwalk crashed to the stage floor mere feet behind them. Omega landed hard, beneath Echo, who spread out to cover her protectively as cables slithered down. Frightened screams rang out from the audience. Quickly, shocked stagehands closed the main curtain.

When all was still, Echo raised his head and stared down at his partner, dark eyes wide with horror.

"Meg? Are you okay, sweetheart?" The words seemed to burst from Echo.

"F-fine, Echo. I, I just got the wind knocked out—"

Suddenly Omega felt her lips covered and her mouth taken in a fierce, sweet kiss. Simultaneously she felt her Winchester & Tesla pressed into one hand, though how Echo had known where she had stashed her warp pocket containing the weapon, she had no idea—let alone how he had reached it through all her costuming. The all-too-brief kiss ended abruptly, and

Echo was standing beside her, helping her to her feet, even as frightened stagehands and cast members came running to see about them.

"Go to your dressing room and lock yourself in until I get there," he ordered in a low voice. "Now. I'll be there soon."

"Be careful, Echo," Omega said, clutching his sleeve, and he nodded.

"Always. Get going, Meg."

The two Alpha Line Agents moved swiftly in opposite directions.

* * *

"Meg, it's me," Echo said, as he knocked on her dressing-room door, knowing his voice would be audible to her through both the door and the transponder. Fractions of a second later, she unlocked and opened the door for him, as he removed the headset. He saw to his relief that Omega had gotten out of her constricting costume and wig, and into her gym clothes, by that time; she would be far more able to handle an emergency situation without the voluminous skirts and petticoats of her costumes—which had been one of his concerns in her taking the role.

Echo pushed the door closed and locked it securely, and the two Agents stood there looking at each other wordlessly for a long moment. Then suddenly, they were in each others' arms, and Echo bent his head to his companion's, watching the sapphire eyes flutter closed, as he covered her lips with his own. Omega moaned softly as her lips parted in invitation. Echo accepted the invitation with a sigh, closing his own eyes and tightening his arms around his partner, as Omega's fingers laced themselves into the dark hair at the nape of his neck. No gentle urging, this; it was possibly the most intense, most passionate kiss Echo had ever shared.

At last Echo ended the kiss, but instead of releasing her, he slipped one hand up into her upswept hair and pulled Omega's head to his shoulder, closing his eyes again.

"Damn, baby. I thought I wasn't going to get there in time," he said in a low voice. "I knew you couldn't really run yet with that foot and ankle, and I thought I was gonna watch you get crushed, right in front of me. Just like I did in that damn dream, last night. Which I'm starting to think wasn't a dream at all." Abruptly he released her.

"That was no accident, Meg," Echo said then, controlled fury hidden behind a businesslike demeanor; no one but his partner, and possibly his Director, would have recognized the intensity of his anger in those moments. "The support cables had been heavily nicked on one side, then the catwalk set to swinging. The stress snapped the damn cables, and the weight of the whole catwalk on one fly-rail cable was more than the compromised brake could handle—it's busted, fifteen ways from Sunday. And then I found this." He handed her a note. "It was attached to the catwalk."

Omega glanced at Echo, then read the computer-printed note. It was succinct.

*E—you're next.*

"Not an A with a period this time," she observed. "It's an E. With no period. Like the abbreviation of your code name."

"You noticed that too, huh?" he growled.

"Yeah. Which means this time, it was somebody who knows who you really are. Somebody who knows who WE really are."

"Exactly. I've already called it in. Along with the notion that the idea for tripping you up last night MIGHT have been planted in the bitch's mind, in order to set you up with an injury that would have prevented you getting out from under, tonight."

"Ooo. Good point. Not that she wasn't already predisposed."

"Yeah. Anyway, Fox wants us both out of here A.S.A.P.," Echo informed Omega. "Like he pointed out, more and more it's looking like you an' me could be the real targets...which is what Slug told you, your first night onstage. So India and

Romeo are coming in to finish investigating tonight. The rest of the performance is cancelled. So is tomorrow's performance." He shook his head. "They got repairs to do, anyway. To the fly-rail system, to the catwalk setpiece, to the stage boards..."

"I kinda figured," Omega remarked. "So I changed out of that darn period dress into something where I could help you better." She gestured at her leggings.

"The only help I need right now is for you to faint."

"What?" Omega asked, confused.

"The leading lady just fainted from shock and fright. Her lover is going to carry her away from the danger and take her home."

"Oh, I get it," Omega said with a smirk. "This is our extraction cover."

"You got it."

"All right. Ready?"

"When you are. No, wait. We want everybody to be able to hear this." Echo unlocked and cracked open the door by almost a foot. "Okay, go."

Omega groaned loudly, closed her eyes, went limp, and toppled forward. Echo caught her and let her sag against him, then he cried out.

"AH! OH, NO! Meg? MEG?! Say something, honey! Oh, dammit! Wake up, sweetheart! Help! Somebody help!" Echo bent slightly to gather up Omega in his arms and carry her; she lay still in his gentle embrace. He kicked the door open, making as much noise as he could, and carried her out into the corridor, where several actors and stagehands met him, attracted by his cries.

"Oh!"

"Oh, no!"

"What's wrong?"

"What happened now?!"

"She must have fainted," Echo explained, voice and expression conveying intense worry. "It was a helluva scare, what with that damn catwalk nearly crushing her. I'm getting her outta this blasted cursed theater and taking her home, where she'll be safe." He moved toward the backstage exit, carefully bearing his 'helpless' burden. Outside, stagehands helped him get a limp Omega into the passenger seat of the Corvette and strapped in, and stood in concern, watching as the two Agents drove off.

* * *

Several blocks away, Echo turned to his partner.

"Okay, Meg, you can 'come to' now."

No response.

"Meg?"

Still no response.

"Shit, Meg, don't play games with me; I'm not in the mood for it. That was a helluva close call," Echo said irritably, jabbing her in the shoulder with his index finger. Omega sat up with a start.

"Oh! I'm sorry, Echo; I must have dozed off after you put me in the Corvette," Omega apologized sheepishly. Echo studied her in concern.

"Meg, are you sick or something?"

"No, Echo, my sleep patterns are just hosed up, what with the last month of...shit. My stupid body doesn't know when bedtime is."

"Are you sure? You nearly get pancaked, and then fall asleep?? Damn, I thought I was cool in a crisis."

* * *

"Yeah. And you've still got the market cornered on cool, don't worry. I just went out 'cause I closed my eyes too long—I really am kinda tired, an' I think maybe there's still a little of last night's pain meds in my system. I noticed I didn't have quite my usual energy during tonight's performance, despite my best efforts. That was a lot of fun, being carried out like that," Omega changed the subject. "That was probably the most fussin' I've had over me since I was a kid."

"You liked my performance tonight, I take it?" Echo grinned.

"...Yeah," Omega said, suddenly uncertain of the veracity of specific events that had occurred earlier in the evening, given his blanket, rather comprehensive, wording. "There go Romeo and India." She pointed at another black vehicle as it passed in the night. "What's on tap now? I guess dinner and dancing are out...again..."

"Right. We go home, grab a bite—sandwiches again, I guess, dammit, or maybe another casserole—and wait to see what Romeo and India turn up," Echo told her.

* * *

*'Performance,'* she thought, as Echo concentrated on driving. *He called it a performance. How MUCH of it was a performance? Was the kiss in the dressing room part of the performance? What about the one on stage, where everybody could see? Maybe...both of 'em were an act. It would sure make sense, in the context. After all, he's had members of the chorus constantly coming on to him, the whole time; it would sure help reinforce the cover story that he and I are lovers. I notice nobody's tried to hit on ME, though. Surprise, surprise.*

*What if all of it was a kind of a performance? Even the other day, when he told me he was interested in me from a romantic standpoint? Maybe what he really wants is just that whole 'partners with benefits' thing that I wondered about at first. Like, for when he's in between girlfriends or whatever. After all, I pretty much flung myself at him, at The Beach, a few weeks ago. Maybe he figures he's doing us both a favor or something.*

Omega shot a considering glance at her partner, who seemed as absorbed in thought as she was. He did shoot her a querying look, however, modifying it with a meaningful glance at her foot; he raised his eyebrow, and she nodded in reassurance. Echo nodded, smiled, and returned his attention to the road.

*Surely he really cares, though,* she pondered. *At least to SOME degree. I think even his smiles are warmer, more affectionate, since we developed our 'thang,' as he gets a kick out of calling it. But,* she realized, *wouldn't he call it something different if he were really serious about it growing? I don't wanna be nothing more than his fall-back, when he doesn't have something better going.*

"Baby?" he asked then, shooting her another look, and seeming deeply concerned. "You're awfully quiet over there. Are you sure you're feeling okay?"

"Yeah, Ace, I'm okay," she asserted. "I was...kinda thinking over the evening's events, I guess you could say."

"Good." And he shot her a warm, brilliant smile, the dark-chocolate-brown eyes conveying what looked to her like a hint of desire. Omega could have sworn her insides flip-flopped with yearning.

She spent the rest of the trip to Headquarters trying to determine how she could find out what Echo really wanted from her...without embarrassing herself in the process.

* * *

Echo dropped Omega at her quarters, telling her he was going to the Agency research library to check on something, and Omega wandered around the apartment for a few minutes, smiling happily, still floating from the effects of that last smile Echo had given her. She went into the bedroom and replenished the water in a certain small bud vase on the bedside table; it held a stargazer lily and a scarlet hibiscus, right next to a certain pink resin cube containing a red rose. Gradually an idea formed, a way of determining exactly how serious Echo really was about their romantic relationship, and she decided to act on it.

Omega went into her kitchen and prepared a simple, elegant supper, instead of the basic sandwiches Echo was expecting. Then she got out her mother's china and set a formal table for two, dimming the lights in the dining room area, and placing two taper candles on the table.

She took a luxurious soak in the bathtub rather than a shower, then slipped a set of black silk lounging pajamas—India had convinced her to purchase them at the same time she got the turtleneck evening dress—over equally silky skin, leaving her hair down. Then she waited for Echo.

And waited.

And waited.

Finally she called his cell phone.

"Echo? It's Omega. Is everything all right?"

"Fine, Meg," Echo's voice sounded absent, distant. "Whatcha need?"

"Nothing," Omega replied hastily. "You just hadn't come back for dinner, and I wondered if I needed to meet you, maybe give you a hand."

"No. I can handle everything fine by myself."

"Oh..." Omega winced, thankful he wasn't there to see. "Well...are you gonna be long? I've got dinner ready, and, well—"

"Oh, no, Meg, don't wait on me. Go ahead and fuel that supercharged metabolism of yours. I'm checking out some things here in the library, then I'm going to the Core, to have Lima or Bravo pull up some stuff for me, whichever one is on duty. I'll probably be a while. I'll see you in the morning."

"Oh," Omega said again, face falling. "Okay. Good night, Echo."

"'Night, Meg." Echo hung up.

*Not Angel-voice,* she thought, staring at the phone as her heart sank into her toes. *Not even baby. Just plain ol' Meg. I guess it really WAS an act—all of it. But I thought...the other night, and earlier tonight...but what would he want with a half-alien...thing...like me, anyway? Echo deserves better. Maybe he really meant it, to a point, only he just kinda wants me around when he's between girlfriends or something. I'm...convenient, I guess. And after all, there was that whole mess at The Beach. So he probably figures I'd enjoy the attention, especially after watching me get dumped by Mu.*

"I give up," Omega sighed, finally defeated. "It's all pointless. I should have known better...I DID know better. I simply...let myself get encouraged, get my hopes up, when I should have listened to India to begin with."

Appetite evaporated, she cleared the dining table, put away the food, hung the silk pajamas out of sight in the very back of the closet, and went to bed.

* * *

Omega dragged herself out of bed the next morning only with some difficulty. The foot and ankle were stiff—she had forgotten the therapy exercises the night before, in all the various forms of excitement—but functional, and she ran through the exercises to work out some of the stiffness before doing anything else. She showered and dressed in a Suit, then drifted into her living area, flipping on the television and staring at it listlessly from the couch. After a while, Echo wandered in.

"Morning, Meg," he greeted his partner with a gentle smile as he came through the back door.

"Morning." Omega's voice was flat, expressionless. She didn't look up, but continued staring at the TV. Echo paused, studying her.

"You got breakfast ready?"

"Oh—no." She still didn't look up.

"Well...want me to fix something, then?" He moved over to the couch to stand beside her.

"No. I'm...not very hungry."

"Meg...are you SURE you're okay?" Echo's brows drew together. She looked down then.

"I...yes, I'm fine, Echo." Omega stood just as Echo bent over her; the lips intended for her forehead found only air, and he frowned. "I guess I'd better finish getting ready," she said, headed for the bedroom.

"Meg?"

"Hm?"

"Are you...feeling sick?"

"What do you mean?" Omega stopped in the bedroom door.

"Is...your stomach upset, for instance?" Echo studied her intently.

"No..."

"But you are tired."

"Well, yeah."

"And not sleeping well."

"Right."

"And you've thrown up almost every day for several days now..."

"Yeah. Echo, where are you going with this?" Omega puzzled.

"Meg," Echo said softly, "come back over here and sit down." Echo sat in the corner of the sofa; Omega joined him, and they faced each other on the couch. "I need to ask you a really personal question, baby. I know it's gonna embarrass you, and it ain't gonna do me any favors there either, but it's important, trust me." Echo leaned forward, resting his forearms on his knees. Omega's forehead creased, and she watched him, mystified.

"Okay..." she murmured.

"Meg, where are you in your cycle?"

"What?!"

"Let me try it another way: Could you be pregnant?"

"Echo!! What are you saying?! I don't—I haven't—" Omega was appalled. Echo took her shoulders gently.

"Meg, I know you haven't. But Wright sexually assaulted you. He wasn't successful in fully raping you, but that doesn't mean..." Echo's face drew in pain. "And you WERE under the influence of some really powerful...biochemistry. I mean, given the genetics and all, I have to wonder...how effective the birth control...I mean..."

* * *

Echo broke off as Omega went white to the lips.

"Oh no...oh, dear God, no...please..." She drew her knees tight to her chest, wrapped her arms around them, and rested her forehead on them. "No no no no no no no..."

Echo's eyes narrowed in sympathetic pain; instinctively he drew Omega against him. With that one caring gesture, Omega suddenly came completely apart emotionally. She turned to him, burying her face in his shoulder and sobbing hysterically;

she had cried fiercely some weeks earlier, at his beach house in Ipswich, from the stress of the stalking and near-rape, but that had been mild compared to this panic-stricken response. Echo merely held her, his eyes closed, pain etched in his face, and let her cry, venting the agony, the horror and fear.

Slowly the sobbing subsided. A silent Omega, drained of strength, simply rested against Echo.

"Meg...what will you do?" Echo whispered then, very gently.

"I...don't know." Her voice was hollow, devoid of emotion.

"Terminate?"

"I...I don't believe...I...God, help me..."

"I didn't think you would." Echo nodded. He paused for a moment, suddenly uncertain. "Meg, if...well, I wanted to... dammit." Echo stumbled to a stop, paused and gathered his words, then plunged ahead. "Meg, if you're pregnant, you're going to need help, and the baby's going to need a father figure." Gentle fingers lifted her chin from his shoulder. "Meg, I'm here. I'll help, I swear. We can...we can apply for a life partnership and merge our quarters. We can add a nursery; you've seen from Alpha Two's quarters, life partners get bigger combined living spaces than individual agents. Our quarters as life partners will be a little bigger than both our quarters now, put together...especially if, if there's kids..."

"Echo, that's sweet, and...and I appreciate the, the magnitude of the offer, but...it's SO much harder than that. Way the hell more complex." Omega began to cry again.

"What do you mean?"

"Echo, if I really am..." Omega couldn't bring herself to say it, "and if Mark Wright is the biological father, then I have to make the most awful choice imaginable: Kill my child, or let my child kill you. Because, sooner or later, it will try."

"Oh, shit," Echo breathed, "I forgot all about the programming."

"Right. A genetically-programmed assassin whose sole purpose for being is to kill you." She patted her belly. "It won't be human, Echo. It may look human; I don't know. But it will really be a murdering alien monster." A brokenhearted Omega thought then, long and hard. "Neither option is...acceptable..."

"Meg, either you have the baby, or you don't." Echo looked puzzled.

"Not necessarily," Omega replied, as enigmatic as Echo could be. "Look, Echo, go ahead and call India and let's get the suspense over with, okay?"

* * *

India thoroughly examined Omega in her bedroom. An anxious Echo paced, alone, in Omega's living area, worried sick over his partner's condition. Eventually India emerged from the bedroom; Echo stopped dead.

"False alarm," India said succinctly. "I've got to admit, it had me worried when you told me. Because you're right—the symptoms really looked like it. But the hormonal component isn't there, and there's no sign of a blastocyst, or even a zygote. So...no, she's not pregnant. It's only massive stress and stage fright, coupled with severe and ongoing disturbances to her sleep cycle, just like she figured originally."

Echo relaxed noticeably, even as a tidal wave of relief flooded his being.

"Thank God," he murmured under his breath, fervent. "How's Meg doing?"

"She's...okay...I think. Echo, she asked me for some...really strange favors."

"What do you mean?"

"First, she asked me to promise that I wouldn't tell anyone if she was pregnant—even you."

Echo's eyes narrowed, then closed. He sighed in disappointment and hurt.

* * *

"Then, she asked if I would think about trading partners temporarily and let her help Romeo complete the crash investigation at the theater." India noticed Echo suddenly avoided eye contact at the mention of 'trading partners.'

"...Shit. That's asking for trouble."

"That's what I told her. I also said it was a real gamble. She answered, 'Exactly.' Then it got even stranger."

"I'm listening."

"She wanted me to promise that, if anything 'happened,' I wouldn't let any of the medics try to resuscitate her."

* * *

With a slight, horrified exhalation, Echo froze, his jaw slack; then he turned away. *Oh dear God,* he thought, trying not to visibly cringe. *So that was her alternative solution. I dunno if it's Scylla and Charibdis, or rock and hard place, but she found a third way. If she dies, there is no baby. Of course, I'm not sure I can keep going without her, so it might all end up moot.*

"Echo?" India probed. "You know what that was all about, don't you?" Echo refused to respond, unwilling to breach his partner's confidence. "Echo, tell me."

"India." The brusque voice came from the bedroom door. The two Agents spun to see a closed-faced Omega, wrapped in her robe, standing and watching. "It's no one's business but mine." She gave both Agents stern stares. "And it's no longer an issue anyway."

India nodded slowly, beginning to comprehend.

"Meg, maybe the medics might have..."

"I know, India. Maybe. Operative word being 'might,' not 'can.' I was...investigating options."

"I...understand. Do you need me for anything else?"

"No, India," Omega's voice softened, "not at the moment. Thank you."

"You're welcome, Meg. I'm glad everything's okay."

"Me, too."

"I'm going to rejoin Romeo at the theater, then."

"All right. See you later, girlfriend."

"Bye, Meg."

* * *

Echo was silent through the entire exchange. As soon as

India left, however, he launched in.

"Meg..."

"Let it alone, Echo." Omega's voice held a warning.

"Meg..." Echo pressed.

"Echo..." She duplicated his tone. The corner of Echo's mouth curved up slightly.

"Meg..." he said deliberately. Omega noticed, and her lips twitched in amusement.

"Echo..."

"Mmmeeegg..."

"Echooooo..." Omega began to snicker, and Echo to grin.

"Meg..."

"Ech-ch-cho-ha-ha-ha!" Omega laughed aloud, venting tremendous stress. Echo came over and put an arm across her shoulders.

"That's a lot better, Angel," he told her, dropping a light kiss on her temple. Omega slipped an affectionate, companionable arm around Echo's waist, as her laughter subsided.

"Thanks, Echo," she said softly. "For looking out for me. For being there for me. And for...offering to be there through what could have been the biggest..." She broke off, not sure what to say, unable to find words to describe what would have been an horrific ordeal. "It would have been a nightmare for me. But you offered to help try to make it work. You're always there when I need you."

"Well," Echo replied, shrugging, "it works both ways."

"Not...really." Omega averted her face, withdrawing slightly. "I've never known you to truly 'need' anybody." She pulled away, as surprise and mild dismay washed through Echo.

"Waitaminit," he tried. "What about when Ma was dying? Didn't we talk about this the other day already?"

"Yeah, we did," Omega noted, blunt, "and I pointed out then, that while you needed a friend, it didn't necessarily have to be me. C'mon, let's go report in to Fox. He's probably been waiting for us in the Alpha Line Room for a quarter of an hour already."

"Yeah, he's gonna be annoyed," Echo agreed, putting aside his personal worries for the time. "And we've got some other appointments we need to keep, too."

"Okay. Let's get rolling."

# Chapter 9

Instead of Fox, however, virtually the entire Arcturan embassage awaited the Alpha One team in the Alpha Line Room off the Core, per Echo's request to Fox the previous evening. A wary Omega glanced around, suspicious; no one else was in the room, and one of the Arcturans quietly went to the door, closed, and locked it. Still, by her count, the embassage was short one person.

"Where's Tt'l'k?" she asked Ambassador Zz'r'p.

"He is not here, nor will he be, ever again," the tall, blue telepath told her, in his formal, benevolent way. "After his abhorrent behavior in dealing with you, Omega—the way he exceeded the Director's order and displayed such callous disregard for your and Echo's psychic privacy—it was decided he should be removed from the Arcturan embassage. He was sent home for medical treatment; we have every indication he is exceeding unwell, and that behavior was most likely a symptom of the disease. It does not excuse such behavior, but hopefully it helps explain it."

"You fired his ass," Echo interpreted.

"I should rather term it a...medical discharge...but yes."

"Oh," Omega remembered. "I'd forgotten, in the general hubbub lately. Yeah, I think I do recall Fox telling me about that, a while back. While I was...on leave, I think." She tiptoed around her reaction to how Fox and Alpha Two had feigned her partner's death in order to force an end to what was essentially a stalemate in the Wright situation.

"Yeah, me too. Good," Echo responded with grim satisfaction, understanding and allowing Omega the euphemistic reference. "Now, Zz'r'p, you and your people know about my dream the other night?"

"Yes," Zz'r'p confirmed.

"Wait. What dream?" Omega wondered, confused. "You said something about that last night, but I never had a chance to ask you about it..."

"Oh, that's right; you don't remember it, on account o' the pain meds. Okay. The night before last—the night you busted your foot—I had a dream," Echo explained. "It was as vivid as a flashback, but it wasn't a flashback, because it hadn't happened yet. And when it did happen, it wasn't exactly the way it was in my dream."

"I...don't get it."

"I dreamed I saw you getting crushed under the chandelier, Meg," Echo told her. "At the theater. And I couldn't get to you to shove you outta the way, 'cause there was a small army of Marcies an' Jakes in my way, grabbing onto me and shit." He shook his head. "And DAMN, was it realistic. Except for the small army, I guess. Then last night, it happened almost exactly the same way, except it was the catwalk setpiece, and there wasn't anybody around me to stop me getting to you...thank the good Lord."

Omega blinked for several moments, startled.

"Whoa," she finally murmured, concerned. "That sounds a LOT like...like Slug's initial probes of me, last year, before he began his end game."

"What she said. And exactly. So I also guess y'all know about Meg's theory?"

"Yes, Echo. Fox discussed it with us already." Zz'r'p nodded.

"Is it possible, then?" Omega asked, deeply concerned. "Is it reasonable that Slug's psyche may still be...on this plane of existence? Or is it a half-baked idea?"

"It is just possible," Zz'r'p admitted, as his companions nodded agreement. "There are techniques for placing...nd't'lq... how shall I translate? Psychic twin? Pieces of the mind? ...into another being. Upon physical death, the rest of the psyche may then follow, if that is the telepathic being's wish. But we are not certain it could be done surreptitiously, without the host being's knowledge."

"Why?" Echo asked.

"Two reasons," Kk'q'r, Zz'r'p's colleague and an expert on the subject, replied. "First of all, it is nearly impossible to accomplish without the host's active permission."

"Cooperation, one might even say," Zz'r'p added.

"And the second reason is that it typically produces an... intense awareness...of each other in both entities," Kk'q'r finished. "There may be other techniques, somewhere in the Great Spiral, that the Deltiri do not know but that Snails do. But we have discussed it among ourselves, and we feel that nd't'lq placement is the most likely to suit your situation...or at least, to be an analog of that situation. It would require an actively-cooperating host, however, so you would need to look for such a one."

"I don't get it," Echo muttered to himself.

"I'm not sure I do, either, Echo," Omega told him quietly. The diplomatic team took a moment to conclave telepathically, then Zz'r'p turned to Alpha One.

"Perhaps a demonstration is the best way," he suggested. "I would not propose it if I did not know of your mutual trust and closeness. But Omega now has sufficient telepathic ability to accomplish it, with some assistance in refining the technique. And Alpha Line's history has already proven a loose telepathic bond exists between you."

"You're proposing Meg puts a piece of her head inside mine?" Echo verified.

"Something like that," Zz'r'p confirmed. "But it is not just a 'piece.' It is more like a 'clone' of herself. Her mental self."

"Hm..." Echo's brows drew together. Omega studied him only a moment before turning to the Arcturans.

"No." Her voice was firm. "Echo isn't comfortable with that."

"Actually," Echo murmured thoughtfully, "we could get rid of the damn headset and transponder, too..." He looked at

Omega as her shoulders drooped, and she sighed. "You don't have to do this, you know."

"Don't I?" Omega met Echo's eyes. "We have to understand, at least. And you're right, we could communicate instantly. Not to mention, if it really is Slug, I could maintain a telepathic block for both of us, like we talked about the other night." She turned away from her partner with another sigh. "Do it, Zz'r'p."

*Very well, Omega. Let me show you what to do.* Zz'r'p's voice sounded in her head. He then proceeded to illustrate the process for her.

*Oh, I get it,* Omega said, studying the concepts Zz'r'p showed her. *Like...this?* Somewhat awkwardly, she tried to duplicate his instructions.

*Very good,* Zz'r'p approved. *That is an excellent first effort. Let me help you refine your efforts only a smidgen, and it will be ready.* After a few moments of joint activity, Zz'r'p told her, *There. Now for Echo. Echo, can you hear me now?*

*Loud and clear, Zz'r'p,* Echo's voice said. *Is Meg here, too?*

*I'm right here, Ace,* Omega told him.

* * *

*That's funny,* Echo mused.

*What is?* Omega asked.

*Well...your thoughts kind of echo,* Echo observed. *You know, reverberate. Like there's...I dunno. A duplicate telepathic 'line' or something. Or two of YOU.*

*Good, very good,* Zz'r'p interjected. *You already perceive her nd't'lq, Echo. Now let her in. Drop your mental defenses.*

Echo obeyed, and Zz'r'p directed Omega deep into Echo's being. Omega was diffident, proceeding with extreme caution, fearful lest she inadvertently violate her partner.

*It's all right, Meg,* Echo told her then, sensing the source of her discomfort. *Relax. I trust you.*

*I'm glad you do, because I sure don't,* Omega replied.

*Then let's make it simple. Zz'r'p, how about this?* Echo

indicated a 'location' in his mind/being to the other two members of the link.

*Exactly where Omega's nd't'lq needs to be placed,* Zz'r'p confirmed. *Your instincts are excellent, Echo. But initially, do not open to her. Let her try to place it there without your help. Do not fight. Simply remain passive.*

*Okay...* They sensed his mental shrug. *Any time, Meg.*

*Umph.* Omega grunted mentally as she tried to reach the location in Echo's mind. *It's like...running into a rubber wall. Or a 'soft' force field.* She tried again to penetrate the appropriate part of Echo's mind. *Unh. I just bounce off.*

*Echo? Do you sense anything?* Zz'r'p asked.

*Yeah. I can...'feel' Meg bumping around in here. Kind of like a mental tickle,* he teased.

*Oh, hush, you,* she told him. But Echo and Zz'r'p could both sense her mental smile, and shared their amusement. *Behave, you two,* she reprimanded them both.

*All right, baby. I was just trying to get you to lighten up a little. You're too worried about me. It's all fine.*

*He is right, Omega; he is completely relaxed and unconcerned. And yet you cannot enter his deepest mind without his permission. Echo, is it not true that you could hold her at bay indefinitely like this, with little or no effort?* Zz'r'p asked.

*Yes, I think so,* Echo mused. Zz'r'p nodded.

*And her enhanced abilities, relative to yours as a non-enhanced human, are not small. Now, let her in.*

Abruptly Omega sensed an invitation from Echo, and she entered the recesses of his mind unhindered.

*Good. Now offer your nd't'lq, as I showed you earlier,* Zz'r'p commanded. Omega followed his instructions. *Now, Echo, you accept it.*

*What do you mean, accept it?* Echo queried.

*Take it in. 'Adopt' it,* Zz'r'p tried.

* * *

*You mean...* Echo said, and Omega suddenly felt a mental

sensation unlike anything she had ever experienced: Total, unquestioning acceptance of her entire being, right down to the smallest detail—her greatest strengths, and her deepest flaws, all accepted without hesitation. It felt something akin to a warm, gentle, very intimate embrace.

*Ohhh...* she sighed involuntarily.

*That is precisely what I mean, Echo,* Zz'r'p verified with a mental smile. *Now...*

"...back outside," Zz'r'p said. "There. Tell me what you experience now."

"Well, I definitely know he's/she's there," the two Agents said in perfect unison, then glanced at each other.

"Ooo, this is gonna be different," Omega murmured. "It's a lot...closer...than I expected."

"What she said," Echo agreed.

"Yes," Zz'r'p confirmed. "It can be very intimate. That is why, for Arcturans, it is the culmination of the wedding ceremony."

"What?" the two Agents responded simultaneously, startled.

*Echo, I didn't know—I didn't mean—oh, Echo, I'm so sorry,* Omega stammered mentally.

*Calm down, Meg, I already picked up on that,* Echo told her. "Zz'r'p—"

"No, Echo, you are not," Zz'r'p replied aloud to the yet-unspoken thought. "It is only a part of the ceremony, this is not Arcturus VII, and you are Terrans of Division One. Until such time as the Agency charter is amended to include marriage, it would not be binding even had we performed the entire ceremony. And yes, Omega, it is reversible. Echo, you can reject and expel Omega's nd't'lq at any time. Likewise can you retrieve it, Omega."

"Would it hurt Meg?" Echo asked, perturbed by the notion. "She seemed to...like it...when I accepted it..."

"Because it was effectively an acceptance, an affirmation, of her total being, and that is how she experienced it," Zz'r'p explained. "Yes, she will experience nd't'lq expulsion as... equally total rejection. I...am surprised."

"Why?" Alpha One asked together.

"Once it was established, I did not expect you—either of you—to consider breaking the bond."

* * *

Echo stared at Zz'r'p, who returned it, head cocked to one side, and Echo abruptly realized that Zz'r'p knew—completely—how he felt about his partner. Suddenly Echo sensed mental activity, and spun toward that partner.

"Meg? What are you doing?"

"Pulling out, Echo," Omega told him. "We understand the process now. There's no need to maintain the connection. And I have lots of experience in what it's like to be stuck with a telepathic link you don't want. I'm not going to do it to you."

Echo glanced meaningfully at Zz'r'p, who nodded. Then Echo looked back at Omega.

*Meg, you're projecting,* Echo told her telepathically.

*What? Why are you thinking at me?*

*Privacy. The Arcturans have blocked us off so we can talk. You're projecting, Meg.*

*I don't understand.*

*You're assuming I'm uncomfortable with this situation. I'm not. Not only is the link with my best bud, who also happens to be my girl and the partner I trust with my life, I think this is a really damn good way to fight Slug. It enables you to maintain a link between us without effort or outside help. If we'd had this before the catwalk fell, you would've immediately known what I saw, started moving in time to accommodate that bum foot, and been out from under by the time I could even make it onstage. You're the one who's uncomfortable, Meg. I don't blame you in the least, though; your telepathic experiences, by and large, have been...unpleasant, baby.* Echo directed sympathy and concern at her. *But, Meg, I swear to you I won't 'abuse the situation,' I think you put it the other day. Let's just try it for a little while.*

*I know you won't abuse it, Echo,* Omega responded, and Echo felt her absolute trust. *I just...*

*Meg, if I didn't trust YOU, I'd never have allowed the demo in the first place. I think I trust you more than I've ever trusted anybody in my life. And...you've never violated that trust. Ever.* Echo experienced the wave of warmth that suffused his partner at his declaration, and he smiled. Then a realization struck. *Meg?*

*Yes?*

*What are you afraid of? What are you trying so hard to hide?*

* * *

Omega reeled back from Echo's perceptive thought.

*Echo, don't go there,* she begged. *In less than a month, I've had nearly every aspect of my being laid bare to friends and strangers alike. Allow me what scraps of privacy I have left. Just know that I'll never willingly violate your trust.*

*I know that, Meg. And I'm not worried about it. That wasn't why I asked.*

*Why, then?*

*I wanted to help.*

That gave her pause.

*There's...nothing you can do to help, Echo,* she finally told him. *It's just...a hopeless situation, is all. A lost cause. From the very beginning. It's better that I bury it deep and...try to forget.*

* * *

*Meg? Is there someone—?* Echo felt his gut wrench.

*Don't, Echo. Please. Don't go there. I know you mean well, but it'll only hurt. Leave it be, for my sake.*

Abruptly, he sensed as Omega erected a mental wall, effectively ending the conversation without breaking the bond, as Echo had no idea how to circumvent it.

"All right, Echo, you win," Omega sighed aloud. "How long do you want to keep it up?"

Echo sighed as well.

"I won't add to your bad experiences, Meg," he told her. "If you want your nd't'lq out of my head, do it. Take it back. I won't try to stop you."

A puzzled Arcturan diplomatic team observed the exchange, bemused.

"It's all right. I do trust you, Echo," Omega avowed. Echo studied his partner, dimly sensing her struggling to eliminate the discomfort she felt.

*Are you afraid I'll accidentally run across something, and it'll embarrass you?* he mused.

*Yes,* came the immediate and unexpected response through the psychic wall, and Echo's eyebrow cocked.

*Are you afraid that IT will embarrass you, or that I will embarrass you?* he wondered.

*Both. Either. It doesn't matter; it's all the same in the end. But the only way YOU could embarrass me would be accidentally,* she told him. *I know you'd never do it deliberately.*

"So...wait. You can 'hear' me through the firewall block thing you put up?" he asked out loud.

"Yes, if you're 'talking' to me."

"Directly or indirectly."

"Yes. I think you were only wondering to yourself just now, but you directed it at me," Omega explained. "I thought I'd answer for you."

"So I can also hear you if you're 'talking' to me." He cocked another quizzical eyebrow.

"Right."

"But not otherwise."

"No. Except some...sensation, some emotion...will probably still filter through." She shrugged.

"Are you comfortable with that?"

"More or less," Omega hedged.

"Well...can you live with it, then?" Echo rephrased.

"Yeah, I guess so."

"Okay, then let's try it this way for a while. Can you put up a protective block around both of us?"

"Let me see..." After a few minutes of concentration, Omega turned to the familiar blue alien. "Zz'r'p, check Echo out."

"Very good, Omega," Zz'r'p commended immediately. "Your blocking skills have become truly excellent over the last couple of years. You are quite successfully protecting Echo against three of us, singly and in concert."

"Okay. We've got the defense. Now we need a strong offense," Omega replied.

"And believe you me, I intend to do some serious offending," Echo muttered.

"What he said. Thanks, y'all," Omega told the Arcturans.

"You are more than welcome, Omega," Zz'r'p responded. "Truthfully, we desired to atone to you for the actions of one of our number—even though he is no longer numbered with us."

"It was never your fault, y'all, any of you. But I appreciate it all the same," she told the aliens with a gentle smile. "If y'all will excuse us, Echo and I have some planning to do now."

"And we have to go see the Director," Echo appended.

* * *

As Alpha One headed across the Core, aimed for the ramp up to Fox's office, Echo thought at his partner. *Maybe you feel better after all that.*

*How so?*

*You ought to feel needed now.*

*I...don't get it.* Omega was puzzled.

*You said you'd never known I 'needed' anybody. Well, you should know now. I need you.*

*What?!*

*Meg, I really can't adequately protect myself against Slug's mind attacks. I need you to protect me mentally,* Echo admitted. *That way, I can protect you physically. Teamwork, baby. Like we always do.*

*Oh. Okay. Yeah, I suppose,* Omega agreed, still hesitant.

"So you should feel better, Angel-voice," Echo said, and grinned.

"If you say so..."

Echo sighed.

* * *

Romeo and India reported their findings to all three of their supervisors—the Agency Director, and the Chief and Assistant Chief of the Alpha Line department, assembled in Fox's office.

"...So whoever th' hell it was, it wasn't a damn Snail," Romeo expostulated, as Fox scribbled notes to himself.

"Right. It was a relatively tall biped," India confirmed, "judging by the evidence of arm reach, digital manipulation, and stride."

Omega and Echo nodded simultaneously. *Still could be Slug, Echo,* Omega told him.

*I know. Working jointly with another entity. Just like we are. Determined to finish his plan. Just like we'll both finish this investigation, no matter what... 'happens.'*

Omega glanced at her partner, curious. *What do you mean?*

*I've been thinking.* Echo met the blue eyes. *If something should...happen...on this mission, it's more likely to happen to you, because you're out there on stage and more vulnerable, and so I want you to come in here with me.* Echo tapped his temple wordlessly, and Romeo and India gaped. Even Fox raised an eyebrow, surprised. *Then I'll get your body back to the medlab as fast as I can, so the medics can clone it or get it into a regen pod or something like that. Then I'll get Zz'r'p to help, and we'll transfer you back, once your body is fixed.*

*You'd do all that?* Omega blinked, touched. *Just to keep me—*

*Yes.* Echo's answer was simple, firm, and confident. *In a heartbeat.*

"Awright, it done finally happened," Romeo broke in on the wordless conversation. "They gone all Vulcanian on us."

"Is it true?" a curious India asked. "Are you two...different?"

"Yes," Omega answered.

"—And no," Echo finished. "We're as human as ever— no, Meg, don't even think it," he added, as she opened her mouth to remark on her alien genetic component. "But we've been conferring with the Arcturans to see if Slug could still be alive."

"And?" Alpha Two asked in unison.

"Yes, he may still be alive, after a fashion," Omega answered. "Zz'r'p showed us how it could work—"

"—And this is the result," Echo added without missing a beat. "We decided to run with it, at least for now, as being the best way we have to combat a telepath."

"Well, well," Fox remarked finally. "This should prove interesting. I don't think such a thing has ever happened before in Division One. How are you two...enjoying this latest twist in your partnership?"

"It's...a little disconcerting, Fox." Omega glanced apologetically at Echo. Echo explained.

"Meg's had too many 'mind-rapes' over the years, Fox," he said softly. "It's proving a bit...disturbing...for her. I'm good with it, though. But I'm trying to help ease her mind on the sitch, literally."

Fox nodded, and Romeo and India glanced at the floor. Omega simply sighed.

"So, Romeo, did anyone see a stranger in the theater? Something or someone out of place?" Echo returned the conversation to its proper subject.

"Naw, Echo," Romeo responded. "Nothin' unusual. Nobody who wasn't s'posed to be there."

"That argues for someone in the show," Omega noted. "Blast. I like everybody in the show." *Hmm...on the other hand...well, I guess we need to check backgrounds. Echo, what do you think?*

*Go for it, Meg. Research like that is your specialty anyway. Correction—one of your specialties, Angel-voice.* Both Agents smiled.

"All right, I'll get on it," Omega said.

"Okay, y'all gotta cut that shit out when you're in a meeting, guys. This is gonna get damn confusing f'r the rest of us," Romeo averred.

"Amein," Fox agreed.

* * *

*C'mon, Angel,* Omega heard much later as she worked on pulling up background information on the cast and crew with Lima. *You're still on a twenty-four hour clock. I've got all the departmental reports done and collated. Let's go home. Bravo and Lima can finish for you and report the results later. I'm hungry. And you gotta be starving, with that hyped metabolism.*

*What's the word on tomorrow's performance, Ace? Have the repairs been made yet? Are people even willing?*

*Yeah, baby, Mike says the repairs are done, and he 'outed' Alpha Two as the 'investigators' brought in to take care of things. So when you see 'em at the theater, act like you don't know 'em. But that's what it took, to get everybody back on stage for another performance...which,* he pointed out, *was necessary; not only would they go bankrupt from refunding all the tickets, if the show closes we'll never manage to find out what's going down. Or where Slug is. But the company was scared. And I can't say as I blame 'em. I'll be glad to get this one solved and in the bag.*

*All right. Just a sec.* "Hey, guys," she told Bravo and Lima, "Echo just reminded me it's time for me to go. I gotta get some rest before tomorrow's performance, so I have to be on a normal Earth-day schedule. Can y'all finish here for me?"

Both young men nodded vigorously.

"Sure thing, Omega," Lima agreed. "Besides, what you don't know about research, cross-referencing and stuff...wow! Me an' Bravo had already learned a lot, just in the first five minutes. Never mind spending the last several hours working with you."

"Yeah," Bravo averred. "And we weren't exactly stupid on the subject, before. But there's no problem. You run off and get some shut-eye. We'll see what we can get pulled together for you, then pop it to you and Echo when we're done."

"Good. Thanks, guys." Omega waved, and headed out of

their joint office—which happened to be immediately under Fox's office—to meet Echo at one of the Core's exits, en route to their quarters.

* * *

They entered Echo's front door, and two ties were promptly loosened, Suit jackets unbuttoned. "That's better," Omega remarked, as they tossed jackets and ties across one of Echo's armchairs.

"Yeah. First things first, though—let's go get that transponder out from behind your ear."

"Okay."

They meandered through the back door and into Omega's bathroom—noting along the way that the recliner was now back in the den, and the extra side table gone—and she pulled the transponder kit out of the middle right drawer of her vanity. "Here," she said, plunking it down on the countertop. "Oh good, Facilities left the stool. Would you mind doing the honors, Ace? I think you can see what you're doing better than I could."

"Not a problem. Gimme a cotton ball and some alcohol, and I'll have it out in a minute."

Omega dragged over the requested items from their position on the vanity top, and parked herself on the stool, her back to her partner. Echo studied the spot behind her ear with a critical eye, then gently fingered her skin.

"Right here?"

"Yeah, that's it. Can you feel it?"

"Yeah. It's kinda behind the mastoid bone."

"That's it, yeah."

"Okay, baby, hang on. It might sting a little bit."

"I know. It did when I put it in, too."

Echo swabbed the area thoroughly with alcohol; then, while he waited for it to dry, he fished the extraction tool from the implant kit and popped the sterile seal on it. Then he lined it up with the tiny transponder chip.

"All right, Meg, here we go," he murmured. Omega

grabbed the edge of the countertop with both hands, and Echo inserted the extractor. It immediately grabbed and secured the chip, and he withdrew it gently. A tiny bead of blood welled from the small wound. He laid the extractor tool to one side, then got a fresh cotton ball, wet it with alcohol, and swiped it across the little puncture wound.

Omega hissed as the alcohol stung the open wound, and her knuckles whitened where she held the countertop, then gradually eased.

"Damn," she grumbled. "Nothing burns like alcohol in a raw place."

"Ain't that the truth." Echo got a small spot bandage from the extraction kit and applied it to the wound, thereby ensuring any additional blood seepage didn't stain her clothing. "There we go, baby. Whatcha want me to do with the implant kit?"

"Just leave it there and I'll take care of it later. We might want that thing again one of these days, so I'll run everything through the sterilization mode and put it away."

"Okay."

Omega slid off the stool and they headed back into Echo's quarters.

* * *

"Whatcha want to do about supper?" Echo asked at that point. "Want to go out?"

"Actually, I think I'd rather not go out, if you don't mind," she told him. "I know we keep trying, and now we actually have a chance, but...I'd like to...not be around so many people tonight." She tapped her temple. "I gotta get a little more used to this."

"Ah, okay. That makes sense. A quiet dinner at home, then—just us."

"Nothing fancy," Omega protested. "I'll settle for slapping together a couple sandwiches and eating in front of the TV."

"Again."

"Again."

"All right. Let's do it, then." Echo got up, and they sauntered into his kitchen.

"Oh, waitaminit, I've got some stuff," Omega said, disappearing into her own apartment as Echo extracted sandwich ingredients.

* * *

She returned a few minutes later, with several small trays of finger-food items from the previous evening's abortive repast. Echo cocked an eyebrow at the rather 'fancy' addenda to the menu, but said nothing, either audibly or mentally, and Omega didn't volunteer anything.

Silently they assembled sandwiches, and tucked several of the finger foods—assorted crudités, cubes of smoked Gouda and Cheshire, sliced fruit—she had prepared the previous evening onto their plates. Omega took hers into the living area, sitting down on Echo's couch with a sigh. Echo joined her.

* * *

"Tired?" he asked, just as she stuffed the huge sandwich into her mouth.

*Good timing, Ace,* she thought ruefully, and he grinned.

"Sorry." A hungry Echo tied into his own sandwich with enthusiasm.

*No, I'm not really tired,* she told him mentally while eating. *Just...trying to unwind. I've been rather busy in recent weeks.*

"That's an understatement," Echo teased, around a mouthful.

*Says the master of the art form,* Omega retorted. *Honestly, Echo, God Himself could appear in this room, and you'd merely remark that we had an important Visitor.*

Echo almost did a spit-take, and started laughing.

"Oh, damn, Meg, am I really that bad?" he chuckled finally.

Omega swallowed, then rejoined, "Worse."

"Shit. Sorry."

Omega shrugged, polishing off the last bite. *Nothing to apologize for. That's just you. I got used to it a long time ago. I'm okay with it. It kinda makes life...unusual, sometimes. I don't get caught off guard quite as much as I used to, at least.*

She set her plate on the side table.

"Well...how about I try to improve it a bit?" Echo proposed, similarly dispensing with his empty plate and slipping a companionable arm around his partner's shoulders.

"If you did that, you wouldn't be you anymore, and nobody would know what to think." Omega grinned.

"Even you?"

"Especially me. I'd be convinced someone was impersonating you," she avowed. "Or that another shapeshifting doppelganger had showed up in Headquarters."

"I'm sure you could come up with some way to tell, Meg," Echo ribbed, gently pulling her closer. "You're pretty resourceful."

"Oh, yeah, I suppose," Omega remarked, sobering. "But then I'd have to figure you out all over again."

* * *

"Would that be...so unpleasant?" Echo murmured, his lips barely grazing her temple. He leaned forward then and bent his head, feeling Omega's warm breath on his lips. Abruptly, she averted her face, and Echo felt the firewall reinforce itself. "Meg? I...I thought—"

Omega pulled away and stood.

"I don't feel like rehearsing tonight, Echo." She headed for the back door.

* * *

"Rehearsing?" Echo repeated blankly. The brown eyes were dark with an admixture of emotions.

"Yeah. Your overall performance last night—the last few nights—ought to have gotten you a Tony," Omega said quietly from the doorway. "Considering how different it is from reality, you make a very persuasive panic-stricken lover."

* * *

She disappeared into her darkened quarters. Echo sat staring after her for a long minute; then his eyes closed, and his head dropped back onto the couch, as he suddenly understood the reason for her reaction.

"Damn," he whispered. "How do you fight someone else's insecurity?" He sighed, then groaned, "Meg, what am I going to do with you?" He listened intently.

But whether audible or telepathic, he got no answer.

* * *

Instead of sleeping, Omega spent the night on the Headquarters roof with her telescope, stargazing and maintaining a protective telepathic block around Echo. Shortly after dawn, she heard the confused, mildly-distressed mental query.

*What the hell?! Meg? Where are you, baby?*

*On the roof, Echo. I'll be down in a minute.* She began stowing her equipment and shutting down the electronics.

*Aw. You were up all night.* It was a statement.

*Yes. I kept the block up. That way, we were both safe from any...intrusions.*

*Damn.*

*Some coffee would be appreciated.* Omega started downstairs. *Preferably pretty strong.*

*You've got it, Meg.* Echo's response was immediate.

* * *

Echo met her at the front door of her quarters with a steaming mug. *Here,* he told her, handing her the mug of coffee, made just as she liked it, with plenty of cream but no sweetener. *Fox said Bravo and Lima emailed us the results of the research, by the way. I haven't taken a look; I figured that was your right, since you did the work with 'em.*

"Thanks." Omega took the coffee and sipped it. "I'll check it in a minute."

*Want some breakfast?* Echo headed for his kitchen.

"Not really. I'm not hungry." Omega continued sipping the coffee as she moved into her study and booted the laptop. She sat down and logged on, then brought up her email.

*Meg, are you back on the stimulants you used during Slug's original attack on you?*

"Yeah; I went by the medlab after you went to bed last night and had 'em give me a 'script. I have to stay awake somehow, Echo," Omega called over her shoulder. "I'm already damn tired. If I fall asleep, you know the telepathic block goes down. And that could be disastrous, at this point."

*Then you need to eat. Those things rev your metabolism. And it's not slow, to begin with. You'll burn fuel faster than a starship. I know it also puts the kibosh on your appetite, as Fox would say, but you need to try, baby.*

"All right," Omega sighed. "Fix me something."

*What?*

"Anything. Surprise me." Omega studied the email from Fox's executive assistants. "By the way, why are you thinking to me instead of talking?"

*Why not? It's easier. Besides, I'm...kinda getting used to it. I figure I need to practice, anyway.*

*Okay, I'll join you,* Omega caved in. *It IS easier than yelling across both apartments. Well, blast an' damn,* she said blankly, all at once.

*'Blast an' damn' what?*

*We hit a dead end. There's absolutely no cross-correlation between Slug and any member of the cast OR crew, that the boys could find,* Omega told Echo. *Nor yet even the producers or theater staff.*

*So no one at the theater was ever in a position to even encounter Slug?* Echo clarified.

*Apparently not.*

*But no strangers have been seen in the theater...* Echo mused.

*Well, we are dealing with a telepath,* Omega reminded him. *Capable of projecting mental images. Like in the mirror. So maybe he just faked everybody out, and made himself LOOK like somebody they knew.*

*Yes, but damn, Meg, that's a lot of minds to fool simultaneously. Slug never could do that before. Maybe Zz'r'p could. Maybe. But he'd have a helluva migraine afterward.*

*But what if the symbiotic relationship boosted his ability or something?*

*Hm. That's...well, I got no way to evaluate that, baby. Do you?*

*No. And, well, based on some comments Zz'r'p made when I mentioned it a while back, I don't think the Arcturans know how, either, Ace.*

*Okay. So we leave it as a possibility, but until we have more evidence, it's a dead end.*

*So what do you think we should do?* Omega asked, moving on to the rest of her email.

* * *

*Mm,* Echo considered as he prepared breakfast. *I think...I think we'll keep Romeo and India with us at the theater. That would help us cover it better. They can handle out front; we'll cover backstage. And the cast and crew will feel better for the 'official investigators' being there, anyway.*

*True. All right. Lessee, then. With a little extra effort on my part...mmph...* Echo felt Omega concentrating hard, *you and I ought to be able to see through the mental disguise—at least partly. And that'll be enough to tell if there IS one.*

*Damn, Meg,* Echo remarked, surprised, *you have gotten really good at this blocking stuff over the last few years.*

*I...I don't want...I keep thinking, if I can only make it better, stronger, then the next time...but...but it's never strong enough...I'm never good enough...*

Echo felt the intense pain, even through the firewall, and he stopped breakfast preparation, prepared to head to her side immediately.

*Meg, you shouldn't expect to be as strong as someone who was born a telepath, honey. At least, not at this point.*

*So I shouldn't even try? That's kind of like saying I shouldn't...fight a rapist, because most men are bigger and stronger than me, and I'll lose. No, I still have to try. At least to maybe hold him off long enough for help to arrive, never mind to use some of my advanced training. I only...I wish...it hurts so bad, Echo.*

There was a long silence between the two Agents. Echo, in his kitchen, suspected Omega was crying, and finally he ventured, *Meg—do you want me to come in there, and give you a shoulder to cry on?*

* * *

*No. I'm...okay. Or, well, I'll BE okay.*

Omega paused for a moment and wiped her face with one hand to obliterate the tear stains, staring unseeingly at the computer screen as she considered matters.

*You know, to tell the truth,* she finally told him, *I really would like to talk with you about it. You've got a way of cutting through the extraneous garbage to the stuff that's important. It helps me sort things out. It would probably help my sitch now.*

* * *

*Okay. I'm listening.* Echo put the finishing touches on breakfast. It was Omega's favorite—scrambled eggs, bacon, biscuits, and honey.

*I can't, Echo. I don't know how. Even telepathically.*

*Why not?* He set the table.

* * *

*I can't give you a frame of reference.* Omega deleted the routine emails on system status, then filed the shift reports from Alpha Line.

*Meaning?*

*Echo,* Omega said bluntly, thoughts full of ironic, black humor, *when was the last time you were raped? Physically or mentally?*

*You and I talked about that the other day, a little bit. You described what the Cortians would have done to me.*

*Yeah...but you hadn't thought of any of that, really, until I said something. You figured they'd kill you first, right? Or just enslave you.*

*Well...yeah.*

*Okay. So when was the last time you WERE actually violated, or knew you were in danger of being violated, like that?*

*Actually, mentally, at the same time Tt'l'k did it to you, a few weeks back. But I couldn't really tell it, I guess. I couldn't even feel it happening. Physically? During our little Dallas diversion, back when we made our first effort at going on vacay,* Echo replied. *Well, Zzs tried, anyway. But she didn't get very far.*

*Exactly. How concerned were you during the attempt?*

* * *

*Well, some. For a second or two there, I thought I was in big trouble.* Echo began bringing out the food. *But in general? Not very. Frankly, I was more worried about her biting my tongue off when you told me to kiss her and tickle the roof of her mouth. But rape? Not so much, I guess.*

*Because...?* Omega pressed. *Zargothians are a lot stronger than humans, after all.*

*I wasn't in any real danger,* Echo responded. *I'm not exactly inexperienced. And you and half of Alpha Line were close by.*

*All of Alpha Line,* Omega corrected. *That's my point, Echo. You weren't worried because you were never in a position of complete vulnerability. You have no idea what it feels like to be completely overpowered—no force, no strategy, nothing that you can do to help yourself. No. Way. Out. So how can you comprehend the...the emotions I have? The helplessness, the worthlessness. I thought I was so strong, so combat-ready! But no. I'm...nowhere close. I've been mind-raped—several times. And knew it. And the only reason I wasn't physically raped was because I managed to hold Mark off long enough that you got in there...and you were bigger than him, and stopped it. I mean, if I'd been awake, he'd never have got that close...but I wasn't. I was almost completely pinned down by the time I woke up and realized what was happening. And none of that counts the kind of physical violation that Slug did when he 'enhanced' me.* Echo heard her mental sigh. *Maybe on this mission I've found my true calling—target.*

Echo winced, then tried changing the subject. *Come and get it. Breakfast is ready.*

* * *

*I'll be there in a minute. I just got one more email. Go ahead and start eating,* she told him.

*Okay.*

Omega clicked on the last file, a message from the Los Angeles Office. Then she gaped in shock and dismay.

* * *

*Hi Meg,*

*I was thinking about you and just wanted to tag up and find out how you're doing. I know you've been through the wringer lately, and I gathered from what Echo said the other day that I didn't help with that any. I'm sorry about that; I never meant to hurt you. I honestly thought I was getting out of the way for what—or rather, who—you really wanted to be with. I want you to be happy, even if that's not with me.*

*I heard that you and Echo have started going out, and I sincerely hope that works out well for you both. He's a lucky man, and I tried to make sure he knew just how lucky, when he called.*

*But turn about is fair play. If he doesn't treat you right, you come tell me, and I swear I'll fix his little red wagon for you, if it's the last thing I ever do. And...well, if it doesn't work out with you and him, tell me that, too. I'll come back, and I think you and I will make a damn fine couple.*

*Is the latest mission going okay? Stay safe, all right?*

*Love,*

*Mu*

* * *

Echo sat down at his dining table and loaded his plate, beginning to eat. Moments later, a furious Omega suddenly appeared in the doorway.

"Echo—why didn't you tell me you talked to Mu?" she demanded.

* * *

The dining room was silent as Echo sat, staring at her blankly in confusion, as he tried to understand the antecedent to her query. Then recollection returned, and he lightly struck his forehead with the palm of his hand.

"Shit," he replied, "that's right. I'm sorry; it slipped my mind completely with everything else that's been going on. He asked about you and...sent his love."

"Why did you call him?" she pressed. He sensed the mental firewall become rock-solid, and blinked in concern.

*That ain't good,* he thought. *'Fess up, boy. No matter what. She's gotta know she can trust you. You went behind her back, and it's upset her...because there's still something she's scared of me finding out, and she's wondering if I'm trying to figure out what.*

"I wanted to know why the hell he dumped you," Echo admitted, as open and straightforward as he knew how to be. *Oh damn,* he thought, as soon as the words were out of his mouth. *That was NOT the way to say that. Now she REALLY believes I'm trying to figure out what she's hiding.*

"Why? So you could decide if you oughta risk being seen with me?" Omega lashed out.

"That's not fair, Meg, and you know it," Echo replied, firm, though the accusation hurt him. *Yup, that's what she thinks, all right. Way to go, Echo, son. Time to take it in a different direction, and ensure she knows my real motivation.* "Did it ever occur to you that I might have been trying to find out if I had a serious rival?"

"Yeah, right," she said, tone dripping sarcasm. "The only men willing to fight over me are alien psychopaths and brainwashed rapists." She glared at him. "So what did he say? That I was a little too 'exotic' for his taste? Or was he honest enough to admit that he didn't want to be seen with a kludged-together inhuman creature, created to be a sleeper assassin, a murdering Frankenstein's monster?"

A shocked Echo was shaken to his core at the anguished wrath that poured from his partner, betraying her inner self-loathing.

"Actually, Meg," he admitted in a quiet voice after a pause

to gather his thoughts, "I think maybe he's in love with you."

* * *

"Oh, now there's a good one. Men in love always dump the object of their affections and run clear across the continent." Omega rolled her eyes in disgust and folded her arms.

"They do," Echo responded, his voice still quiet, "if they think that's what will make the lady in question happy."

She noticed that he'd dropped his gaze and was no longer looking at her, but the pain on his face and in his eyes was still detectable; she knew him too well not to see it. *And I caused that pain,* she thought, trying not to cringe. *The one man I wouldn't hurt for the world. But he went behind my back! What was he trying to find out? The stuff I'm too ashamed to tell him? Did he think I'd tell Mu, but not tell him?*

Then what he'd just said hit her conscious mind.

"What?" Omega stopped her mental and oral tirades, startled; the statement fit perfectly with what Mu had said in his email. "Wait. Where the hell would Mu get an idea like that?"

* * *

"He thought you were interested in...someone else, so he got out of the way, Meg," Echo told her, dodging the detail of who the 'someone else' was. "Was he wrong? Do you want him back? I'll call him for you, if you like..." Casually, Echo started to put a forkful of egg into his mouth, then abruptly set it down, untouched. *If I so much as shovel that into my mouth, never mind try to choke it down, I swear I will throw up, right here,* he realized.

"You're serious, aren't you?" Omega asked, patently stunned.

"Yes." Echo stood slowly, feeling like his chest was ripping open.

"Where are you going?"

"To...call Mu for you." He turned for his study, but Omega laid a restraining hand on Echo's arm.

"No. Let it go, Echo," she said softly. "I'm...sorry. For

railing at you, for hurting you, and for hurting Mu. I didn't realize he felt like that. I'm...still not sure I believe it. But he deserves better than...than me."

"Meg, I said it once before—if the two of you are in love, your genetics don't matter."

"I know, Echo. And if Mu AND I were in love, maybe I might agree with you."

"You don't—?" Echo glanced at her swiftly, needing to verify what he thought he'd just heard. Omega shook her head.

"Mu is really sweet. I like him a lot. Maybe I could learn to love him, in time. But I...don't." She sighed, suddenly looking incredibly tired. "You know, I had a really old great-aunt who's probably turning in her grave right now." Omega chuckled ruefully, and sat down at the table. "At around ten-thousand rpm's, I'd estimate. The graveyard's probably humming."

"Why?" Echo asked, sitting back down himself and trying to resume his meal, dawdling a bit to let his churning stomach settle back down, as Omega filled her plate.

"She used to tell me that, if I didn't watch out, I'd lose all my 'beaus.' Let them 'slip through your fingers,' was the way she put it, I believe it was. See, she was born not too long after 1900...uh, sometime during World War I, I think, though it might have been a little earlier...and to her, not winding up an 'old maid' was more important than considerations of love."

"Let me guess—she was an 'old maid,'" Echo ventured.

"Yeah." Omega grinned lopsidedly. "How'd you ever guess?"

"Oh, lucky shot." Echo grinned back, feeling his gut finally release and relax. "I take it you don't agree with her?"

"You are correct, sir. Not to mention a good cook." Omega was rapidly depleting her breakfast rations. "You made my favorite."

"I was trying to tempt you."

* * *

"Huh?" Omega glanced up, trying to hide the startlement. *Tempt me? To do WHAT, exactly...?* she wondered, confused.

263

"You needed to eat. I was trying to coax you into eating well."

"...Oh. You did a good job." Omega tried not to smear her hand across her face, as she grasped that he meant a different sort of temptation than she had reflexively assumed. She poured great quantities of honey on her biscuit, then took a huge, sticky bite. Mouth full, she lowered her guard and proceeded to think to him. *You're right, I never have agreed with my great-aunt. And neither do you.*

*That's true,* Echo replied, resuming his own meal, *but how did you know?*

*That's easy.*

*Oh?* The syllable came with an unverbalized invitation to elaborate.

*Echo, in all the researches I've done through the historical archives in recent months, I've found lots of references and photos of you. But you were always either alone, or with X-ray or Romeo. Being privileged to have you as my best friend, and consequently knowing what I know, it isn't hard for me to figure out why there was never a lady agent...make that a lady, period...on your arm—even at the social functions. Even though you've told me you had a couple of girlfriends, over the years. I think the reason ended up being named 'Chase.' You weren't serious about the others; you were, about her.*

Omega watched as Echo studied his empty plate intently, unconsciously fingering the handle of his coffee cup, before he wordlessly drank from it.

* * *

As he set the mug down, however, he felt a sudden wave of sadness and grief breach the abruptly-strengthened psychic firewall, and he glanced at his partner.

"Meg?"

"Hm?"

"I'm all right, Meg. I'm past that. I swear I am, baby. Don't let it get you down. It's...been over a year now since Slug... took her away. You know what they say about time."

"That's good, Echo," Omega smiled gently, but Echo saw the lonely ghost in her eyes again—the same one he'd seen at intermission when he first took her to see *Phantom*. "Except getting past the grief doesn't automatically imply getting over missing her. I've suffered more than enough loss of my own to understand that much." But before he could formulate a reply, she stood, efficiently cleared the table, and went into his kitchen, where she loaded the dishwasher. "There. Now I'll go get ready for work. Guess I've—we've—got another performance tonight."

Echo caught the amended remark, and tried to correct her mistaken impression.

"Meg, I—"

"Give me 'bout a half-hour to shower and change, Ace, and I'll be ready to go," Omega said, vanishing through the back door.

Echo sighed.

# Chapter 10

By the time Alpha One arrived at the theater, Alpha Two had swept the premises, meeting them at the backstage door.

"Nah, man," Romeo noted, when Echo asked. "We ain't found another thing."

"What he said," India averred.

"Well, that's good, I guess," Omega decided.

"Yeah, and it fits," Echo agreed. "The perp strikes a big blow—thank God, it missed—and then lays low for a while, waiting for another opportunity once we've let our guard down."

"Or else tries a different venue," India suggested.

"Mm. Possibly," Echo concurred. "Either way, we don't need to let our guard down."

"At ALL," Omega added.

"Yup," Echo said with a nod. "All right, guys, let's go. Romeo, India, I want you to stay here until after closing curtain tonight, in case Meg and I need backup. All right?"

"Works for us, Echo," India agreed. "This situation is starting to get serious, and Meg's foot is still finishing up healing, I gathered from Zebra."

"Yeah; 'sides, we ain't got another assignment currently," Romeo said. "We 'uz just fillin' in for Alpha One, runnin' the department, an' we can help ya do that an' still help with this too."

"Uh-huh," India averred. "Consider us your tag-team."

"Good. You two cover the front of the house—the lobby, box office, restrooms, concessions, as well as the auditorium proper: the audience seating, all that—and I'll handle backstage and the control booth," Echo instructed. "I pretty much know my way around it by now, anyway, and it would take longer than we've got to show y'all around that. Meg has the onstage, live stuff, obviously. Between the four of us, we ought to be able to cover things pretty well."

"All over it, boss-man," Romeo agreed, and they split up.

* * *

Shortly before curtain, after Omega was in costume and makeup, a knock came at the door.

"Who is it?" she called, nibbling on a cracker to help provide sustenance to get her through the show, without further upsetting her stomach; she had thrown up earlier from her usual stage fright.

"It's Sofia, dear. I...wanted to check on you."

"Oh, okay; come on in. The door's unlocked, and I'm already in costume."

The door opened, and the prima donna entered, closing it behind her.

"There you are. You look all right..."

"Yes, I'm fine," Omega offered the other woman a guarded smile. "Echo got me out from under the other night, and kept me safe."

"Oh, how wonderful," Sofia averred, almost purring the words. "Our own personal hero, right, my dear girl?"

"Pretty much, yes," Omega agreed. "I was sure glad to have him there, the other night."

"Then I'm sure you won't mind if I, ah, borrow him tonight? After the show, I mean," Sofia wondered. "You see we're, um, well, let's just say that there MIGHT have been a 'scary theater phantom' that showed up in my condo this afternoon, and I need our hero to come...'chase it away.' You understand, I'm sure?"

"Oh," Omega said, sitting up straight, startled. "Do we need to come handle things?"

"No, no, no, my dear, don't bother your head over it," Sofia said with a smile. "We've worked this all out, and I'm sure you wouldn't want to be a fifth wheel."

"Ah. It's...like that," Omega observed, her heart falling as disappointment and hurt swept over her. Somehow, she managed to keep it off her face.

"Oh yes." Sofia smiled again, a complacent, self-satisfied expression.

"You and, and Echo, worked it out?"

"Who else would you think, dear?"

"...All right."

"I knew you'd understand."

As Sofia let herself out, Omega turned back to the mirror and sighed.

Abruptly her stomach lurched, and she leaped to her feet, running into the tiny bathroom to purge her gut again. Only this time, it had nothing to do with stage fright.

* * *

The performance that night went relatively well, though everyone in the company, onstage and backstage, was jittery and anxious. The fly-rail system for the catwalk had been almost completely replaced, and performed flawlessly; the dents and dings to the catwalk had been cosmetically disguised, and its structure reinforced, while the damaged boards in the stage had been replaced.

During intermission, Alpha Two reported in to Echo, while Omega changed costumes in her dressing room, and prepared herself for the next act.

"Nah, man, we ain't seen nuthin' at all," Romeo declared, while India nodded. "Looks like you 'uz right, an' whoever it is holed up to wait f'r another chance."

"Good," Echo said. "Let's see if we can't keep him holed up." He nodded. "Y'all keep doing what you're doing; I'm gonna go see about Meg."

"Let me know if that foot is hurting her, Echo," India told him. "I'll swing by and treat it, if she needs me to."

"Thanks, India; I will," Echo said, offering a slight smile. "But I expect she'll be okay; she's been looking pretty good on it all night."

"Great, then. And yes, she's a wonderful actress and singer."

They split up, and Echo headed for the dressing rooms.

* * *

"Oh, hey Ace," Omega greeted her partner as he slipped through the open door of her dressing room, while Cecile, hairpins in her mouth, adjusted the wig Omega wore. "Has Sofia talked to you yet?"

"Huh? Sofia? No, why?" Echo wondered.

"Um, she said she thought the, ah, 'Theater Phantom' had showed up at her place, or something like that," Omega said, staring into the mirror and applying fresh lip color...which had the desired effect of ensuring she didn't have to meet his eyes. "Wanted you to, uh, 'go over and check things out,' I think."

"Oh, shit," Echo said, eyes widening. "Yeah, that needs to be checked out. Weird."

"Um, yeah."

"Okay, I'll go find her now," Echo said, checking his wrist chronometer. "I might have enough time to talk to her before second act curtain, if I can find her in time."

"All right," Omega agreed "See you later, Ace."

"Later, Meg."

And he was gone.

*Without so much as a 'Break a leg, Angel-voice,'* she thought, stifling a sigh.

* * *

Echo didn't find Sofia before the curtain; there were too many people milling around the house proper.

So he slipped backstage again as the lights began to dim for the second act, and saw his partner safely through to the final curtain. He applauded, proud, as she took her bows with the cast, and murmured congratulations as she scurried past him, headed to her dressing room. She threw him a tired smile—completely understandable, given her lack of sleep—and kept going.

Echo turned to follow.

* * *

But before Echo could even pass through the offstage door into the dressing area after the final curtain, he felt a hand on his arm, and instinctively spun, still on alert.

"OH!" Sofia exclaimed, stepping back in surprise. "It's just me, darling. I'm so sorry; I didn't mean to startle you. I suppose I should have thought."

"That's okay," Echo brushed it aside. "After the other night's little incident, I've had to be...kinda wary tonight."

"I can imagine..."

"Listen, Meg told me we needed to talk," Echo said. "I went looking for you at intermission, but couldn't find you. Something about maybe the phantom showing up in your house?"

"Yes," Sofia said, her face crumpling. "Strange things have been happening all day today, Alec! It's so frightening! I could hardly wait to get out of my condo and come here for the evening! I was hoping you, ah, and your partner, might be free to come by and check on things. It would make me feel SO much safer! If you don't, I'll just have to go to a hotel. I can't possibly feel safe until you have a look."

"Mm. Well, it makes a certain sense," Echo decided. "Whoever it was pulled a major event the other night; it stands to reason, like I was telling Meg earlier, that he would want to—"

"Might it not be a she?"

"Well, it could be, and in a way it might still be, but the actual perp showed himself to us early on," Echo explained.

"Oh. So you KNOW it's a 'he.'"

"Exactly." Echo nodded. "Anyway, we expect him to go into hiding for a while, after bringing down the catwalk set. And it might be that he'd try to follow someone home and hole up in a cast member's house, rather than risk getting found somewhere in the theater."

"Oh dear!" Sofia shivered. "Now you simply MUST come over and check my condo!"

"Okay. Let me line up a few things first, check with Meg, and then we can head to your place. Did you drive?"

"Silly man, I don't even have a car," Sofia laughed. "I took a taxi."

"Okay, then you can ride in the 'Vette, and I'll drive us over to your place."

"That will be fine," Sofia almost purred. "Shall I wait for you in the bar?"

"Won't that be closed?"

"No, not if I'm there. They usually keep it open for at least half an hour after closing curtain anyway, in case some of the patrons want refreshment before they leave." Sofia shrugged. "It brings in a surprising amount of revenue, that way."

"Right. I'll come find you, and we'll head out, once I get my ducks in a row," Echo agreed.

"See you soon, dear," Sofia said, headed for the front of the house.

* * *

"Meg," Echo said, as his partner pared off the bulky costume with little Cecile's help, "I finally found Sofia and talked to her. And I thought—"

"Don't worry about it, Echo," Omega replied, bending over so Cecile could assist her in easing off the heavy wig; unfortunately, they had had to secure it with quite a few hairpins earlier—because it had slipped rather alarmingly during one of the dance numbers—and it was proving tricky to find all the pins in order to release it from Omega's own hair. "Ow. There's another one, Cecile."

"I see it, Miss Meg. Hold on."

"Uh, okay, so, Echo," Omega continued, staring at the floor while Cecile worked, "don't worry about me. I'm pretty tired anyway, so I'm just gonna go home. You go ahead and, uhm, take care of Sofia."

"But..."

"Ace, it's all right," Omega said in a soft voice. "You make sure she's...'safe,' and I'll see you in the morning." The wig finally came off, and Omega straightened up, holding her back and neck. "Ohhh...that feels SO much better."

"I'm sure it does," Cecile said with a giggle. "It's heavy,

271

but it isn't quite tight enough."

"If it was any tighter, I think it would crush my head," Omega declared. "I've about got a headache tonight as it is."

* * *

"Meg, is everything okay?" Echo wondered then, sensing an odd jumble of emotions filtering faintly through her mental firewall.

"Everything's fine, Echo," she told him, calm and quiet. "I'm just...tired tonight."

"And headachy," a mischievous but sympathetic Cecile added.

"And sorta headachy," Omega agreed. "So shoo. Run on and see to Sofia; I'm sure she's waiting."

"Yeah, she's in the bar," Echo noted. "But...do you need me to take you home?"

"No, I've already made arrangements. I'll be fine. Go see to her."

"Well...okay," Echo finally agreed.

He turned and left.

* * *

*There's more going on here than meets the eye, and it isn't like Meg not to want to provide backup for me,* he decided, as he slipped out of the dressing room. *So there's two possibilities that I can see. Either this is legitimate, and I need to check out Sofia's place to see if Slug has managed to find a way to hole up there...in which case, I need backup...or Sofia has Meg convinced of something in order to get me over to her place alone...in which case, I need backup. Of a different kind, but backup, just the same.*

He stopped right inside the backstage door, thinking.

*I need to find Alpha Two,* he decided, and struck off, headed for the opposite side of the theater.

* * *

"Sure thing, Echo," Romeo agreed. "But we can't go with ya quite yet."

"Why not?" Echo wanted to know.

"We promised we'd run Meg by Headquarters," India said. "She's really tired, she said, and wanted to get home as soon as possible, and take something for a looming headache."

"That's basically what she just told me," Echo noted. "Okay, do that, and I'll text you the address. But I want you to hurry up and get Meg home, then come immediately. I'm not keen on taking on a telepath without backup someplace nearby."

"No problem, man," Romeo averred. "We'll 'fly low,' if you need us to."

"Well, I dunno that you need to do THAT," Echo said with a grin. "I'll take my time getting over to Sofia's place, and try to give you plenty of time. But come on pretty quick, okay?"

"Right," India said.

* * *

"I don't get it, Meg," Romeo said, as he drove the Lexus toward Headquarters to drop off Omega. "If you don't really have a headache...why ain't you with Echo, over checkin' out th' actress-lady's place f'r the perp?"

"Because there is no perp," Omega sighed from the back seat. "At least, not at her condo. Sofia came by before the show and gave me a heads-up that she and Echo had arranged a...a liaison...after the show. I guess Echo just figured that, what with him an' me having a cover story as lovers, it didn't do to be too blatant about it."

India and Romeo glanced at each other, puzzled and worried.

"Meg, I really don't think that that's what's—" India began.

"Guys, I simply don't wanna talk about it," Omega murmured. "Just because I don't have an actual headache—but believe me, I AM teetering on the brink of a nasty one, so I haven't lied to anybody—doesn't mean I'm not worn out. I'm tired, I only wanna go home and crash, and what Echo does on his own time is his business."

"What about th' mental block thing?" Romeo asked.

"Oh!" Omega said, sitting up straight and pulling out her

273

cell phone. "Thanks for reminding me, Romeo! I guess maybe I need to call Zz'r'p and ask for a little help, there. My sleep cycle has been screwed up too long; I have gotta get some sleep, or I'm gonna trip over my own feet in tomorrow night's performance. If not sooner."

"Meg, I still think," India tried again.

"Shush," Omega said, pointing to the phone she held to her ear. "Zz'r'p? It's Omega. I'm not disturbing you, am I? It's not too late? Oh, good. Listen, I have a favor to ask..."

* * *

"I got a bad feeling about that," Romeo grumbled, after letting Omega out near one of the Headquarters entrances and watching her safely inside the building. "Th' pretty lady is startin' to get some weird ideas in 'er head."

"I've noticed, and I don't like it, either," India agreed, equally unhappy. "I can't think, after what I saw on Echo's psych profile, that he'd turn around and start an affair with another woman. Not when he's that crazy about Meg."

"Wait. I thought you figgered he 'uz only tryin' t' make Meg feel better?"

"I changed my mind after seeing that psych profile. Like, a hundred and eighty degrees. He's nuts about her, Romeo."

"He is?! You know that? F'r sure?"

"No, I don't KNOW that, but I'm better than ninety-nine percent certain."

"Cool." Romeo shot his partner and mate a delighted grin. Abruptly he sobered. "Then what th' hell is goin' on? What was that all about?" He jerked a thumb back in the general direction of Headquarters.

"I'm not sure, but I have the feeling we're starting to see some serious psychological reactions to the shit she's been through lately, honey," India decided. "And maybe there's a certain manipulative, privileged bitch used to getting her own way, who's trying to take advantage of Meg's problems in order to cut Meg out and try to take Echo for herself?"

"Uh-oh," Romeo muttered. "In that case, we better lay

down tracks an' get over there t' back 'im up, like he asked, and fast."

"Yup," India agreed. "I only wish we could have gotten Meg to listen to the fact that Echo set us up as his backup... which means he's NOT trysting with this 'Sofia' bitch."

"I hear ya. But ya know what? Meg's reaction sounded t' me an awful lot like it hurt too much t' even discuss it. Which means..."

"You think Meg is as crazy about Echo as Echo is about her?"

"We c'n hope, hon. F'r their sakes. Lissen, I wanna get us over t' this condo an' sweep it an' have done. Maybe if we c'n clear th' place fast enough f'r Echo, we c'n get him back to Headquarters b'fore Meg crashes f'r the night, an' she'll see he wasn't interested."

"That's...a really good idea. Let's burn rubber."

"All over it!"

* * *

Sofia was quiet as she sat in the passenger seat of the Corvette, while Echo drove her home. This suited him fine, as he was focused on figuring out what was likely going on at her condominium. He had quizzed her while they got under way, but she had been extremely vague in her responses, and had had very little in the way of hard data or clues to provide him. She could not even give detailed descriptions of any unusual events, simply resorting to, "Things have just been acting very strange all day, and I had a feeling like I wasn't alone."

*So either she's a receiver, and is picking up Slug's 'broadcasts' without meaning to,* he decided, *or there's something really fishy about all this. Either way, I'm not in any hurry to get there. Not until I got backup handy.*

Consequently he took his time driving, hoping that Alpha Two could drop Omega off at Headquarters and still meet him by the time he arrived at Sofia's building.

But when he pulled into the parking garage's visitor area, there was no sign of the black Lexus.

*Shit, dammit to hell an' back, as Meg would say,* he thought, unsure whether to be concerned or annoyed.

* * *

Echo had Sofia unlock her front door, then put her behind himself, drew one of his blasters, and led the way inside, easing through the door, ready for anything.

But there was...nothing.

Echo straightened up from his partial crouch and looked around, lowering his blaster, but still searching the room with his eyes...

...Which was why he wasn't expecting what came from the rear.

There was the sound of the door closing quietly, then soft hands encircled him from behind, and Sofia slid around his body, under his arm, to smile up at him.

"What the...?!" he began, trying to move Sofia to one side. "Stay behind me, Sofia. It could be dangerous."

"Nonsense, darling," she purred. "We both know you're right where we both want you to be. Well, maybe not QUITE," she amended, nodding at something deeper in the apartment. "The bedroom is over there, after all."

"Hellfire damnation!" Echo cursed. "You don't mean to tell me—"

And suddenly Sofia was all hands.

She put both palms on his chest, sliding them around, underneath his jacket, and managing to dislodge the left side of the garment; a quick grab-and-jerk on her part pulled his Suit jacket half off his body, as the left sleeve slipped down over his hand, the shoulder ending up hooked around his elbow. The same hand slid down his back, across one buttock, and along the outside of his thigh, just as the other arm encircled his torso. Sofia pressed her breasts against his chest, resting her cheek against his breastbone, before he could free a forearm enough to push her back—one hand still held his blaster, and the other was caught in his jacket sleeve.

She reached for the blaster in his hand, evidently intent

276

on removing it from his grasp. He thrust it upward, out of her reach; the move jerked his left arm upward, as his jacket yanked it up like a sling.

"OH, no you don't!" he growled. "Keep your hands off my weaponry, dammit!"

"All I want to do is to lay it down, dear heart," Sofia purred. "You won't be needing it."

"The hell you say!"

This dance went on for several minutes; unfortunately, holding the blaster over his head opened up Echo's torso to Sofia's attentions, and further bound his left arm, still stuck in his sleeve. She began caressing his chest, sliding her hands around his ribcage, as she deposited kisses on his shirt front, and he had as much as he could do to keep her from removing his other blaster from its holster. He backed up several steps, but she only followed him, her arms wrapping around him.

Echo tucked his right arm, forcing the forearm down between his body and Sofia's, keeping the blaster pointed to his left and his finger out of the trigger guard. Then he shoved her away with that same forearm, hard, and she staggered back. He made a quick decision and holstered the weapon, deciding that the danger he faced was more immediate and less deadly than the blaster warranted.

But before Echo could readjust his jacket and free his imprisoned arm, Sofia was back. She grabbed his tie, and one quick, deft, twisting jerk pulled the knot undone—suddenly the loose ends of his tie were dangling down his chest.

"Holy shit!" he exclaimed in surprise. "How the hell did you do that?!"

"Experience, darling," Sofia breathed with a seductive smile. "Unlike your poor dear partner, I'm not new at this game." And suddenly one hand squirmed between the buttons of Echo's shirt, finding skin and fondling. Her other hand reached for the shirt's buttons. Echo grabbed that hand with his lone free hand, yanking it away from his body.

"—The hell?! Gronk! Stop that!"

"You don't really mean that." She pushed her hand farther inside his shirt, groping toward one breast.

"Dammit, Sofia, what the HELL do you think you're doing?!" he cried. "Get your damn hands off me! Shit, cut that out! Get your hand outta there! Glag'gub'it! Let go, dammit! Son of a bitch! Will you just STOP IT?! Damn! Sofia, what the hell are you trying to do?! Mierda!"

"Darling, isn't it obvious? You want to be seduced, and I plan on doing the seducing. Now just calm down and quit worrying; I promise this will be a lovely evening, if you'll only relax and let it happen." She pressed him backward. "Just keep going; that's right. Right over here. The sofa is right behind you, darling. Relax and sit down. I've got this."

"The hell you say! I don't appreciate being brought here under false pretenses, Sofia! Especially when I've told you repeatedly that I'm not available, dammit! Abdab!"

"Oh, of course you are, darling. You wouldn't have come here if you weren't. You're a smart boy; you knew what was in the wind, but you came anyway."

"Only because you told me that the bastard Theater Phantom was here, and you were afraid to come home, damn you!"

"Now, now, sweetheart, just—"

"HELLFIRE! SONUFABITCH! GET YOUR DAMN HANDS *OFF* ME, G'DANK'EN GR'UB!"

The front door opened and Alpha Two walked in.

"What th' hell is goin' on here?!" Romeo demanded, as he and India took in the scene.

* * *

An incensed India placed a sullen, red-faced Sofia in an armchair and stood guard over her while Romeo helped Echo get his clothing back in order.

"Thanks, guys," Echo murmured. "I lost count of how many arms she's got. India, can you scan her and make sure she's not from Uzshei?"

"I already did," a sardonic India declared, flat. "She's

human. Just the two arms. But evidently she knows how to use 'em pretty fast."

"No shit."

"Is there anything even here?" Romeo wondered, as Echo finished re-tying his necktie.

"I doubt it," Echo decided, shrugging to adjust the positioning of his Suit jacket. "But I suppose, given she did register a complaint to us, we need to be thorough and sweep the place anyway."

"Damn," Romeo grumbled. "This 's gonna be a helluva waste of time."

"Ain't that the truth," Echo said. "India, would you mind ensuring she stays right where she is, while Romeo and I check out the place?"

"It would be my pleasure, Echo," India said, throwing the prima donna a glare that would melt lead. "I'm glad to help out my department chief, friend, and mentor. Let alone the man who's been named the Assistant Director, and future Director."

Sofia's red, flushed face paled slightly.

* * *

Sofia had a large, opulent condominium that actually covered more than one floor, so it took Romeo and Echo some little time to sweep it properly and ensure no other entity was, in fact, there.

"Which is a waste of time, like you said," an annoyed Echo noted, "but we have to do it."

"I know," Romeo muttered, continuing to help his former partner scan the dwelling. "It jus' makes me mad when I realize how she groped th' hell outta ya, an' Meg at home mopin' by 'erself."

"Wait," Echo said, stopping dead. "Why is Meg moping?"

"I'm not completely sure what went down, but evidently Ms. Grope-y in there," Romeo jerked a thumb over his shoulder, "mos' likely told th' pretty lady that you an' her had a little thang goin' down." He shrugged. "That's what me 'n India think, anyway. She wadn't talkin' to us much, though, so

I can't tell ya, positive."

"Aw, damn," Echo griped. "So Sofia managed to upset Meg into the bargain."

"SOMEthin' was sure upsettin' 'er," Romeo allowed, "but she wouldn't say what. What she DID say was that you an' Grope-y 'uz meetin' up, an' Grope-y told 'er it wadn't anything t' do with no perp."

"I'm getting really tired of the bitch—Ms. Grope-y, you called her? It fits—sticking her nose in between me and Meg every chance she gets," Echo continued his complaint. "If it wasn't for the fact that she's the one we're ostensibly trying to protect, and that she and Mike are good friends, I'd be about ready to say the hell with this whole damn mess, go back to Headquarters, and spend some quality private time with my partner."

"Y'all serious, then?"

"Aw, hell, I dunno, Junior," Echo sighed. "I'd like us to be. But Meg is so...on edge...all the time lately, I'm not sure if I'm ridin' a roller coaster or traversing a mine field."

"Or ridin' a roller coaster THROUGH a mine field," Romeo chuckled, nudging Echo with an elbow, urging him to lighten up.

Echo took the hint, and tried to offer a laugh, but it was weak. Finally he simply shook his head, and they resumed scanning the deluxe condo.

* * *

"I gave Ms. Sofia a little talking-to," India said several hours later, in the condominium building's parking garage. The Lexus was parked next to the Corvette, and the three Agents were doing a quick tag-up before heading home to Headquarters. "I basically told her that if she ever pulled a stunt like that again—if I even so much as HEARD of her putting her hands on any Division One agent, but especially you, Echo—she would NOT like the consequences. And I pointed out that since I used to be an ER doc, and now have access to galactic tech, I know how to cause extreme unpleasantness without causing...

PERMANENT...or detectable...harm." India chuckled, a grim, wry sound. "I don't think she'll try that again."

"Good," Echo noted. "You can get away with that easier than I could, in the circumstances. And this conversation never happened."

"Got it," Romeo and India said together.

"So neither of you found anything?" India asked then.

"Not a thing, babe," Romeo averred. "Me 'n Echo are a hundred percent convinced she made up th' whole damn thing, just t' get him over here so she could try 'n seduce 'im."

"Although she's got a damn odd idea of what constitutes seduction," Echo noted.

"Well, I think she's completely discounted Meg in her calculations," India decided. "She looks at her and sees the uncertainty, the aftermath of the whole Wright stalking thing, plus leftovers of discovering Slug's machinations...and that's ALL she sees. She has no idea how capable, how intelligent, how truly badass, Meg really is, because Meg's in a bad place right now."

"Speaking of which, if what Romeo mentioned to me is right, I need to get home to Meg pretty soon quick," Echo said. "We got no Theater Phantom here, so it was a huge time sink, when I could have spent some time with my partner."

"I agree, and I think that's an excellent idea," India agreed. "Let's go home, guys."

They piled into their respective vehicles and headed out.

* * *

Upon arriving in the agents' housing section of Headquarters, Omega had entered her apartment, still hopeful. *After all,* she thought, *maybe it wasn't how Sofia made it sound. Maybe he wanted to interview her for more clues or something. He might still come home and want to be with me.*

But as the clock on the wall continued to mark off the passing seconds, seconds became minutes, and minutes became hours, the female Agent began to lose hope.

Finally the hour arrived when she had stayed up as late as

she dared, given the show schedule the next day. She went into the bedroom, closed the door, prepared and went to bed. As she reached for the bedside lamp switch, she saw the rose in the resin cube. She picked it up and turned it about in her hands, studying it as she did so, as she did every night.

Then, instead of finishing the nightly ritual and kissing it—a habit only interrupted a few times in recent weeks, when the man who had given the rose to her had shared the room with her, making the ritual too revealing of her emotions— she reluctantly placed it back on the nightstand with a sigh, switched off the light, and scooted down in the bed, pulling the covers to her chin before turning on her side and curling into a tight ball of pain.

She cried herself to sleep.

* * *

Several hours after Omega went to bed, Echo finally arrived home. Without hesitation, he headed straight for the 'back door' between his and Omega's quarters, only to find her apartment dark, the bedroom door most of the way closed.

*Aw, damn,* he thought, disappointed. *She must have gotten tired of waiting and went on to bed. I thought I'd never get done at Sofia's place, so I could come to Meg. Well, at least I can let her know I'm here.*

He moved to the bedroom door, opening it and slipping inside.

Omega lay quiet, curled in the bed, dimly lit by the soft orange glow of the night light in the corner; her soft, slow respiration told him she was asleep. He smiled, tiptoed to the side of the bed, and sat down gingerly, reaching for the bedside lamp, turning up the brightness barely enough to see his partner, wanting to look at her for a few minutes before betaking himself to his own bed. Then he did a double-take, brows knitting in chagrin.

The tearstains on her face were obvious. *She cried herself to sleep, when I didn't come in a reasonable time,* he realized, biting his lip, troubled. *Dammit. She really IS gonna be upset.*

He reached out and brushed a wisp of spun platinum from her face, and she stirred at the light contact, then red-rimmed sapphire eyes flickered and opened.

"Echo?" she whispered, voice hoarse and low.

"Yeah, it's me, baby," he told her, keeping his own voice quiet. "I'm finally here."

* * *

Omega pushed up on one arm, trying to wake up and focus. *He's here,* she thought. *And he came to me. Maybe it really was only a business thing. I wonder what he found.*

Echo leaned toward her, his intent to kiss her plain. She stretched upward to meet it, welcoming the sign of his affection.

Then she smelled it.

Sofia's perfume.

All over him.

A tsunami of betrayal washed over her.

* * *

With a slight smile, Echo leaned in to kiss his partner. Abruptly, and to his shock, Omega pulled back, averting her face. The mental firewall solidified into granite.

"Get out," she practically growled, tone low and threatening.

"Huh? What's wrong?" he wondered, confused. "What did I do?"

"Do you think I can't smell her perfume all over you?" Omega demanded, and Echo blinked. She threw a glance at the clock, checking the hour—which was either very late, or very early, depending on one's point of view—then scowled. "You've been with her all night. I don't know what kind of games you think you're playing, Echo, but I want no part of it. Go play with her, if you've a mind to."

"Baby, I didn't—"

"GET OUT!"

If they hadn't trained so much together, Echo would never have seen the slap coming. But he instinctively threw up a hand and caught her forearm in mid-swing.

"Stop that," he told her, stern. "Hear me out, at least."

"I don't need to. I know what happened."

"Obviously you don't, or you wouldn't have just tried to clock the guy who wanted to kiss you."

"Past tense," she sighed, dropping her gaze to the blankets.

"What?"

"Just go on to bed, Echo," Omega murmured, sudden anger gone, replaced by morose dejection. "I'm not gonna take advantage of...recent events...so don't worry."

Echo merely stared at her, still confused.

"What the hell are you talking about, baby?"

"Kissing me, versus kissing her," she whispered. "She's beautiful, she's talented...and she's a normal human. I'm... anything but. I get that it's probably something you've been curious about for a long time by this point, so now you've got your answer. She's the better choice." Omega turned away, lying down and curling up, her back to him. "Now turn out the light and go to your own room, and let me sleep. I have performances to deal with, and to try to stay alive through...at least long enough to capture the perp."

*Aw shit,* Echo thought, in a blend of annoyance, upset, and deep concern, not even trying to hide it from her—not that she showed evidence of picking up on it through the nd't'lq, given how hard her mental wall was at that moment. *Here we go again with the 'I'm not human' mess. I get why it upsets her... at least, as far as she'll let me in to see it, anyway...but every time I think I've got her worked through it, it crops back up. I'm starting to get worried, though; this is getting worse and worse, ever since Wright showed up, with that whole pile of shit. She doesn't need to lose it, not in the middle of a dangerous operation like the one we've got. It could get one or both of us killed. And worse, it sounds like she's starting to not care.*

"All right, I'll go back to my room...for now," he agreed. "But we're gonna discuss this in the morning."

"There's nothing to discuss."

"Yes, there is. And we ARE going to discuss it."

Echo leaned over and kissed Omega's cheek. She flinched,

and tried to shy away; the reaction hurt him deeply, but he hid the fact. He switched off the bedside lamp, rose, and turned for the bedroom door.

"Good night, baby," he told her. "Sleep well. We'll talk tomorrow."

And he was gone.

* * *

When Omega woke the next morning, Echo was sitting on the bedside, clad in lounge pants and t-shirt, moccasin slippers shoved on his feet, watching and waiting for her to awaken. The faint scent of chicory coffee floated through the air.

"Wha...?" she wondered, pushing up in bed and groggily rubbing sleepy eyes. "Has something happened?"

"No," Echo said, "and yes. No, there's not a mission-type emergency or anything. But we do have a little issue I promised to discuss with you. A certain personal issue. If you won't let me tell you, will you at least let me show you telepathically?"

"I...really don't wanna see, Echo," Omega murmured, heart sinking. "Like I told you last night, she's the better choice. Don't...don't worry about it."

"Omega, she's not MY choice!" a red-faced Echo exclaimed, intensely frustrated, and Omega stared at him, shocked by his vehemence. "She's playing her damn head games again! Now, I dunno what the hell she told YOU, but she told ME that she'd apparently had the Theater Phantom show up at HER place, and she was afraid to go home alone! Given she's worked with Mike long enough to know who he really is and where he's from, she also knows who and what we are, and she asked me to come back and check the place out! I THOUGHT she'd asked BOTH members of Alpha One to come, but I knew you were tired, so I didn't think too awful much about it when you chose to come home alone—I figured you needed to crash, especially if you had a headache threatening...like you claimed." He raised an eyebrow, and she understood the unspoken question.

"O-okay..." She stared at him. "I, uh, I didn't actually have a headache yet, but like I said, one was threatening, Ace, I swear. I was getting those twinges, you know? And I did come home and take half a dolocet. It...helped. So did...did getting some sleep."

"Good. I'd have brought you home myself, except Sofia was insisting that she had to have SOMEone with her, somebody capable of handling the situation, or she wouldn't feel safe. And somehow, I didn't especially want to bring her by Headquarters while I ran you home, and end up with her seeing where we lived, let alone the heart of the Agency; I was afraid she'd just show up on our doorstep at some point. Or worse, tell some of her human friends. Worst of all, BRING some of her human friends."

"Um, all right. That all makes sense, Ace."

"But I'm not stupid; I figured I'd want backup, one way or another," Echo continued. "If it WAS Slug, I'd need help. I didn't figure you'd leave me out to lunch on the telepathic block, but I wasn't sure how bad your headache was..."

"No; I called Zz'r'p last night and asked him to, uh, discreetly put a 'guard' around you," Omega murmured. "And he did; I made sure I felt it go up before I would drop mine."

* * *

"Thanks, baby," he replied, settling a little. "So I trusted you to keep me safe from a mental attack, one way or another; I just wasn't sure how you were gonna do it and get any rest. That worked fine, what you did. BUT...I figured either I was letting myself in for a physical attack, or...well, it was fishy; she couldn't give me ANY details of what had supposedly happened to scare her so bad. Therefore, I started to suspicion that Sofia was maybe playing head games again...so I grabbed Romeo before we ever left the theater, and had Alpha Two meet me at Sofia's place."

"Huh? Romeo?"

"Yeah. So he and India both came over, after they dropped you off here," Echo explained. "Only they didn't get there until after Sofia tried to make her move on me. Which, I guess, is where I got her perfume on me that you smelled last night. DAMN, but she's got arms like an octopus! Only don't tell Klack I said that; I wouldn't want to offend him!" He flashed her a slight smile, and Omega snickered despite herself; the amiable and mischievous octopus agent Burbulon Vex, aka Klack, was stationed at the Atlantis Office, and was a good friend of the Alpha One team. "Evidently that woman has some really strange ideas about what constitutes seduction, because she seriously thought that's what she was doing, but... shit! I guess she figured if she could get a significant part of my clothes off, she could have her way with me or something. Like, maybe she thought I was only playing hard to get or... whatever."

"Oh?" Omega murmured. "Aw geez. And?"

"Oh HELL no," Echo declared. "I don't take off my clothes for just anybody, baby. I'm not even quite ready to do that for you yet, though I like the idea a whole lot." He shrugged. "I think if we found the right combination of timing and mood, you an' me, no problem. But it hasn't happened yet. And I'm not willing to push it. SHE was."

"Okay; fair enough. Keep going."

"All right." Echo didn't attempt to hide his pleased response to her request to continue, considering how hard she had tried to avoid it, only moments before. "Anyway, India and Romeo interrupted her attempts to get my jacket, shirt, and tie off, so they can confirm that I wanted no part of her, because I was cussing a blue streak in multiple languages when they came in, and Sofia turned twelve shades of red as soon as she saw 'em. I'll call Romeo for him an' India to come over here and tell you, if you want me to." Echo jerked a thumb over his shoulder.

"No," Omega said, her voice quiet, eyes wide. "I believe you, Ace. Or, well, I would like to get their description of that scene, just for shits and giggles!" she admitted, then snorted. "I guess it WAS hard, because we don't want to offend somebody we're trying to protect, but..."

"Exactly! DAMN," Echo exclaimed. "I was right before not caring, though! She managed to grab my tie just right to yank it and undo the knot, though I dunno how; that knot is supposed to be designed not to loosen or tighten until the AGENT gets ready—that way a perp can't try to choke you with it or something. But maybe I'm not the first Division One agent she's been around; I dunno. So she's got my tie undone and she's yanked my jacket off one shoulder and got my arm tangled in the sleeve, and the blaster's in my other hand, so I got NO hands to do anything. And she's reaching for the buttons on my shirt—she actually got one hand inside my shirt; I've already showered twice since I got home—and I'm pushing off hands and backing up...and thank GOD we left the front door unlocked, because that's when Alpha Two came in." He shrugged. "At that point, Sofia finally backed off. I redid my tie, refastened several shirt buttons, and got my jacket squared away, and then India ensured Sofia stayed put, while Romeo and I did a detailed sweep of her condo, just for the sake of thoroughness, 'cause Fox woulda had a herd of longhorns if we hadn't. Which condo is mondo huge, and took for-damn-ever. It woulda gone faster if all three of us could have worked on it, but none of us wanted Sofia up and roaming around! And— surprise, surprise—we didn't find one damn thing. I talked it over with India and Romeo once we got back to the parking garage for her condo, and we're all convinced she made up the whole thing, just to try to get me over there, alone."

"Oh dear," Omega murmured, then chuckled. "I'm sorry, Ace. I don't mean to laugh; I just keep sorta picturing this scene from some comedy film..."

"No, that's okay," Echo offered, shaking his head with a wry grin, and secretly relieved to see her mood had changed. "I get it, and it probably did look like that, I guess. Though I was a little too busy at the time to think about it!"

"I'll bet!"

"Do you wanna see it from my point of view now?"

"Um...maybe. I..."

*Just look, baby. It's okay. You're not gonna see me doing anything that'll make you unhappy, though you probably won't be happy with Sofia.*

*Um. Okay.*

So Echo showed her a few moments of memory of the incident, from his perspective—which was really all it took to show her ALL of it, it had happened so fast. Omega was incensed for her partner.

*Whoa. Did she actually try to grab your butt?*

*Uh. Damn. I guess she did, at that. It all went down so fast, I actually missed it. It's like, suddenly she had twelve hands, and they were goin' everywhere, an' I was just tryin' to get 'em all away from me. If I'd had two seconds' respite to get my left arm untangled from my Suit jacket, she'd never have managed as much as she did, but I think she did that deliberately, for exactly that reason. Frankly, I'm surprised she didn't try to grab my crotch, but I do believe she honestly thought she was being seductive, so she might have thought that was too much, too soon. If she'd managed to get much more of my clothes undone, she probably would've, though. I think she was goin' after a nipple, as it was; she just didn't get her hand far enough into my shirt.*

*If she had, I mean grabbed your crotch, what would you...?*

*Well, let's put it like this: Dad and Ma raised me to be a Southern gentleman—you know that; I try my hardest to be one around you, honey—but years in this job have taught me certain reflexes. Never mind the adult comprehension, based on experience, that not everybody is deserving of the 'Southern gentleman' treatment. If she'd grabbed the family jewels, if Sofia had really tried that, I expect India would have needed her medikit upon arrival. Repairing a busted nose and ensuring it heals straight is hard even for galactic tech, though. She might not have been a leading lady anymore when I got done, if she'd tried it.*

*Okay. I, uh, I'm sorry I left you to her attentions, Ace. What she communicated to me was kinda different than what she told you.*

*What did she tell you?*

*It wasn't so much what she SAID, as the way she said it. You know what I mean? She made it sound like you two had arranged it, and the whole 'need to have the condo checked' was only what y'all were telling people to avoid gossip. I mean, our cover story was that you were with me, so people had to think...*

*Okay, I get that picture. Look, baby. I'll be honest with you. I do think Sofia is a beautiful woman. And if Romeo and I were still partners—meaning, you and I had never met— then I might have responded to her initial advances. Maybe. Emphasis on maybe, and might have; and given her slightly weird predilections, I doubt it would have lasted much past a couple dates and possibly a smooch session, especially if last night was any indication. But none of that is the case. I've got somebody beside me that I enjoy having beside me. Somebody I like being around, a lot, and that I want to eventually have around ALL the time. As in, 24-7. Or, well, 48-7, I guess. And that somebody is you, not her.*

*O-okay. Are...are you sure?*

*Absolutely positive.*

*All right.* There was a silence. Then Echo heard a mental giggle, and Omega added, *I bet it still looked like a comedy scene. From outside your perspective, at least. INSIDE your perspective, not so much. I could sense your annoyance. And I don't blame you at all.*

*Yeah. Probably. If nothing else, it might make a good scene for a romantic comedy or something, I guess.*

*Maybe so. But you know what?*

*What?*

*If I'd been there, I'd 'a punched her lights out. I'm flat, downright furiously angry about it. You'd have had to put me on report. I'd have lit into her like a freakin' buzz saw. And she'd 'a had a helluva lot more than a broken nose when I was done.*

*That...you're gonna think this is stupid, baby, but...that makes me feel really good.*

They were quiet again for a moment, as both of them took in what had happened, and what their respective reactions meant.

"Seriously, ask India and Romeo," Echo suggested aloud after several more moments. "I won't mind, and I won't be offended. They can probably give you a better idea of what it looked like. I expect it WAS pretty funny, after a fashion. Now that I think about it, Romeo did have kind of an odd look on his face when he and India came in and saw the scene."

"Like maybe he was trying not to laugh?"

"Exactly. Although it changed from 'trying not to laugh' to 'seriously pissed off' really damn quick, once the full scenario hit him."

"Okay."

"Now, are we all right, you and me?"

"I...guess so, yeah."

"Good. Can I have a kiss now?"

"Um, about that," Omega began, and Echo furrowed his brows, worried. "Would you mind...easing back just a smidgen? I'm not saying stop," she hastened to add. "I'm only...I mean, with everything that's going on, I..."

"You're struggling a little bit?"

"Yeah, kinda. More than a little, if I'm honest. If, if we hadn't gotten thrown into this mission right off," she tried to explain, and Echo could sense her inner turmoil through the nd't'lq, "we could have sorta eased into it more, and maybe I'd have the time to think, and to get used to it and be...more confident in it...instead of, of knee-jerking all the time, and default assuming that..."

"Oh. I get it," Echo decided. "Too many distractions."

"Bingo." Omega looked relieved that he understood. "I think that's one reason why Sofia is doing what she's doing; she senses my lack of confidence, how I'm still trying to get used to the idea that you and I can have...THAT kind of, of relationship...and she's..."

"Taking advantage of it," Echo finished for her, in tacit agreement. "Yeah, that makes a lot of sense—and now that I think about it, I believe India mentioned something last night about that being her take on it, too. Okay, baby. Then how about this?"

He took her shoulders in gentle hands, then leaned forward and placed a soft, chaste kiss on her lips. She reacted fast enough to return it in kind.

"There's our good-morning kiss," he told her. "Nothing too distracting, but enough to remind you of who and what you are to me. Which thing is my very special partner. In every sense of the word."

"That'll work," she murmured, offering him a shy smile. "Thanks for understanding, hon."

"I told you to begin with, we'd go at the pace you were comfortable, baby," he reminded her. "If you need for the relationship-development stuff to slow down while we work through a complicated, dangerous situation, it makes sense to me, and I have no problems doing that." Echo stood, and held out a hand. "I made a whole pot of strong coffee earlier. Now, let's go get you a mug of it, and see about breakfast."

* * *

The majority of the day was spent in their quarters, watching TV, reading, and talking; Omega's call was not until the early evening, so Echo chose to let her rest as much as he could. He was glad that Zz'r'p had worked with his people and allowed her to get some sleep the previous night, while still ensuring that Alpha One was protected.

"And Zz'r'p already contacted me," she told him, tapping her temple, "and said he and his colleagues would take turns keeping us shielded in an extended block until we got ready for the theater tonight, anyway. So if I decide to take a nap, I can, and we won't have any problems with it."

"That works," Echo decided. "Damn, I wish the Arcturan envoy had been this large last year, when we had our big run-in with Slug."

"Ain't it the truth," Omega agreed. "That trade negotiation extension he worked out with Sugar at the end of the year really helped open things up diplomatically, I think."

"Yeah."

But as he watched her, seeing her tension and general dispirited mood, Echo began to fully grasp that down time, especially emotional down time, was what his partner needed now, and that was something he could ensure. More, she seemed to truly appreciate the fact.

So Echo chose cheerful, entertaining movies from his collection—a lot of them were funny animated films—thereby getting Omega to laugh. He kept their conversation light, telling jokes and tales on himself, from childhood all through his career as a Division One Agent—which, he noted with pleasure, seemed to delight her. He pressured her for nothing, not even her attention. He ensured she ate well and nutritiously, and that she stayed flexible and physically comfortable. When she did take a short nap, right after lunch, he tucked a throw around her and tiptoed around, allowing her to sleep. After a few minutes, he sat down in the armchair close by, and simply watched her sleep.

*And after all,* he decided as he sat and watched over her, *probably what we need to do when this is all over, is head off up to the beach house in Ipswich again for about a week. That way she can relax and unwind with no pressure and no deadlines. She's not gonna get her energy completely back until this is all over and she has extended time to rest. But we can handle this, for the time being.*

She woke half an hour later, still tired, but in a much more cheerful mood.

By midafternoon, when it was time to start thinking about getting ready to go to the theater, she was joking with him again.

# Chapter 11

The theater sets had been positioned for curtain, the tech crew had set props, and most of the cast were already in the dressing rooms warming up and applying makeup, by the time Omega and Echo arrived at the theater, somewhat later than usual. Romeo and India met them backstage.

"Hey, hey, it's the man an' his pretty lady," Romeo said, and grinned as they walked up. "Still got th' head thing goin', you two?"

Echo and Omega didn't even glance at each other, but India saw the twinkle of mischief in brown and blue eyes alike.

"You—" Omega began.

"—know—" Echo added, timing perfect.

"—it—" Omega continued, without pause.

"—Junior," Echo finished.

"Oh, this is gonna be a weird evening." India rolled her eyes. "Conjoined twins, connected at the mind."

"Something like that," Echo acknowledged.

"Hey, um, 're y'all...okay?" Romeo wondered, trying to be delicate. "I mean, last night was a big steamin' pile o' horse shit..."

"I'd have called it ass shit," India muttered darkly, "and we all know who the ass was, damn her."

The other three Agents stifled snorts.

"I love this woman," Romeo declared, putting an arm around his life partner, who offered a sardonic smile. "She ain't afraid t' call 'em like she sees 'em. So. Guys? Y'all good?"

"I think so, Junior," Echo considered. "We had a long talk this morning, Meg an' me, once she woke up good. And I explained stuff, and she told me what Sofia had led her to believe, which was way different from what Sofia told ME. Anyway, she knows what really happened. Though I think she's gonna want a description of the whole clown-car routine from you guys!" he added, and Omega stifled a giggle.

"Huh?" India said, confused.

"Oh!" Romeo exclaimed. "I think they mean what it looked like, when we walked in on Sofia's shit, an' Echo all tangled up in 'is own coat?"

"Exactly," Omega said, grinning wider. "I know it wasn't REALLY funny, 'cause Echo showed me what went down from his perspective." She tapped her temple. "But I kept picturing this scene from a rom-com or something!"

A doubtful India looked askance, but Romeo snorted.

"Yeah, okay," the younger man agreed. "Later on, when we got time, I'll tell ya. An' you're right; I ain't never seen Echo in a sitch like that before!"

"Okay," Echo agreed with a sheepish grin. "Meg? You never did answer the man. Are we...good?"

"Oh. Yeah, we're good, Romeo," Omega said with a soft smile. "Thanks for asking."

"No prob, pretty lady. I'm jus' glad things worked out. Me 'n India 'uz worried boutchu last night—worried 'bout the whole mess. Hey, Echo, th' theater's clear, man," Romeo reported then. "India an' I been all over it with a fine-toothed comb."

"Twice," India added. "Out front and backstage, both times. Sir Michael helped out on the backstage part, so we know our way around now."

"Good," Omega replied. "In fact, that's great. Can y'all keep patrolling the house and the stage areas a while longer without Echo?"

"Sure, Meg," India volunteered. "Why?"

"Yeah, Meg, what's up?" Echo glanced at his partner, curiosity engaged.

"Nothing major," she noted with a grin. "Another lesson in the art of theatrical makeup. You had an assignment, remember? I'll grant, it's been a few days since we've had a chance to think about it, but hey."

"Oh, yeah," Echo recalled, and Alpha Two stared at him as if he'd lost his mind. "I'm supposed to paint your face. You want me to do it tonight?"

"It's as good a time as any. You said you thought it might come in useful, one of these days, if you knew how, too. And we got Alpha Two backing us up tonight, so you should have some time to spare, to do it."

"Good points, all. Okay."

"Wait, wait, wait," Romeo interrupted. "Echo, you gonna play in Meg's makeup shit? I thought you hated that crap."

"Well, I hate the way it feels on ME, yeah," Echo admitted. "But Meg is teaching me a few things about how it can be used to change or modify your appearance, and I'm starting to see how the skill could be useful, especially if we should ever happen NOT to have access to more high-tech disguises. And she knows how to do it. So I figured it might be a good thing to learn." He shrugged. "I don't necessarily wanna wear it myself, though I would if I HAD to. But broadening the skill base can only be a good thing, ya know?"

"Yeah, I guess it makes sense," Romeo decided, somewhat skeptical.

"I think it makes really good sense," India declared. "Meg, after this is all over with, maybe you can do a departmental seminar?"

"Ooo, there's an idea," Echo said. "How 'bout it, baby?"

"I...would consider that," Omega conceded. "Might I have a volunteer as a model, there, India?"

"You bet," India agreed immediately.

"Bingo," Echo said.

"Y'all think it's that important?" Romeo wondered.

"It could be, in the right circumstances," Echo determined. "And it's a lot more interesting than you'd think, based on our one film experience, Romeo."

"Awright. I guess I'll give it a shot, then."

"You two had better get going," India said, glancing at her wrist chronometer. "You don't wanna be late for curtain."

"Right," Omega said, getting in gear. She grabbed Echo's tie and tugged lightly, affectionately. "Let's go, Michelangelo."

* * *

Omega went into the bathroom and washed her face while Echo removed his Suit jacket, hanging it alongside her costumes on the wardrobe rack, and rolled up his shirt sleeves. Then she came back into the dressing room proper and sat at the makeup table, tired despite her afternoon's rest; Echo ducked into the bathroom and washed his hands, assuring they'd be sanitary when he worked on his partner's facial skin. When he came back into the dressing room, Omega was still sitting, staring into space with an absent expression.

So Echo stood, waiting. Omega glanced up at him.

"Well, come on, Ace. Let's get started." She waved a finger toward the makeup kit.

"I...was waiting for you to throw up..."

"Oh. Blarg. There. All done."

"C'mon, Meg," Echo chuckled. "I don't wanna get halfway into this, and you suddenly have to toss it."

"Actually," she admitted quietly, "I already did. Before we even left our quarters to come here, while I was getting dressed to leave." She sighed. "I thought you would have picked up on it through the nd't'lq." She shook her head in mild annoyance at herself. "That's actually why I got sick earlier than usual; I had the time to think about it today. And I was trying so hard to damp down the stage fright so it wouldn't affect you through the nd't'lq, I got all anxious and wrapped around the axle, and ended up making it worse."

"Oh," Echo realized. "So that's why my gut tied itself in knots earlier. I couldn't figure out what I ate to mess it up, and nothing settled it. It finally just calmed down on its own." He pondered. "Now that I think about it, I bet I can determine when you got sick last night, too...only..." He frowned, considering. "Did you barf twice last night?"

"Um, yeah, I did," Omega confessed. "I, uh, Sofia's little head games kinda upset me, and, and I hadn't gotten my tum quite settled from the first barfing session, so..." Omega blushed.

"Aw, honey. All right; that makes sense now," he decided.

"I'm sorry, Ace." Omega hung her head, embarrassed.

"'S okay, baby. Pitfalls of being conjoined twins connected at the mind, I suppose. I'm kinda...pleased...that, well, not that you were upset," Echo admitted. "Just that you cared enough TO get upset, I guess. I hope that makes sense to you." Omega nodded, so Echo sat down and prepared to begin work. "All right, tell me how to do this."

"Well, there's several schools of thought behind the various application techniques," Omega explained. "You can use sponges, brushes, or fingers to apply the stuff. I've seen really talented makeup artists that used any or all of the above."

"What do you tend to do? I saw you using brushes the other day..."

"I use a little of all of it," Omega noted. "I like to apply my moisturizer with my fingers, because I can feel if I've applied enough or too much that way. The grease stick foundation, I dot directly on my face, 'cause it's in a swivel-up tube like a fat lipstick, then I blend it with a sponge. If I can't find a sponge, my fingers will do okay, but it won't be as smooth, I don't think. The powder stuff tends to work better with brushes, at least for me, though I've used shaped sponges. Heck, I've even used fingers in a pinch. You just gotta pick the right finger; around my eyes, I'd use my little finger, but for my cheeks, I might use my thumbs..."

"Okay, I can see that. So first...you said moisturizer, right? Because it keeps your skin from absorbing the makeup?"

"Right. Here it is." She handed him the tube. "I got a spare sponge here if you'd rather use that."

"No, I understand the idea of 'feeling' it as it goes on," Echo averred. "I'll use my fingers." He didn't tell her it was partly because he wanted to be able to touch her face, feel her smooth skin under his fingers, and he tried hard to keep that thought hidden behind the mental firewall she had established, not sure how she would take it, especially given recent events. *But she's already beautiful,* he thought. *If I can do justice at all to the image I've got in my mind, by the time I'm done, she'll look drop-dead, awe-inspiring, flat gorgeous onstage.* "How much do I use, to start?"

"Take the tube and squeeze a little bitty dollop on your index and middle fingers," Omega said, apparently unaware of the thoughts and emotions he was trying hard to keep under control, much to his relief. She reached for the tube. "Here; let me show you, the first time." She squeezed a small blob onto his fingertips. "There. Now, if this were my everyday makeup, that would cover my whole face with a very thin film. But it needs to be a bit heavier for stage makeup, so see if you can get that to cover one cheek and most of my forehead—say at least half my forehead. If you need to use more, though, do it—it isn't gonna hurt anything; some days, my skin is drier than others. Then use another dollop the same size, and you should be able to get the rest of my face—the other cheek, the rest of my forehead, nose, upper lip, and chin. Sometimes it works better if you apply a slightly smaller blob to the cheek and forehead, and then a teensy little dab to my nose an' chin. About that much again should get my neck and throat, though you'll probably have to use a smidge more for that area."

"I need to do that, too?" Echo blinked. "Your neck, I mean."

"Yeah. Take it down all the way past my collarbones, if you can. I've got some low necklines, and the makeup needs to fade out, along about there. So make sure you blend the edge out, real well, when you apply the foundation. I'll show you what I mean, once we get there."

"Okay. Um...past your collarbones, you said?" Echo said, frowning.

"Yeah. Don't look so worried," Omega said with a grin. "Be glad I don't have any serious cleavage showing in this one!"

"*I* wouldn't mind if you did," Echo declared, raising a rakish eyebrow and offering her a mischievous grin. "I just didn't want YOU thinking I was getting a little too friendly, baby."

Omega snorted, then laughed.

"You're definitely a red-blooded, All-American, straight male, Ace," she decided. "Well, maybe that should be 'All-Earth,' but you know what I mean."

"Well...let's just say that I can appreciate beautiful women," he noted, applying moisturizer on her left cheek. "Especially the one I work with."

"Aw. That's sweet. Thank you."

"Just like the hot tub conversation, I meant it."

"I know."

Omega coached him through moisturizer, base, and contouring, then leaned back slightly and closed her eyes, resting her head on the chair back.

"That looks great; you're really getting the hang of this, Ace. All right, hon, you're on your own now. You've seen my costumes, so you know what color palette to use, and you've seen me apply it a couple times now, and you know how I blend it to avoid hard lines and keep everything subtle. Do my eyes next, then lips, then cheeks."

"Ooo-kay..."

Echo considered the relaxed face for a moment, pondering what specific color scheme to use, then selected eye shadow colors and commenced work with a characteristically steady hand. He moved on to eyeliner, applying it to upper and lower lids and 'winging' it slightly at the outer corner, as he'd seen her do, then stared at the mascara tube.

*I am NOT thrilled with this mascara shit. And this eyelash curler thing looks like a damn torture device,* he thought to himself in very decided terms. *If I try this, I'mma hurt her eyes or something. And that would be...bad.*

*All right, Ace,* the response came, *no sweat. I'll get it. It does take some getting used to. And yes, you can injure an eye if you're not careful. Finish the rest, then. Unless you want me to do the rest.*

*No, I can do that,* Echo replied, in some relief. *I just didn't wanna risk hurting you. I'm not tryin' to get outta the job or anything. It's kind of interesting, to tell the truth. I wanna see what I can make of it.*

*Okay. Go for it.*

He outlined her lips with the brownish-pink lip pencil, carefully painted on the same combination of lip colors as he had for the prior performance, then turned to her blush. He applied it, then leaned back and looked at it.

*Unh-uh,* he decided. *Not enough.*

So he added more, periodically leaning back and checking the intensity, until it was the same level she had achieved previously, whenever he had watched.

*Sorry, Angel, I refuse to think 'hooker,' not where you're concerned,* he thought, and grinned. To his satisfaction, he sensed vague amusement reflected back at him, so he continued with his task.

A few moments later, he surveyed his finished work. His lips parted to allow a slight exhalation of awe and desire, and the already-dark eyes grew darker, the pupils dilating—the room seemed to him to grow brighter—as he studied the calm, lovely face.

*I did it,* he thought in wonder. *Somehow, I did it. That's exactly how I wanted her to look for the show. Damn. She's... utterly, stunningly...exquisite.*

"Meg?" he said softly, cupping his hand around her cheek. She made no reply, but her head lolled over against his hand, her cheek resting in his palm, and he smiled. But when he tried to slide his hand back into her hair, he realized he was supporting her head.

"Meg?" he asked again, reaching out to her mentally. All he got was an incoherent jumble of images, flashes of dreams. "Oh, shit," Echo whispered, shaking her lightly. "She really is worn out. Honey, wake up. Wake up, Meg. Come on, sweetheart, wake up."

"What? Oh!" Omega came to her senses with an alarmed start. "Is everything all right?! Slug didn't—?!"

"No, no, Meg, calm down. Everything's all right. You just dozed off."

"Oh, wow. I'm really sorry, Echo," Omega murmured, still not fully alert. "When I hurled earlier, I musta lost the stimulants...it hadn't been that long since I'd taken 'em, but I thought it had been long enough to absorb 'em all, or at least enough. Maybe not, though."

"It's all right, Meg. No harm done," Echo soothed. "Do you want some more now?"

"Yeah. I better, if I'm gonna get through the performance." Omega yawned prodigiously.

Echo dug through her duffel and produced the bottle, extracting a capsule and handing it to her. Omega swallowed it dry, and a few moments later, she was back to normal.

"Okay, Ace, I've got the block back up," she told him, pushing her chair up to the dressing table in order to look into the mirror. "Now hand me the 'torture device,' would you? Oh WOW! GOOD job, Michelangelo...!"

* * *

The flawless performance was completely mind-blowing to Omega's impressed partner, as usual. Afterward, Echo took a wiped-out Omega home, leaving Romeo and India to secure the theater; given everything that was going on, Alpha One had largely given up on attempting to go out after the performances.

On the way home, Echo called Fox, requesting that the Arcturans telepathically secure the Headquarters building again, so his weary partner could get some well-earned rest. The Arcturans, concerned for their human protégé, promptly agreed.

Omega tumbled into bed as soon as she got home, and slept like the dead.

* * *

The next morning, a much better-rested Omega was up and about before Echo. She began breakfast preparation, but postponed actually cooking anything until Echo should indicate he was ready. When he failed to appear in a reasonable time, however, Omega became concerned.

"Echo?" she called, knocking on the back door's frame.

*In the bedroom, Meg,* came the mental answer, and she headed for Echo's bedroom door.

"Are you all right, Ace?" Omega grasped the doorknob. "You're kinda behind schedule this morning...by a lot, actually."

*No. I'm a long way from 'all right.'*

"Are you sick?"

*Yes.*

"Still in bed?"

*Yes.*

"Okay. I'll have you feeling better in a few minutes. I'm coming in."

*No, you're not.*

"What, are you sleeping in the buff again?"

*Yeah. I started feeling a little off before I crawled into bed last night. I thought I'd sleep better that way, at least for the night. And therefore, I am flat-out stark naked this morning. You need to stay out. That being only one of the reasons.*

"Echo, I'm doing theater." Omega grinned as she opened the door. "I've seen naked men before."

*Not this one, you haven't.*

"What are you worried about? You've got the covers pulled up to your neck." Omega offered the ill man a soft, teasing smile as she stepped inside. "Fever chills?"

*Hell, yeah. I feel like shit.* A listless Echo turned his head to look at her. *No, I take that back. Shit doesn't feel this bad.*

"Flu?"

*Yeah. Harrnakian, I think. Judging by the symptoms, at least.*

"Mm. You really do feel lousy, then. Harrnakian influenza is about the worst thing going. And I can speak from personal experience on that." Omega moved to Echo's side. She laid a light hand on his forehead as she sat on the edge of the bed.

*Meg, stop. Clear outta here, like five minutes ago. Of all people, you do NOT need to risk getting this shit.*

"Huh. You don't feel feverish...at all," Omega observed, shifting her hand from his forehead, to his cheek, to the back of his neck. "I think there's some antipathogen around here somewhere. Let me think...where the hell did I put it...?"

* * *

*Meg, I can't choke it down even if you find it.* Echo's eyes narrowed in pain as he tried to swallow. *My throat feels like it's been sandblasted. Now get outta here before you catch this shit and hose the damn mission. You couldn't possibly sing, like this. You probably couldn't even talk. The good Lord knows, I can't, right now.*

But Omega ignored him.

"Like I'm gonna let you lie here and suffer. Right." She stood and moved toward Echo's bathroom.

*Meg, for the last time...GET OUT!!*

So loud was the mental shout that Omega paled almost white; her entire body was paralyzed for a split-second. Abruptly and without a word, verbal or mental, she spun on her heel and walked out. The bedroom door slammed closed behind her.

Echo closed his eyes and turned his head to the wall, pain written on his face that was not due to any illness.

* * *

Shortly thereafter, another knock came on Echo's bedroom door. "Echo, it's us. It's Alpha Two," India's voice said through the door. "I know you can't talk. We're coming in to see about you." Romeo and India entered and moved over to flank the ill man.

"How'd...you know?" Echo croaked hoarsely.

"Shush, you. Save that voice. Meg called an' asked if India would come by an' check on ya," Romeo offered. "Said you might have a rip-roarin' good case of th' Harrnakian flu. We hadn't left f'r the theater yet, so we swung by her quarters, and she let us into yours through the back door."

"Echo, Meg said you yelled at her," an accusing India stared at him as she scanned his vital signs.

"...Sort of," Echo admitted, somehow managing to scratch out the words through his raw throat as he put a weary hand to his temple. "Didn't mean to. Head thing. Not used to it yet, and I was way louder than I meant to be. I just didn't want her to catch this crap, an' I was worried 'cause she kept insisting on tryin' to help, so I guess it had an adrenaline pump behind it."

"Open your mouth and let me see your throat," India ordered, and Echo obeyed, as she shone a light into his mouth. "Oh, wait. I get it, now. You didn't want her to risk getting sick, when she has to perform in the show, so since you couldn't talk, you 'raised your voice'...only you're not used to the mental conversing yet, and overdid it."

Rather than speak when it hurt so much, Echo simply nodded by way of reply. India continued her examination, producing a stethoscope and using it to listen to heart and lungs, then tapping his chest lightly while listening.

"And, knowin' Meg, she 'uz determined to help, regardless o' whether she risked contracting it or not, so she 'uz nosin' around all over, tryin' 'a check on ya an' shit," Romeo remarked, understanding. Echo nodded again, grimacing in pain from even that slight motion.

"This is...really strange," India declared after a few more moments spent examining Echo.

"What?" Echo rasped.

"You've got all the symptoms of Harrnakian influenza, all right, but you have absolutely no sign of infection," India explained. "Your temperature is normal, your throat looks fine, there are no signs of increased antibodies in your bloodstream..."

"Waitaminit, hon," Romeo interrupted. "He's sick, but he ain't sick?"

"That's right," India replied. "Echo, I'm not quite sure how to help you. I can give you some analgesics to ease the discomfort, but that's about it. There's no infection to fight. We need to get you down to the medlab right away, and see if we can figure out what's going on..."

"Perhaps I can help," a formal voice said from the door. Zz'r'p entered the bedroom as they turned to look.

"M' damn bedroom's worse'n Grand Central Station," Echo muttered, sounding not unlike he had been gargling gravel. "C'mon in an' join the party, Zz'r'p. Let's see what you can do."

"No offense, Zz'r'p, but how can you help?" India asked.

"Because, when Omega notified Fox and me of Echo's condition," Zz'r'p elaborated, "she informed me that she dozed off last night at the theater."

"Yeah," Echo grated. "Just for a couple minutes, though. Nothing happened."

"That you were aware of," Zz'r'p corrected. "It is entirely likely that this is a...call it a 'telepathic virus.' Rather than a true illness, a subconscious suggestion has been placed into your mind, causing your nervous system to replicate the symptoms and make you feel pain and discomfort, even though your body shows no sign of actual infection. It would be intended to at least disable you. It would also prevent you—or your colleagues, here, but especially you—guarding your partner at the theater, by diverting attention to curing your supposed mysterious illness. You, the one person with whom she now has a telepathic connection, who can watch from offstage, and immediately warn her if you spot anything amiss."

"Ooo," Romeo said, scowling, "sneaky."

"Very," Zz'r'p agreed.

"...Don' get it," Echo ground out. "Meg knew?"

"She suspected—especially after Agent India examined you," Zz'r'p said.

"But she ain't here," Romeo protested. "How is she gonna know what India found?"

"But she is here, Agent Romeo, for all intents and purposes." Zz'r'p looked meaningfully at Echo, who nodded and touched his forehead.

"But...can't she handle it, if she knows?" Echo managed to force out through the pain in his throat. "She's already 'there,' if you know what I mean."

"I strongly suspect she could," Zz'r'p admitted. "She told me exactly where in your psyche to look. And I have already verified its presence, as soon as you invited me to try; it is not merely a theoretical situation."

"Why didn't she, then?" India asked.

"Omega said that she never goes where she isn't wanted," Zz'r'p said, an enigmatic look on his blue, fishlike face.

In deep pain that was no longer physical, Echo closed his eyes.

* * *

After Zz'r'p's ministrations, a tired—but no longer sick—Echo crawled out of bed, showered, and dressed for work. But when he exited his bedroom, he stopped dead.

The back door was closed and locked.

"Aw, shit," Echo muttered, wincing. *C'mon, Meg, don't do this,* he thought. *You know why I had to get you out of here. I thought it was a real virus, and I was trying to protect you, honey.*

There was no response; Echo didn't even sense the firewall. It was as if their telepathic link had simply ceased to exist. At that thought, Echo swiftly checked his being for his partner's nd't'lq. It was still there, but oddly inactive. *As if Omega has simply...gone dormant,* Echo finally decided, *like she's hibernating or something. Meg, open the door, honey.*

No response.

"A.T.L.A.S.S., voice authorization override Alpha-One-Echo-Black," he murmured to the household security computer, and the latch clicked. Echo opened the door.

Omega's quarters were empty. A note was propped in the recliner.

*Ace—*

*I know now who the Phantom is. The 'illness' you got was the last piece in the puzzle; it told me who, and why. Unfortunately, it's somebody nobody expects, because they don't know he's still around. I've gone to the theater to take care of the matter. Don't bother coming; you need to stay home and rest. It's me he's really after, anyway, not you. And I know what to do.*

*We're beyond the turning point. From here, there's no return.*

*Goodbye, Ace.*

*—Ω*


"Oh, damn," a horrified Echo whispered, dropped the note, and sprinted for the door.

* * *

Omega entered the theater alone, as conspicuously as possible, eliciting many queries regarding Echo's absence. Omega answered them all the same way, in character as the actress/lover.

"Oh, the poor baby came down with the flu. He just feels awful! I'm sure he'll be up and around in a day or two, though."

Then she called for her dresser.

"Cecile," she told the young woman, "I need your help tonight."

"Of course, Miss Meg," the assistant replied. "What do you need me to do?"

"Well, you know how I always get stage fright before the show?"

"Yes, ma'am."

"Since Echo isn't here, will you keep me company? I want you to be really happy and cheerful, and take my mind off my stage fright."

"Of course, Miss Meg," the little dresser said, and grinned. "I've got some funny stories I can tell you about Sir Michael— some inadvertent pratfalls, things like that. I know he won't mind."

"Perfect," Omega said with a smile. "Keep me in stitches. We'll have the entire theater wanting to know what's so funny!

One other thing...”

“What's that?”

“I'm a little tired tonight, and I'm afraid of coming down with Echo's flu,” Omega elaborated her story. “I was wondering if we could do most of my costume changes in the wings, rather than my having to run all the way back here to the dressing room...”

“Oh, yes; that won't be a problem at all, ma'am. In fact, up until a few weeks ago, Miss Sofia did all her changes that way, too. We just decided to try it this way for a little while, after Jake's little backstage ‘hidey-hole’ made an embarrassing situation—he tried to pull me in there, see, when I was only waiting for Miss Sofia to come offstage; it almost ran us late for her next cue, and she was not happy! Neither was I! He has a thing for brunettes, male or female, and Mr. Echo and I were unlucky enough to get his attention, I guess. I'm glad he's finally gone; Miss Sofia tried to get him fired after that little incident! But he sucked up to the producers, and they gave him another chance.”

“Oh my!” Omega exclaimed, shocked. “Nothing... happened, did it? I mean, he didn't...”

“Oh, no, no, nothing like that! In fact, he gave me a wide berth after that,” the little dresser acknowledged with a wicked smirk. “He tried to grab my breasts and had one hand in the waistband of my pants, so before he could do anything else, I kneed him in the groin as hard as I could, and he let go. It was the second time he'd tried something like that on me, and I warned him the first time, so I did what I said I'd do! We didn't see him anywhere near his ‘hidey-hole’ the rest of the night, and he was ‘out sick’ the next night!”

“HA!” Omega laughed uproariously. “I know THAT technique! GOOD for you!”

“Yes! Don't worry, I'll be waiting for you as soon as you come offstage, for each scene,” a grinning Cecile reassured the Agent. “No delays allowed! I'll have everything ready for you, I promise.”

"Cecile, you're a gem!" Omega said with an affectionate grin, and the petite assistant beamed. "I'll tell you what. You're so helpful tonight, I'll let you leave early, and I'll take care of my own costumes after the show, for a change. It'll give me a chance to unwind after the performance, anyway. How does that sound? You can slip away to meet that handsome boyfriend you told me all about."

"Oh, Miss Meg, thank you! That would be wonderful!"

"It's set, then. Come on, let's go get ready."

* * *

Echo skidded breathlessly to a stop in the vehicle hangar beside an empty space.

"Dammit, of course she took the Corvette," he cursed, panting. "What else would she take?" Quickly, he pulled his cell phone.

"Romeo," he barked. "Are you and India at the theater? WHAT?! She reassigned you? You're WHERE?! Shit. Listen, forget the reassignment. Swing by Headquarters and pick me up. We're headed for the theater. And Junior? Fly low, if you know what I mean."

* * *

Cecile was as good as her word, keeping Omega laughing uproariously, so much so that actors and technicians stopped by to join in the fun, as the sounds of gaiety emanated through the dressing room door. And when the performance started, the faithful dresser met Omega offstage without fail, with the appropriate costume in hand.

When intermission arrived, Cecile tried to convince Omega to return to the dressing room to rest, but Omega refused, on the pretext of being too restless to relax.

Act Two began with a blonde undercover Alpha Line Agent in wig and costume, on high alert.

* * *

Three anxious Division One Agents pulled up to the theater in a single vehicle. As they hit the backstage entrance, Echo whispered, "India, you and Romeo check the house—box office, lobby, bar, concessions, offices, and as much of the auditorium as you can unobtrusively manage. I've got backstage."

"Got it," India murmured, and she and Romeo moved out rapidly.

Echo stood for a moment, considering strategy, then went into action. Swiftly, almost ninjalike, he swept the backstage area, including the fly-rail.

All was clear.

He stopped, puzzled, and pondered for long moments before pulling a spectral imaging scanner from his pocket and heading for the dressing rooms.

* * *

Omega had just come offstage after her solo when she realized she had a vague awareness of Echo's presence in the theater.

"Oh, Ace," she muttered under her breath, heart breaking, "don't you even trust me to do this? Well, it doesn't matter. After I'm done tonight, the Theater Phantom will be gone, and you won't have to worry about me any more. Ever again."

She sighed, then focused on the costume change for her next scene.

* * *

Echo entered Omega's dressing room and headed straight for the makeup table. He aimed the spectral imaging scanner at the mirror and activated it.

Moments later, he was staring down at a red light next to the detailed readout on the instrument, a grim, satisfied smile on his weary face.

"Bingo," he said.

* * *

Omega moved into position beside Michael, and he nodded at her, smiling. Then he leaned over and asked in concern, "How's Echo? Have you heard from him?"

"Actually, he just arrived in the theater a few minutes ago," Omega whispered back. "He seems really tired, but he's up and around."

311

"How do you know all that?!" Michael asked, surprised. "You just came offstage."

"I'll tell you later," Omega responded. "The scene's about to start..."

* * *

Echo was still investigating Omega's dressing room, intent on doing one last verification of his results, when the psychic blow fell.

A blinding pain erupted in his head, and everything went dark.

* * *

An alarmed Omega inhaled sharply in the wings as she awaited the next scene. She turned to her acting mentor.

"Michael, tell the stage manager to hold the lights. I have to go—now."

"What's wrong?!"

"It's Echo." With no further explanation, Omega gathered the costume's skirts and sprinted through the offstage door. In the corridor, she paused only long enough to peel the hindering costume off as a unit, flinging it aside and running on in the flesh-toned unitard she wore underneath; she forgot about the wig, not that it mattered—it didn't hinder her movements, so it wasn't worth bothering about.

*Echo?! Echo, answer me!* Omega snapped their link into full activity, a hard block around them both. She had extended her block to include Echo as soon as she had sensed him come into the theater, since she knew it meant he was likely out from under the protection afforded by the Deltiri embassy at Headquarters; but it had evidently been insufficient, given her distractions with the performance. *That, or my perp is just that much stronger,* she considered, worried.

*Mmmh...Mmmeg...* Echo's thoughts were barely coherent as he responded immediately to her call. *S-sorry I...y-yelled...*

*What? Oh, that. It's okay, hon. Don't worry about it. Are you all right?*

*Head...blow...light...head out...dark...*

*Light? Head out? Oh! Someone knocked you out?*

*Mmm...hmm...*

*I wonder who?* Omega thought sardonically, cold raw fury blazing within her.

*Didn'...see...think it was....*

*I already know, Echo,* Omega told her partner. *And he's big trouble. Listen, hon', I've got to pull my nd't'lq.*

*No. Don't. Why?*

*We're up against a powerful telepath. Ace. You're out of the fight. I intend to get to you before he takes you out permanently, which is what he intends in order to get back at me—and then he intends to kill me, too. I'm effectively weaponless, even though I've got my Winchester & Tesla. Hand-to-hand isn't nearly fast enough to stop a telepath. I'll have to fight him on his level. So I need all the mental resources I can get. I was planning on something like this anyway. And I don't want to risk any telepathic feedback frying you.*

*Mnh...dan...danger...*

*Yes, Echo, I know. It's very dangerous. But there really isn't any other way.*

Omega neared the dressing room containing Echo and the telepath and began to move stealthily.

*You...get hurt?*

*Probably.*

*Worse?*

*Probably.*

*Nnnooo...*

*Echo, I have to. You'll die otherwise. He WILL kill both of us if he can.*

*But if you...pu-ll out...some-thing...happen...*

*I know,* Omega told him. *If something bad happens, I'm gone. I'll have to do this fast, and pray it works. Echo, do you think you can manage a very basic mind block? Just for a few seconds?*

*Yes.* The thought was bleak.

*Do it, Ace. I'll try to keep sheltering you from the outside, as best I can. Maybe it'll help, some.*

A very rudimentary block went up around Echo's psyche; Omega recognized the pattern, and realized that, from long exposure, Echo had automatically and instinctively based it on her own. Which, she decided, was good; if they were lucky, the perp wouldn't recognize the difference between Echo's and Omega's, until it was too late...or at least until Omega could make her move.

*All right, Echo, here goes.* She began pulling her nd't'lq back within herself.

*Stop. Please, Meg. Nooo...don't...please...*

*Almost there, Echo. Hang on, Ace. It'll be over soon.*

*Do- don't...* Echo tried to hold on, failed.

*Echo...* Omega maintained a last, tenuous contact, trying to figure out how to say goodbye to this man she respected, admired, and adored; she fully expected her mind to be destroyed in the coming fight, but she could see no other way—at least, this way, Echo stood a chance of survival. She sighed, at a loss. Finally she settled for, *Remember me, Echo. I love you to pieces, hon.*

She severed the link.

*MEG!!* She heard the last reverberations of the agonized mental shout as she burst into the room and projected the most powerful mental blast she could muster...

...Directly at the tall blue Arcturan looming over Echo.

* * *

Tt'l'k spun, caught off guard by Omega's combination of physical stealth and hard telepathic block. He lashed out mentally, just as the full force of Omega's enraged attack struck him.

Omega staggered, but Tt'l'k went down under the raw, icy fury of the woman who now unleashed another telepathic barrage on the former assistant ambassador. The irrational alien 'heard' only three words from the blonde Agent; they were cold, clipped, tight.

*You hurt Echo.*

And suddenly Tt'l'k was afraid.

* * *

The silent battle raged for several more seconds, then it was over.

Both combatants toppled to the floor and lay, still as death.

* * *

Echo regained consciousness a few minutes later, with a nasty headache raging in his head and a raw, hollow emptiness somewhere inside, as if a part of him had been ripped out... of his heart, and his mind. He sat up with a groan, then with a wordless exclamation, scrambled for Omega's limp form. He felt for a pulse, and nodded to himself in relief, then he gently opened her eyelids to check her pupils.

"Thank God," he whispered; it was a fervent prayer. Quickly he verified that Tt'l'k was alive, then Echo pulled his cell phone. "Alpha Two, report to Omega's dressing room immediately," he barked. "Code Alpha One-Black. Agent down. Notify the stage manager and Headquarters, in that order, and call for backup. I'm beginning a preliminary exam on Meg."

He replaced the cell phone, then pulled Omega into his lap and held her, trying hard to ignore the fact that it was the exact same positioning that his counselor had insisted upon to combat his PTSD. Carefully, he tugged off the costume wig and tossed it aside, checking her ears for signs of hemorrhaging. There was none, and Echo smoothed perspiration-damp platinum strands back from his partner's forehead as Romeo and India burst in.

"We had 'em stop th' show. What th' hell happened?!" Romeo exclaimed, taking in the scene as India rushed to kneel beside Echo.

"Grab Tt'l'k," a grim Echo ordered, and Romeo unquestioningly started restraining the unconscious alien, even as India reset her scanner for Deltiri and quickly scanned Tt'l'k. "He's the Theater Phantom. He got the drop on me, and knocked me in the head mentally. Meg picked up on it through the nd't'lq, and stopped him taking me out completely. He probably would've taken me out instantly the first time, if she hadn't already had me inside her telepathic block."

"WHAT!! How?! And why is he even here??" India asked, resetting her medscanner again and scanning Echo's head quickly before starting on Omega. "Okay, Tt'l'k is gonna be out for a while, according to my readings, so lemme take care of you guys first. You've got a slight concussion, Echo. Nothing serious. It probably happened when you fell, after Tt'l'k nailed you mentally. I didn't think Meg had any weapons to speak of, and she's not holding anything now. How on earth did she take down Tt'l'k?" she reiterated.

"We keep forgetting, Meg IS a weapon," Echo said quietly, looking down at the woman in his lap as India examined her. "Or at least, she was designed and intended to be one. She had her Winchester & Tesla in a concealed carry, but at this kind of short range, like she pointed out to me, that wasn't gonna be nearly fast enough. So she broke our link to consolidate her mental resources—and boy, has she got 'em; plus she wanted to protect me from any possible neural feedback—then apparently attacked him TELEPATHICALLY...with everything she had." He shook his head. "I wasn't connected with her, by then, and I was unconscious, to boot...but I could still sense the, the energy, the mental forces, raging around me. It was..." He shook his head again. "I got no words. Like being stuck between two Tesla coils on max, I guess. Thank the good Lord I was inside the telepathic equivalent of a Faraday cage."

"Oh, no," India whispered, looking at Echo in shock, and Romeo's face held an expression of horror. "That could mean—"

"I know," Echo groaned, closing his eyes and bowing his head. "So did she. I...I think she...intended it, all along."

"Her dresser said nobody's been in here since th' opening curtain, Echo," Romeo said quietly. "She set a trap for 'im. With herself as bait."

"Oh, damn, damn, damn," India murmured, resuming

her examination with increased intensity. After a moment, she looked up and told the two men, "Well, so far, so good. There's no sign of organic damage. We won't know about... other damage...until she wakes up."

"If she wakes up," Echo whispered. The three Agents waited, silent and tense.

"She's comin' around," Romeo observed at last, as Omega sighed softly.

"Mmnh..."

"Meg?" an anxious Echo asked. "Meg, can you hear me?"

"Mmmh...mm-hm."

"Do you know who I am?"

"Mmm-hmm..."

"Who am I, Meg?"

"Echooo..." Omega's head lolled onto Echo's chest, where she sighed and relaxed instinctively, trying to nod off again.

"Meg, do you remember what happened?" India asked intently.

"Uh-huh. Tt'l'k...gonna kill Echo. Stopped 'im."

"Pretty damn good, too. Dude's still out," Romeo remarked.

"And gonna stay out for a while, based on my preliminary scan. Honey," India said to the semiconscious form in Echo's arms, "try to wake up. I need to check you."

With a protesting groan, the blue eyes opened, to gaze up into worried brown eyes. Omega was silent for several minutes, studying Echo's face, as India re-checked her pupils.

"Meg?" an uncertain Echo finally queried. "Baby, talk to me. Say...SOMEthing. Anything. Are you okay?"

"Mmm." Omega winced. "Would y'all mind keepin' the volume down? I swear it feels like I've got a cranial cavity big enough to put Jupiter through." She rubbed her forehead with the heel of her hand.

Echo and India sat back in relief; all three of the anxiously-waiting Agents grinned.

"She's just fine," Echo observed in satisfaction...

...But she wasn't, quite.

# **Chapter 12**

"...Then I found out about Echo's dream, and I realized he'd been probed, just like Slug did to me in the early days of my being an Agent. Only gastropoids don't have long ranges, and we'd pretty much determined that who- or whatever was doing it was remaining around the theater district, because nothing ever actually happened AWAY from the theater," Omega explained later in Fox's office. She was surrounded by Fox, Echo, Romeo, India, Michael, and Zz'r'p.

"Right," Echo agreed. "We figured whoever it was, was holing up in one of the storerooms, because most theaters have lots of storage areas—for costumes, props, sets, set dressing, all that stuff—many of 'em not even accessed on a regular basis. And as long as it allowed for access to the theater where *Phantom* was being staged, it didn't even have to be the SAME theater. Which, we eventually figured out, meant it wasn't likely to be a gastropoid at all, Slug or otherwise."

"Then why didn't you figure it out sooner?" Fox wondered.

"Because we weren't sure what kind of effect it would have on his abilities, if Slug managed to...'transfer brains,' let's say," Echo said. "I mean, conceivably it could have boosted his range, if a different brain was powering his abilities, or something."

"Never mind the fact that Slug apparently showed himself to us, right off the bat," Omega reminded them.

"Okay, that all makes a certain sense," India decided.

"Indeed, it might be just possible," Zz'r'p agreed. "I would say unlikely, but stranger things have happened. And we still know little of gastropoids."

"Only, when I finally realized that 'Slug' knew visual details of what went on when Tt'l'k...invaded my privacy, I knew it couldn't be Slug," Omega noted.

"Why not?" Romeo asked. "Slug woulda been usin' somebody with eyes."

"True, Agent Romeo," Zz'r'p interrupted, "but Omega is correct. Snails have no eyes, consequently there was no visual processing center in Slug's mind. Even with access to the information, he would have had little or no way to interpret it. He might reflect it back, much as Slug did to Echo last year, in order to appear to be Omega, but he could not have described the image. Therefore, it was a sighted telepath plaguing the theater."

"One with a range that didn't depend on physical distance," Omega added. "Someone who knew us, Echo an' me, and would be able to recognize and find us, even from Midtown Manhattan all the way over to Williamsburg in Brooklyn."

"Which is way farther than Slug could do," Romeo recalled.

"And THEN I remembered that Zz'r'p had enclosed Echo in a block the other night, so I could get some sleep," Omega reminded them. "While he and Alpha Two were scoping out Sofia's claim that the Theater Phantom was in her condo. Only her condo was farther from Headquarters than the theater, and Zz'r'p never had to LEAVE Headquarters to do it. Never mind that I've mentally communicated with him when he was on another continent. Which said that a Deltiri had the range to do it, easy."

"True," Zz'r'p confirmed. "Deltiri telepathic communication is, as nearly as we can determine, based on a kind of quantum entanglement. Distance is not a significant factor, if we know the other being."

"And all of that combined pointed to one being," Echo added. "The one that Meg and I were semi-directly responsible for getting canned."

"Tt'l'k was..." Omega paused, searching for the right word.

* * *

"Pissed," Echo said succinctly, finishing the thought without need of a mental link. Omega bit her lip, wincing. Echo drew his brows together, concerned about her reaction.

*Damn,* he thought, disappointed. *I'd hoped sharing that link would have brought us even closer together. Hoped maybe she'd grasp how I felt and return it. Instead, I think it's backfired. I think she's shoving me away. But I still don't think she gets how I feel about her. It's just the whole concept of the mental contact; she didn't want it because of what's been done to her in the past, and it's left her uncomfortable around me. And,* he added, glancing around the room, *the others see it, too.*

* * *

"...Yeah," Omega agreed after a patently uncomfortable pause. "He'd lost a cushy position because of us. Never mind the fact that he'd resented my working with Zz'r'p to hone my mental skills, from the moment he realized it was happening."

"What?" Fox demanded, surprised.

"Why?" Romeo wondered.

"Because she is human," Zz'r'p explained. "And in his mind, therefore, 'beneath' such skills and training." He gave the Deltiri equivalent of a shrug. "Open-minded, it seems, he was not."

"Damn bastard," Romeo grumbled...almost, but not quite, under his breath.

"Amen," Michael averred.

"That," Fox agreed.

"But I thought you sent him back to the homeworld weeks ago," India observed.

"We thought we had," Zz'r'p admitted. "It turns out that he studied up on the various incidents with Slug—historic, and more recent—and figured out how to use some of the gastropoid's mental techniques. Most notably, the ability to make another sentient think they were seeing one thing when they were really seeing another. And apparently—I would say, likely due to his illness, which tends to make its victims... heedless of possible harm, if not outrightly megalomanic, at least in the latter stages—he was willing to take considerable risk with his own psyche to do it. Which meant he was unafraid, even cocksure, to take on many minds at once...and evidently managed it as a consequence." The alien ambassador shook his head. "When one is confident and unafraid, one's mental capacities are strengthened considerably. He walked completely away during the ship boarding, right under his guards' noses, as you humans would say...with no one the wiser, until he did not get off with them at Deltir. Even then, it was assumed that he was somewhere in the spaceport on Deltir, and so the embassy here was not notified...until I received Omega's urgent message to verify his whereabouts, this very afternoon."

"And that was the confirmation of the deduction. He knew my psyche well enough to know how to bait a trap, from nearly a year of working with Alpha Line," Omega added. "So he decided to pay us back, Echo an' me—in spades."

"Well, it's one payment that'll wind up delinquent. We'll do more than 'fire his ass' this time. So which one of you figured it out?" Fox asked with a grim smile. "Or did you do it...'together'?"

"Both of us figured it out—independently," Echo said, shooting a glance at Omega, who was staring fixedly at a corner of Fox's desk. The room's other occupants exchanged confused, pained looks as they watched the interaction—or lack thereof—in the Agency's number-one team—the team that, heretofore, had always been so very close.

"Ah," Zz'r'p interjected smoothly. "Omega, I did notice your nd't'lq had been withdrawn from Echo. This occurred during the battle?"

Omega nodded.

"There is a sense of...rejection?"

She nodded again.

"Emptiness?"

Echo and Omega both nodded.

"This is quite normal," Zz'r'p explained. "The dissolution of an nd't'lq bond generates a deep sense of loss, usually in both members of the bond. And, though I know of no other instances of a human member in such a bond, it is not rare for Deltiri to take other planets' species for mates; we have been a spacefaring race for a very long time. Upon the death of a spouse, while the nd't'lq remains within the surviving bondmate, the...'connection,' we will say...is gone, unless the dying spouse wished to be...mm, restored, we will term it. Unfortunately, that is not always possible. And unless such restoration occurs, the sense of 'being' gradually diminishes; this eventually results in the dissolution of the nd't'lq as well, and the surviving mate often goes into a deep depression as part of the grieving process." The Deltiri shrugged. "Of course, that usually occurs after a lifetime of mating, but even short bonding periods produce great pain upon loss of the bond."

"That explains a lot," Echo muttered.

"Indeed, Echo. And you cannot yet re-establish the nd't'lq by yourself, can you, Omega?"

"...No."

"Then I will assist, if you like. And can even help Echo place his in you, to make it a full bond."

The others smiled then, believing they understood Omega's behavior. So they were surprised when Omega failed to respond. Echo laid a light hand on her arm.

"How about it, Meg? You're already the first Agent on Broadway. Wanna be the first permanently telepathic—not to mention the closest—team in all of Division One?"

"I...I don't think so, Echo," Omega said after a pause, and Romeo saw that look like pain flash again through Echo's eyes. "I don't want you to be...constrained...like that." Omega's voice was very quiet, and the room was silent when she finished speaking.

"Meg, are you okay, honey?" India asked gently.

"Everybody keeps asking me that. I'm not okay, I've never been okay, and I never will be okay," she grumbled under her breath. "And in the end, nobody really gives a shit." There was a long pause, as the others stared at her in dumbfounded shock. Omega finally raised her head and spoke in a normal tone, albeit one in pain. "I've still got a nasty residual headache, India. My head is splitting, and I think I need to take some of those meds you gave me."

"Then you'll need to lie down, girlfriend. You'll be loopier than a ride on Coney Island five minutes after you take it, otherwise."

"Is it the same stuff Zebra gave me for the busted foot?"

"I think so, yeah. Lower dose, though."

"Okay. Fox, would you mind if I called it a day?"

"There's debriefing and paperwork, Omega," Fox reminded her, and she winced, instinctively rubbing one temple.

"Go ahead, Meg," Echo said quietly. "You're hurting. I'll handle it." Omega nodded and left.

* * *

"Damn," a deeply worried Romeo muttered after her departure, "th' pretty lady's walled everybody off now—even Echo."

"I think maybe it's a delayed coping mechanism," India observed. "She's blocking off all external emotional stimuli until she deals with the psychological fallout from the stalking and rape attempt. As well as this latest pile of horse manure, which, when you think about it, pretty much spins off of that anyway. She's not superhuman, after all."

"That would make a great deal of sense." Zz'r'p nodded. "That is why she rejects the bond with Echo. She has a considerable amount of anger and pain bottled inside, I believe. And that is understandable, given her history. I think, among other things, she does not wish to subject him to that bottled emotion. Such things have a way of...fermenting, if we may extend the bottle analogy. And I am sure she recognizes that."

Echo shot the alien telepath a meaningful look. *Among other things is right,* he thought at the alien, who nodded subtle agreement.

"Why do you think that, though?" Fox asked. "She may just be in a bad mood because of the headache. I could tell it was a faktish duzi, merely by looking at her eyes."

"Because, when we interrogated Tt'l'k, he indicated he was overpowered, not completely by force of mind, but by sheer, raw fury. He sincerely thought she would kill him. It is my considered opinion that she COULD have, had she so chosen, given her mindset in those moments. And she may well have caused some sort of permanent damage to him, though everyone in our...chain of command, let us term it... is agreed that there was no other way, and told her so before she attempted it, when she proposed it this afternoon. Had she not done as she did, Echo would be dead at the very least, and possibly Omega as well. But Tt'l'k is now so traumatized that he has effectively retreated into himself. For all intents and purposes, Tt'l'k is in a catatonic state of his own creation, at least externally. We were able to reach him telepathically, but he has gone deep within, and did not want to respond to us— we gave him little choice. I think we will have no difficulty getting him back to Deltir this time, as he is too afraid to stay on Earth, though healing him now is problematic."

"But...why?" Echo wondered. "Why did Meg even try to do it that way? HOW did she do it?"

"Because when she discussed it with us, immediately prior to going to the theater, when we—and I mean the entire staff of the embassy—brainstormed it, none of us could see how she could combat him any other way and hope for both of you to survive," Zz'r'p noted. "She did not make her decision in a vacuum, Echo. She came to us with her idea; unfortunately, we could offer no better alternative, for she had already thought it through very carefully, and she is nothing if not intelligent, logical, and creative. And we, the embassy staff, are not trained in...dueling, we will call it; interrogation is one thing, but combat quite another! So while we could have tried to take him on, the high probability was that we would fail, and he would still manage to kill Alpha One. The only being who stood a chance of success was Omega herself. That said, we did give her several important pointers as to HOW to do it. Which it seems she took heed of, and they did indeed help, I have gathered."

"HOW?" Echo reiterated. "I mean, I know she's got above-human ability in this respect, but...even she admits she's not on your level, Zz'r'p. I'm glad it worked, but damn. I don't understand why Meg's still with us."

"You truly do not know, Echo?" Zz'r'p asked.

"No. I have no idea. All I know is that it was strong as hell, because I could feel it, raging around outside my head."

"Yes, it would have been incredibly powerful, that showdown. Apparently, he—Tt'l'k—committed the one act which unleashed everything our dear youngling Omega had held in check for so long...all the rancor, all the hate, all the rage, all the bitterness, the pain, the loathing and disgust. It seems Omega 'said' but one thing to Tt'l'k," Zz'r'p reported. "But that one statement tells the tale, and reveals how deep was the anger—the raw, fierce, scarce-controlled fury—she turned upon him in those moments. And it was that incredible, unrestrained, pure anger which made her more than a match for an innate, trained telepath."

"And what was it?" Fox wondered. "What in the name of HaShem could she have said that would reveal all that? Let alone scare Tt'l'k as bad as you indicate?"

"Three words," Zz'r'p declared. "She said, 'You hurt Echo.'"

They all turned and stared at the head of Alpha Line.

* * *

"...And you'll pass on my invitation?" Michael asked Echo. "I've given the entire cast and crew an...amended... explanation of what happened. The humans only know that there WAS a 'phantom,' but think it was a human trying to cause havoc after being turned down at the casting call, and the two of you were investigators trying to catch the phantom before it hurt somebody—and then of course, you brought in some colleagues to assist, after Meg got hurt. The offworlders know the whole truth, at least in so far as I knew it before I left to come here...and I'll tell them no more, because it's private, I think. But they all, humans and offworlders, want her to have that opportunity."

"I'll be glad to pass it on, Mike," Echo agreed. "I can't swear she'll do it, but I'll pass it on."

"Very good, then, and that is all I could ask. I'll talk to you both later. Ta-ta," he said with a smile, and departed.

* * *

"That's promising," Fox observed after Michael was gone. "There's some serious good will we've made at the theater, if they want her to do that."

"Yeah," Echo agreed. *The problem is likely to be getting her to do it,* he thought.

* * *

"My friends, now that we are at last down to the core of our little group, I must admit—I am very concerned about Omega," Zz'r'p admitted after several more moments, during which they all silently pondered recent matters. "Never mind the other...events...she has experienced in the last few weeks. And I have reason to suspect that her response to those events has been...mm, escalated...by Tt'l'k yesterday, at the same time he implanted the telepathic 'virus' in Echo, while she inadvertently slept—if not even earlier, as there would have been opportunity; I suspect he was attempting to increase his advantage by doing even more damage to her self-esteem and general sense of self. And the breaking of the nd't'lq bond, voluntary though it was—at least on her part," the ambassador amended, glancing at Echo, "is likely to create some additional... emotional difficulty for her, to add insult to injury."

"What about Echo?" Fox wondered. "He was the other side of that bond."

"Yes, and I can tell he is not unaffected," Zz'r'p noted. "But nor is he already dealing with multiple unresolved post-traumatic stresses. One way or another, our Omega has many issues that need working out, in her mind and heart, else there will be serious repercussions. And sooner rather than later, in my estimation."

"Do they need the nd't'lq re-established?" India queried.

"It would likely be optimum," the Deltiri agreed. "But even

when it was in place, I believe she largely shut Agent Echo out of the full link. Is that not correct, Echo?"

"Yeah," Echo confirmed with a sigh. "She was...something was bothering her, pretty damn bad, though I don't know what," he said, aborting what he had been about to say, lest he violate her privacy. "She...well, let's just say she was afraid I'd pick up more than she wanted; I asked her, point-blank, about that, and she admitted that was the problem. She flat wasn't comfortable with...'full access,' I guess you could call it. Not so much because she thought I'd go nosing around as much as that I might stumble over something, from what she told me; she does trust me, and I try hard to be worthy of that trust. But I think it's a kind of knee-jerk reaction to the whole multiple mind-rapes thing, especially after Tt'l'k did what he did. Privacy issues. Really, seriously damn big...privacy issues."

"Mm," Fox murmured, offering nothing more. But his expression made Echo wonder if the Director knew, or suspected, more than he was telling. And he wondered what it was.

*Not out of rank curiosity,* Echo thought, stifling a sigh. *Just...because I'm worried sick about her. She's obviously in pain because of whatever it is that she's afraid to tell me, and I hate to see her hurting that bad. I wish I knew what I could do to help. But if she won't tell me, there's nothing I can do. And I refuse to go prying, or even trying to figure it out on my own, though I might be able to; I'd almost be willing to bet there's been enough clues she's inadvertently dropped. But no. That's as much a violation of her trust as poking around inside her head without her permission, as far as I'm concerned. She'll tell me...when and if she can.*

"Echo," Zz'r'p offered, "I can provide a bit of...of mental assistance...for you, that should help smooth over the pain of Omega's absent nd't'lq, if you like. I expect it feels rather as if an important part of you has gone missing..."

"That's exactly what it feels like, Zz'r'p," Echo confessed. "And it's kinda...raw."

"Because it is fresh," Zz'r'p said with an understanding nod. "Will you allow me to help? It will only take a moment."

"Be my guest," Echo said with a wave at his own head, inviting the alien into his mind.

* * *

*Excellent,* Zz'r'p said. *I tried offering this to Omega earlier in a 'private' conversation, but her responses were...curt, succinct, in the extreme. Not quite rude, because she considers me a friend, but she was...not receptive.*

*Yeah, I have the feeling that the aftermath of all this is gonna be a bit of a mess,* Echo agreed. *You heard her remarks about 'not being okay.'*

*I did. I also heard them mentally. The rest of you barely heard her; in her mind, however, she was screaming.*

*Oh boy. That's NOT good.*

*No. But I am here now to help you. We will help her deal with her problems as soon as she allows us in to do so.*

*All right. Go ahead and do what you need to do,* Echo agreed.

Zz'r'p reached into Echo's mind, locating the empty hollow where his partner's 'clone' had been, and gently smoothed over the psychic tears left, where the male Agent had already begun bonding with it. Echo felt his being relax as the raw feeling departed, though there was still a lingering emptiness.

*Is that better?* the blue alien asked.

*Yeah. That helped a good bit. Thanks. But...there's still an empty place.*

*I know, and I am sorry; I can only do so much. You did not merely accept her nd't'lq,* Zz'r'p noted. *You were actively making it part of your own being.*

*I...guess so.*

*You love her. Deeply.*

*...Yeah.* Echo shrugged. *I figured you already knew that, from when we came to you to ask about Slug, and his attitude toward partnerships.*

*Well, I did,* Zz'r'p agreed. *I knew, well before that, truthfully.*

*But only now, when I see what having her nd't'lq meant to you, do I realize the depth of that love. No wonder her reaction to your acceptance of it was so strong; you did not merely accept it, you welcomed it, cradled it, protected it. You wanted it. Wanted it as part of your very being. Wanted it to be part of your bonding, your...marriage. Assuming we can manage such an eventuality for the two of you.*

Echo felt himself flushing, but said nothing; he only hoped the others in Fox's office didn't notice. *Or at least don't correctly interpret the cause,* he decided.

*They see it, but think it is part of the process,* Zz'r'p told him. *And I do not plan to disabuse them of the notion. Echo, if...I can help, I will be glad to do so, my friend. It is likely to be more difficult before it becomes easier, however. This situation has been developing ever since her programming kicked in last year, and she found out what she really was, why she was really here, and what had been done to her. Arguably, it has been developing in her subconscious since the 'enhancements' were performed on her as a child. Try not to take her reactions personally, no matter what she may say or do; she is in terrible pain, but she cares for you, a great deal.*

*But she doesn't love me. Not the way I do, her.*

*I did not say that. But right now, she is simply not in a position to deal with it. She is lashing out—at everyone, let me remind you; not only you—because she is afraid. The pain, the anger, the despair she feels...* Echo sensed the other male mentally shake his head. *You have no idea what she is dealing with, even with all the memories with which she has trusted you. Never mind the possibility that Tt'l'k exacerbated it. I... am very concerned for her, in this moment.*

*Me too.*

*You do understand that she is holding you at a distance because she considers you unattainable, don't you?*

*I...no, I didn't. Is this that whole 'hero thing' causing problems again?*

*Exactly. And at least in part, I suspect one of the reasons she blocked you from experiencing the bond to its fullest extent is because she most likely believes that, if you see her as she truly is—which, of course, in her view is the animalic monster she believes herself, especially after the 'breeding attempt'— you will be repulsed. She will not only lose you as any kind of a potential romantic partner, but as a friend and as a working partner into the bargain. At least, that is how she sees it. That, I think, is her deepest fear. I have yet to determine if she understands that her current path, in pushing you away, is guaranteed to produce that very thing, if taken to its ultimate lengths. Then again, she may very well be conscious of it, and feel it is what she deserves. That it is ALL she deserves.*

*Aw, hell. Is there any way to get her to understand that I don't care about all of that?*

*Love her. Love her as hard as you can, as unconditionally as you can, and make sure she knows it. Though until we can get her some counseling and healing, you may have to be subtler than you would like.*

*I'll do whatever it takes, Zz'r'p.*

*Good, because I need for you to do something, Echo, for me, but more importantly, for her.*

*What?*

*If you can, get her to come to me, so that I may do for her what I just did for you, as well as to search for and undo anything Tt'l'k did. It will help, at the least. If we do not, I fear she will rapidly sink into a grave despondency. And that... could prove fatal, in the end. If for no other reason than she becomes reckless. I believe she has been wandering in this direction for quite some time, at this point; I have noticed a distinct lack of valuation of her own life for at least a year now, especially in preference to those she cares about, and it seems to be increasing. Does this match your observations?*

*Damn, does it ever.*

*It is as I feared, then. Deep, chronic depression is one of the most dangerous mental states I know; combined with post-traumatic stress, it is that much more perilous. She is, in my estimation, teetering on the edge of the abyss.*

*I'll do the best I can, Zz'r'p,* Echo agreed promptly. *I can't promise anything, though. Meg can be stubborn.*

*I know. But if you cannot, no one can.*

* * *

"Better now?" Fox queried his oldest human friend, when Echo and Zz'r'p came up for air.

"Yeah, a little," Echo agreed. "It doesn't feel quite so... raw...at least."

"Good," India averred. "One down. Now if we can get Meg to actually TALK to somebody, preferably a counselor, but any of us here would do, too..."

"Some of us here are trained counselors," Zz'r'p reminded the physician with a smile.

"That's...more complicated," Echo admitted. "I've tried getting her to talk to me, and she was actually willing to do that a couple times, but she's told me she doesn't even know where to start. I even tried when we still had the telepathic thing going, and she still didn't know how. And I don't think she can face telling a perfect stranger."

"Well, we jus' gotta work on comin' up with some options f'r the pretty lady, I guess," Romeo decided.

There was nothing the others could add to that.

* * *

Echo entered his quarters and headed straight for the back door.

"Meg?" he called into the darkened apartment of his partner. Spotting the partly-closed bedroom door, he moved over to it and knocked lightly. No answer.

"Meg?" he asked again, pushing the door open gradually. The bedside lamp was on, but it was dimmed to its lowest level; Omega lay on the bed nearby.

Omega had stripped off jacket, tie, holsters, and shoes, and lay curled on the bedspread in shirtsleeves and sock feet, her back to the door, apparently asleep. Echo studied the still form briefly, then walked over to the side of the bed.

"Meg, Michael has an invitation for you."

No response.

"Meg, I know you're awake. I don't like being ignored."

The form on the bed sighed.

"I'm sorry, Echo. I just...don't feel like talking."

"Why? It's only me."

"I just...I just don't."

Echo sat down on the side of the bed and began gently massaging his partner's tight shoulders.

"Meg, what's wrong, honey? What's bothering you? Tell me, and I swear I'll try to help you work it out."

"...Nothing. Everything," Omega responded, inconsistent and uncaring. "I don't know." Echo felt her shoulders tense even more, and she suddenly punched the pillow. "I can't do anything right."

"What??" Echo exclaimed, startled. "Meg, you just successfully finished a damn nasty little mission. And took on a telepath on his own turf, and WON. You left Tt'l'k with a taste of his own medicine—you came out of what he did to you, but he's pretty much catatonic, according to Zz'r'p, because he's scared to death of you! I'd say that's doing a whole damn lotta something right."

"Echo, you don't understand!" Omega cried in frustration, turning over to look at him.

"Then tell me. Explain. I'm a good listener."

"I...I can't," Omega said miserably, burying her face in the pillow she had just attacked. "I can't."

"I thought you trusted me," he murmured in a low voice, pained.

"I do," Omega groaned. "But I still can't. Please, Echo. Don't be mad..."

"I'm not mad." His voice was still low. "Mad isn't what I am right now."

Omega understood his meaning, and the shoulders beneath his hands began to shake.

"See what I mean?" she sobbed, and he stared down at

her, horrified that he had made her cry. "I can't even treat you right!"

Echo turned her gently onto her back and gathered her up to let her cry against his shoulder, totally confused as to the reason for her reaction, but still accepting its sincerity. She pushed away.

"Echo, please don't," she begged. "It only makes it worse."

"I...make it worse?" Echo felt himself pale slightly, as agony shot through his being. Omega nodded as she wept.

"You're being so understanding, and I'm such a fool."

"Understanding?!" Echo expostulated, intensely frustrated. "Shit, Meg, I don't understand one damn bit of this whole situation! What the hell is the matter?!"

Omega froze then, staring up at Echo's face.

"You...you really don't, do you?" she whispered, seeming astounded. She sat up, wiping her face with her hands. "Echo... give me a minute and wait for me outside, will you?"

* * *

From the den, Echo could hear water running in the bathroom sink; this was followed by splashing water, then the water shut off. After a few minutes Omega, clean face free of tears, followed Echo into the living area and sat down on the couch, patting the seat beside her. Echo joined her.

"All right, Ace, so what did 'Sir Michael Primo Uomo' want?" Omega tried to joke. It fell flat, but Echo appreciated the attempt.

"He wants you to come back to the theater for an encore performance..." he glanced at his wrist chronometer, "uh, that would be tonight—damn, it's gotten late—now that 'T.P.' is gone," Echo said and smiled, going along with her effort to lighten the mood.

"Oh. I...don't think that's a good idea."

"Why not?" Echo asked. "You'd have no distractions, for a change. And you're still Division One's one and only 'Angel-voice'. And now we know it really IS your voice—not Slug's."

"I'd only mess it up."

333

"No, you wouldn't. You never messed up any of the other shows, and those were all done under stress, and some of 'em were done with a damn busted foot! Besides, I'd like the opportunity to see you perform—from the audience, for a change—without having to worry about someone taking a potshot at you. And who knows when, or even if, I'll get another chance? It's not like Division One agents star on Broadway on a regular basis," Echo deadpanned. Omega smiled wanly then, and agreed.

"All right, Ace. I'll do it for you. Tonight?"

"Yep."

"You'll be out front, in the house?"

"In the Agency box. Where you and I saw the show together."

"Okay."

* * *

Echo was already seated in the theater, awaiting the curtain, when he felt the light hand on his shoulder.

"Hello, Echo," Sofia purred, sitting beside him, "I...do hope you don't mind if I...join you. The house is sold out—this is the last seat—and I really want to see your partner have a chance to perform without any worries other than the show. Oh, look, there's Sir Andrew," Sofia remarked, waving. "How good of him to come."

"Well, actually—" Echo began.

"Meg is really very talented, you know," Sofia remarked, in her typical babbling way. "I've been pressing the producers to offer her a position as one of my understudies; Kate wants to go home for a few months, in any case...and you and I both know, that's a long way! I understand they offered, but Meg declined."

"I don't—"

"Sshh," Sofia said, as the house lights dimmed. "Curtain..." Echo sighed.

* * *

The performance seemed to go fine, although Omega's

334

voice faltered once, in her first scene. Echo wasn't certain, but he thought it was because she had been distracted, looking for her partner; at least he saw her glance his way. It never occurred to him that she had not only seen him in the dark auditorium, but had seen his companion in the box, and—given her current state of mind, especially in the wake of the nd't'lq withdrawal—assumed they were together.

After that, her performance seemed to soar; Omega poured her heart and soul into her music, almost as though she needed the emotional release. The remembrance number fairly tore Echo's heart out of his chest—or would have, if Sofia had not been clinging to his arm and murmuring accolades for his partner. *I appreciate the praise for Meg,* he thought, annoyed, *but I do wish she would shut up so I can pay attention.*

The audience was spellbound, and more than one cheek was wet at the end of the love song. When the chandelier 'fell' at the end of the first act and Omega fled it in apparent fear, the entire house gasped and cringed away from the stage. Echo felt a thrill of pride in his beloved partner.

* * *

Sofia stuck like glue through intermission, much to Echo's exasperation; no amount of hints, direct statements, or bluntly going off and leaving her, deterred her from remaining at—or at least near—Echo's side. She was, however, careful about how she touched him, and kept glancing about with a guilty look, as if half-expecting a certain wrathful physician-Agent to come out of the woodwork.

Echo had wanted to visit Omega backstage at that point, but he flatly refused to disturb Meg with Sofia's inconsequential chatter. He never thought that his visit—complete with surreptitious eye rolls regarding his erstwhile and unwelcome companion—might have reassured her, instead of annoying her.

Act Two, if anything, was better than Act One. Omega's solo was heart-rending in its lonely wistfulness, and seemed to pour out her grief over losing those she loved. Echo wondered briefly if everyone else in the audience had the same sensation that she was singing to them.

* * *

The play's events spiraled rapidly, then, to a climax. When Michael's last, plaintive notes faded, the stage grew dark, the music ceased; a prolonged hush fell on the audience.

Then it erupted.

When Omega and Michael took their curtain call together, the entire house came to its feet in a standing ovation. Echo's dark eyes shone with pride and tenderness as he leaped to his feet and applauded his partner with intense enthusiasm, and Sofia studied his face thoughtfully, then nodded to herself. When the curtain came down for the last time, she excused herself.

"Thank you for the company, and the spare seat, Echo," she told the undercover Agent. "Your...partner...is brilliant. And I have no doubt she saved my life—and yours, if the report I had is to be believed—by being willing to do what I could not have even attempted; I heard all about the...confrontation...from Michael, you see. She is...truly...impressive. Obviously, it does not do to underestimate her! Would you give her my deepest thanks? I...need to see Sir Andrew, before he gets away..."

And with that, she was gone.

* * *

In some relief, Echo made his way through the auditorium and around the backstage to the dressing rooms, greeting and being greeted by cast and crew as he progressed. When he reached Omega's dressing room, he knocked on the door.

"Angel-voice, it's Echo."

Silence.

He pushed the door open.

The dressing room was empty, all sign of his partner expunged as completely as if a special containment team had swept through.

* * *

They met, purely by accident, at the entrance to the

Headquarters building at dawn the next morning, as they both finally headed home.

"Hi, Echo," a subdued Omega, dressed in her usual Suit, greeted her partner. "Did you and Sofia enjoy the performance?"

"Huh? Sofia? You knew Sofia was there?"

"Yeah. I spotted you both in the box. Did you like it?"

"Yes," Echo said shortly. "Sorry I missed you afterward."

"I figured if I...wasn't there," Omega shrugged, "you wouldn't feel obligated, and you and Sofia could have a nice evening together." They entered the building, their usual lock-step completely out of synch. "Where did you take her to dinner?"

"Dinner." Echo looked blank. "Oh. Actually, we...didn't eat dinner. I...completely forgot."

"I...see." Omega hid a wince and glanced pointedly at her wrist chronometer. "I guess you did have a nice evening."

* * *

"Did you know Sir Andrew was in the house last night?" Echo asked casually, reading Omega's assumption in her reaction and remarks. He also saw the wince she tried to hide, and it gave him a bit of hope in an otherwise disappointing interaction.

"Oh! No, I...didn't know. Did...did he enjoy the performance?" Omega asked, her sudden agitation betraying her concern that the show's creator enjoy her depiction.

"I rather think so. He gave you a standing ovation," Echo observed. "But you can always ask Sofia. She left with him right after the curtain call. Which, I might add, was a huge relief, since she didn't have an invitation to the box. I did gather the house was sold out, however." He raised an eyebrow just as Omega glanced sharply at Echo's very un-regretful face while they entered the elevator. Echo punched their floor. "Did you spend the evening with Michael?"

"No. He did invite me to dinner. But I...wasn't hungry."

"What did you do? Did you go out with some of the other cast members?"

"...No. I...honestly don't really remember what I did," she admitted. "I...had some thinking to do."

It was Echo's turn to glance sharply at his partner's drawn, somewhat pale face. "Have you eaten breakfast?"

"No."

"Did you even eat dinner after the performance?"

"...No. Like I said, I...wasn't hungry."

Echo punched the stop button.

"Let's go grab something. We can talk." He started to punch the ground floor button. Omega's hand covered his, stopping him, then withdrew quickly.

"I'm kind of tired, Echo. I think I'd rather take a quick nap, if you don't mind. I need to start kicking back over to Division days."

"...All right," Echo acquiesced, hiding the puzzled frown.

* * *

After naps, Alpha One resumed a normal shift with a simple city patrol. At the end of the day, Echo turned to the unusually-subdued woman at his side in the Corvette.

"How about dinner and a movie, Meg?" Echo smiled. "Let's get back to that business of you going out with your best friend."

"Echo—don't." Omega gazed fixedly out the side window. His smile faded.

"Why?"

"Because we both know it's going nowhere."

"I don't know that. I don't know anything of the kind."

"Oh, come off it, Echo!" Omega burst out. "I'm tired of this. Do you honestly think you're convincing me? No self-respecting man would willingly even look twice at a helpless, incompetent, inhuman thing like me! That's why Mark Wright had to be programmed to mate with me! All you're doing is reminding me. So just stop it!"

*Damn,* Echo thought, as his eyes narrowed in pain. *I'm thinking I just heard confirmation of Zz'r'p's notion that Tt'l'k messed with Meg's emotions. I've heard her make comments similar to that lately, but that one was kinda over the top. I mean... 'helpless'? 'Incompetent'? Hell.* "Meg, don't—" he tried.

"Echo," she sighed, staring at her hands, "let's just go home. I'm tired."

"Meg, listen to me." Echo brought the Corvette to a halt at a red light.

"There's nothing to discuss."

"Yes, there is. I understand what you're feeling—"

"Do you?" Omega's gaze was piercing.

"Well, all right, I think I understand why you're feeling this way. Telepathic rapes, physical rapes, stalking. You're lonely—" Suddenly Echo heard the car door latch click. He turned, but by that time Omega was striding swiftly down the sidewalk.

But the Corvette was stuck in traffic, and Echo could only stare after her, bewildered.

* * *

Over the next couple of days, Omega continued to withdraw farther and farther, obviously in deep, intense pain.

Insofar as possible, Echo continued to act as if everything were normal. Omega, however, occasionally found thoughtful, even affectionate, little gifts cropping up around her apartment—a volume of poetry, a box of Belgian chocolates, a single stargazer lily in a bud vase, a six-pack of her favorite chocolate stout. Uncharacteristically, she seldom acknowledged them.

When Omega began to request that Echo remove her from active duty, he went to Fox. They discussed the situation together, just the two of them, and decided it would only reinforce Omega's negative mindset to remove her from duty. A quick call to Zebra confirmed their suspicions. However, they concluded, it was possible to subtly reduce Alpha One's duties, in order to ease the stress on Omega without it being obvious.

What WAS obvious to them both was that recent events

had simply been more than Echo's partner—or anyone else, for that matter—could easily take in stride, and Omega desperately needed some space. "And some counseling, if we can ever convince her to take it," Fox added, and Echo agreed.

What was obvious to neither of them was what, if anything, they could do to improve her mental state.

* * *

India slipped up beside Echo as he leaned on one of the catwalk rails, all alone, surveying the Core, several days later. If India had had to put a word to the faint hints of emotion she detected in the inscrutable face, she would have called it despair. Her heart went out to this reserved man she considered a close friend, almost a brother.

"Echo?"

"Oh, hi, India." A subdued Echo turned to greet the Alpha Line's field medic. "How's it goin'?"

"Pretty well," she replied. "You?"

Echo shrugged, but otherwise didn't reply.

"Meg still hasn't opened up?"

"Opened up? Hell, no. If anything, I think she's withdrawing deeper." Echo stared down at the Core's main floor, unseeing. "I don't know how to reach her any more. I don't think she wants to be reached."

"Well, that's not too uncommon with PTSD."

"I know. Been there, done that. But she's not even trying to come out of it or get help—not now. I'm not sure she even wants to. Especially if Zz'r'p is right about that whole nd't'lq thing, and how it's affecting her. And," he added, "given how it's made ME feel, I can believe it. Plus, I think he's probably right about Tt'l'k having thrown his own monkey wrench into the works, judging from a couple things she's said that...didn't really make sense, otherwise."

"How's her self-esteem?" India asked, concerned.

"What self-esteem?" Echo shot back. "Meg was a little uncertain when she first joined the Division, yeah, but some experience under her belt fixed that. I know she quit thinking

340

of herself as human, or even really as a woman, for that matter, when she discovered that Slug genetically engineered her. But at least she accepted herself. Now..." Echo's voice trailed away.

"Have you tried taking her out?"

"She won't go."

"Have you tried talking to her?"

Echo nodded.

"She changes the subject—or leaves." He shook his head. "The other day while we were on patrol, she actually got out of the car, ducked down an alley, and walked home." He shrugged. "Okay, we weren't really still on patrol, or I'd have had to take disciplinary action. We were already on our way home. But we were still over in the East Village! I have no idea if she walked the whole way, caught a taxi, or what—she won't tell me."

"What else have you tried?" India pressed. Echo threw her a cautionary look, and the medic understood it—*Don't push into the private stuff. Don't even go there.*

"I've tried...a number of things. She won't let me get close enough to try much."

India sighed.

"Do you want me to try talking to her—either woman to woman, or doctor to patient?"

Echo shrugged.

"You can try, I guess. Good luck with that. She isn't listening to Fox or me, and I think even Zebra has tried to get her to come down for at least a friendly discussion of matters. But Zebra said she never showed up. Fox and I are lettin' a lotta stuff like that slide, because a reprimand isn't gonna help, and will probably actually make things worse. And Fox trusts me to know her, so he's going along with it." He shrugged. "I don't think she wants to be like this; I think she's just...given up. She's buried under the weight of the emotional avalanche, so to speak, and doesn't see a way out. Unfortunately, I can't figure one out, either."

"Hey," India said, a light bulb going off, "isn't Meg's birthday coming up in a few days?"

"Yeah..." Echo shook his head. "I tried to get her to let me take her out for that—without being obvious about, 'I'm taking you out for your birthday'—but she's..." Instead of finishing, he sighed. "I'm about out of ideas, India."

"Well...what about a birthday party?"

"How the hell are you going to get her to it?" Echo wanted to know. "It's all I can do to keep her on patrol. She's even asked me, as department chief, to relieve her of duty. Three times."

"On what grounds?!" a shocked India asked.

"Unfit for duty."

"Oh, shit. She's halfway down the tubes, then."

"Yeah. Exactly. And augering in."

The two Agents were silent for several minutes, thinking. Then India said, "What about a surprise party?"

"Surprise party?" Echo considered. "Hm. Knowing Meg, that might work. You wanna invite the entire Agency, or 'just the family'?"

"Umm...what about this?" India brainstormed. "The actual party is just the family—Meg and you, me an' Romeo, Zebra and Fox, and your mom, if she can get away from the Ranch— but we collect happy-birthday messages on the sly from anybody else in the Agency that wants to..."

"That works," Echo said, raising his eyebrows. "Fox can help get the word out about the messages. And it oughta be a good morale-boost for Meg, to see how many people care about her."

"Just so, as Fox would say," India agreed. "Now for details. When and where?"

"Not her actual birthday," Echo said emphatically. "We're, um, on-duty and have a, um, a special assignment. Something I threw around a bit of clout to get. And I plan to take advantage of the fact, if you get me."

"Yeah, that's okay. How about the day before, and Romeo and I throw it at our quarters? We're off that day, and that gives us a couple more days to plan it."

"So are we. Done," Echo replied. "I'll talk to Fox about the Agency messages, and I'll also make sure Meg gets there, somehow, if I have to throw her over my shoulder and carry her. You and Romeo put the rest of it together."

"Got it!" India grinned.

* * *

When Echo entered his quarters, going through to his bedroom to change, he found the latest sonnet, lying on his pillow. Unable to converse with Omega about her feelings any other way, Echo had struck on her romantic nature and love of poetry, and had, two days earlier, left a quotation from Shakespeare on her dresser, written in his firm, spare handwriting. Appropriately, it had been from *The Rape of Lucrece*.

* * *

*...What uncouth ill event*
*Hath thee befall'n, that thou dost trembling stand?*
*Sweet love, what spite hath thy fair colour spent?*
*Why art thou thus attired in discontent?*
*Unmask, dear dear, this moody heaviness,*
*And tell thy grief, that we may give redress.*

* * *

The next day, he had found a note in Omega's characteristic stylized hand, lying in his recliner. It was from Shakespeare's Sixty-Sixth Sonnet.

* * *

*Tired with all these, for restful death I cry,*
*As to behold desert a beggar born,*
*And needy nothing trimm'd in jollity,*
*And purest faith unhappily forsworn,*
*And gilded honour shamefully misplac'd,*
*And maiden virtue rudely strumpeted,*
*And right perfection wrongfully disgrac'd,*
*And strength by limping sway disabled*
*And art made tongue-tied by authority,*
*And folly—doctor-like—controlling skill,*

*And simple truth miscall'd simplicity,*
*And captive good attending captain ill:*
*Tir'd with all these, from these would I be gone.*

* * *

*That's not good.* Echo's brows had knit with worry as he read. *I know exactly what she's saying, with this. She feels like her whole life is upside-down and inside-out, and she's tired of all of it. That first and last line, though...those really worry me. Well, at least I got her to respond. Let's see what I can come up with to answer...*

* * *

That night, Omega had gone to bed, to discover another note lying on her pillow, weighted by a stargazer lily. It was the Fifty-Third Sonnet.

* * *

*What is your substance, whereof are you made,*
*That millions of strange shadows on you 'tend?*
*Since everyone hath, every one, one shade,*
*And you, but one, can every shadow lend.*
*Describe Adonis, and the counterfeit*
*Is poorly imitated after you;*
*On Helen's cheek all art of beauty set,*
*And you in Grecian 'tires are painted new.*
*Speak of the spring and foison of the year;*
*The one doth shadow of your beauty show,*
*The other as your bounty doth appear,*
*And you in every blesséd shape we know.*
*In all external grace you have some part,*
*But you like none, none you, for constant heart.*

* * *

Now, fresh from brainstorming with India, Echo read Omega's response to his all-out attempt to buoy her flagging sense of self-worth by expressing his own honest admiration and affection. She had chosen Sonnet Twenty-Nine.

* * *

*When, in disgrace with fortune and men's eyes,*

*I all alone beweep my outcast state,*
*And trouble deaf heaven with my bootless cries,*
*And look upon myself and curse my fate,*
*Wishing me like to one more rich in hope,*
*Featured like him, like him with friends possessed,*
*Desiring this man's art and that man's scope,*
*With what I most enjoy contented least;*
*Yet in these thoughts myself almost despising.*

* * *

Echo studied the quotation, puzzled.

"Wait just a damn minute," he said, frowning. "Something's wrong here. Wha— wait! It's missing lines," he declared, and began counting lines in the poem. "Yeah, it's definitely missing five whole lines! Where's that book of sonnets..."

Echo hurried into his study and grabbed the book of poetry from one of the myriad shelves of books there, then flipped over to Sonnet Twenty-Nine.

*Here we go,* he thought. *Here's what it's missing.* And he read.

* * *

*Haply I think on thee, and then my state,*
*(Like to the lark at break of day arising*
*From sullen earth) sings hymns at heaven's gate;*
*For thy sweet love remembered such wealth brings*
*That then I scorn to change my state with kings.*

* * *

"Huh. That has a whole different mood and attitude; it's happy and full of love. I wonder..." he murmured aloud. "Was the other one missing anything?"

Then he rushed into his bedroom and snatched the previous day's note from his dresser, counting lines again. Taking the two notes, he strode purposefully back into his study.

Echo spread the two handwritten missives out on the desk, side by side, then pulled a volume of Shakespeare off the shelves. He spent some time comparing the handwritten copies to the printed versions, then he muttered, "That's not the end of that poem, either! Now why did she leave out..." Echo sat down at the desk to slowly peruse the sonnets in full.

"Ooo," he murmured, as he read the full text of Sonnet Sixty-Six.

* * *

*Tired with all these, for restful death I cry,*
*As to behold desert a beggar born,*
*And needy nothing trimm'd in jollity,*
*And purest faith unhappily forsworn,*
*And gilded honour shamefully misplac'd,*
*And maiden virtue rudely strumpeted,*
*And right perfection wrongfully disgrac'd,*
*And strength by limping sway disabled*
*And art made tongue-tied by authority,*
*And folly—doctor-like—controlling skill,*
*And simple truth miscall'd simplicity,*
*And captive good attending captain ill:*
*Tir'd with all these, from these would I be gone,*
*Save that, to die, I leave my love alone.*

* * *

When he had finished, he laid the tome down, turned the chair, and stared thoughtfully at the wall.

"...Save that, to die, I leave my love alone," he murmured. "She left that out, too. And ONLY that, on that poem. But... why? What's the key, here?" Echo pondered the matter for long moments, before it hit him that in both cases, the 'speaker' was discouraged, even severely depressed—which fit Omega's current mental state—but in both cases likewise, the 'speaker' was then encouraged and uplifted by thoughts of his or her beloved.

*Not the one who loves her,* he realized. *The one SHE loves. And that would be the one thing keeping her going, it sounds like. The question is, who does she love?*

Abruptly a vidcall conversation with Mu floated into his memory.

*'Mu, who...do you think Meg does want...to be with?'*

346

*'You.'*

And he smiled.

"Good," Echo murmured. "I can work with this."

* * *

Two days later, Omega appeared, alone, in Fox's office.

"What can I do for you, Omega?" Fox said gently, looking up from his desk.

"Fox, I...I'd like a transfer," Omega said in a low voice.

"You and Echo want to transfer?" Fox responded, surprised.

"No, Fox. *I* want to transfer." Azure eyes dropped to the floor as a shocked Fox studied her.

"Does Echo know?"

"...No."

"Why do you want a transfer?"

"...Personal reasons."

"Mm-hm. I see," Fox replied in a deliberately knowing tone. Omega shot a startled, somewhat panicked look at him before he continued. "Transfer where?"

"Off-planet."

"Oh, of course. Halfway around it isn't good enough for YOU," Fox muttered under his breath.

"Excuse me?"

"Nothing." Fox met Omega's dull, dispirited eyes. "Request denied."

"But...but, Fox..." Omega was stunned. Those same dull eyes grew wide in something that looked to the Director very like full panic. It was an expression he had never seen there before, and it pained him to see.

"Denied, Omega," Fox said firmly. Then his voice softened. "Close the door, Omega." She stood and complied. "Now sit back down."

As Omega seated herself, Fox told her, "Omega, my dear tekhter, I won't let you make the kind of mistake you just asked for. You're struggling right now, in grave pain, or you'd never have considered such a thing. You and Echo are a team, Omega. A very, VERY...special...team. I kvell every time I see the two of you in action! I am not stretching the truth in the least when I say that, in all my travels, I have never seen a partnership like yours; it is unparalleled for its ability, its potential...and its understanding. Oh, I know what you think, how you feel," Fox forestalled her comment with a raised hand as she opened her mouth to protest, "yes, I DO, because I've been there myself, after being freed from the concentration camp. You and I have discussed my personal history a little bit—though perhaps not enough to help you, and I'll rectify that soon, when you're better able to cope with it—so you know I DO know what you're thinking and how you're feeling, tekhter, and I understand your pain...but you're wrong. You're in too much pain to see things clearly."

"What...what do you mean?" Omega's voice was so low, Fox had to lean forward to hear it.

"You know exactly what I mean, maydele. Cut Echo some slack. He's trying his absolute damnedest to be there for you, but he can only go so far if you won't meet him part-way— he's standing right beside you, yet you don't acknowledge him or his efforts! And while you may not be able to see it at the moment, the rest of us can—he's hurting, meyn teyere, badly, because he can't reach you. Because you won't let him. When he wants to, so much." Fox paused. "When did you lose faith in Echo, Omega?"

"What?! I never lost faith in Echo, Fox!" Omega all but gaped at her Director and father figure.

"So, it is as I suspected—it was yourself you lost faith in." Fox nodded, his decades of wisdom coming to the fore. "So much so, that you now find it impossible to accept others' faith in you."

Omega stared at the floor, then abruptly pushed out of the chair and turned toward the door.

"You're not dismissed, Omega." He let a hint of warning enter his tone. Omega froze. "Sit back down, please."

Omega turned slowly and returned to her chair in front of Fox's desk. He sat in silence and watched her for long moments before speaking again. She tried not to squirm in mental discomfort and what appeared to the older man to be intense anxiety. *Unlike others who have sat in that chair, and gotten that same warning,* he realized. *She isn't sullen or defiant. I don't think she has it in her to be either right now...not that she's prone to such attitudes anyway. No...she's afraid.* And suddenly that same wisdom borne of decades of experience flashed comprehension into Fox's mind. *She's afraid, because she thinks her world is collapsing, and she has nowhere to go, no way to run...and no way to stop it. She needs a bulwark... and I think I know just how to give her one. Or rather, to remind her that it's there. That it's always been there.*

"Omega, do you know why Echo has faith in you?" Fox asked then. "Because you never let him down. He's told me that."

"I know," she replied in a low tone. "He's told me, too."

"Then why—"

"Fox," she interrupted, "this...is a little bit different."

"Where have I heard that before?" Fox muttered. "Omega, do you trust Echo?"

"Absolutely." Her voice was firm. It was the first thing she had said with any degree of confidence since entering Fox's office that day. In point of fact, the Director decided, it was likely to have been the only thing in which she had acknowledged confidence in the last several days, possibly weeks. "With...with my life," she added.

"Then trust him now, meyn kind," he advised her. "Even if you can't trust yourself. Trust in Echo's faith in you. He has...a great deal of it. More than you could possibly realize, at least right now. And lean on that. You'll find you can, you know."

Omega looked up and met Fox's eyes, and he saw that the panic had left them, replaced by a kind of confusion mingled with what he took to be a desire to believe him. Then she nodded thoughtfully, hesitantly.

"Good, tekhter. Now go home and think about what I've said."

A weary, despondent Omega rose and exited Fox's office, shuffling down the ramp to the main floor, then slowly left the Core.

* * *

On Alpha One's day off, a jeans-clad Echo returned from running mysterious errands all day and stuck his head through the back door.

"Meg?" he called, then blinked. Omega slouched in her recliner, channel-surfing on the TV; she wore no makeup, her hair was down and unkempt, and she was wrapped in pajama top and an old, battered, terrycloth robe. A half-empty bag of potato chips lay on the end table beside her; an empty beer stein, its interior coated with partly-dried foam, and several empty stout bottles sat next to it. "Meg, did you spend all day in bed?" Echo asked softly, shocked at the uncharacteristic behavior.

"Part of it," she shrugged, offhanded. "It wasn't worth gettin' up and gettin' dressed. An' there wasn't anybody around who cared one way or the other."

"Well, there is now," Echo responded, smiling in encouragement at her despite his deep concern. "India just called. She and Romeo want us to come around the corner and have dinner with 'em. So go shower and throw on jeans and a shirt, and let's go."

Omega stopped channel surfing and looked up at him with a dull gaze.

"Thanks, but you go on without me, Echo," she sighed. "I'm...not hungry anyway."

"No." Echo stood his ground.

"What?" She looked up at him, startled.

*Good,* he thought. *That got her attention.* "I said no. I'm not going unless you go."

"But why?" Omega was mildly exasperated, and it showed.

"Because you're my partner. Because you're my closest friend. Because, contrary to what you seem to think, I like having you around. Because I care. Because I like the company.

Because I like talking with you. Because you make me think. Because we have the coolest conversations. Because I feel like I'm missing half my head and most of my insides without you. Because I prefer being with you to anybody else on the planet. Or any other planet. Stop me when you've heard enough. Because I get a kick out of your jokes. Because you get MY jokes. Because—"

"All right, all right! Enough," Omega interrupted, the ghost of a smile finally appearing on her face—the first Echo had seen there in days. "I get the message. I suppose nothing will satisfy you except my getting ready and going with you?"

"You know me well."

"All right," she huffed in mild annoyance...but Echo noticed she capitulated. "Jeans and a shirt, you said?"

"Yep."

"Give me twenty minutes." She heaved herself out of the chair and meandered toward her bedroom.

"You've got it." Echo grinned and watched as his partner closed her bedroom door.

* * *

While Omega got ready, Echo stepped into his own bedroom, closed the door, and pulled out his cell phone, hitting a speed dial.

"Badass to Soldier. Yes, message delivered. No, doesn't have a clue. Affirmative; arrival in T minus..." he glanced at his wrist chronometer, "say sixteen minutes. Right. Badass out."

* * *

"Echo," Omega called, standing in her black silk robe in her bedroom, damp hair combed but not yet braided, "you got a minute?"

"Sure, Meg, whatcha need?" Echo said, coming to her bedroom door, which she had opened partway upon exiting her bathroom. Missing the way his eyes widened and darkened upon realizing that she was ONLY wearing her robe, Omega sighed.

"I'm a little bit brain-dead," she admitted, gesturing at her

351

open closet. "I can't decide."

"Uh, what, you want me to help you pick out your clothes, baby?"

"Well, at least kinda, like, help me decide on options, I guess." She pulled out a couple of pairs of jeans, holding them against her body by turns. "Which?"

Echo cupped his chin in his hand, considering. Then he pointed. "I like the skinny jeans on you more than the flared-leg, I think," he decided. "Unless you're gonna wear cowboy boots. Then you'd need a pair of stacked jeans, I guess."

"No, I think it's been too hot for boots; I was thinking sandals or maybe athletic shoes. Okay. Skinny jeans tonight." Omega tossed the selected jeans onto the bed. "Now, for a top, I got black, white, t-shirt, polo shirt, silk blouse..."

"A silk blouse is a little much for tonight, I think," he told her. "But a t-shirt is probably more casual than you'd want. They wanna cheer you up, so India's been cooking all day, I think."

"Oh! Bless her heart," Omega murmured, touched by the other woman's thoughtfulness. "All right; a polo shirt, then?"

"That ought to be fine, yeah."

"Black or white?" Omega pulled out two shirts, one in each color.

"Hold 'em up and lemme see," Echo said. Omega promptly held one to her face, then the other. "I dunno, baby. You're kinda pale, and they're both washing you out today..."

"Well, I guess I can apply a little makeup," she considered. "I don't want India thinking I'm sick or something. The medlab has been on my case enough as it is, wanting me to come see one of their counselors or...whatever. Is either one better?"

"Um, I think maybe the white is a LITTLE better."

"All right." Omega tossed the white polo shirt onto the bed beside the jeans, sticking everything else back into her closet and closing the closet door. "Okay, shoo, Ace, while I get dressed. And thanks."

"Uh..." Echo hesitated. Omega looked up.

"What?"

"This is gonna sound stupid..."

"Nah. What?"

"Can I come back and watch you put on your makeup?" Echo asked, an inquisitive expression on his face. "I kinda got interested in the theater makeup thing, and I wanted to see how your everyday makeup is different."

"I guess so, if you're really that interested," Omega agreed, and shrugged. "Give me a few minutes to get dressed, then bring a chair in from the dining table. You can sit and watch me; it won't take long."

"Okay."

* * *

Echo waited outside the bedroom door until Omega opened it and waved him inside. She was dressed, but her hair was still loose, and she did not yet have on shoes and socks. He followed her as she padded barefoot into the bathroom, then plunked down his chair in the doorway, turned it backwards, and straddled it. Omega picked up a comb and ran it through her hair, then sectioned off the front and began to French-braid it.

"Oh!" Echo said, watching. "So that's how you do that."

"Yeah," Omega agreed. "Have you never watched me braid my hair?"

"Not really, no," Echo noted. "I've been around when you've done it, of course, but usually I was busy doing something else and never had time to sit and do nothing BUT watch. That's interesting. You just keep adding pieces in...this side, then that side, then this side..."

"Right. Then, when you get to the nape of the neck, it turns into a regular braid," she said, following suit. "Like this."

"Here," he said, reaching for her hair. "I can braid this last bit for you. Shiitsooyee taught me how to make braided horsehair stuff, like hatbands an' junk, so I know how."

"Um, okay," Omega agreed, letting him take the strands and finish the braid.

353

Echo focused on what he was doing, secretly enjoying the feel of the silky strands in his fingers; moments later, he had reached the end of her hair, and she handed him the elastic, which he nimbly wrapped around the smooth, sleek braid, roughly an inch from the end of the hair.

"There you go," he told her. "All done. It's really shiny today; did you do something to it?"

"I added a deep conditioner to it, while I was still in the shower," Omega told him, cleaning off her face with a baby wipe. "It felt awfully dry and kinda brittle, almost, when I got ready to wash it. Scrunching it all up and sticking that wig on it night after night, and then sweating like a horse, didn't do it any favors, I think."

"Never mind barfing every night, AND losing your appetite from the stimulants," Echo added, as Omega picked up a tube of cosmetics. "You're bound to have lost some nutrients in there."

"Ooo. I didn't think about that. Yeah, good points. I might need to ask India about a nutritional supplement to take for a few weeks." She squeezed a small amount of the makeup from the tube onto a small facial sponge.

"Waitaminit. I thought that was your moisturizer. It looks exactly like the other tube we used at the theater..."

"It is."

"It looks like foundation."

* * *

"It's kinda both, and the tubes look similar 'cause it's from the same cosmetic line. It's called a tinted moisturizer. It's lighter than a standard foundation, and it serves the purpose of both. It's got a sunscreen in it, too. For every day, I don't use a whole lotta 'goop,' as you like to put it." She applied the tinted moisturizer, which evened out her skin tone, then studied herself in the mirror. "Ugh. Dark circles under the eyes. Those have gotta go."

"Have you not been sleeping well?"

"Um, well, not exactly," Omega admitted. "I've...kinda

been having a lotta dreams an' stuff."

"Bad ones?"

"...Sometimes."

"What about?"

Omega shook her head.

"Mark, Slug, the theater phantom, you name it, Ace," she confessed. "Sometimes one from column A, one from column B...that kinda shit."

"Ouch."

"Yeah. So let's see if I can cover this up a little bit. Or India really WILL have a cow." She reached for a concealer stick, dabbing it on the offending areas and blending with her fingertips, patting gently to spread the concealer over the delicate skin. "That's better. Okay, a bit of powder..." she suited action to deed, "some eyeliner..." a coppery-bronze crayon outlined her eyes, contrasting and emphasizing their azure hue. Then she smudged it with a cotton swab to soften the line, and reached for a compact and a long-handled brush. "...And a swipe of blush, and I'm done." Within moments her cheeks appeared more flushed. "Rather than fool with lip color, I'm gonna just use some lip balm," she decided, reaching for the balm. "I'm only gonna eat it off anyway, if we're having dinner over there."

"Yup," Echo agreed. "That's way cool, baby. Other than the eyeliner, which is really subtle—and REALLY makes your eyes go 'pow,' by the way, and they're gorgeous, to begin with—I can't hardly tell you're wearing ANY makeup."

"Which is the point." Omega offered him a slight smile. "Day to day makeup doesn't have to do nearly as much as stage makeup. I wanna even out any blotchiness, protect my face from getting sunburned, and keep it moist. The eyeliner is mostly only to help bring out my eyes, and I don't always even bother with blush. But you're right; I'm a little washed-out today. I've...I've just been...tired." She shook her head. "Of everything. Tired of me most of all, I think."

"I know. I get it. But I've been worried, honey."

"I...know. I'm...sorry." Omega sighed. "I've been a pain in the ass...to everybody. But to you, most especially. When you've stuck by me through all of it, and deserve way better treatment than I've given you lately. And I'm really, really... sorry."

"Thanks, baby, but it's okay. What brought this on? I've been trying to talk to you for days."

"Aw, Fox turned into my dad the other day and gave me a talking-to," Omega admitted, without telling him why she was in Fox's office to begin with. "Anyway, he managed to get outta me that, well, that I'm second-guessing myself. And third-guessing, and fourth, and twelfth and forty-fifth and...you get the idea."

"You're not trusting yourself any more. Yeah, I picked up on that."

"So he asked me if I trusted you, which of course I do, and he told me that, if I couldn't trust myself, I should trust your assessment of me...or something like that. Lean on you, he said. I've been thinking about it a lot, and..." Omega drew a deep breath. "You gotta help me, Ace, but...I'm gonna try. I'm gonna trust...your take on things. I'm gonna trust YOU. Because I can't seem to trust me right now."

"Great!" Echo said, his dark eyes warming. "I'm SO awful glad to hear that, I can't tell you, honey! What can I do to help? What looks like being the worst issue? If we can figure that out, we'll start by tackling it."

"I dunno. That's kinda the problem! I can't seem to get my head above water, Ace," she told him with a deep, frustrated sigh. "It feels like my whole life kinda rose up and dogpiled me, if you understand what I'm trying to say."

"I think so, but try me."

"Uhm, lessee. Okay, remember a few weeks ago when I told you that I kept wondering if I'd done something different, paid more attention, not gone stargazing that night, if Slug might not have got me? If it would have made a difference?"

"Yeah?"

"Like that. About EVERYTHING. 'Should I have done that, should I do this, what if I had done the other thing instead?' Over and over and over. About every damn little thing! Until I'm ready to SCREAM! And THEN I think, 'None of it would have made any difference anyway; I'm hopeless.' And it all goes to hell in the proverbial handbasket! I know everybody thinks I need to talk to a counselor; I mean Zebra has been on my case about it ten million ways from Sunday, and I know I probably should—but I can't! I can barely talk about it to YOU, and you pretty much know everything, or almost everything," she explained. "How the hell am I supposed to tell it all to some stranger?"

"What if I came along and helped, by doing some of the telling for you?" he offered.

"No," she murmured, shaking her head. "There's stuff there that even you don't know, remember. I'm...I can't..."

* * *

"You never got that resolved in your mind up in Ipswich, did you?" Echo recalled. "Wright showed up, and you got punted into the high surf..."

"Yeah, and that kinda ended the whole, 'Meg needs some quiet introspection time,'" she pointed out. "BOY, did it."

"Okay. But I wouldn't have to be there for all of it. I could just, like, come in and help you set up the whole scenario and history for the counselor, then bug out and let you two hash it over." Echo paused, as sudden inspiration struck. "OR..."

"Or?"

"Meg? Zz'r'p already knows all of it, right? I mean, he deprogrammed you..."

"Um, yeah, I think he does. At least as much as you do, anyway, BECAUSE OF the deprogramming; no way I coulda told him all that, any more than I could tell you. I, I think it's... kinda gotta be shown, you know? Why?"

"Well, isn't he certified as a counselor? And you trust him. You're friends with him, and he already helps train your mental abilities. And you don't have to TELL him, you can SHOW him. Exactly like you were just talking about. All you have to do is remember it, and he'll experience it with you...like I did, with your memories of Slug's kidnapping you."

Omega stared at him, sapphire eyes wide in shocked comprehension, jaw slack.

"Holy shit, Ace," she murmured, stunned. "Why the hell haven't any of us thought of that before now?"

"So it's a good idea?"

"That's the best idea I've heard all week. I'mma give him a call tomorrow."

"Better make it the day after," Echo warned. "Remember, we've got that mission tomorrow. And we'll need to travel to get to it."

"Oh, okay. Yeah, I forgot. Day after tomorrow, then."

* * *

But Omega's mood, which had begun to lift a bit with the interaction with her partner, dipped somewhat at the reminder.

*Does he not know what tomorrow is?* she wondered. *I mean, he doesn't have to make a big deal over it, like I kinda did for him. Because after all, his mom was possibly dying, if Zebra couldn't overcome the cancer. But some sorta acknowledgement woulda been nice. A card or something.*

* * *

"So...do I need any jewelry or anything for dinner tonight, do ya think?" she tried, wanting to get her mind off her partner's apparent lack of recognition of the day.

Echo stood, moving the chair out of the doorway, as Omega walked across the bedroom to her dresser.

"Look at me," he ordered, but gently. Omega turned and met his assessing gaze. "Nah, I think you're good as is," he decided. "Only if you want to bother."

"Maybe the star earrings that Romeo gave me, last Christmas," she considered, opening her jewelry box. "I'm already wearing India's charm bracelet." She picked up the earrings and slid them into her ears, then shoved her feet into black sandals. "There. Okay, Ace, let's go visiting for dinner."

"Sounds good, baby," he said, offering his arm to her. She took it, and Alpha One sallied forth...

...For the first time in nearly three weeks.

# Chapter 11

Omega, escorted by Echo and clad in her skinny black jeans and the white polo shirt, walked into the gaily-decorated joint quarters of Alpha Two, where Romeo, India, Dihl, Zebra and Fox awaited Alpha One. As soon as she entered, everyone shouted, "SURPRISE!" and she was promptly covered in hugs, kisses, and congratulatory wishes. Fox and Zebra provided firm, affectionate hugs, but the more effusive kisses were exclusively the province of Alpha Two, although Echo, beside her, added an affectionate shoulder-squeeze and peck on the temple into the hubbub, and Dihl offered a motherly kiss to her cheek.

Omega shot Echo a sardonic sidelong glance.

"You won't go without me, huh?" she muttered, trying to hide how deeply she was affected by their thoughtfulness.

"Nope. There wasn't any point in it." Echo grinned.

"So how many of the 'becauses' did you make up on the spot?"

"None." Echo took his partner by the hand and drew her over to India's dining room table with the others. "I coulda gone on a lot longer. C'mon. The others have been waiting for us; we took longer than I thought. Let's eat."

Romeo and India had contrived to concoct a tempting menu of Omega's favorite dishes—partly by consulting with Echo and Dihl—and they were pleased to see her eating a little better as a result. The fact that Echo had come up with an acceptable compromise that would enable his partner to begin to deal with her issues helped ease her tensions, and when he quietly mentioned it to the others, there was a general exclamation of relief.

"Oh, honey, I am SO glad to hear that," Zebra admitted. "And Echo, that was a brilliant idea."

"Indeed it was," Fox agreed. "It's a pity that no one thought of it sooner; Omega could already be well into her emotional and mental healing."

"Echo thought of it now," Dihl noted, sanguine, "Omega has agreed, and that is all that is important. Her healing will come in time."

"It's good to see you again, Dihl," Omega confessed. "Echo and I have both missed you."

"Well, I would not have missed this little celebration for anything, my dear girl," Dihl averred. "But just so you both know, I have discussed the relative needs here and at the Ranch with Fox, Zebra, and Zarnix, and for the time being, I will be splitting my time between the two facilities. Is...this acceptable to you both?" she wondered.

"It's fine, Ma," Echo agreed. "I know how much that ranch means to you. And I'm glad you're enjoying working in the Agency. But I gotta admit, I'm glad you'll still be around here some, too."

"Good," Dihl said. "Omega?"

"Oh, I don't really have the right to an opinion," Omega murmured.

"Nonsense!" Dihl exclaimed. "Is this not a family, right here?" She waved her hands around the table. "Are you not my son's partner and best friend? Of course you have the right to an opinion! Besides, don't think for one moment that I haven't heard about the fact that the two of you have been going out together!" Dihl watched in amusement as Omega blushed fiercely, and even Echo colored a bit. "Now, tell me, dear child: are you all right with my spending part of my time at the Ranch?"

"Well, um, since you put it like that," Omega said, voice a bit strained from embarrassment, "I, uh, I agree with Echo. I know you love the Ranch, but I'm...I'm glad you're gonna be around here some, too. I...missed you. I really enjoy how you and Echo have been helping me recreate the family recipes that nobody until me thought to write down, and I miss it. An' the other stuff we do, too. I miss our time together, you an' Echo an' me."

"Then, since I am back for at least a month, we will do that very thing on Alpha One's next day off," Dihl decreed. "How does that sound?"

"Great," Omega said, smiling, and the others grinned.

* * *

"It's working," Zebra breathed to Fox. "She actually smiled. And it went all the way to her eyes."

"I noticed," Fox confirmed. "It sounds like the very invitation to dinner opened up a conversation with Echo, and his idea was positively brilliant."

"It was," Zebra agreed. "And it's one she's willing to work with, too. I don't mind telling you, I was getting damn worried."

"I don't mind admitting that I was, too."

"Awright, you two," Romeo called from the other end of the table, "quit wit' th' canoodlin' an' makin' out, down there. Yeah, I'm talkin' to you, Fox! B'tween y'all, an' me an' India, an' Echo an' Meg, we ain't got that many rooms!"

"OH good grief!" Omega exclaimed, formerly pale face now flaming; Echo flushed slightly, as well. "Y'all are all life partners! We just dated a couple times, guys! We're not...like THAT."

"Yet," Romeo teased.

"Oh hush, you," India said, elbowing him, rather to Alpha One's joint relief.

* * *

At the end of the meal, India brought out a wonderfully gooey chocolate birthday cake, whimsically decorated with question-mark candles. Omega's eyes widened.

"Whoa! It's huge," she murmured, after blowing out the candles.

"Uh-huh," India grinned. "I checked, and we've got seven chocoholics here. It should be big enough—I hope!"

Omega chuckled softly then, causing the others to smile, just before she queried, "But why question marks? It's easy enough to find out my age..."

India's grin got bigger.

"Yeah, but Division One Agents have no past, therefore we have no age. I knew there were perks to this job, Fox!"

"Besides," Echo added, teasing, "I thought Southern belles were ageless."

"Now you know what that special 'face goop' of mine does," Omega retorted, sticking out her tongue, and everyone laughed.

"This is way more like it. Th' pretty lady done got her smiles back," Romeo murmured the aside to Echo, who nodded, then offered a forkful of his cake to Omega, who was busy cutting slices for the others.

"Here, Meg. The birthday lady should at least get the first bite."

"Okay," she responded absently, opening her mouth to give Echo a target for his fork as she juggled cake and plates.

At the last possible instant, Echo's hand, normally rock-steady, abruptly twitched; the enormous bite of chocolate cake smeared across his partner's face. The room's occupants froze in shocked surprise, waiting to see what happened next.

"Ooops," Echo said innocently, dark eyes twinkling.

Omega sat still for a long moment. Then she scooped up a just-sliced hunk of cake in one hand. She stood, turned, and deliberately licked icing off her lips, raising the slice of cake.

"Echo, this cake is really good," she remarked, a spark in the blue eyes. "C'mere, you, and try some."

Grinning, Echo backed off, as his partner advanced on him.

"No thanks, Meg, I'm on a diet."

"Uh-huh. India, I promise I'll clean the carpet."

"Okay," India replied, as she, Romeo, Dihl, Zebra, and Fox watched the standoff with large grins.

Omega gradually, subtly, maneuvered an unconcerned, mischievous Echo into a corner; when he suddenly realized what she had done, his eyes widened, and he glanced around for an escape route. Just as he took his eyes off her, she made her move, bringing the cake straight up, close to his chest, and directly into his face.

"Mmph!" he grunted, as chocolate cake filled nose, eyes, and mouth.

"See?" Omega asked, as the five watching Division One agents exploded in laughter. "Good stuff, huh?"

"Yeah, Meg," Echo chuckled, managing to get free of enough of the gooey cake to see, breathe, and speak, "good stuff. Here." He began gently wiping the debris off Omega's face with his napkin. When he was finished, he started on his own face.

"No, let me, Ace," Omega said softly. "You can't see what you're doing, and I nailed ya pretty good." She took the soggy paper napkin from him, then made a face. "India, hand me a couple more of these things," she said.

"Nah, girlfriend," India decided, and ducked into the kitchen. "You need this." She emerged with a roll of paper towels and a bottle of water. A grateful Omega exchanged the icing-soaked napkin in her hand for the roll, ripping off several sheets of toweling, then opening the water bottle and moistening the towels. The others finished eating as Omega cleaned up Echo, then a good-humored Alpha One sat down and actually ate the last two slices of cake.

"Damn, guys. That was some mighty fine cake, as my Dad might have said," Echo declared, as everyone pushed back from the table, but chose to remain seated and chat.

"Oh, he sounds just like him," Dihl murmured, clasping her hands in pleasure, and the others smiled.

"Yeah, it was good," Omega agreed. "Did you make it, India?"

"Sure did," the physician averred, slipping one hand under the table. "I'm glad you liked it."

"It was nummy!"

"Good."

"It was all good," Echo averred, and affirmations went around the table. "That was a delicious meal, India. Thanks."

"Yeah—" Omega began. But she didn't get a chance to finish.

"Time for th' gifts!" Romeo exclaimed then, and he and India deposited a package each in Omega's lap.

* * *

Omega blinked for a few moments without moving, and gradually the others became aware that she was blinking back tears. Echo knelt beside her chair and rested his hand comfortingly on her back, rubbing lightly in a soothing fashion, hoping that his pheromones would still help settle her roiling emotions.

"Meg?" he murmured. "You okay, baby?"

Omega looked up then, eyes glistening. "Do y'all know how much you mean to me?" she whispered, then choked. The others glanced down, deeply affected, as she added, "Thanks for being so patient with me lately—especially you." She nudged Echo. "I know I've been a pain. To all of you."

"'S okay, pretty lady," Romeo replied quietly.

"Yes, Meg, we understand," India added in a low tone.

"I'm just glad you've finally agreed to talk to someone about it all," Zebra murmured. "I've been SO worried about you, honey."

"More, child," Dihl said, voice soft, "thank you for saving my son's life once more."

"Indeed. You did a truly excellent job, tekhter, catching and overpowering the 'Theater Phantom,'" Fox added, gentle and encouraging, "and saving the life of your partner—my oldest living human friend, and unofficially-adopted son—into the bargain."

Omega looked greatly startled for a moment; she evidently had been viewing events drastically differently from the others.

"...It's been no problem to allow you some opportunity to deal with the fallout from recent events on your own terms," Fox continued.

Omega smiled shyly at that, then glanced questioningly at Echo.

"You know I'm here," he remarked. "Now...go ahead and open those gifts. I'm curious."

Omega stared at him oddly for a moment, then turned her attention to India's present. It turned out to be a white halter-top evening gown, slim-fitting, with tiny knife-pleats running its length. Omega immediately stood and held it against herself, trying to imagine it on and accessorized.

"It's a Marilyn dress," Echo remarked, watching with a smile. "Only longer."

"What?" Omega asked, as Romeo and Zebra looked blank; Fox nodded, and India beamed.

"A Marilyn dress," Echo reiterated. "You know—Marilyn Monroe."

"Oh! You're right," Omega realized.

"I KNEW at least ONE of you would get it," India declared, pleased. "That's why I got it—I could just see Meg in that role!"

"It's lovely, India," Omega said with another shy smile. "Thank you. But I really don't have any need for it now. Well, I always have it, if I ever have to go undercover in 'high society' again. Or maybe if the Agency has another big soirée or something, I suppose."

Omega folded it carefully and replaced it in the box, as Fox, Romeo, Dihl, Zebra, and India glanced in concern at the man beside her, whose shoulders, they noticed, suddenly didn't seem as squared as usual.

Omega turned to Romeo's gift, pulling off wrapping paper. She opened the box and dug through tissue paper, pulling out a filmy material.

"Oh! Romeo! What on earth?!" Omega exclaimed, blushing as she realized that the pale blue silk in her hands was a gown-and-peignoir set.

"I figured a Broadway star oughta look th' part, even when she's asleep," Romeo said, and grinned. Two pairs of male brown eyes met surreptitiously over Omega's shoulder, and gleamed at each other. Omega chuckled.

"Now all I need is to have breakfast served to me in bed,

and I'll look the perfect diva. Yeah. Like that happens in the Agency."

"You never can tell, Meg," India teased, poking Romeo in the ribs. "It happened to me just the other day." Romeo grinned knowingly.

Omega smiled at the affectionate couple, then sighed. Fox interjected quickly, before Omega's spirits could sink too far.

"Zebra, my dear, I think it's your turn."

Zebra smiled and rose, going into the bedroom and returning with a large, bright-red gift bag which had been taped shut at the top. She held it out to Omega.

"Here you go; happy birthday, honey," she said, as Omega took it. Echo offered the knife blade on his multitool, and Omega slit the tape across the top, reaching in and pulling out a plush microfiber blanket, which had been sublimation-printed with a certain very familiar image of the Orion Nebula...which, upon request, Echo had provided to Zebra from the data obtained during Omega's starship-pilot training mission.

"Ooo," Omega murmured, hugging the fluffy blanket to her chest. "Soft, warm, AND pretty."

"It's a throw," Zebra noted, "so it isn't intended to be big enough for the bed, although I've used 'em on the bed before, especially if, say, I'm cold but Fox isn't. But it's big enough for two to cuddle under it on the couch, and I speak from personal experience on that." She ribbed Fox, who grinned, then she winked at Echo.

"I think we can make good use of that, once the weather starts turning colder," Echo decided. "Maybe snuggling up and watching a movie marathon on our day off, or something. Never mind naps on the couch."

"Yeah. Especially if we do any more Antarctic missions," Omega agreed, catching her lower lip between her teeth for a moment.

"Oh HELL no," Echo decreed. "I know you've got all the appropriate wardrobe now, but that was a wee bit much, baby."

"No shit," India averred. "I used more frostbite ointment

on you that night, Meg, than I've used in all the time I've been a doctor before AND since. Besides, you need to be careful—between that, and the crash on the protoplanet and the like, you're a bit more prone to hypothermic issues now than you used to be."

"Oh," Fox said, pulling his omnipresent tablet from a warp pocket and recording the information. "That was good to know; I just put it in her file, for future reference."

"Okay," India said. "It's definitely something to consider, when assigning Alpha One."

"Yeah, honey, I can provide you a bit more information on that later," Zebra told her spouse.

"Guys? I was joking," Omega noted in a flat tone, crossing her eyes, and the others snorted or snickered. Echo smeared his hand down his face.

"Well, okay," Echo capitulated. "But you haven't been doin' a lot of that lately, honey, and nobody recognized it."

"What he said," Romeo confirmed. "Sorry."

"No problem," Omega said, offering a wry grin before sobering with a sigh. "I can see where that mighta been confusing. I'm...sorry."

"No, no; none of that," Fox murmured. "No recriminations, tekhter. Not even from yourself."

"ESPECIALLY from yourself," Echo interjected.

"That," Fox agreed. "Not tonight. On with the celebration! Dihl?"

"Yes indeed. And here is my gift, daughter," Dihl said, laying a large, flat, square box, gaily wrapped in multicolored paper, in Omega's lap. "I think you will like it. More, I think my son will appreciate it, as well."

Omega ripped off the paper and opened the box. Inside was a loose-leaf notebook with a cover. It read,

*The McAllister Family Recipe Cook Book*

A certain intimately-familiar family holiday picture

comprised the artwork on the cover.

Lying next to the cookbook in the box was a small package of various dried herbs, each in its own small bottle. Omega knew it came straight from the Ranch's herb garden, and each one was apparently selected with care in regard to the recipes contained in the cookbook.

Omega blinked in shock.

"You...you collected 'em? All of 'em?" she whispered. "My family's recipes?"

"All of them that we have managed to recreate to this point," Dihl said with a smile. "Echo helped a bit, scanning the recipes your mother wrote down on index cards, hidden away in your tiny recipe box in the kitchen, and sending them to me. We have had this particular little project under way for a few weeks now, he and I, you see. And it is loose-leafed so we can add pages as we go." Dihl shrugged. "I hope you do not mind that I added an appendix in the back, with most of the recipes you requested from Joe at the Ranch. And I collected and dried the herbs myself, ensuring you had everything you might need to make all the recipes in the book. I will provide more when they are done drying."

"It's wonderful," Omega said, giving the older woman a prolonged hug. "And it means a lot. Thank you. Thank you both."

There was a kind of reverent silence for a few moments, as the others took in the scene. Finally Fox pushed back from the table and stood.

"Omega, you'll have to come in here for my gift," he told her, leading the way through Alpha Two's dining room door into their living area. Omega's eyes grew round at all the extra hookups on Romeo's wide-screen flat TV. "Sit down right there," Fox said, pointing, and Omega sat in the middle of the couch, where he indicated. Echo sat down on her right, Fox on the left. Romeo and India moved the coffee table out of the way, then sat down at Omega's feet, facing the television. Dihl took the armchair beside Echo's end of the sofa; Zebra sat in the recliner near Fox. "Romeo," Fox requested, "will you do the honors?"

"Absolutely, Fox," Romeo said, fishing a special remote from its hiding place under the couch. He aimed it at the TV and hit a button. Nothing happened that Omega could see, but Romeo carefully timed off thirty seconds on his wrist chronometer, then hit another button. The screen came to life.

"HAPPY BIRTHDAY, OMEGA!!" The room filled with the shout from dozens of voices piped over Romeo's stereo speaker system, as agents and aliens alike clustered in the Core and congratulated her. Omega gaped, then covered her O-shaped mouth with one hand. Alpha-Four's Agent Golf stepped forward, as Alpha Line ranked itself and saluted.

"Omega, Alpha Line chose me to be the spokesman for the department tonight. We'd like to wish the best assistant department chief in the whole damn Agency a happy birthday and best wishes!" A cheer went up from the assembled department. "Echo's told us you've been a little under the weather for the last week or so—and after that mission at the theater we all heard about, no wonder!—but he explained it was why you haven't been at your desk very much, and we're sorry. Get to feeling better soon, okay? Echo's a helluva lot grumpier when you're not around to keep his disposition sunny!" The entire Core laughed, and Omega smiled. Echo's cheeks seemed slightly duskier than usual, but he grinned good-naturedly, as Alpha Line applauded.

* * *

Fox's assistants waved then, from a console in the corner, and brought up a message on one of the Core's big wall-panel screens. It read,

*Happy Birthday Ω*<br>*Winner of the Divvy*

"The what?" Omega asked, confused. "What am I supposed to have won?"

Fox laughed aloud. "It was Lima's idea," he explained. "They said it's the Agency's version of a Tony award. It isn't like we could allow you to be eligible for a Tony, more's the pity, so they wanted you to know...basically, what the entire Agency thought of your performance!" He nudged her with an elbow and grinned. "But I don't think it has nearly as stringent rules for awarding!"

"Like, none!" Lima piped up, and both of Fox's assistants laughed. "We just thought it would be fun!"

"Oh!" Omega had to chuckle, as well; beside her, Echo snorted his amusement. "Thanks, guys! What does it look like?"

"It looks exactly like this!" Bravo held up a small, polished monolith of black granite on a white marble base. "And it's really exclusive!"

"Yeah!" Lima agreed. "Only one has ever been awarded!"

"Or probably ever WILL be awarded!" Bravo added, nearly doubling up with mirth.

"Okay," Omega said, and grinned. "I know exactly where I'm gonna put it on my bookshelves." Everyone else laughed, and the two assistants beamed in delight.

* * *

Madrid, the British weapons designer, stepped into view then. Almost four dozen familiar faces from several departments clustered behind him.

"Cheerio, old girl," he grinned. "Oh, perhaps I shouldn't have used that particular phrase today." Guffaws fairly permeated the Core. "R & D, Sciences, and the Weapons departments—not to mention myself personally—wish you the very best on your birthday, my dear, and would like for you to know how much we've enjoyed our collective associations with you."

"Thanks, Madrid," Omega replied warmly, as her companions smiled. "It's always fun to work with y'all in all three departments, and y'all do really good work."

"So do you," Madrid added. "We got together all three

departments and reviewed our records when Fox told us about this little celebration for you, and we discovered that you've contributed more scientific discoveries, as well as offensive, defensive, and support equipment concepts, to the Division One organization than any other agent in our history."

"Well, well," Fox interjected, "it sounds to me like a commendation is in order."

"Our point exactly!" Madrid smiled. Omega was speechless.

* * *

The Arcturan embassy personnel moved into the camera's focus. "Omega, congratulations on the anniversary of your nativity," Zz'r'p spoke very formally. "We make you the gift of a standing offer: If and when you decide you wish to re-establish the nd't'lq, we will happily provide the necessary assistance."

"Thank you, Zz'r'p," Omega said with a smile, then added mentally, *but it really isn't my decision to make.*

*I understand,* came the unspoken reply; Zz'r'p never missed a beat, and Omega decided he had been expecting a mental response. *Nevertheless, the offer remains. And I have already been made aware of your desire to see me for your counseling. A greatly-relieved Echo texted me earlier this evening with a 'heads-up,' as he would say, and I have tentatively penciled you in for the day after tomorrow at 0400 D1, if that will suit.*

*That would be...great,* Omega agreed. *And thank you, once again.*

*It is ever my honor, youngling. Will you let me perform one small item of healing right now? It will only take a few seconds, and no one will know it is happening, but I promise you, it will help how you have been feeling.*

*All right, I guess so.*

* * *

*Echo,* Zz'r'p's voice sounded in the male Agent's head, *Omega has agreed to let me smooth over the missing nd't'lq. This should help stabilize her emotional deterioration, until I can begin counseling her.*

*FANTASTIC!* Echo almost shouted mentally, so great was his relief. *Wups, sorry. Too loud.*

*No problem, as you like to say,* Zz'r'p said with a chuckle. *I have some experience with INexperienced telepathic communications.*

He broke the link, and Echo glanced at his partner. Seeing the distant look in her eyes, he realized she was deep in communication with the Deltiri, and he quickly turned to the others, making several gestures to indicate that Omega had agreed to let Zz'r'p help her.

"Oh, thank HaShem," Fox breathed.

"Lotsa that," Zebra averred, and the others nodded assent.

* * *

Omega allowed Zz'r'p to enter the deep recesses of her mind, and abruptly the pain she had been experiencing diminished, as a soothing feeling washed over her being. Even her uncertainty felt lessened.

*Oh, wow,* she thought in relief. *I dunno what you did, Zz'r'p, but that feels...better. A lot better.*

*I did two things, Omega. First, I verified that Echo was not the only one that Tt'l'k implanted with subliminal suggestions, most likely that evening you fell asleep at the theater, though possibly earlier; in YOU, he inserted a...programming module, let us call it...that was making your mental state worse. That has now been removed.*

*Tt'l'k did...you're kidding.* Omega was so stunned even her mental voice was bland.

*No, I am not. When I discovered his subliminal 'illness' suggestion in Echo, I began to worry about what he might have done to you at the same time, and when I saw how fast your emotional and mental condition deteriorated, I was convinced of it.*

*Well, you said he'd been studying Slug's techniques. I guess it stands to reason he'd try a small programming attempt.*

*Indeed. Perhaps it is as well that he has been taken out of general activity.*

*Yeah. But I didn't WANT to hurt him that bad. He made me really mad, yeah, attacking Echo that way, when Echo had never done anything to him. But I wouldn't have killed him, and I still hope I didn't leave him...you know.*

*I know. If you wish, I will keep you apprised of his medical treatment.*

*I'd like that, yes.*

*Only do not expect much; his condition would have been difficult to treat, in any event. With the overlay of his fear and catatonia—self-induced, let me add—well, the prognosis is... that much worse.*

*Aw, damn. Awright. You said you did a couple of things to me, just now.*

*I did. As for that second item of healing—I simply smoothed over the 'raw edges' where the link with Echo had been,* he told her. *I did it for Echo the other day, and he said it helped him, as well.*

*The nd't'lq removal hurt him, too?* Omega wondered in consternation. *But...I didn't really think he would...I mean, he doesn't have telepathic tendencies...I never meant to hurt...*

*I know you didn't, and so does he. But he cares very deeply about you, my dear. I think you do not realize how much. You mean the world to him.* Zz'r'p paused, considering, then added, *You are rejecting the nd't'lq partly based on the notion that he does not want it. But you should know that he DID want it, that he treasured it as much as he treasures his partner...because it WAS his partner. I think you should seriously reconsider recreating the link between you.*

*Oh,* Omega told him, surprised. *I'll...think about that. Maybe we can talk about it in our counseling sessions. Then, if...if it makes sense, I'll...ask him. If he wants it back, I mean.*

*I think that a good idea. And you may find his answer... unexpected. All right; back outside, for now.*

* * *

As the surprisingly-swift telepathic conversation and healing ended, with no one in the Core the wiser for its occurrence outside of the Arcturan embassage, the entire diplomatic contingent nodded.

Then Zz'r'p stood straight and tall, smiled...and bowed, granting the astonished Omega the ultimate honor—Arcturans reserved formal, full bows for only the most highly-respected persons. Moments later, and without hesitation, the rest of the embassage followed suit.

Alpha Two, Zebra, and Dihl gaped at the unexpected honor; Fox pressed his lips together, hiding a knowing smile. Echo didn't try to hide his proud grin. Then he leaned over and gently nudged his partner.

"Way to go, baby," he breathed in her ear.

Omega smiled.

* * *

*It is done,* Zz'r'p told Echo then. *The smoothing over of the nd't'lq connections...and more.*

*What more was there?* Echo wondered. *Well, other than the counseling an' stuff.*

*A little... 'subroutine,' let us call it...which Tt'l'k implanted in Omega's sleeping mind at the same time he gave you the 'telepathic virus,'* Zz'r'p explained. *It was this attempt of his at using Slug's style of mental programming which has resulted in your partner's sudden, rapid, emotional deterioration— essentially, it accelerated the process that was already occurring. The 'subroutine' was not especially sophisticated— another probable indication of his illness—but it was effective, nevertheless. That has been halted and expunged as of mere seconds ago; her response was positive and immediate, and I think her prognosis is now much better than it was, thirty seconds ago. I wanted you to know.*

*Oh wow,* Echo thought. *That's...great.*

*Yes. And she and I begin the rest of the healing, the day after tomorrow.*

*Zz'r'p...* a grateful Echo began.

*Hush, youngling. I 'see' that already; you have no need to say more. And do not worry about trying to subtly notify the*

375

*others with you—the rest of her Agency 'family.' I will handle that momentarily, in the same fashion I notified you.*

*Okay. But I'm gonna say it anyway: THANKS.*

*You are very welcome, my friend.*

* * *

A raucous chattering came from somewhere off-screen just then. A tolerant, amused Zz'r'p simply pointed downward.

"Tilt down," Fox commanded, and the camera controller obeyed, revealing a grouping of enthused Hypothenemoids, led by Irokin.

"Hiya, Meg!" the beetle-like aliens exclaimed cheerily, all together. "Happy hatching-day! Echo has our gift! Make the pretty lady happy! Enjoy!"

"What?" Omega laughed. "Slow down, y'all. You said Echo has the gift you sent?"

"Yeah, Meg," her partner answered. "Let's just say we won't have to get coffee for at least six months." Echo grinned.

"Ooo, good job, guys!" Omega gave the little creatures a thumbs-up. "What kind?"

"Chicory coffee, straight from the New Orleans café!" Irokin replied, waving a prehensile antenna in response; it kinked around in a reasonable mimicry of a thumbs-up back at Omega. "High-octane!"

"My favorite! Even better!" Omega responded in enthusiasm. Her six companions glanced at each other and nodded subtly.

* * *

A small-screen image formed within the larger one. In it stood the aliens and agents of the Ranch, the field station in Texas. Joe Beck, the Haepergen overseer, stood front and center. "Hi, there, little lady. Remember me?" he said.

"Hi, Joe!" Omega exclaimed. "Good to see you! I gotta come by there sometime and ride Celeste again!"

"You do that," Joe said with a grin. "Come on down with Dihl, next time she's here. An' bring Echo with ya. Anyway, we here at the Ranch just wanted to wish a happy birthday to the purtiest partner Echo's ever had!" In the background, all the ranch hands waved their hats and cheered.

"Sorry about that, Romeo," Omega shot an apologetic glance at her friend. Romeo grinned.

"Th' day somebody tells me I was Echo's 'prettiest partner' is th' day I plant a big fat wet one on Echo."

"Please," Echo held up his hands and averted his face, a mock grimace on his features, "stick with Joe's assessment, everybody!" All three locations—the apartment, the Core, and the Ranch—exploded in laughter.

* * *

The camera in the Core zoomed out then, showing the entire gigantic room behind the small-screen image of the Ranch, jammed wall to wall with celebrants. Inhabitants of both locations were waving and yelling enthusiastically. Fox turned to his Agent.

"Happy birthday, Omega," he said quietly.

"Thank you, Fox," she responded softly. "Thank you, EVERYBODY." Both images showed enthusiastic responses.

"There are other greetings, from quite a few of the other Offices, including one from Agent Burbulon Vex in the Atlantis Office," Fox noted, "but since they're all in rather different time zones from ours, and/or on different shifts, they chose to record them. I'll have those downloaded to your laptop by the time you get home tomorrow evening, and you can view them then."

"That's...wonderful," Omega murmured, touched.

"There's one more live birthday greeting for you," Fox added. "Romeo?"

The remote clicked; the small-screen insert disappeared, and the image on the big screen changed. A lone agent stood there.

"Mu?!" Omega exclaimed, surprised. Romeo and India shot shocked glances at Fox. Echo's sober eyes flicked across Omega's startled face as she stared at the screen.

"Happy birthday, Meg," the agent onscreen said, subdued.

377

"How are you?"

"I'm...all right."

"Can I...talk to you...alone?"

* * *

Omega nodded, and the others stood and filed through the door into the dining room. India closed it behind them, and the six Division One agents stood silent. Finally India ventured to speak.

"Fox...are you sure that was...wise?"

"I put out the invitation Agency-wide, India. Mu responded." Fox shrugged. "It's better if they have a talk, I think. It gives them an opportunity for closure—one way or the other." He shot a worried glance at a slightly pale Echo, who stood impassively, waiting.

* * *

"Okay, honey," Mu said, once the others had gone and the door was closed, "now tell me the truth. You don't have to put up a front for them any more. How are you really doing?"

"I told you...I'm fine."

"Come on, sweetheart. I know you better than THAT. You're pale, you're tired, you look discouraged and almost scared, and you're still not smiling as much as you oughta be. Besides, when I called Fox the other day to answer his general request for anybody that wanted to wish you happy birthday, I asked how things were going, and he admitted you were having a rough time of it."

"Oh," Omega said, wondering what—and how—to answer to that. "Well, um, yeah, a little, I suppose."

"How are...are things going with you and Echo?"

"All right. We just completed a mission, and brought in the perp."

"I'm glad, but Meg, quit trying to dodge. That's not what I meant, and you know it. How are you doing as a COUPLE?"

Omega's gaze faltered despite her best efforts, and she glanced down.

"Uh-huh," Mu said, in a knowing fashion. "Fox said

something about you two having to set up a telepathic link to combat that perp you just brought in, and how you weren't comfortable with it. Echo didn't do anything, did he? Like, something to MAKE you uncomfortable with it? Because if he did, I swear I'll come back and give him a taste of his own medicine. And the medlab will be patching up his busted nose...and maybe more...when I'm done."

"Oh! NO!" Omega exclaimed, shocked. "No, Mu, it was nothing like that! No, it was...it was the whole concept that bothered me," she admitted. "Between Slug and Tt'l'k, I... look. I never asked to be made a telepath, even a low-level one like I am. I read enough science fiction as a kid that, even when Slug...did what he did," she avoided direct commentary on the details, "I wouldn't have wanted it if he'd offered it to me on a platter. And I don't understand how telepathic races can handle it; I mean, it seems to me that there's just some things that are meant to stay inside our own heads, you know?"

"And Slug and Tt'l'k both pulled all of that out." Mu watched her, his concern obvious.

"...Yeah. And in Tt'l'k's case, then proceeded to tell God an' everybody what he found."

"Damn."

"Yeah. So...no, Echo didn't do anything. His mama raised him to be a gentleman, and I told her a while back, she did a damn good job."

"Wait. You've met Echo's mother?"

"Yeah, and so have you. You just didn't know that's who she was."

Mu paused to think, staring into space for long moments, before realization spread across his face.

"It's Dihl, isn't it?" he asked then. "Dihl, from the medlab? One of the best medtechs they've got in the place? There's a resemblance..."

"That's her," Omega said with a smile. "Only don't tell anybody, okay? We don't need another vengeful old enemy going after her, too."

"Ooo. Right. Okay. I swear I won't say a word."

"Good. And thanks. She's really sweet, and...well, she thinks I've saved Echo's life, and, and Echo's my best friend and she's his mom, so...we kinda got to know each other, just because, you know, and..."

"No, I get it. Now you like her for her own sake, and she feels the same."

"Right."

"But, um, Fox told me you were pushing Echo away," Mu diverted the conversation back to its original topic. "So...are you and he..."

It was Omega's turn to avert her gaze.

"I'm not sure it was ever 'like that,' Mu," Omega finally murmured. "I think it was a combination of me being available and, and convenient, and Echo feelin' sorry for me, and...him being between girlfriends."

"The hell you say!" Mu expostulated. "That time he and I talked on the vidcall? There was a look in his eyes like I've never seen there before. The man's crazy about you, or I'll eat my tie and cufflinks for lunch!"

"Wha-what?" Omega said, looking up, startled.

"Listen to me close, honey," Mu told her, his own face drawing in pain. "Echo. Is. In. Love. With. You. I'd stake my career on it—I DID stake my career on it. If he hasn't told you so yet, it's probably ONLY because he doesn't know how. Especially if you've been all depressed, like I sorta gathered from Fox."

"But, but...Sofia..." Omega stammered.

"Wait. Tell me about this Sofia," Mu demanded.

* * *

After Omega explained, and Mu made her go through each incident with Echo and analyze them, including respective aftermaths, he shrugged.

"Honey, I think you played right into her hands," he decided. "She wanted him for herself, and tried her damnedest to cut you out. Given your mental state after all the shit you've been through, you let her, and chose to project onto Echo the notion that he had to want her more than you, because you felt he MUST, 'cause you're so down on yourself right now that you can't imagine anybody might seriously want you. HE was the one that kept cutting her off at the knees, because you wouldn't. And because she was probably annoying as all hell."

"But...but how do you KNOW that? Have you talked to him again since...?"

"Nah, I don't need to; I already know. Because I'm a guy, and I know how us guys work," he said with a wry grin. "By this point, if he never sees her again, it'll be too soon."

"Um...okay..."

"Uh, listen. This is something I kinda have to ask, honey, so please understand, I'm not trying to take advantage of anything, but...well. If...if you've decided Echo isn't...isn't the guy you want...maybe I could come back, and we could try again...?"

* * *

After a good ten to fifteen minutes, the door to the dining room opened, and the others watched as Omega came through.

She was smiling gently as she walked up to Echo, who unexpectedly turned away.

A flash of shocked hurt crossed her face.

* * *

Echo watched as Omega emerged from her confab with Mu, a soft smile on her face, and his guts knotted.

*They're back together,* he thought, watching that soft smile, his heart threatening to shatter. *I've lost her. I did everything I could, everything I knew to do; I even gambled on some shit, and it wasn't enough. She doesn't love me. Not like that. Not like I wanted her to.*

He braced himself, steeling himself as best he could for the news he expected to hear from her lips. But there was no way for the male Agent to find a means of dealing with the news he anticipated, and remain indifferent...or even look as if he were.

*I can't stand it,* he thought, and turned away.

* * *

Finally beginning to feel confident of Echo's affections after Mu's revelations, Omega headed straight for him, wanting to discuss matters with him...or at least let him know that she was open to a private discussion.

But to her shock, her partner took one look at her...and turned his back.

*Wh-what?* she wondered, as the pain of public rejection shot through her like a slap in the face, and she felt her face blanch. *But...but Mu said...I thought...oh. Oh. I...I guess maybe...Mu was wrong, after all.*

* * *

"Uh-oh," Fox breathed to Zebra and Dihl, flanking him, as they all watched the interaction. "There went some major crossed wires."

"No shit," Zebra whispered.

"Oh, my poor children," Dihl said under her breath, as she continued to watch. "Why can't you just TALK to each other...?"

"Because they are both so reserved, and so used to understanding each other better than ninety-nine times out of a hundred, that it doesn't occur to them that it's needful," Fox remarked. "So in the one percent—probably well LESS than one percent, truthfully—of such occasions when they do NOT understand, they usually don't REALIZE they didn't understand, and..." Fox subtly spread his hands, evoking the current situation.

"Damnation," Dihl grumbled.

"Lotsa that," Zebra agreed.

* * *

Romeo could stand it no longer.

"What did he say? Are you two goin' out again?" he demanded of Omega.

"Romeo!!" India protested, shushing him, as she watched a pale Echo in concern.

"We talked," Omega said, nodding. "He apologized. And...

so did I." She paused. "No, junior, we're not."

"Did 'e ask you out?" Romeo caught a sharp jab to the ribs.

"In...a manner of speaking," Omega evaded.

"But you said—?" Romeo got a punch in the side.

"I already told you." Omega was patient.

"Why not?" Romeo pressed, as India smacked him.

"That's between Mu and me, Romeo." Omega refused to say more.

"Meg," Echo turned to face her, "it wasn't the damn DNA thing again, was it?"

"No, Echo." She sighed. "The truth of the matter is, as we chatted, he let a couple things slip about his new partner, some little things she's done, and I realized that SHE likes him, and is attracted to him. So I clued him into the fact, and he sat up and took notice, rather startled...but seeming...intrigued." Omega shrugged. "It was...interesting to watch."

"Ooo," Romeo murmured, considering. "That works out good for them."

"Yeah, it does," Omega agreed. "I think that might turn out being a happily-ever-after, in the end—at least, if he can shift gears enough to truly accept it. It sure looks like I'm followin' in Great-Aunt Marjorie's footsteps, though. Maybe neither of us was right."

"I don't believe that, and neither do you," Echo responded; the others listened intently, curious. But neither Agent elaborated.

"Whatever." Omega shrugged.

"Do you...WANT him back...?"

"I could have had him back, just now, if I had," Omega sighed. "But...no. It wouldn't have been fair, to him or me. Or Zeta."

"What...do you want, then?" Echo wondered.

"Maybe...we can talk about that tomorrow," Omega suggested, seeming a bit shy. "You know, while we head out on our mission, or while we're staking things out, or...something."

"...Okay." Echo shrugged, but the others thought his

shoulders straightened a little.

"Good." Omega turned to India, Romeo, and Fox with a smile. "You three plotted this, didn't you?"

"With a little help," India confessed. "Okay, a lotta help. Especially from Echo, though Zebra and Dihl definitely threw in their four bucks' worth apiece."

"Thanks, y'all. All of you. I...really needed this tonight."

"We know, pretty lady," Romeo said, hugging her. "Y'r fam'ly loves ya, ya know. We jus' wanted t' make good an' sure that you knew it, if ya get me. I kinda think you'd forgot it f'r a while. This 'uz a reminder, sorta."

"Meg," India murmured, joining the embrace, "I know it's hard, feeling so vulnerable. And I know it feels like you've been vulnerable for...well, it's been about a month since Wright showed up, but I bet it feels like nearly forever. I've—kind of—been there with...well, remind me some time to tell you about the ER stalker we had at my hospital, and who got kinda fixated on me, specifically. But, honey, you have to realize something: you're not vulnerable any more. Stop and think. You took out one of the strongest telepaths the Agency has ever seen—on his own turf." India pulled back and looked into Omega's eyes. "Zz'r'p said that Tt'l'k expected you to kill him...and he also said, Zz'r'p I mean, that he had no doubt, if you'd wanted to, you COULD have killed Tt'l'k. That's powerful, honey."

"That's not merely powerful, it's impressive, Omega. Damn impressive—as much for the innate moral stance you took in NOT killing him, even as much as he'd put you and Echo through, as for the total command of the situation it revealed in you," Fox added, taking her hand in both of his and squeezing it, just before pulling her into a brief fatherly embrace. "Remember how you did it—and why," Fox added in her ear, in a whisper meant only for her, and she gave him a subtle nod in reply.

"Damn impressive is right," Echo finished, putting an arm around his partner-companion. "I'll put it this way, Angel-voice—I'd hate to get you that pissed at me." Omega smiled at him. "Now, Fox—did you save that last bottle of champagne from her opening night?"

"I did, indeed," Fox said, turning. "It's chilling in India's kitchen."

* * *

"Better?" Echo asked his partner at the end of the evening, as they walked around the corner to their own quarters.

"More or less," Omega smiled. But Echo saw that the lonely ghost was back, deep in the blue eyes.

"Do you think you might be up to that road-trip assignment tomorrow, then?" Echo asked. "And, like you suggested, maybe we can talk about some stuff while we wait on the stakeout."

"Sure. Why not?"

* * *

Echo brought the Corvette to a stop, hidden between several large clumps of sagebrush, parked, and switched off the ignition. As he and Omega opened the vehicle's doors, the sounds of the west Texas desert night made themselves heard. Echo led the way farther into the brush. When they had traversed some little distance, he stopped and turned.

"Do you know where we are, Meg?" Echo asked. Omega turned in a slow circle.

"Oh!" she exclaimed then. "Yes! I do! This is where I had my telescope set up, observing, when Cartman ran over it trying to get away from you! We're on the Ranch!"

"Right!" Echo grinned. "Down near the south end. It's where we met."

"That feels...strange," Omega remarked.

"What? Why?"

"After all this time, it seems like...I've always known you."

"Oh. I know exactly what you mean, baby." Echo chuckled. "Sometimes I start to make an offhand comment to you, about a family member, or an old high school friend, or something like that. Something from my past, my childhood, and whatnot. But then I stop, thinking, 'She won't know who the hell I'm talking about.' And it catches me off-guard every time."

Omega checked for 'critters,' then sat down on a low boulder in the moonlight. Although it was near midnight, the stone was still warm from the daytime heat.

"I'd still listen, Echo. You know you're always welcome to share any part of your life with me that you choose."

"Really?" Echo remarked, an unusual inflection in his voice, as he jammed his hands into his trousers pockets.

"Of course," Omega responded. "The good Lord knows, turn about is fair play. There's virtually no part of my life that you haven't shared. Especially in the last, oh, month."

"Well...maybe one or two," Echo deadpanned. "But there's one part of your life that's important today. Happy birthday, Meg." He pulled a small gift box out of his pocket and handed it to her. She smiled.

"I was wondering if you'd forgotten, as...hectic...as things have been lately," Omega told him, unwrapping the small box and opening it. She inhaled sharply when she saw what was inside. "Ohhh..."

"Do you recognize the stone?" Echo asked, as she gaped at the box's contents.

"Judging by the way the moonlight is behaving in it, is it a hyperdiamond?"

"Bingo, baby. It's tough and beautiful all at once, like its new owner."

It was a pure, water-clear hyperdiamond solitaire ring. The beautiful, incredibly hard, blue-white stone had been formed and faceted via galactic techniques...in the shape of a star. The setting was made of some alien precious metal alloy that Omega didn't recognize; in some angles and lights, it appeared gold, in others, silver.

"Echo, it's gorgeous," Omega murmured, gazing at the jewel. "I've never seen anything like it. I didn't know they could be grown that big, never mind with that clarity. I...didn't know you could cut a hyperdiamond in that shape, either. I didn't know you could facet a hyperdiamond, period!"

* * *

"Well, you can find most anything, if you've got the whole universe to shop in." Echo made light of it. "Do you understand why I chose a star?"

Omega nodded, smiling.

"Of course. Lone Stars, Broadway stars, movie stars, shooting stars, protostars, starwatching, stargazer lilies, starships. It had to be a star." She extracted the ring from its case and put it on her right hand. Echo sat down beside her.

"No, Meg," he said softly. "It goes here." Echo removed the ring from her right hand, and slipped it on the third finger of her left hand. It fit perfectly. "There."

Omega looked at the ring on her finger, then raised her eyes to meet Echo's, a question in the azure depths. Echo watched as the question changed to expectancy. Finally the blue eyes faltered and looked down. Omega reached for the ring to remove it. Swiftly Echo covered her hand.

"No," he said. "Leave it there. Please." Then he sighed and looked away. "Meg...I know there's a question I'm supposed to ask now. But I can't ask it." Echo glanced at her; the confused, hurt expression in her eyes made him look away again, pain knotting in his chest. When he next spoke, that pain expressed in his voice, and he found he couldn't disguise it. "I can't ask it, because I can't follow through on it. Yet." He stood, and stared into the starlit darkness. "But I've talked it over with Fox, and with Romeo—because they're both pretty much in the same boat. Meg, we've decided to petition the Ennead to amend the Agency charter on the matter of, um, conjugal relationships, essentially immediately—at a high priority, at least. And maybe, if we can convince 'em..." He shrugged, turning toward her. "THEN I can ask you that question. Anyway, I thought, in the meantime...you might like to wear that."

Omega stood and moved to stand in front of him.

"I'm still waiting," she murmured. Echo turned to her, taking her hands in his.

"For what?" he whispered, letting his dark eyes reveal his uncertainty.

"You've explained why you can't ask the question, and I understand that...but I still haven't heard the declarative statement," Omega told Echo, her entire attitude evocative of hesitancy and insecurity. "It usually...comes first. And it's... just as important. Maybe more." She shrugged. "I mean...we had our little 'thang' and all...sorta-kinda, I guess, given how messed up my head has been. I'm sorry for all the, the bumps and potholes, we ran into along the way, because of that. But part of the reason why I haven't felt confident in that 'thang' was because...I never heard that declarative statement..."

"Oh, damn," he said, eyes widening. "I've said everything but, haven't I? I...guess I figured...you already knew; you know me so well, about so much. But I suppose a telepathic firewall works both ways, huh?"

Without waiting for an answer, Echo pulled his partner into his arms and bent his head to murmur a few words softly in her ear.

"I love you, baby. With everything I've got. I can be clueless sometimes about, about 'feelings' shit, so it took me damn long enough to realize what I had, right beside me. But like I've told you, I'm not a robot, and I DID finally realize it. I just didn't know what to do with it; I wasn't even sure if YOU were interested, and I didn't wanna risk breaking up the best partnership in the whole damn galaxy, if you weren't. I decided I'd rather be beside you as partners and best buds, than not beside you at all." He pulled back long enough to look down at her. "When I told you a couple weeks ago in Ipswich that the only things I was really afraid of were variants on losing you, this is why. I'm head over heels in love with you, and I know I'll never have anybody like you again, ever." He shook his head. "Forget the galaxy. Forget the Coalition, Aleancë, PGLEIA, all of it. YOU are the center of my whole damn universe."

Omega bit her lip, offered him a wobbly smile, then hugged him hard, burying her face in his chest for a moment. He held her close, remembering her current emotional and mental fragility and letting her regain a sense of emotional equilibrium, then pulled back a little, and took her chin in one hand, holding it very gently.

"There," he whispered then, tilting Omega's chin to gaze into the shining sapphire eyes. "Is that what you were waiting for?"

* * *

"Yes." She smiled up at him, almost deliriously happy. He dropped his hand and encircled her with it once more.

"Now...it's your turn." Echo waited, looking steadily at her. With a shock, Omega suddenly realized the arms around her were tense.

"Echo?! You mean you don't know?? Damn, honey. I thought the whole planet—the whole flippin' galaxy—had it figured out by now. I even pretty much told you, that day Zz'r'p helped us figure out about the gastropoid stuff, though maybe I wasn't as direct about it as you needed to hear, 'cause I was so scared. But...yeah. That was one of the reasons I've been so embarrassed and humiliated around you lately—I thought you knew! And, and especially after the nd't'lq withdrawal, the, the loss an' depression from the feeling of rejection...plus, I guess, probably that little programming module of Tt'l'k's— which, now that I think about it, I'm willing to bet he knew how we felt, and deliberately tried to throw a monkey wrench in it—well, it all left me feeling, and believing, you weren't interested, so..." She shrugged again. "I thought you knew how I felt, and...didn't want it."

"Ohhh," Echo breathed in comprehension. "So that's what all that meant."

"Yeah." Omega tenderly brushed a sensitive fingertip along Echo's cheekbone, and he tilted his head slightly to increase the contact; she cupped her hand, and he rested his cheek against it. "Of course I do," she said softly. "I love you so much. How could I not?"

* * *

It was all Echo had waited for. He drew Omega closer and

kissed her, a lingering caress that sealed a bond long-awaited.

At last they ended the kiss, but not the embrace, content to hold and be held, to laugh and talk in low tones.

"Do you know where I was when I first fell in love with you, Ace?" Omega asked.

"No. Where?"

"Right here. This very spot."

"Here?" Echo blinked in surprise. "But, Meg, neither of us has been back here since—"

"Since we met," Omega finished. Echo stared down at her, astounded.

"From the beginning??"

"From the first moment," she averred. "At the risk of sounding ridiculously full of it, I think it was love at first sight...probably because my subconscious already kinda knew you, thanks to the programming...but now I KNOW that Slug had nothing to do with that!"

"How?"

"Because, what with all of the...remembering, the analysis, I've had to do in recent weeks, I was mulling it all over the other day, and I suddenly picked up on a tiny tidbit of an inadvertent exchange—mostly feelings, not real thoughts; not full ones, anyway—that happened during our confrontation with him last year," Omega told him. "I think he must have picked up on how I felt, see, and it made him...ANGRY."

"Huh. So Zz'r'p was right about that. He really didn't like the idea that his intended tool and his intended target might fall for each other."

"Nope. Not. At. All. I've got to admit, though, I hadn't consciously realized it, myself, at that point. In fact, I didn't realize how I really felt until..." she shook her head. "Until we were ready to head out and chase the Glu'g'ik medium, back at Halloween, last year—remember how I told you that day we researched gastropoids, that I'd started wondering if we could take our relationship up a notch, along about then? And then I gave up on the idea when I discovered the origins of the genetics Slug spliced in? That was why—it suddenly dropped on me like a ton o' bricks that I was crazy in love with you. I remember the exact instant it hit me, too. I dunno if you'll remember, but when I stopped dead in the hall, and made that remark about trying to figure out if I had all my weapons on me?"

"Uh...yeah, now that you mention it, I do."

"Well, that was true, but it was because I'd just recognized that I'd fallen hard for you, and all conscious awareness of everything else...pretty much defenestrated!"

"Oh damn, baby! Your brain kinda flew out the window, huh?"

"Did it ever! It's a wonder I didn't trip over my own feet and fall on my face, I was so out of it, for a moment there." They laughed. "How 'bout you?"

"It...took me a little longer," he admitted. "And I fought it for...a long time. Even after I finally figured it out. Longer than I should have."

"Because of Chase?"

"Yeah. But not for the reason you might think. See, I just didn't want to go through all that pain again—and maybe end up by losing you, too, if you didn't want me the way I wanted you. Then I changed my mind somewhere along the way; I think I started grasping what life without having you that close to me would mean. But then you acted like...well, then you ignored all my little feelers. I thought you weren't interested," Echo said quietly.

"Ohhh, no!" Omega leaned her forehead against Echo's chest, chuckling. "What a comedy of errors. So that's what all that meant. See, by that time, I'd already decided you weren't interested, couldn't possibly be interested...I thought it was the whole DNA thing, never mind the entire assassin mess—I mean, I was trying to look at it from your point of view an' be sympathetic and understanding, and I thought, 'who wants to wake up with their assassin in bed next to 'em,' you know? So I quit looking for 'feelers,' which woulda been long before you even thought to put any out! And so I tried to...to get on with my life, get over it, get over you, but...nobody else really wanted me either, and you were always right there so I couldn't forget, only I didn't want you to NOT be there, and..."

Echo nudged her head up with his own. "Well...better late than never, I guess," he grinned at her.

"I guess." Omega smiled back. "Just, um..."

"'Um' what?"

"Well, I've still got the counseling to go through," she pointed out. "And I'm sure, based on what you went through after the Cortian incident, I'm gonna have some ups and downs..."

"Okay, I get it, and I'll be patient. For you, I can have all the patience in the world, sweetheart. I just have one thing to ask."

"What?"

"Don't shut me out, baby," Echo told her. "I CAN help with all that, I swear I can. Whenever you're feeling uncertain, I can be there. We can talk, we can cuddle, we can kiss, we can go for a walk, we can just be together; we can do any damn thing you want that helps you feel better about yourself and your life. But I can't do it if you don't let me in. I don't even mean telepathically. Just...let me BE there for you."

Omega dropped her head and buried her face in his chest.

"Okay," her muffled voice emerged from his shirt front. "I know now, you really do love me, and...and I don't have to hide how I feel any more..."

"So THAT'S what you were doing."

"Um, yeah, mostly. There's...there's still a couple things I, I need to get up the nerve to tell you. But maybe Zz'r'p can help with that, too."

"All right," Echo said. "Until you get to where you can tell me whatever that last little bit is, I'll be patient, and I swear I won't pry."

"Hokay."

"Now look up here."

Omega raised her head, and Echo almost gasped at the look of utter love in her eyes. He kissed her then, and nothing more was said for a long time.

* * *

Finally they broke the kiss, and she felt Echo's arms tighten around her.

"You know, Meg," he said, "Romeo remarked, not too long ago, that when you found the right man, it'd be 'a helluva romance,' to use his words."

"It already is, Echo," Omega breathed, tilting her head back to meet his lips again.

Just before his lips closed over hers, a streak of light high above Echo's head caught her attention. "Oh—it's a late Perseid." She smiled. "That's appropriate. Look, Echo, there goes another one."

* * *

Echo's eyebrows rose, but his head didn't.

"The only star I'm interested in just now is right here, in my arms," he informed her. "And I'm trying my damnedest to kiss her, if she'd pay attention."

Omega laughed, a happy, melodic sound, and Echo noticed that the lonely ghost in her eyes had vanished—he suspected and hoped, for good.

* * *

"Sorry, honey," she chuckled, submitting joyfully to his kiss and finding, shortly thereafter, that she didn't miss the meteor shower at all.

They were still in each other's arms when the headlights of the shipping truck appeared through the brush, over near the road, where they'd hidden the Corvette.

"Oops, that's our cue," Echo said, raising his head to identify the light source. "U.S. Immigration and Customs Enforcement agents—"

"Jack Alanson and Loretta Anderson," Omega finished. They grinned. "Hey, at least we both like some of the same musicians," she pointed out.

"Yep. Among a helluva lot of other things. Ready to get back to work, Meg?" Echo asked, raising a querying eyebrow.

"Let's do it, Echo," Omega replied, chin held high.

And moments later, both truckers and illegal aliens saw two Division One Agents, one male, one female, stride confidently together out of the night.

# Author Notes

There are, as always, the usual suspects to thank: my husband, Darrell Osborn, who always does such wonderful cover art, and my supportive parents, Steve and Colene Gannaway. There is also my editor for this tome, Courtney Galloway. In addition to reading the finished manuscript and helping me polish, she helped me work out several things in the course of the plot and character development, and I thank her profusely for all of the helpful discussion.

This book and the previous book have been mildly complicated by Mom's stroke and ensuing family upheavals, and it's been hard to focus enough to write and prep for publication—even when I was actively writing, Mom's situation was never far from the front of my mind. I'm happy to report to my fans that as of this writing, she is doing VERY well! She is walking pretty much on her own (sometimes with the aid of a walker), is practicing signing her name again, and can get in and out of the car by herself. We are starting to look toward bringing her home, though rehab exercises and therapy sessions will continue for some time to come. My mom is strong and brave, and I can't tell you how proud I am of her!

~Stephanie Osborn

Huntsville, AL

May 2018

# About the Author

Stephanie Osborn is a former payload flight controller, a veteran of over twenty years of working in the civilian space program, as well as various military space defense programs. She has worked on numerous Space Shuttle flights and the International Space Station, and counts the training of astronauts on her resumé. Of those astronauts she trained, one was Kalpana Chawla, a member of the crew lost in the *Columbia* disaster.

She holds graduate and undergraduate degrees in four sciences: Astronomy, Physics, Chemistry, and Mathematics, and she is "fluent" in several more, including Geology and Anatomy. She obtained her various degrees from Austin Peay State University in Clarksville, TN and Vanderbilt University in Nashville, TN.

Stephanie is currently retired from space work. She now happily "passes it forward," teaching math and science via numerous media including radio, podcasting, and public speaking, as well as working with SIGMA, the science fiction think tank, while writing science fiction mysteries based on her knowledge, experience, and travels.

For more, go to http://www.stephanie-osborn.com/.

# Don't miss any of these highly entertaining SF/F books by Stephanie Osborn!

The *Division One* series by Stephanie Osborn:
*Alpha and Omega*
*A Small Medium At Large*
*A Very UnCONventional Christmas*
*Tour de Force*
*Trojan Horse*
*Texas Rangers*
*Definition and Alignment*
*Phantoms*
Coming soon:
*Head Games*
*Break, Break, Houston*


*Alpha and Omega* (ISBN: 978-0-9982888-0-2 e-book/ 978-0-9982888-1-9 print ) by Stephanie Osborn

Dr. Megan McAllister was already a pretty unusual human—NASA astronaut, professional astronomer, polymath—when she encountered the man in the black Suit that night in west Texas. What Division One Agent Echo didn't know, when he recruited her to the Agency, was that she was even more special.

But he'd find out, soon enough.

Stephanie Osborn, aka the Interstellar Woman of Mystery, former rocket scientist and author of acclaimed science fiction mysteries, goes back to the urban legend of the unique group of men and women who show up at UFO sightings, alien abductions, etc. and make things...disappear...to craft her vision of the universe we don't know about. Her new series, Division One, chronicles this universe through the eyes of recruit Megan McAllister, aka Omega, and her experienced partner, Echo, as they handle everything from lost alien children to extraterrestrial assassination attempts and more. [First book in the *Division One* series]

* * *

*A Small Medium At Large* (ISBN: 978-0-9982888-2-6 ebook/978-0-9982888-3-3 print) by Stephanie Osborn

What if Sir Arthur Conan Doyle was right all along, and Harry Houdini really DID do his illusions, not through sleight of hand, but via noncorporeal means? More, what if he could do this because...he wasn't human?

Ari Ho'd'ni, Glu'g'ik son of the Special Steward of the Royal House of Va'du'sha'ā, better known to modern humans as an alien Gray from the ninth planet of Zeta Reticuli A, fled his homeworld with the rest of his family during a time of impending global civil war. With them, they brought a unique device which, in its absence, ultimately caused the failure of the uprisings and the collapse of the imperial regime. Consequently Va'du'sha'ā has been at peace for more than a century. What is the F'al, and why has a rebel faction sent a special agent to Earth to retrieve it?

It falls to the premier team in the Pan-Galactic Law Enforcement and Immigration Administration, Division One—the Alpha One team, known to their friends as Agents Echo and Omega—to find out...or die trying. [Second book in the *Division One* series]

* * *

*A Very UnCONventional Christmas* (ISBN: 978-0-9982888-4-0 ebook/978-0-9982888-5-7 print) by Stephanie Osborn

It's Christmas in NYC, but for Alpha Line it's anything but a Silent Night: The Agency has a mole, leaking classified information to toy manufacturers and film producers alike, and the Agents are in danger of losing their anonymity. To complicate matters, the Prime Minister of Lambda Andromedae III, complete with entourage, has arrived to negotiate a new trade agreement with Earth. Worse, the more paranoid Division One field agents look at Omega's recent history with the Agency and suspect they have identified the mole!

Simultaneously, the discovery of a grim countdown in the most incongruous place possible—the Christmas tree at Rockefeller Center—augers the threat of horrific events on Christmas Eve itself.

Meanwhile, Omega is struggling to adjust to her very first Christmas in the Agency, made more difficult by the exposure of parts of her past long hidden from her conscious mind.

Will Omega be able to refute the accusations, or be punished for crimes she did not commit? Will the internal conspiracy expose the Agency? Or will efforts to thwart it see Echo—and Fox—caught up in the accusations as well? What is the meaning of the countdown to Christmas Eve, and will any of Alpha Line survive it? [Third book in the *Division One* series]

* * *

*Tour de Force* (ISBN: 978-0-9982888-6-4 ebook/978-0-9982888-7-1 print) by Stephanie Osborn

Alpha One is participating in Omega's very first First Contact diplomatic operation. Unfortunately, it's going to split up the team—the Cortians, a race from the Sagittarius Dwarf Galaxy, have stringent requirements, and that narrows down the list of "candidate exchange students" to...Echo. ONLY Echo. PGLEIA's top Division One Agent, the man being groomed to be the next Director...and Omega's partner. A plum assignment, for the pick of the crop.

But Omega doesn't see it that way, though she can't—or won't—explain why. She is determined to stop the mission from going forward. At any cost.

Why is Omega trying to scuttle a diplomatic mission? What is she seeing that more experienced Agents aren't? Why won't the others listen? Is something bigger, more menacing, happening to her—to them? Will— CAN—Alpha One survive? [Fourth book in the *Division One* series]

* * *

*Trojan Horse* (ISBN: 978-0-9982888-9-5 ebook/978-1-947530-00-3 print) by Stephanie Osborn

After returning the healer Doron to his homeworld of Edeptis, Echo takes Omega on a training run to make her a PGLEIA-certified starship pilot—celestial navigation, extra-vehicular activity, emergency repair, planetary surveys, you name it. And he secretly delights in seeing Omega's joy at finally fulfilling a childhood dream.

But when the Cortians show on the scene, intending to take Alpha One into custody for crimes against the Cortian Amalgam, the resulting dogfight severely damages the *Trojan Horse*, causing it to crash on a primitive protoplanet. Both Echo and Omega are badly injured, and it will take both of them working together to survive in the wreckage, while more Cortian vessels search for them overhead, and Fox and the rest of Alpha Line try to fight their way through to rescue their friends and colleagues. [Fifth book in the *Division One* series]

* * *

*Texas Rangers* (ISBN: 978-1-947530-01-0 ebook/978-1-947530-02-7 print) by Stephanie Osborn

It's time for Alpha One to take a vacation! Traveling to the Ranch, a field station in western Texas near the famed Pecos River, the pair relax and unwind, riding horseback, picnicking, and generally having fun...

...Until they discover a team of alien assassins—the original JFK hit team, no less—sneaking across the landscape and headed to Dallas, to take out the current President on a campaign junket!

Meanwhile, back at Headquarters and unknown to him, Echo's estranged mother—who believed him killed years before, when he entered the Agency—lies unconscious in a regeneration pod, while the medlab staff, led by Zebra, works frantically to save her life: Shortly before their vacation, Omega discovered that Naalin Bryant had developed a particularly virulent form of cancer.

Can Alpha One infiltrate the assassin team without being killed? Can Alpha Line stop the assassination of the U.S. President? And can Zebra save Echo's mother's life and return her to her son, or will Echo lose one—or both—of the two women who mean the world to him? [Sixth book in the *Division One* series]

* * *

*Definition and Alignment* (ISBN: 978-1-947530-03-4 ebook/978-1-947530-04-1 print) by Stephanie Osborn

When another enhanced human, Mark Wright, unexpectedly shows up at the Agency, Alpha One discovers that they still aren't done with Slug's machinations and levels of planning: Wright is there for Omega, and the NEXT generation of assassins will be GENETICALLY programmed to kill Echo! Thus begins a bizarre, inverted manhunt as the telepathically-brainwashed Wright chases Alpha One across the planet, using the pre-programmed mental link that Omega can't fully block, to follow her anywhere Echo can take her... [Seventh book in the *Division One* series]

* * *

The *Burnout* series by Stephanie Osborn
*The Fetish*
*Burnout: The mystery of Space Shuttle STS-281*

Coming soon:
*Escape Velocity*


*The Fetish* (ASIN: B007YATGG8) by Stephanie Osborn

In *Burnout: The mystery of Space Shuttle STS-281*, Dr. Mike Anders buys a small spaceman fetish from a Zuni elder at a trading post. But there's a story behind this little lapis spaceman carving. What is it, and how did it come to be?

* * *

*Burnout: The mystery of Space Shuttle STS-281* (ISBN: 1-60619-200-0) by Stephanie Osborn

How do you react when you discover the next shuttle disaster has happened...right on schedule?

*Burnout* is a SF mystery about a Space Shuttle disaster that turns out to be no accident. As the true scope of the disaster is uncovered by the principle investigators, "Crash" Murphy and Dr. Mike Anders, they find themselves running for their lives as friends, lovers and coworkers involved in the investigation perish around them.

* * *

*Sherlock Holmes: Gentleman Aegis* series by Stephanie Osborn:
*Sherlock Holmes and the Mummy's Curse*
Coming soon:
*Sherlock Holmes in the Wild Hunt*
*Sherlock Holmes and the Tournament of Shadows*


*Sherlock Holmes and the Mummy's Curse* (ISBN: 1-51888-312-5) by Stephanie Osborn

Holmes and Watson. Two names linked by mystery and danger from the beginning.

Within the first year of their friendship and while both are young men, Holmes and Watson are still finding their way in the world, with all the troubles that such young men usually have: Financial straits, troubles of the female persuasion, hazings, misunderstandings between friends, and more. Watson's Afghan wounds are still tender, his health not yet fully recovered, and there can be no consideration of his beginning a new practice as yet. Holmes, in his turn, is still struggling to found the new profession of consulting detective. Not yet truly established in London, let alone with the reputations they will one day possess, they are between cases and at loose ends when Holmes' old professor of archaeology contacts him.

Professor Willingham Whitesell makes an appeal to Holmes' unusual skill set and a request. Holmes is to bring Watson to serve as the dig team's physician and come to Egypt at once to translate hieroglyphics for his prestigious archaeological dig. There in the wilds of the Egyptian desert, plagued by heat, dust, drought and cobras, the team hopes to find the very first Pharaoh. Instead, they find something very different... (First book in the Gentleman Aegis series)

*Sherlock Holmes and the Mummy's Curse* is a Silver Falchion Award winner.

* * *

The *Displaced Detective* series by Stephanie Osborn:
*The Case of the Displaced Detective: The Arrival*
*The Case of the Displaced Detective: At Speed*
*The Case of the Cosmological Killer: The Rendlesham Incident*
*The Case of the Cosmological Killer: Endings and Beginnings*
*A Case of Spontaneous Combustion*
*Fear in the French Quarter*


*The Case of the Displaced Detective: The Arrival* by Stephanie Osborn is a SF mystery in which brilliant hyperspatial physicist, Dr. Skye Chadwick, discovers there are alternate realities, often populated by those we consider only literary characters. Can Chadwick help Holmes come up to speed in modern investigative techniques in time to stop the spies? Will Holmes be able to thrive in our modern world? Is Chadwick now Holmes' new "Watson"—or more?

And what happens next?  [First book in the *Displaced Detective* series]
* * *

*The Case of the Displaced Detective: At Speed* by Stephanie Osborn
Having foiled sabotage of Project: Tesseract by an unknown spy ring, Sherlock Holmes and Dr. Skye Chadwick face the next challenge. How do they find the members of this diabolical spy ring when they do not even know what the ring is trying to accomplish? And how can they do it when Skye is recovering from no less than two nigh-fatal wounds?

Can they work out the intricacies of their relationship? Can they determine the reason the spy ring is after the tesseract? And—most importantly—can they stop it? [Second book in the *Displaced Detective* series]

* * *

*The Case of the Cosmological Killer: The Rendlesham Incident* by Stephanie Osborn

In 1980, RAF Bentwaters and Woodbridge were plagued by UFO sightings that were never solved. Now, McFarlane, a resident of Suffolk has died of fright during a new UFO encounter. On holiday in London, Sherlock Holmes and Skye Chadwick-Holmes are called upon by Her Majesty's Secret Service to investigate the death.

What is the UFO? Why does Skye find it familiar? Who—or what—killed McFarlane?

And how can the pair do what even Her Majesty's Secret Service could not? [Third book in the *Displaced Detective* series]

* * *

*The Case of the Cosmological Killer: Endings and Beginnings* by Stephanie Osborn

After the revelations in *The Rendlesham Incident*, Holmes and Skye find they have not one, but two, very serious problems facing them. Not only did their "UFO victim" most emphatically NOT die from a close encounter, he was dying twice over—from completely unrelated causes. Holmes must now find the murderers before they find the secret of the McFarlane farm. And to add to their problems, another continuum—containing another Skye and Holmes—has approached Skye for help to stop the collapse of their own spacetime, a collapse that could take Skye with it, should she happen to be in their tesseract core when it occurs. [Fourth book in the *Displaced Detective* series]

* * *

*A Case of Spontaneous Combustion* by Stephanie Osborn

When an entire village west of London is wiped out in an apparent case of mass spontaneous combustion, Her Majesty's Secret Service contacts The Holmes Agency to investigate. Once in London, Holmes looks into the horror that is now Stonegrange. His investigations take him into a dangerous undercover assignment in search of a possible terror ring, though he cannot determine how a human agency could have caused the disaster.

Meanwhile, alone in Colorado, Skye is forced to battle raging wildfires and tame a wild mustang stallion, all while believing that her husband has abandoned her. Who—or what—caused the horror in Stonegrange? Will Holmes find his way safely through the metaphorical minefield that is modern Middle Eastern politics? Will this predicament seriously damage—even destroy—the couple's relationship? And can Holmes stop the terrorists before they unleash their outré weapon again? [Fifth book in the *Displaced Detective* series]

* * *

*Fear in the French Quarter* by Stephanie Osborn revolves around a jaunt by no less than Sherlock Holmes himself—brought to the modern day from an alternate universe's Victorian era by his continuum parallel, who is now his wife, Dr. Skye Chadwick-Holmes—to famed New Orleans for both business and pleasure. There, the detective couple investigates ghostly apparitions, strange disappearances, mystic phenomena, and challenge threats to the very universe they call home.

It was supposed to be a working holiday for Skye and Sherlock, along with their friend, the modern day version of Doctor Watson—some federal training that also gave them the chance to explore New Orleans, as the ghosts of the French Quarter become exponentially more active. When the couple uncovers an imminently catastrophic cause, whose epicenter lies squarely in the middle of Le Vieux Carré, they must race against time to stop it before the whole thing breaks wide open—and more than one universe is destroyed. [Sixth book in the *Displaced Detective* series]